A Few Late Roses

Anne Doughty

HEADLINE

First published in 1997
by HEADLINE BOOK PUBLISHING

First published in paperback in 1998
by HEADLINE BOOK PUBLISHING

10 9 8 7 6 5 4 3

ISBN 0 7472 5821 X

Typeset by CBS, Felixstowe, Suffolk

Printed and bound in Great Britain by
Clays Ltd, St Ives plc

HEADLINE BOOK PUBLISHING
A division of Hodder Headline PLC
338 Euston Road
London NW1 3BH

A Few
Late Roses

Prologue

My mother never talked about the past. What happened long ago was over and done with, water under the bridge, as far as she was concerned. She was wrong, of course. You can't ignore the past. It always remains part of you. It shapes your present and your future and if you do try to ignore it, you could well end up as she did, bitter and disappointed and so out of love with herself and the whole world that she cast a dark shadow all around her.

That was how she nearly ruined my life.

Even in her dying my mother managed one final, bitter act. The morning after she died, my brother remembered the sealed envelope she had deposited with him some years earlier. He assumed it was a copy of her will, the provisions of which she'd quoted so many times we already knew them off by heart. It was indeed her will. But with it was a document he had not expected, a letter of instruction, hand-written in her own firm and well-formed copperplate.

'Jenny dear, what in the name o' goodness are we gonna do? Shure I had it all arranged with her own man and the undertaker down the road from the home. Hasn't she upset the whole applecart?'

1

I knew he was badly shaken the moment I snatched up the phone in the bedroom where I was already packing. The steady, well-rounded tones that made him such a success with the patients in his Belfast consulting rooms had disappeared. I hadn't heard Harvey sound like this since we were both children.

'What d'ye think, Sis?'

I wasn't surprised he'd had arrangements already made. For two years she'd been bedridden and almost immobile. She'd been at death's door so many times that the kind-hearted staff at the nursing home became embarrassed about calling us yet once more to the bedside.

'What exactly does it say, Harvey?' I asked.

'"I wish to be interred with my own family in the Hughes apportionment situated in Ballydrennan Churchyard, County Antrim, and not with my deceased husband George Erwin in the churchyard adjacent to Balmoral Presbyterian Church on the Lisburn Road."'

He read it slowly and precisely, so that I could imagine her penning it, her lips tight, her shoulders squared. The more angry and bitter she was about something, the more formal the language she would use. In a really bad mood, she'd end up sounding like a legal document as she piled up words of sufficient weight and moment to serve her purposes. Consistent to the very end, I thought, as I listened.

'And there's a bit about the flowers,' he added dismissively.

'Oh, what does she say about flowers?'

'She wants flowers. She says this idea of asking people to send money to some charity or other is a lot o' nonsense and quite inappropriate.'

'She would, wouldn't she?' I laughed wryly. 'Shall we send a pillow of red roses, Harvey? Or one of those big square wreaths that say "Mum", like the Kray brothers', when they were let out of prison for their mother's funeral?'

I heard him expostulate and made an effort to collect myself.

'Sorry, Harvey, I'm not quite myself at the moment. I just can't believe she's gone. I'm all throughother, as she might say. In fact, when you rang I was standing here with one arm as long as the other when I'm supposed to be packing.'

He laughed shortly, but seemed comforted.

'You're the boss, Harvey. You backed me when Daddy died,' I said gently. 'If you want to go ahead with the Lisburn Road as planned, I'll not object. We're the only ones concerned, let's face it.'

'You're shure, Jenny?' he went on, a trace of relief already audible in his voice.

I stared round the disordered bedroom where two cases sat open and small piles of panties, Y-fronts, shirts and blouses were already lined up. I sat down abruptly, sweat breaking on my forehead.

'No, no, I'm not sure, Harvey,' I said weakly. 'The minute I spoke, I knew it wouldn't be right. Isn't it silly? Can't we even get free of her when she's dead?'

In different circumstances, a countrywoman wanting to be buried with her family in the place where she was born could be a matter of sentiment. But there was no question of that with our mother. She'd never gone back to Ballydrennan after her father died, not even to visit her sister Mary who lived with her family only a few miles

3

away. What was more, she'd never had a good word to say about the place. No, there was no question of sentiment. Only of spite.

Daddy had done all he could to give her what she wanted while he lived. When he died, he'd left her with a house, a car and a decent income. Now, one last time, she was rejecting him in the most public way possible. But something at the back of my mind told me we had to go through with it.

'Harvey, I'm sorry, but I think we've got to do it. I can't give you a single good reason why we should, but I have to be honest,' I confessed. 'I'm not being much help to you,' I ended up lamely.

'Yes, you are, Jenny. Being honest's the only way. Took me a long time to see you'n Mavis were right about that. But you were. I'm much beholden to you, as they say,' he added, with a slight, awkward laugh.

'Maybe there has to be one last time, Harvey,' I said quickly. 'But it'll make a lot of extra work for you.'

'Don't worry about that, Jenny,' he replied easily. 'Ring me when you've got your flight time and I'll pick you up at Aldergrove.'

Two days later, in the crowded farm kitchen of our only remaining Antrim relatives, I took a large glass of whisky from the roughened hand of one of the McBride cousins and wondered how I could add a good measure of water without attracting attention. Before I could move, a huge figure embraced me.

'Ach, my wee cousin.'

Jamsey McBride had always seemed large to me. When

he'd carried me about on his shoulders as a little girl, he'd been like a great friendly bear, his remarkable physical strength offset by a surprising gentleness of manner.

'Jamsey!' I replied as the whisky sloshed in my glass.

'Ach, shure Jenny, how are ye? Begod, shure I haven't laid eyes on ye since your poor fader went. God rest his sowl, he was the best atall, the best atall. That mus' be neer twenty year ago now. Dear aye, ye'll see some changes in this place since last ye wor here. Aye, changes an' heartbreak too.'

His eyes misted and I looked down into my glass to give him time to recover. Jamsey's eldest son had been killed by paramilitaries early in the eighties and he still couldn't speak of it without distress.

'Now drink up, woman dear,' he urged me after a moment. 'Shure ye'll be skinned down at the groun'. Yer fader usta say that wee hill the church stan's on was the caulest place in the nine glens.'

So I drank my whisky as obediently as a child and listened to the ring of his Ulster Scots and tried to keep the tears from springing to my own eyes. No, it was not sorrow. Not tears for my mother or her passing, or even for Jamsey's son, whom I had barely known, but tears of regret for the world I once knew, the people and places of my childhood.

Standing there in the large modern house that had replaced the low thatched cottage where my aunt and uncle began their married life, I mourned my links with the land and that part of my family who still lived closest to it. For these were people my mother had no time for, people whose hard-working lives she despised, whose successes and failures she treated with indifference or contempt.

A red-faced figure appeared at my elbow, the neck of a bottle of Bushmills aimed at my glass.

'No, Patrick, no,' I protested, laughing. 'If I have any more, I won't be able to stand up in church, never mind kneel down.'

He laughed aloud, clutched me by the arm and turned me to look across the crowded kitchen.

'Jenny, is that yer girl over there forenenst that good-looking dark-haired lad?'

'Yes, that's Claire and her brother Stephen,' I nodded. He winked at me, and pressed his way towards the next refillable glass.

Jamsey watched his brother work his way across the room and was silent for a moment.

'Gawd Jenny, we're all gettin' aul,' he began, sadly. 'But that girl of yours is powerful like her granny. In luks, I mane,' he added quickly.

'I'm glad you added that, Jamsey,' I said, laughing. 'My mother could be a bit sharp.'

'Ach, say no more, say no more,' he muttered hastily. 'Shure, don't we know well enough she'd no time for the likes of us. But yer Da was a differen' story. Ye've got very like him, Jenny. D'ye know that?'

'It's my grey hair, Jamsey. I see it's in the fashion round here as well.'

'Ach, away wi' ye,' he laughed, dropping a heavy hand on my shoulder. 'Shure you've only a wee wisp or two at the front, an' me has no hair atall, no moren a moily cow has horns. Tell me, d'ye like England, Jenny? Is it not too fast fer ye? Boys, I go over for Smithfeeld Show ivery year and the traffic gets worser. 'Twould run ye down and niver stop to cast ye aside.'

After the warmth and noise of the big kitchen, the chill of the October day took my breath away when we stepped outside. I shuddered so violently that Claire came and linked her arm through mine. 'Get Daddy,' I saw her mouth to Stephen, as the whole party set out on the short drive down one glen and into the next. A little later, the four of us walked up the rough path to the small grey church. Down by the gate, the cars were parked erratically on the grassy verge of the minor road, as if their occupants had gone fishing in a nearby lake or were playing football in someone's field.

From behind the massed clouds that had threatened rain as we left McBride's farm the sun suddenly appeared, casting one side of the deep glen into such dark shadow that the whitewashed houses gleamed like beacons. The church was in the light. Beyond its low hill and the curve of the Coast Road, full of the whiz of Saturday afternoon traffic, the white-capped rollers sparkled as they crashed on the rocky shore.

We followed the coffin into the empty, echoing church, its pale, peeling walls dappled with sunlight that fell through the high, undecorated windows. As we filled the first row of dark wooden pews, the undertaker's men manoeuvred in the tiled space below the pulpit and placed the coffin on trestles so close to us I could have reached out and touched it.

We waited for the minister to appear and ascend to his vantage point. The silence deepened and the damp chill of the air and dead cold of the hard wooden bench began to eat into me. But, as the minister threw up his arms and made his opening flourish, I forgot all about being cold. At the first resounding reminder that we are all born to die, I heard, not the words, but the accent. Sharper and quite different from Jamsey's slow drawl, his speech and his turn of phrase took me straight back to childhood, just like Jamsey's had.

I did try to listen to the words from the pulpit but all I could hear were voices from the past, telling jokes and stories. Tears sprang to my eyes and I had to dab them surreptitiously while pretending to blow my nose.

'She tried to take that away as well,' I said to myself.

I stared at the wooden casket in disbelief. Yes, it was true. As far back as I could remember, she had tried to stop me visiting our relations in the glens. If it hadn't been for my father I wouldn't even have known they existed.

I shivered, tried to concentrate on the sermon, on the carved oak of the pulpit, on the scuffed wooden top of the untenanted harmonium. Anything to keep my mind away from what she had done. I wanted to weep as inconsolably as the child I had once been.

'Brethren, let us pray.'

I breathed a sigh of relief as we shaded our eyes and bent our heads discreetly forward. It was so long since I'd been to a Presbyterian service I'd forgotten about not kneeling down. I hadn't even warned Claire or Stephen, but they seemed to be taking it in their stride. I glanced sideways at Claire and found her grey eyes watching me from beneath her shaded brow. She smiled at me encouragingly.

I couldn't think what on earth she and Stephen were making of the funeral service with its emphasis on repentance and the shortness of our mortal span. Their grandmother had never to my knowledge repented of anything and she had lived to the ripe old age of eighty-eight.

We stood up to be blessed and remained standing while the black-coated figures hoisted up their burden; one oak coffin with brass handles as specified by Edna Erwin, late of this parish, as per Harvey's letter of instruction.

While we were in church the wind died away completely. When we emerged, a few handfuls of people marked out by our formal clothes as mourners, we stood blinking in the sunlight. McBride cousins in dark suits and well-polished shoes, elderly ladies wearing hats and hanging on the arms of sons or grandsons, a few people from Balmoral Presbyterian Church, discreet in grey or navy. Together, we found ourselves by the church door, bathed in the sudden warmth of the low sun.

Borne aloft on the stout shoulders of the undertaker's men, the coffin glinted as we scrunched along the gravel on the south side of the church, tramped across the rich green sward beside the recent burials, and stepped cautiously onto the newly beaten path that meandered between the overgrown humps of unmarked graves and the tangles of long grass still laced with summer wildflowers.

Here, in the oldest part of the churchyard, in a burying place far older than the church that now stood empty behind us, we waited till the last able-bodied person had made the journey to the graveside. Beside my own small family stood Harvey and Mavis, their son Peter, and Susie their younger daughter. Beyond, the dark figures of Jamsey and Patrick McBride with their wives, Loreto and Norah. A dozen people altogether. Most of whom she disapproved of one way or another.

Words were spoken and the first shower of earth from the chalky mound piled up beyond the damp trench spattered on the shiny surface of the oak casket. Suddenly, the air was full of a rich, autumny perfume. The sun's warmth playing on the mass of waiting flowers had drawn out their sweet, spicy smells.

Standing there by the open grave, I felt a surge of pure joy. Joy in the brilliance of the sky and the sparkle of the sea, joy in my own reconnection with this place I had once known so well, and joy in the three people dearest in all the world to me, who stood so close by my side, so ready to comfort me as I so often comforted them.

It was a moment of totally unexpected wellbeing I shall never forget. As I listened to the fall of earth and pebbles and the familiar words of the committal, I could think only of the joys of my own life, the happiness of my home and family, the success of my work, the pleasure of friends, the problems and difficulties survived and overcome. As the damp earth obliterated the polished plaque on which my mother's mortal span had been clearly visible, Edna Erwin, 1902-1990, I remembered yet again that this moment of joy might never have been if she'd had her way. However mixed and variable its character, my happiness these many years could just as easily have been buried in my past.

I stood in the sunshine, the rhythmic crash of the breakers and the peremptory call of the jackdaws etching themselves into my memory. It was twenty-two years, almost to the day, since the weekend that had changed the course of my life. It was time I went back and found out what really happened that weekend.

Chapter 1

The door clicked shut. As the footsteps of my sixth-formers echoed on the wooden stairs, I put my face in my hands and breathed a sigh of relief. My head ached with the rhythmic throbbing that gets worse if a fly buzzes within earshot or a door bangs two floors away. There was aspirin in my handbag, but the nearest glass of water was on the ground floor and the thought of weaving my way down through the noisy confusion of landings and overspilling cloakrooms was more than I could bear.

I made a note in the margin of my Shakespeare and closed it wearily. I enjoy the history plays and try to dramatise them when I teach, but today my effort with *Richard III* and his machinations seemed flat and stale. Hardly surprising after a short night, an early start, and an unexpected summons to the Headmistress's study in the lunch hour. After that, I could hardly expect to be my shining best, but I still felt disappointed.

I stretched my aching shoulders, rubbed ineffectually at the pain in my neck, and reminded myself that it was Friday. The noise from below was always worse on a Friday afternoon, but it came to an end much more quickly than

13

other days. Soon, silence would flow back into the empty classrooms and I might be able to think again.

I looked around the room where I taught most of my A-level classes. Once a servant's bedroom in this tall, Edwardian house, the confined space was now the last resting place of objects with no immediate purpose. Ancient textbooks, music for long-forgotten concerts, programmes for school plays and old examination papers were piled into the tall bookcases which stood against two of the walls. Another tide of objects had drifted into the dim corners furthest from the single dusty window: a globe with the British Empire in fading red blotches; a bulging leather suitcase labelled 'Drama'; a box inscribed 'Bird's Eggs'; a broken easel; and a firescreen embroidered with a faded peacock.

There were photographs too, framed and unframed, spotted with age. Serried ranks of girls in severe pinafores, accompanied by formidable ladies with bosoms and hats, the mothers and grandmothers of the girls who now poured out of the adjoining houses which made up Queen's Crescent Grammar School.

I wondered yet again why the things of the past are so often neglected, left to lie around unsorted, neither cleared away nor brought properly into the present, to be valued for use or beauty. I thought of my own small collection of old photographs, a mere handful that had somehow survived my mother's rigorous throwing out: Granny and Grandad Hughes standing in front of the forge with my mother; my father in overalls, with his first car, parked outside the garage where he worked in Ballymena; and a studio portrait of my grandmother, Ellen Erwin, clear-eyed, long-haired and wistful, when she was only sixteen. That picture was one of my most precious possessions.

My husband, Colin, says I'm sentimental and he finds it very endearing. But I don't think it's like that at all. I think your life starts long before you're born, with people you may never even know, people who shape and mould the world into which you come. If I were ever to write the story of my life, it would have to begin well before the date on my birth certificate and I couldn't do it without the fragments that most people neglect or throw away, like these faded prints at Queen's Crescent.

The throb in my head had eased slightly as the noise level dropped from the fierce crescendo around four o'clock to the random outbursts of five minutes past. Another few minutes and I really would be able to get to my feet and collect my scattered wits.

I stared out through the dusty window at the house opposite. In the room the mirror image of mine, there were filing cabinets; a young man in shirt sleeves bent over a drawingboard under bright fluorescent tubes. On the floors below, each window framed a picture. Girls in smart dresses sat on designer furniture, in newly decorated offices with shiny green pot plants. They answered telephones, made photocopies and poured out cups of Cona coffee, disappearing with them to the front of the house, to their bosses who occupied the still elegant rooms that looked out upon the wide pavements of the next salubrious crescent.

Colin would be having tea by now. Outside the large conference room in the thickly carpeted lobby, waitresses in crisp dresses would pour from silver teapots and hand

tiny sandwiches to men who dropped their briefcases on
their chairs and greeted each other with warm handshakes.
Beyond the air-conditioned rooms of the beflagged hotel, I
saw the busy London streets, the traffic whirling ceaselessly
round islands of green in squares where you could still
hear a blackbird sing.

Daddy would probably be in the garden. He might be
talking to the tame blackbird that follows his slight figure
up and down the rosebeds as he weeds, working steadily
and methodically, as if he could continue all day and never
get tired. 'Pace yourself, Jenny,' he'd say, as he taught me
how to loosen the weeds and open the soil. 'No use going
at it like a bull at a gate. Give it the time it needs. Don't
rush it.'

He was right, of course. He usually was. A mere two
hours since I'd been summoned to Miss Braidwood's study
and here I was, so agitated by what she'd said that I'd
gone and given myself a headache when I had the whole
weekend to work things out.

I glanced at my watch and thought of all the things I
ought to be doing. But I still made no move. My mind
kept going back to that lunchtime meeting. I looked round
the room again. This was where I worked, where I spent
my solitary lunch hours, a place where I was free to think,
or to sit and dream. It wasn't a question of whether I liked
it or not, it was what it meant to me that mattered.

Up here, I could even see the hard edge of the Antrim
Hills lifting themselves above the city, indifferent to the
housing estates which spattered their flanks and the roads
which snaked and looped up and out of the broad lowland
at the head of the lough.

At the thought of the hills, invisible from where I sat, I was overcome with longing. Oh, to be driving out of the city. I closed my eyes and saw the road stretch out before me, winding between hedgerows thick with summer green, the buttercups gleaming in the strong light. Daddy and I, setting off to see some elderly relative in her small cottage by the sea or tucked away in one of the nine Glens of Antrim, whose names I could recite like a poem. The fresh wind from the sea tempering the summer heat, the sky a dazzle of blue, we move through meadow and moorland towards the rough slopes of a great granite outcrop.

'Well, here we are, Jenny. Slemish. Keeping sheep here must've been fairly draughty. Pretty grim in winter even for a saint. Can we climb it, d'ye think?'

'Oh yes, please. We'll be able to see far more from the top.'

Bracken catching at my ankles, the mournful bleat of sheep, the sun hot on my shoulders as we circle upwards between huge boulders. A hawthorn tree still in bloom, though it is nearly midsummer, shelters a spring bubbling up among the rocks. We stop and drink from cupped hands. There isn't another soul on the mountain and no other car parked beside us on the rough edge of the lane below. As we climb, the whole province of Ulster unrolls before us, until at last we stand in the wind, between the coast of Scotland on one far horizon and the mountains of Donegal, blue and misted, away to the west.

'Isn't that the Mull of Kintyre, Daddy?'

'Yes, dear. That's the Mull of Kintyre,' he replied, as if his thoughts were as far away as the bright outline beyond the shimmering sea.

Reluctantly, I got to my feet. Daydreaming, my mother would call it, but the tone of her voice would make the weakness into a crime should she catch me at it.

'Jennifer, you have got to get to that bookshop,' I said to myself severely. There was shopping as well and whatever else happened I had to be at Rathmore Drive by 5.30 p.m.

The staffroom door was ajar. Gratefully, I pushed it wide open with my elbow, dropped the exercise books on the nearest surface and breathed a sigh of relief. No one sat on the benches beside the long plastic-covered tables. There was no one by the handsome marble fireplace, peering at the timetables and duty lists pinned to the tattered green noticeboard perched on the mantelpiece. Best of all, no one crouched by the corner cupboard, where a single broad shelf was labelled 'J. McKinstry – English'.

I winced as the light from naked fluorescent tubes flooded the room. Mercilessly, it exposed the peeling paintwork of cupboards and skirtings, layers of dust on leafy plaster interlacings. It also revealed a folded sheet of paper bearing a badly smudged map of the world in an empty corner of the message board. Across the width of what survived of Asia, my name was neatly printed. Hastily, I read the note:

I should like to have a word with you about Millicent Blackwood. Could you please come to me in the Library on Monday at 1 p.m. before I raise the matter with Miss Braidwood. E. Fletcher.

My heart sank as I picked up the tone. Millie, poor dear,

was yet another of the things I had to think about over the weekend. Oh well. I tucked the note in my handbag, switched off the lights and left the building to the mercy of the cleaners.

'Bread,' I said to myself. The pavements were damp and slippery with fallen leaves, the lights streamed out from shops and glistened on their trampled shapes. I looked up at the sky, heavy and overcast. There was no sign at all of the hills. I'd have given so much for a bright autumny afternoon. Then the hills would seem near enough to touch, just down the next road, or beyond the solid redbrick mill, or behind the tall mass of the tobacco factory.

But today they lay hidden under the pall of cloud, leaving me only the less lovely face of the city that had been my home for most of my childhood and all but two of my adult years. Thirty years ago Louis MacNeice called it 'A city built upon mud; a culture built upon profit', and it hadn't changed much in all the years since.

I made my way to the little bakery where I buy my weekly supplies, a pleasant, homely place where bread and cakes still come warm to the counter from behind a curtain of coloured plastic ribbons. In my second year at Queen's, Colin and I used to visit it regularly, to buy rolls for a picnic lunch, or a cake for someone's birthday. It hadn't changed at all. Even Mrs Green was still there, plumper and greyer and more voluble than ever.

She prides herself she's known Colin and me since before we were even engaged. She's followed our life as devotedly as she watches *Coronation Street*. Graduation and wedding, first jobs in Birmingham and visits home. I remember her asking if she might see the wedding album and how she marvelled at the enormous and ornate volume Colin's mother had insisted upon. These days, she asked about the house or the car, the decor of the living room or the health of our parents, Colin's prospects or our plans for the future.

I paused, my fingers already tight on the handle of the door. I turned my back on it and walked quickly away.

'No, I can't face it. Not today.' No one had seen me, but I was shocked by what I had done. 'Jenny McKinstry, what *is* wrong with you?' I asked myself as I hurried on, grateful to be anonymous, invisible in the crowd.

It was something about having to perform a ritual. Having to say the right things, in the right tone. Responding to hints and suggestions in the right way. Taking my cue and playing the part of the young, married, working wife, as Mrs Green wished it to be. She was a good-hearted, friendly woman, but today I couldn't keep up the bright bubble. It would have to be bread from the supermarket.

'Telly, miss. Sixth edition. Telly.'

I put down briefcase and basket and hunted for change. The newsboy had no mac, only the worn jacket of a suit several sizes too big for him. I put coins into his damp, outstretched hand and read the headline as I picked up my things.

Thank God for that. The march was off. I didn't read the details. The fact was enough. One less thing to worry about, for Keith and Siobhan would certainly have marched in Derry and everyone knew the police and B Specials had orders to teach them all a lesson.

'You're a coward, Jenny McKinstry,' I said to myself and wondered if it was really true. Would I have the courage to march if I were a student, like Keith and Siobhan, or would I need to be as politically minded as they both were. Or was the problem more that I was one half of 'a respectable young couple'?

That was the phrase on the bank manager's file. Though it was upside down and in small print, I had managed to decipher it that day when he interviewed Colin about the loan for the car we were hoping to buy. We had laughed over it all the way back to our borrowed flat, where our worldly goods were stacked high, awaiting their final destination. It became a joke between us, a couple of words that encoded a moment in time, when we were happy, looking forward to our new jobs, and our first proper home.

I had stepped into the bookshop before I quite realised it. I turned round at the sound of my name.

'Hello, Mr Cummings. My goodness, you're busy this afternoon.'

'Indeed, we are,' he agreed, nodding vigorously. 'Never known the place so busy. Come on down to my wee office. It might be best if I lead the way!'

I followed the tall, stooping figure between the book-lined aisles to the newly constructed and unpainted cubicle he dignified as an office. Beneath the sloping roof there was space for neither filing cabinets nor cupboards, but from rows of hooks on every vertical surface hung clips full of invoices, pink and yellow and blue. From beneath a small table piled high with similar clips, he drew out two stackable stools.

'Do sit down, my dear. I think we've got them all, but we'd better make sure.'

He unhooked a clip, flipped through it deftly and

extracted a sheet of pink paper. I glanced quickly down it and breathed a sigh of relief.

'Wonderful, Mr Cummings. You've got the whole lot. I don't know how you've managed it but I'm so grateful. I really was caught out, you know.'

He smiled broadly and settled back on his stool. 'You shouldn't make your subject so popular, Mrs McKinstry. Look at the problems it gives your poor bookseller when you come in and tell him your classes have doubled.'

I laughed easily at his mild complaint. Mr Cummings was an old friend. For years we had shared our passion for poetry and our enthusiasm for the young Ulster poets we both knew personally.

'You're very good to take all this trouble over such a small order. Three knights sharing a single copy of *Richard III* does rather cramp the dramatic style!'

He laughed and nodded at the bulging clips all around us. 'There's no lack of orders these days,' he said flatly. 'And you could hardly believe the sales on the fiction side. But it's the quality that counts, isn't it?' he ended sadly.

I nodded silently. When his pleasant face shadowed with regret like this, I always thought of my father. They were probably about the same age, but whereas my father had an air of wry humour about him whenever he reflected upon his life, Mr Cummings always spoke as if his plans had never come to anything and it was now too late in the day to hope for anything better.

'Another year, Mrs McKinstry, and the quality of business won't be bothering me. At last I'll be able to read all the books I've never had the time for.'

I saw the sadness deepen. I was wondering what I could

22

possibly say when he checked himself and turned towards me.

'Which reminds me,' he went on briskly. 'What's this I hear about Miss McFarlane retiring? To the best of my knowledge, she still has several years to go. I remember taking her by the hand to the village school when I was in the top class. Surely she isn't serious?'

'I think Miss McFarlane's mother has been unwell a great deal recently,' I said cautiously.

I saw his lips tighten and his head move in a curious little gesture he always made when someone, or something, had really upset him.

'Quite a character, old Mrs McFarlane,' he said shortly. 'She must be nearing ninety now.'

His tone told me that what I'd heard in the staffroom about Connie was probably not exaggerated after all. At the age of fifty-seven, her mother, it appeared, still treated her like a child. Each morning she got up at 6.30 a.m. to light the fire and see to her mother's needs before she left for school. After school, she did the shopping and the housework. At weekends, Mother liked to be read to and taken for drives in the countryside. Of all this, Connie never spoke, though just occasionally she would refer to 'Mother' in excusing herself from an evening engagement.

'A great admirer of yours, Mrs McKinstry. I'm sure you'll miss her when she goes.'

'Oh, I shall indeed. She's been so kind to me since I came to Queen's Crescent.'

'So, it *is* true.' He nodded to himself and looked quizzically at me over the curious half-glasses he always wore in the office. 'Another new face, perhaps? Or perhaps not. Perhaps a face I know very well?'

I blushed. For all his rather formal manners and old world air, Mr Cummings missed very little.

'Perhaps, Mr Cummings,' I began awkwardly. 'You've guessed, of course. She is going. I have been offered the Department. Miss Braidwood wants to advertise right away, so I've got to decide this weekend. It's not an easy decision.'

He looked so puzzled that I wondered if he'd forgotten about young couples and families.

'It would be a big responsibility indeed,' he offered finally. 'But very rewarding, I'm sure,' he went on quickly, as if he were happy to be back on firmer ground. 'With the new building, I expect you'd have all kinds of resources.'

I nodded and told him about the English workshop and drama areas already planned for the new building on the outskirts of the city. He listened attentively, but when I finished he reminded me that a Department is only as good as the people who run it. He said he was sure he knew who Connie would want.

'The trouble is,' I began uneasily, 'I'm not a free agent. Everyone talks about equality, and women pursuing their own careers these days, but attitudes don't change that quickly. As far as most of my family and relatives are concerned, we might as well be living in eighteen sixty-eight as nineteen sixty-eight,' I said, a sharpness in my voice that quite surprised me. 'Of course, my husband's very understanding,' I corrected myself hastily. 'But his family's a different matter. It's a touch of Dombey and Son, you see. Or rather Grandson, to be precise.'

Suddenly, I was aware of time passing. I stood up

abruptly. Mr Cummings rose too.

'It's hard, Mrs McKinstry, I know it's hard,' he said as
we shook hands. 'But remember, you've only got one life
to live. You can't give your best if your heart's not in it.'

He looked so incredibly sad that I stopped where I was,
ignoring the press of customers around the entrance to his
tiny cubicle.

'I needn't talk, you know. I did what others wanted of
me. But there's a price to pay. It can cost you dear for the
rest of your life.' He released my hand, suddenly aware he
was still holding it, long after the handshake could properly
be said to have ended: 'If you take the job, I expect I shall
have to call you Madam,' he added, with an awkward
attempt at lightness.

'If I take the job, Mr Cummings, you'll have to call me
Jenny,' I replied.

He went ahead of me to the main entrance. At the door
I put my hand lightly on his arm. 'Thank you very much
for your advice, Mr Cummings,' I said firmly. 'If I do take
the job, I'll need every friend I've got. I'll let you know on
Monday.'

I turned away quickly and didn't dare look back at him.
I couldn't trust myself not to burst into tears.

The mizzling rain was heavier now. The dim light of
the afternoon had faded further towards dusk. From the
square-cut ledges of the City Hall came the squabble of
hundreds of starlings as they began to roost for the night.
Double-deckers swished past the office workers who
poured in from the roads and avenues around the city
square. I made my way towards the long queue for the
Stranmillis bus.

'Jenny.'

I stopped in my tracks, puzzled and confused, so far away in my thoughts I didn't recognise the familiar voice.

'Keith!' I exclaimed, as my eye moved up the worn duffle coat and discovered the familiar face of my brother-in-law, smiling and brown after his vacation job.

'The very man. How's yourself?'

'Fine, fine. When did you get back?'

'Only last week. Job was great, paying well, so we stayed as long as we could. Heard things were moving here. Come on an' we'll have a coffee. Colin won't be out for half an hour yet, will he? Tell us all your news.'

'I'd love to, Keith, but I can't. Colin's in London with William John and I'm due up at home at five thirty. I'm running late as it is and you know what that means.'

He reached out for my briefcase, dropped his arm lightly round my shoulders and turned me away from the bus queue.

'Surely I do. I'll run you up. Bella's on a meter round the corner. Come on. We can talk on the way.'

It took me all my time keeping up with Keith's long strides. He wasn't much taller than Colin, but put together quite differently. While Colin was fair like his mother and moved as if he had all the time in the world, even when he was in a hurry, Keith was dark and spare and full of edgy tension. In the last year, he'd grown a beard. Now after a summer in Spain he was deeply tanned and there were fine lines etched round his eyes. His face had lost its youthful look. Though still only twenty-two, it was Keith who now looked the older of the two brothers.

'Keith, what've you done to poor Bella?' I asked as we stopped by his ancient Volkswagen.

'Isopon,' he replied briskly as he searched in his pockets for his car keys. 'I was afraid the rust molecules might stop holdin' hands. Bella's going to have to last a long time. No company car for the prodigal son, ye know.'

There was not a trace of malice in his voice despite the fact that Colin had had a red Spitfire for his twenty-first. You're a better person than I, Keith McKinstry, I thought, as I settled myself on the lump of foam rubber he'd used to mend the collapsed passenger seat. He accelerated as the lights changed and overtook the crawling traffic ahead.

'How's your father, Jenny?'

'Pretty good, thanks. He's still managing to go into work two days a week though sometimes he lets Gladys Huey collect him and bring him home.'

Keith nodded easily. He and my father got on well. On the few occasions the two families had been together they talked agriculture and politics. They had ended up with a considerable respect for each other, even where they had to disagree.

'And your dear mother?' he continued, raising an eyebrow.

I sighed. ''Bout the same. Bit worse, perhaps. I think she's been seeing a lot of your mother. You know how I feel about that. When they're not trying to score points off each other they just reinforce each other's prejudices.'

'You're right there,' he said, with a short, hard laugh. 'I'd a pretty cool reception when I got back. Cut off my allowance for a start. They know fine well I can't get a grant with the old man coining it.'

'Keith, why? What reason did they give?' I asked, outraged.

'Ach, Jenny, it's simple. Quite logical. If I'm independent enough to go against all their wishes in my choice of company and in my course of study, then I may as well be totally independent. Just simple blackmail.'

I looked at him in amazement. How could he be so steady, so easy? How could he possibly manage without a student grant or an allowance?

He shook his head and glanced at me as we drew up at traffic lights. 'So that's that. Know any good hotels that need a waiter? Speek Engleesh var gud,' he went on, grinning broadly.

I had to laugh, but what he'd said wasn't at all funny. 'Oh, Keith, you can't manage a job in your third year, you need all the study time you've got.'

'That's what Siobhan says.'

'Well, she's right. Tell her we'll have to work out something. When can you come to supper? I'll talk to Colin about it. We might be able to help.' I stopped short, aware of the implications of what I'd just said. Unless we could persuade William John to change his mind, the only real way I could help Keith was out of my own salary. And that was bound to cause trouble in both families.

'Did Maisie quote Paisley at you?' I asked as the traffic came to a halt yet again.

'Paisley?' Keith sounded horrified.

'I thought I'd better warn you,' I went on quietly. 'I think the pair of them have been going to some of his services. My mother has a whole set of new catchphrases and you know she's never original. We could even be in for a religious phase.'

'Oh Lord. Your poor father. How does he stand it, Jenny?'

'I honestly don't know,' I said sadly. 'He seems to let a lot of it pass over him. But then I suppose he hasn't much alternative. Daddy's always been a realist, as you know.'

We crawled slowly into Shaftesbury Square and I spotted the newsboy I'd met on the way down.

'So the march is off, Keith. Are you very disappointed?'

He smiled and shook his head. 'The march isn't off, Jenny. Don't pay any attention to the papers. If the organisers can't get it together, the Young Socialists will still march. There's a meeting tonight. It's got to go ahead. It's just got to. Even if there's only a handful of us.'

I opened my mouth to protest and then shut it again. 'And Siobhan's going too,' I said quietly.

'Of course.'

We stopped at the pedestrian crossing opposite the front gates of Queen's. Students streamed in front of us, clutching books and ring files. Five years ago, I would have been among them, walking along this very pavement, hurrying up the hill, past the Ulster Museum, the great grey block of the Keir Building and the familiar shops of Stranmillis village.

'How're we doing?' Keith asked as he accelerated again.

I saw the lights go out in the bakery. 'About half past, I expect,' I said, as casually as I could manage.

'Sorry we've been so slow. The bus would have been even worse.'

We turned into Rathmore Drive and stopped outside

the Victorian villa with the beech hedge that had borne the name of 'home' for me ever since I was six years old.

'I wish we'd had time for that coffee,' he said.

'So do I,' I said unhappily as I got out and came round to the pavement.

He looked down at me and smiled. 'Perhaps she'll be in a good mood,' he suggested lightly.

'Oh damn that, Keith,' I said vehemently. 'It's not my mother I'm worried about. It's time I learnt to cope with her. It's you and Siobhan. D'you think there'll be trouble?'

He nodded easily. 'Of course there'll be trouble. But there's no other way. And you've forgotten something. We do have one weapon.'

I couldn't think what it could possibly be. That was the whole point. All I could think of were crowds of students and young people, unarmed, totally unprotected, up against a force of trained men who'd been ordered to work them over. The thought of it made me feel sick with fear.

'The cameras, Jenny, the cameras,' he said as he leaned into the back seat and brought out my briefcase and basket. 'I can't promise you it won't be nasty, perhaps very nasty, but the cameras will be some protection.'

He stood looking down at me, a slight reassuring smile on his face. 'It's one thing people just hearing about police brutality, it's another thing when they see it themselves in their own living rooms at teatime. And the B Specials know that now too. It's some protection. All right, not a lot. But some.'

I nodded, not trusting myself to speak.

'Now don't worry. I'll give you a ring Sunday night when we get back,' he went on, bending down to kiss my cheek. 'Don't take the Saturday newspapers too seriously. Wait till you get the Sundays.'

I looked up at him and managed a smile. At least I could try to take the comfort he was offering me. 'Good luck, Keith. Give Siobhan my love,' I said firmly. 'Supper next week. We'll make a date on Sunday.'

'Right ye be.'

'Thanks for running me up.'

'And good luck to you, too,' he said, raising his eyes heavenward at the thought of my mother.

'I'll need it,' I said, laughing ruefully as I opened the garden gate and hurried up the crazy paving path between the rosebeds.

Chapter 2

George opened his eyes. The log cracked again in the fire and a spark arced through the air and struck the log basket. Lucky it didn't get as far as the new rug, he thought, as he straightened himself up and reached for the polished brass poker. Edna would not be well pleased if she came home and found a scorch mark on it and the fire so low it was almost out.

He'd been thinking about the specifications for those new tractors Bertie had brought back from the exhibition in Birmingham and the next thing he knew he was away back in Ballymena fitting a new axle on a traction engine with old Willie Prentice. Years ago that was. The only place you'd see that engine now was in a museum. Wasn't it funny the things that came back to you if you nodded off for a minute or two after your lunch.

He glanced at the clock. It was nearly three. Surely he hadn't slept that long. He leaned over for another log without getting out of his chair. He tried to place it in the hottest part of the glowing embers but the pain caught him unexpectedly and the log fell short.

'Bad luck, George, you should've stood up in the first place,' he said aloud. He put a hand to his chest and straightened his shoulders cautiously. 'And if that's the way the wind's blowing you'd better take your pills and forget all about hoeing that rose bed.'

He stood up awkwardly, clutched at the back of his well-worn wing chair and waited for his knee joints to respond to the call for action. His pills were in the drawer of his bureau but as he picked them up he remembered he could never swallow them without water.

The kitchen was empty, spotless and shining. He looked around and shook his head. Surely to goodness the new cleaning lady would suit. He'd heard her working like a Trojan all morning and when she'd brought him his sandwich before she left, it was on a tray with a cloth and had bits of parsley and tomato to make it look nice just like those pictures in the women's magazines. But there was no pleasing Edna these days. It was a long time since she'd had a good word for him. There wasn't much he could do about it now.

He swallowed the pills, rinsed the glass and turned it upside down to drain by the sink. Then he looked at it and thought again. He dried it and put it away. As he closed the cupboard door the pain surged. He put out his hand and held on to the sink.

'Go away,' he said to it. 'Come tomorrow, when it doesn't matter so much.'

He felt the sweat break on his brow and wondered if he should sit down. But the kitchen was not a place where he ever felt comfortable. Edna hated him in the kitchen and if she arrived back from town just now she'd make a fuss and say he'd been doing something he'd been told not to do. How was she to get her jobs done if she couldn't leave him for five minutes? She always said five minutes when she'd been gone most of the day.

'Come on, George, get going. Tell yourself it's downhill.'

He made his way back along the hall and into the dining room. To his surprise the pain began to ease.

'Great stuff,' he said triumphantly. 'Let's get this fire made up while the going's good. Shure, what does it matter if I have to sit here the whole afternoon, so long as I'm all right for Jenny coming.'

Gladys would laugh if she could hear him. His secretary for twenty years and his friend and confidante for most of them, she'd told him only last week that he mustn't talk to himself or people would get the wrong idea.

'An' d'ye not talk to yourself, Gladys?' he asked her teasingly.

''Deed I do,' she replied promptly. 'But I make sure no one's listening.'

He made up the fire and sat down gratefully. The pain had eased a lot but it had left him feeling weak. Or maybe that was the tablets. Whatever it was, he'd have to behave himself today. Rest, the doctor said. Rest. There hadn't been a lot of rest in his life and it didn't come easy to him now. But he could read. Wasn't he lucky he had good eyesight and enough books to thatch houses with, as the saying was.

He picked up a small leather-covered volume from his side table. A spot of Goldsmith in the dying months of the year. *Sweet Auburn*, perhaps. A link with times long past when the world was simpler, if not better. He opened it and looked at the familiar handwriting inside the cover. 'To Daddy with love, because your old copy is falling apart. Happy Birthday, Jenny.'

'Daddy, can we go up to Granny's house before we go home?'

He looked down at the small hand clutching his arm and the earnest regard in the dark eyes. 'It's a bit of a walk for you, love, and it'll be wet after the rain.'

'But I have my boots, Daddy. Granny McTaggart says I could go anywhere in my seven league boots.'

Mary McTaggart laughed and took the brown teapot from the stove. 'Have anither drap o' tea, George. I think ye may go, for she's talked 'bout nothin' else all week. She's had Lottie gae up there three or four times a'ready. She'd 'ave gone hersel' if I'd let her.'

He looked at his watch. Edna would be expecting her back for bedtime at seven and the Austin was not exactly the world's fastest car.

'Please Daddy. I've had such a lovely holiday with Granny McTaggart and she's told me all about you when you were a little boy.'

'Oh dear,' laughed George, looking up at the old woman who had always been so kind to him. 'Has she told you all my secrets?'

'Yes,' said the child promptly. 'But I can keep a secret, can't I, Granny?'

'Oh, ye can do mony a thing, my little lady. I hope yer auld granny is still here in ten years time to see ye.'

'When I'm sixteen and all grown up?' she said, as she fetched a small pair of Wellingtons from a corner of the big kitchen where those of Mary's youngest son and his family were lined up against the wall.

The rain had cleared and the late August sun was warm
on their faces as they avoided the puddles in the farmyard,
George stepping carefully in the brown leather shoes he
wore in town. Five months now since the move. A hard
time it had been. Worries about the loan on the showroom,
the tractors and trailers he had ordered from England, the
cost of the glossy catalogues he'd distributed with reapers
and binders and combines too big and too costly to stock.
The mortgage on the house in Stranmillis, the only one
Edna had liked, was far more than he had planned and the
work it needed took up every hour when he was not at the
showroom. But it had been his own choice. For the first
time in his life he was his own boss. You couldn't have
that and peace of mind as well.

In this last month things had begun to move. The war
years had been profitable for farmers with every bite of
food sure of its market and a good price guaranteed, and
the three years since had been good too, though labour had
to be a problem with wages so low. The farmers were
beginning to spend what they had accumulated, confident
now that the old hard times were past. First they bought a
motor car for themselves, then they put in a bathroom for
the family and then they looked at their old-fashioned and
worn-out farm machinery. Having a tractor was the first
step. He'd be sad himself to see the plough horses go, but
the change had begun during the war on the big farms and
now he was sure the smaller farmers were beginning to
follow on. A tractor could do the work of a couple of men.

Well, it would take a lot of tractors to put Harvey through
his seven years. He'd set his heart on being a doctor and
the sixth form master at the new school said he had every

chance of passing his exams. That had really pleased Edna. In fact, since the move from Ballymena, things had been easier there. She had joined the Church ladies and went out more. Sometimes on a Saturday when he was decorating or fitting up shelves she would bring him a mug of tea. At times she seemed almost content.

'Did you always come this way when you went to school?'

George glanced down at the small figure skipping along at his side. She never walked unless she was thinking about something and then you would see her move one foot at a time, with a dogged deliberation, her brow deeply furrowed. On her first day at her new primary school down the road she had walked solemnly off with her mother and then come skipping home with a friend. That was typical of Jenny. The surprise in his life, the daughter he never expected, closer to him from her earliest years than the son of whom he had had such hopes.

'No, usually I went down beside the stream till I got to the road. I only came this way to see Granny McTaggart.'

'Didn't you get your shoes wet going down by the stream?'

'I didn't wear shoes.'

'But you can't wear Wellies for going to school,' she protested. 'Did you take your shoes in a shoe bag?'

'I didn't have any shoes or Wellies. Lots of children didn't in those days.' He looked down again and saw the familiar furrow as she considered this piece of information. She was walking now with her eyes focused on the toes of her boots and the rough surface of the almost overgrown path.

'Didn't the stones hurt when you tramped on them?'

'Sometimes, but your feet got hard and you didn't notice, mostly.'

At that moment they reached the first of the two streams that crossed their path.

'How did the stream know where to go under the ground?'

'It didn't. It just felt around and wherever it found a hole or a crack, in it went.'

'Do you think it likes being under there?'

George smiled to himself. She could go on like this for hours. And he would be happy to let her for the workings of her mind never ceased to intrigue him. But it made Edna angry. Always asking questions, and such silly nonsense too. She blamed him for encouraging her.

'Look, Jenny, you can see Scotland now.'

'Where?'

He saw her bend down and peer out to sea between two gorse bushes. He laughed at himself, picked her up and felt the soft touch of one arm as she wound it round his neck. She waved the other towards the sea, greeny-blue and flecked with white caps after the passing shower.

'Is that Scotland?'

'Yes, love. That's the Mull of Kintyre.'

'Mull of Kintyre,' she repeated solemnly as if she were learning it by heart.

He stood and pointed out the landmarks of his childhood world, and then, still carrying her, strode up and across the stepping stones to the abandoned house where the thatch had fallen in at one end and been overwhelmed by a tangle of roses, a few of which were still in bloom.

'The door's not locked, Daddy, but Lottie wouldn't let me go in. She says there might be a ghost.'

The door had never had a lock. What was there to steal and who was there to steal it? Andy McTaggart had said it would make a storehouse for potatoes, but young Harry, always more practical, said it was too far away and not worth the carrying. So, after his mother died it had stood empty. He had removed her few possessions, put away the few pieces of delph as keepsakes for his brothers and sisters and planted fuchsias in the couple of three-legged pots which had survived.

He pushed open the door. He was surprised that there was no smell of damp, but then the back windows were broken and it was summer, the flagged stone floor was dry and only slightly dusty. Jenny walked in under his arm and stood regarding the empty hearth.

'What's that, Daddy?' she asked, pointing her finger at the metal crane which still stood over the hearth, the chain dangling, untenanted over the absent fire. He saw flames spring up and shadows move and smelt the soda farls fresh from the griddle. It wasn't all hard. There had been happiness in this place too. He knew now why his mother would not leave when he married in '31. All the things she had loved were here. She had insisted firmly that she would stay and Mary McTaggart, ten years younger and now widowed herself had backed her up. Edna had said these old people can't move with the times. It was better to let them alone.

'Mmm, what's that, love?' he said, collecting himself and looking down again at the two bright eyes that regarded him unblinkingly.

'Have you seen a ghost, Daddy?' she said thoughtfully.

'Perhaps I have, Jenny. It depends what you think a ghost is. Some people think ghosts are just what we remember inside our heads. I was remembering your Granny Erwin and your aunties and uncles in Scotland, and England, and America. I'll tell you about them on the way home in the car if you're a good girl. But we must go now. All right?'

'All right, Daddy, but can I walk across the stepping stones all by myself?'

He hesitated. There was only a little water over the stones, hardly enough to wet his own shoes, but they were always slippery. She might fall and the boulders were rough in the stream bed. She could hit her head. How could he bear to lose this child, never to see those eyes again watching him, trusting, questioning. He felt tears mist his vision. What you love most you fear to lose. But you must face that fear or you destroy something of what you love. That was what his mother always said.

He nodded shortly and saw her run out of the cottage and across the rough grass. Before he had pulled the door behind him and opened his mouth to say a word of warning she was away and across. Standing on the far bank, a small, self-contained figure, she was waving to him.

'Come on, Daddy, hurry up, you said it was time to go.'

He followed her cautiously and reached for her hand as she skipped along beside him.

Remember that, George. Let it be a lesson to you, he said silently to himself. Don't ever try to put her in a cage to keep her safe, he added, as they moved together along the valleyside where the heather murmured and shook with the passionate harvesting of the bees . . .

George woke abruptly, the buzzing still in his ears. Pain oscillated in his chest. Suddenly the room seemed very warm. He leaned back in his chair, wiped beads of perspiration from his brow and thought longingly of the cool air of the glenside in the early morning, of the path he had walked with Jenny in his arms only moments ago in his dream.

The pain began to subside and his breathing became easier. He settled more comfortably in his chair. Lulled by the quiet, the warmth of the fire and the powerful drugs that dilated the arteries of his chest, he dozed off again. As the minutes of the long afternoon clicked past on the broad face of the clock on the mantelpiece, he moved far away in time and place.

The rain came in the night. It swept down the deep glen in soft grey curtains, catching fragments of light from the half-obscured moon. At first, the fine droplets slid over the summer dry grass, then, as the few dark hours of the short night passed, the thin soils became sodden and tiny rivulets began to trickle into the dry stream beds. By the time the sun rose and the sky cleared, the air was full of the splash of brown, peaty water as a dozen streams dashed headlong to the valley floor.

It was not the sudden bustle in the deep-cut watercourses that woke young George Erwin from his dream-filled sleep. It was the steady drip from the thatch and the bright dappling on the ceiling, where the sunlight reflected from the pools of water shimmering in the morning breeze on the swept stone flags outside the cottage. He lay, warm and still, only his eyes moving round the familiar features of his small, bare room.

The tiny window that looked south across the great trench-like hollow of the glen was spattered with raindrops and shadowed by the climbing rose his father had planted for his mother long ago. When he brought his young bride away from the comfortable, slate-roofed house where she had lived with her parents, and taught in the village school, she had come without regret, and made no complaint at the hardness of her new life, but down there, near the sea, where the soil was deep and had been worked for centuries, she'd had a garden and an orchard and he knew that she missed them. To comfort her for the loss of which she never spoke, he sent all the way to Antrim for a pink rose like the ones she had left behind.

Exposed to the strong wind on the valley sides and the thin soils of the crumbling basalt, it had struggled to get its roots down. Seeing its need, his father had collected soil from the lowland stream banks and manure from the farm where he laboured. He'd carried it up on his back and tended the young root with the same warm affection he offered to her and his children. The rose had flourished as their life had flourished. Now, when he was gone, it was his mother's greatest joy. Apart from her children, all grown and gone away except for himself, there was nothing she loved more dearly than her climbing rose.

He could tell by the strength of the light and the shadow of the window thrown on the whitewashed wall that it was late. Usually by this hour he had milked the cow and searched for the eggs laid in strange places by the hens who had gone broody. Sometimes he would light the fire before he set off for school, or dig potatoes for their supper, or tether the goat in some new place where it had not already eaten all the meagre grass. Today there would be no time to do any of those tasks and he wondered why she had not called him an hour ago.

Just at that moment, she did call. A light, soft voice unmarked by the hardship of her life and the loss of so many she had loved.

'Georgie. Time ye were up. It's a grate mornin'.'

He jumped out of bed, poured water from the delph jug into the basin on the washstand, gave his face and hands a perfunctory wipe and pulled on his shirt and trousers. As he opened the door into the big, dark kitchen, he saw his mother was sitting outside. She was already at work. While she sat on one kitchen chair, another close by held her workbox and a pile of napkins. She was turned towards the light, her needle flying, her movements so fast he could hardly follow them. She heard him come, let the damask drop in her lap and reached up to kiss him.

'How mony more?' he asked, returning her kiss.

'Seven forby. But 'tis early yet. He'll not likely be here a while yet,' she said, reassuring him. 'Are ye weary the morn?' she went on, looking at the droop of his shoulders and eyes filmed with sleep. 'Ye were way late last night,' she added gently.

'No, I'm nae tired at all,' he said brightly.

She smiled at him and took up her work, knowing now that he was tired. And how would he not be tired with the jobs McTaggart gave him, and him not strong. She felt her eyes mist as she looked at him, twelve years old and trying to do a man's work with a child's body. 'Away now an' eat a bite, I left it ready for ye,' she said quickly as she concealed the end of thread at the back of her work and trimmed it off neatly with her fine scissors.

'Have ye had yourn?' he asked, his eyes on her hands and the small practised movements she made as she picked up the next napkin and checked that the tracing was in the right place and on the proper side of the fabric.

'Oh, long since,' she laughed as she squinted into the light, moistened the white thread and manoeuvred it into the eye of the crewel needle.

He knew she hadn't eaten, just as she had known that he was tired. But neither felt any shame in their deception. In the important things of their life, their love for the hard but beautiful place in which they lived, their joy in the creatures who shared their bare hillside, and the pleasure of the few books which had survived the struggle to make ends meet, they could be honest. There was between them both friendship and love.

The fire was not lit, though there was turf in the basket and kindling stacked in a corner by the wooden settle. No need of warmth on such a fine summer morning, but without fire there could be no cooking. The empty hearth told him that both the flour sack and the meal barrel were empty. Unless there were some dollars from Nellie in America or a postal order from Glasgow or London, they would remain so. The few shillings from the man who collected the white work would have to go on baker's bread. And in June and July they had to buy potatoes till the new crop were ready to dig. In all the old stories they read on winter's nights, July was the 'hungry month'. As he bit into the dry crust of bread, Georgie wondered why it was only July, for June was just as bad.

Most mornings they had tea, made weak and brewed well over the fire, but he knew that there would be no more tea till after Friday's cart. He looked at the glass of buttermilk set by his plate and winced. He hated its sour taste and the little globules of fat that settled on your upper lip as you swallowed it. But he knew she would be anxious if he left it untouched and drank instead a glass of spring water from the white enamelled pail in the cupboard.

'Drink it, Georgie, ah do. 'Tis good for ye. Ye hav tae build yer strength.'

He imagined he heard her voice, even though she was outside, bent over her work, the sunlight catching the grey in her once dark hair. He knew what she was thinking when she said that, too, though the words were never mentioned between them.

Three years ago, for weeks of the summer he had lain side by side with his younger brother in the room now used only when some of his brothers and sisters came to visit. Between the two narrow beds his mother had sat, hour after hour, wringing bits of cloth in a pail of water cold from the stream to wipe their faces and bodies. He had felt sweat pour from his brow and found his limbs ached so much he could hardly manage to use the chamber pot. It had gone on for weeks, sleeping and dreaming and not knowing which was which. He had had nightmares, called out in his sleep and seen them move his brother to another room. Only at the end of it, when he could just manage to stand again, did they tell him that Jamsey had died from the same rheumatic fever from which he was beginning to recover.

It had taken his brother to the churchyard behind the grey stone church at the valley's mouth. From his place in the schoolroom in the shadow of the church he could see the gleam of the marble stone. The names he could not see, but he had no need, he knew them by heart for they were the history of his family. Despite the rain and wind of these three years, the new letters were still sharp: 'And Jamsey, aged 7, youngest son of Ellen and the above James Erwin.'

He drank the buttermilk as quickly as he could and wiped his lips on his sleeve. On the scrubbed wooden table next to his plate were two brown eggs in a paper bag. He took them up reluctantly, fetched his satchel and reading book, and went out into the sun.

'Tell Mary I'm behind wi' my allocation, I've not baked a bite yet. She'll give ye a piece for school.'

Mary McTaggart was a kind neighbour and had been good to them in many ways. But her husband was a different matter. He had been amiable enough when James Erwin was his tenant and hired labourer, working long hours without overtime and paying his rent without fail. But young George could only manage half a man's work, and even when the hours after school and at the weekends were enough to pay the rent, it no longer brought it in cash. If there was one thing Harry McTaggart liked, it was cash. On the nail.

'Have ye learned yer poem?' she asked, her needle poised over the initials she was working on the damask.

'Aye. Will I say it over tae ye?'

She shook her head. 'Nay, nay, ye'll be late. Ye'll say it for me the night, when the work's away tae Belfast.' She smiled up at him and held out the napkin she had just begun. 'Look, Georgie, these must be for ye. There's half a dozen for G.E.'

He stood looking down at the intertwined letters with their broad satin-stitch bodies and delicate chain-stitch swirls. It had never happened before. In all the allocations, the dozens of pieces she had worked, there had never before been a G.E. He reached out a finger and touched the letters cautiously, knowing full well that a dirty mark would mean a deduction in the payment. She held out the others, five more large squares of finest damask, each traced lightly in blue with his own initials.

He looked at them wistfully. By the end of the afternoon they would be finished, and long before he got back from the farm they would be wrapped in clean cotton rag, tied into a bale with the others and carried up the track to the waiting carrier. He would take them to Belfast and somewhere in the crowded streets of the city, in a warehouse or in a factory shed, they would be smoothed and folded, tied with fine green ribbon and put in boxes lined with soft white tissue. Made in Ireland. Hand finished. In tiny gold letters. So she had told him. And then they would go on their way to those who could afford to buy such things, to some great house in some other part of Ireland, or to England, or across the ocean to America.

'Some day, Georgie,' she said quietly, breaking into his thoughts, 'ye'll have napkins, an' books, an' things of yer own. Make sure ye lissen hard to all the master says. What gaes into your head, Georgie, belongs to ye, e'en when you've nae piece to take to school.'

There were two ways down to McTaggart's farm. You could climb upwards on a rough track till you struck the metalled road and then follow it along for a mile or more, till it dipped into the head of the glen and then rose up out of it again to strike across the plateau to Ballymena, or you could drop down the hillside and pick your way along a narrow path which followed the valleyside just where the overlying basalt met the underlying chalk and the rough, hungry land of the dark rock became suddenly gentler and greener.

George chose the low path and set off downhill between the gorse bushes, the rush of water in his ears. Their own stream from which he carried the buckets for washing and cleaning was in full spate and the broad flat stepping stones his father had placed there were well covered. He stepped gingerly across, the cold water tugging at his ankles, concerned for neither his much-mended clothes nor his bare feet but for the book tucked inside his battered satchel. Once safely across, he took to the straggling grass, still wet from the rain and scattered with wildflowers. Soon the walking became easy. With chalk beneath, the turf was short and springy, dry already after the rain and sprinkled with the yellow stars of tormentil and the blue bell flowers of milkwort.

He stopped on a small, grassy lawn and listened to the muffled roar of a stream in its subterranean course. He tipped back his head and looked up. Over the black, frost-shattered basalt flowed one of the many streams that coursed down the rock-strewn beds they had carved out for themselves. Where he stood, it had already dived deep, seeking out the cracks and fissures in the porous rock. Only in the wettest of winters did these streams overflow their underground routes and flood across the patches of springy turf like this one where he stood wriggling his toes luxuriously in the softness.

Below him the valley lay green and shining in the sunlight, the two grey trackways weaving their way along either side of the river until they met the Coast Road. Beyond the straggling village on the southern side of the glen, an arc of sand dazzled in the sunlight. Blue and barely rippled by the breeze, the sea lay so calm, so tranquil. It was hard to imagine the winter storms churning the waves into great crashing breakers, brown with sand and broken shell, boiling up the beach and snatching hungrily at the concrete base of the new road that took the visitors in their jaunting cars to see the sights of the rocky coast, from The Glens to Ballycastle and beyond.

Across the calm water lay the coast of Scotland, so sharp and clear he felt he could reach out and touch it. He smiled, remembered his father and what he used to say on all the fine summer days like today when he came back into the cottage, calling out for Ellen. 'Boys it's a powerful day, Ellen. Iss tha' clear I ken see them tossin' ther hay o'er in Scotlan'.'

Reluctantly he walked on, his eyes still moving over the valley below. The hawthorn had flowered late, right at the end of May, but it had blossomed so richly the branches looked as if they were laden with snow. The scent lay heavy on the air and he drank it in, savouring it like the smell of delectable food, bread fresh from the griddle or bacon frying over the fire.

As he strode up a small rise where the path opened into a broad track leading to the farm, he must have closed his eyes for a moment to taste its richness, for suddenly he found his way blocked. He was looking up at Andy McTaggart, the eldest of the McTaggart sons, astride one of the big plough horses. Andy stared down at him, the reins in one hand, an elegant-looking whip in the other.

''Tis a gae fine mornin',' Georgie said agreeably as he waited for the horse to get used to his presence and allow him to pass by. But the rider made no motion to let him through.

'Is ther nae shorter way fer ye tae gae doun an' o'er tae the school?' he asked unpleasantly.

'Ther is, aye. But I hae a message for yer mather.'

'Oh, an' what's that?'

Georgie felt the blood rush to his face as he remembered the two eggs in his satchel. For a moment he thought he might make up some message, a greeting, or a bit of news. But it was no good, he knew he wasn't quick enough for the likes of Andy McTaggart.

''Tis for hersel',' he said, flustered.

'Oh aye, it is. We all nae tha'. Come to beg yer piece tae tak tae school. Ye're a beggar, Georgie Erwin.'

The horse shuffled, suddenly uneasy, and McTaggart struck him with the whip. It was not a hard blow but it made a crack that sounded loud in the stillness of the morning. Georgie knew that he was showing off, copying some horseman he had seen when his father took him to the Antrim Races. But the knowledge helped him not at all. He felt his face stiffen and the pleasure of the June day fall away as if a thunderstorm had rolled down the valley and shut off the sun.

'I am nae,' he said fiercely, 'I hae me piece in me bag, so I hae. Ye can tell yer mather I'll be late the day. I hae an errand to the shop.'

So saying, Georgie darted past, his eye level with McTaggart's boot in the short stirrup of the saddle. It was well-polished and so new it had not even been mended. He didn't make for the path down into the valley but struck out between the bushes and the outcrops of rock, indifferent to the sharp stones and brambles he encountered that bruised his feet and tore at his bare legs.

'I'm nae a beggar. I'm nae a beggar,' he said, over and over again as he reached the road and strode out along it as fast as his legs would carry him. And all the while, high above his head, he could hear the crack of the whip and the noise of hoofs on the track that led back to McTaggart's farm.

Chapter 3

When the grandfather clock in the hall chimed four, George opened his eyes again and breathed a sigh of relief. The pain had gone. No sign of it at all. He did feel very drowsy and a bit confused, but he managed to make up the fire without bending over and without setting off the pain again. As the fresh logs sparked and crackled, he sat back gratefully and looked at the clock.

'That's another week over, dear,' he said aloud, thinking of Jenny.

He'd been to her school on its Open Day last year and he could imagine her coming down those stairs with her pile of exercise books and the briefcase he'd bought her when she got her scholarship. He wondered when she would arrive. With her shopping to do and no car to help, it would hardly be much before six. He'd asked Edna at supper time last night but clearly he shouldn't have. She'd snapped his head off. How was she expected to know, she'd said, for didn't Jennifer always suit herself?

It was a sad thing that Edna got so little pleasure from her daughter, but it seemed as if nothing Jenny did ever pleased her. No matter what, her mother still complained. He couldn't understand it himself. But then, he'd long ago stopped trying to understand Edna. He, too, had tried to please her once, but he hadn't managed it. Not for very much of their life anyway.

He sighed, picked up his book and read a few lines. He put it down again. He couldn't concentrate. His mind kept wandering. One minute he was thinking about Jenny and listening for her key in the door, and the next he was puzzling over why Edna had been so very sharp last night when he had only asked a simple question.

He leaned back and fell asleep almost immediately.

He was back in the schoolroom in Ballydrennan. He could smell the turf from the fire which swirled round them when the wind blew down the chimney and hear the squeak of chalk on slate. Above the blackboard was a Union Jack and a map of the world patterned with the brightly coloured red patches of British territory. Morning and afternoon Master McQuillan said prayers. He prayed for the King and the Empire, for rain to plump up the potatoes if it went dry in May, or sunshine for the hay in July, or dry weather for the grain harvest in August and safe journeys for the men going to Scotland to look for work, and God's blessing on the sick children and widowed women the glen so seldom lacked.

The three Hughes sisters came to school together. He used to see them as he came across the river and stopped to dry his feet on the soft grass by its side. Edna was some years older than himself and already a monitor with duties teaching the younger children. She walked straight-backed, unswerving to the door marked Girls, with Mary and Annie by the hand. They always sat as far away from the boys' side as she could get them. Boys were dirty and rough, she said when she scolded them for playing Hide and Seek and Tig with them in the lunch break.

He had never taken any notice of girls when he was at school. There were books on a shelf by the master's desk that could be borrowed during the breaks and he read in every free minute he had. Up at McTaggart's, clearing out stables and byres, he would go over in his mind the things he had read during the day. It was a long time before he began to notice girls and the first time he saw Edna after he'd left school, she completely ignored him.

Working at the farm, George was often sent down to the forge with some item to be repaired. He and Robert got on well together and sometimes George would suggest a mend that was quicker and more effective than the way Robert had been using for years. When he left school, the smith told him there was work enough for two. He could serve his apprenticeship in the usual way, receiving as payment only his daily food, but if he concentrated on the farm machinery and left Robert free to do the work he most enjoyed, the shoeing of horses and the making of gates, then he would pay him a small weekly wage as well.

The first day at the forge came as a blow to George. Well used to hard work, he set off cheerfully enough only to discover he could barely lift the heavier hammers. When he pulled on the bellows to blow up the fire, nothing much happened and he laboured till the sweat ran down his face before he could even move them. Reluctant to admit such weakness, he exhausted himself. By evening he was so weary he could hardly stand. And that was when Edna appeared. Still wearing the long black skirt and high-necked white blouse she wore for her work, she came to bring them tea and thick buttered slices of bread for their evening meal.

It was a summer evening. He looked up from the dark corner behind the hearth and saw her standing in the doorway, the sunlight pouring round her, catching her fair hair and touching her pale skin. She seemed to glow in the warm radiance of the sunlight and yet remain cool and fresh. He was sure that angels must look just like she did. He gazed across at her and saw her give a sudden sweet smile to her father. Then, as he opened his mouth to speak, she shot a glance around the workshop, turned on her heel and went walking up the path to the house, her skirt brushing the daisies in the grass, her back as straight and unswerving as always.

She never spoke to George or acknowledged his presence beyond the barest minimum in the five years he worked with her father. Indeed, if three events had not occurred within the space of as many weeks in the spring of 1930 it is unlikely she would ever have spoken to him again.

The first of those three events George created himself, though he did not know that he had. He had been working in Ballymena as a mechanic with a firm producing traction engines. In April, he finally completed work on the motor car he had bought after it had collided with one of the twisted pine trees on the bog road between Ballymena and Ballymoney. The owner was a wealthy young man who had been happy enough to get rid of it, having barely escaped with his life when the steering column sheared. It had taken George six months to rebuild. On his first free weekend he drove the car home to show to his mother. When she had admired every detail of its construction, stroked the leather of the seats and been driven a few miles up the road and back, George left her to rest and drove down the new road into the valley to visit Robert at the forge.

Robert was delighted to see him. He was well enough, he said, but Lizzie wasn't so good. The doctor had told Edna that it was only a matter of time before her mother was a complete invalid. On the other hand he'd had great news from Toronto. Annie was engaged to be married and was saving up for her trousseau, whatever that was. It seemed her future husband had a big job with a motor company called Ford and she was going to be well looked after. Her intended had promised to bring her home on a visit, as soon as they were married.

When Edna came down the path to call her father to his supper, she didn't recognise George at first. But when she did she smiled at him, ran her hand across the leather seat and said how well he was looking. Within a few weeks it was common knowledge that Edna Hughes and George Erwin were walking out. They were married within the year.

George woke twice more in the course of the afternoon. The first time he got slowly to his feet and went to the window hoping that Jennifer might suddenly appear in the Drive or coming up the garden path. The second time he knew he could no longer avoid going upstairs to the bathroom. As he passed his bedroom, he remembered the little pile of new catalogues. Edna always complained about them if she found them in the dining room but she was still in town and besides, Jennifer would take them back up for him when she came.

Halfway down the stairs he realised he'd made a mistake. They were too heavy for him to carry one-handed and he felt so unsteady he had to keep his other hand firmly on the banister. Reluctantly, he let go of all but one, and watched them bounce and slither their way down the stairs ahead of him.

When he got to the bottom, he manoeuvred them one at a time with his toe through the dining-room door and across to his chair by the fire. He looked at them wryly. Today was one of those days when he knew better than to bend over, but only a contortionist could make them into a neat pile with one foot. He sat down gratefully, opened the volume he was carrying and fell asleep again almost immediately. He did not wake when *Combine Harvesters* thudded softly into the dense pile of the new hearthrug, nor when his wife banged the front door behind her, tramped down the hall and peered round the open door at him on her way to the kitchen.

'A grate help he is,' she said as she dropped her carrier bags on the work surface by the sink. 'He can run off all right to that office of his when the notion takes 'im, but not a hand's turn does he do at home.'

She pushed off the elegant high-heeled shoes that had punished her corns all day and jerked open the larder door for her pull-ons. They weren't there. Without her high heels she looked small and stooped. At sixty-six, with a look of sour discontent on her face, she could have been taken for more. The social graces she considered necessary for her public appearances and particularly for her meetings with Maisie McKinstry she habitually cast off with her shoes. Now, in her own kitchen, she made no attempt to check the catalogue of her discontents.

'Never so much as "Can I help you". Not that he's any use anyway and him so slow. All day to peel a potato. What good is that when you're in a hurry?'

She squinted up at the clock, her eyes narrowing, the lines of her mouth slack. Jennifer would be arriving at half past five. Expecting her supper no doubt, just like her father. He'd sit there till she came and then it would be a different story. Jennifer this and Jennifer that, and would you like a wee sherry, dear. He never asked her if she'd like a wee sherry. Not that she ever drank sherry but it was manners to ask.

She pulled a paper bag full of soda farls out of her carrier so fiercely one of them escaped and bounced to the floor. She picked it up, saw its pale floury surface was unmarked by the fall and put it in the bread bin with the others. These cleaning women were all the same. Everything bright as a new pin the first few times, then you'd only to look to find what they hadn't done.

She put away the rest of her shopping, collected a colander full of potatoes from the sack in the larder, and filled the basin with hot water. As the warmth released the smell of earth, unbidden and unwelcome the voice of her old grandmother came to her from the long past.

'Ed-na, Ed-na,' it called, high-pitched, peremptory.

'I'm busy,' she called back, knowing it would not have the slightest effect.

'I've slipped down the bed.'

'Not far enough, ye haven't,' she muttered as she dried her hands and went into the small, dark bedroom.

Mary Anne lay barely visible, her bright eyes peering over the mound of disordered bedclothes, her small head overhung by the pillows. She watched the girl's every move. Critical. Malevolent.

'Where's Lizzie? Where's yer mather? It's her place to cum up and see ta me.'

'She's nae well hersel'. Ye know that.'

'An' what's wrong wi' her, a young thing like her? She's no right to be takin' to her bed at her age. Lift me up. How canna ate me supper lyin' doon? Is it not near ready yit?'

Edna tried to lift her up but the old woman grabbed at her arms and almost pulled her over. Edna breathed in the odour of her unwashed body. It smelt of age, of decay. Like the cottage itself with its rotting thatch and damp walls. She hated coming here. And she hated this old woman who bossed her around just like her mother did. Always wanting something. Edna this and Edna that. Fetch and carry. Well, she'd show them. She'd show them all. She'd get out of this place if it was the last thing she did. And they could rot together for all she cared.

She rinsed the potatoes and dropped them noisily into a copper-bottomed saucepan. Every time she washed those filthy potatoes George had brought home from some farm or other, it reminded her of the old days. Well, she wasn't going to put up with that. The past was over and gone. And good riddance. She'd give the rest of those dirty old potatoes away. The women on the garden produce stall at the Autumn Fayre would think they were just great. More fool them. Then she could go back to buying clean ones at the supermarket. George would never notice the difference.

'Hello, Edna. Can I do anything to help?'

She turned, startled by the quiet voice. 'Oh, so you're awake,' she said sarcastically.

'Can I lay the table?' he continued mildly.

'Well, you know where the cloth is.'

He nodded to himself and turned to go. Something had upset her. But what was anybody's guess. Sometimes she didn't even seem to know herself.

'And you might just redd up those catalogues lying round the place,' she shouted as he closed the door gently behind him.

She bent down to the fridge and pulled out the casserole she had cooked the previous day. She caught the handle of a small china jug. It fell over and spilled milk down into the crisper drawer, showering a limp cabbage, a handful of carrots and a couple of mouldy tomatoes.

That was just typical of what she had to put up with, wasn't it? Maisie McKinstry didn't have to wear herself out bending down and poking around in her fridge. All her stuff was eye-level. But then her husband had money. William John McKinstry could buy and sell George Erwin and not even notice it. The man might have no education and no manners, but he did have a bit of go about him. And that was one thing you could never say about George. If he'd ever listened to her he might have made something of himself. He could have done just as well as any McKinstry if he hadn't been so pig-headed.

She turned the oven full on, pushed the casserole in and banged the door. If it hadn't been for her they'd still be stuck in that wee house in Ballymena. He said they couldn't move till he had some capital behind him, but that was just an excuse. What capital did William John have? And now Maisie could have anything she wanted.

'Shure why don't you and George buy a nice wee bungalow down at Cultra, Edna? Surely George doesn't haff to go on working,' she said aloud, exaggerating the sweet-as-pie tone Maisie had used over lunch.

She'd passed it off, said George didn't feel quite up to a move. She wasn't going to let Maisie McKinstry think they couldn't afford it. But George wouldn't move for her or anyone else. He had always done exactly what he wanted with never a thought for her. And Jennifer was every bit as bad. Like father like daughter. If it weren't for Harvey, her life would hardly be worth living.

The phone rang with a peremptory note. She hurried into the hall. Out of habit she composed her face muscles in just the same manner as she did when it was the doorbell. She picked up the receiver.

'I'd have phoned you earlier, Edna, but Karen said she saw you in Brand's and you and Mrs McKinstry were having a day out, so I didn't want to bother George. How is he, Edna?'

'Oh, he's fine. Working away as usual,' she replied automatically. It was only Mary Pearson from the other side of the Drive about the church flower rota and as usual she was looking for information. Well, she wasn't going to get any. 'I'm just getting a meal, Mary, can we have a chat another time?'

'Oh, yes, how thoughtless of me. I forgot. Karen did say Jenny was coming this evening. In fact, Edna, I think a car has just stopped at your house. I'll see you at the P.W.A. meeting on Monday and we can arrange things then. 'Bye.'

Edna dropped the receiver as if it had suddenly become hot and hurried in her stocking feet into the sitting room. The curtains on the large window that overlooked the front garden and the road beyond were still undrawn. The room which ran the full depth of the house was empty and dark, except for patches of light where the street lamp outside had begun to flicker in the low light of the overcast evening. Cautiously, she edged herself into the one place where she had a good view of the garden gate but could not herself be seen.

A car had stopped, but it couldn't possibly be anything to do with her. It was an awful old thing with white patches here and there as if someone had been trying to mend it. Probably some workman coming to collect his money on a Friday night from some of the better neighbours who were having improvements made.

She was just about to draw the curtains to shut out prying eyes when she saw a movement and drew back. Someone was getting out of the car. She'd just wait and see who it was.

'My God,' she breathed as she recognised the familiar figure. 'Has that girl no sense at all?'

She peered forward as a second figure, equally familiar, unwound itself from the driver's seat and stood leaning against the car door looking down at her daughter.

'Keith McKinstry,' she said to herself, her voice thick with fury. She was sure Mary Pearson would be looking out of her upstairs window to see who it was. Of all people, it was that beggar. She'd never liked him but she'd thought if he was clever enough to study law at Queen's he'd have more wit than to go running around with a crowd of

Catholics and troublemakers. Young Socialists, was what they called themselves. So Maisie said. Though to her credit she and William John had told him where to go. Letting them down like that after all they'd done for him.

He was getting something out of the back seat of the car now. What was it? Only her basket and her briefcase. And there she was standing there looking up at him, all big eyes and smiles. As she watched, Edna saw Keith McKinstry bend down and kiss her on the cheek.

'Oh, that's very nice, isn't it, in front of all my neighbours,' she began furiously.

She would have said more but Jennifer had turned away and now had her hand on the garden gate. She scurried down the hall, shut the kitchen door firmly behind her and pushed her feet back into the high heels which she had kicked under the kitchen table. Then she took out the scouring powder and began to clean the sink vigorously.

Chapter 4

I looked back over my shoulder as I put my key in the lock. Beyond the shrubs and trees that screened one side of the Drive from the other, the black and white shape of Keith's Volkswagen headed for the main road. I waved, but he didn't see me.

I closed the front door behind me, tucked my baggage under the hall table and hung up my coat. At the end of the hall, the kitchen door was firmly shut. The crash of pots and pans escaped to greet me. A bad omen. The dining-room door was ajar and I caught sight of my father as I passed. He had been listening for me, his newspaper folded on his knee. He raised a hand in greeting but said nothing.

As bad as that, I thought. I opened the door of the kitchen and went in. When my mother is in a good mood, she leaves it open, so she can hear the phone and the doorbell. When she's not, she shuts it tight and her hearing becomes even more acute. On such occasions any delay on my part is seen as an unfriendly act. Conversation with my father becomes rudeness to her. On a really bad day she treats it as an act of conspiracy.

'Hello, Mummy, sorry I got held up.'

She turned round from the sink, a look of feigned amazement on her face. 'Oh, so you've arrived after all,' she said sarcastically. 'I'd given you up half an hour ago.'

'The traffic gets worse all the time,' I replied easily.

The signals were clear. Whatever I said would be wrong. All I could do for the moment was try to ignore them.

'Now you can't tell me, Jennifer, that it was the traffic kept you since four o'clock,' she began, slapping down her dishcloth on the draining board. 'You may think I'm a fool, but I'm not that big a fool. Give me credit for some sense. Please.'

The 'please' was squeezed out with such self-pity, I could hardly bear to go on looking at her. The lines of her face were hard and her careful make-up did nothing to soften it. Indeed, the Gala Red of her lipstick only accentuated the tight, unyielding line of her mouth. I felt the old, familiar nausea clutch at my stomach.

If Colin were here, she'd be fussing over the dessert she'd made especially for him, making polite inquiries about William John, arch remarks about young directors and comments about hard-working young men needing good suppers at the end of a busy day. It required a fair amount of tolerance but it was better than this.

'I had to go into town about the A-level texts,' I said coolly. 'I thought you said "the usual time" on the phone.'

'That's the first I've heard of it,' she snapped, turning her back on me and continuing to scrub. 'You must've been buyin' the whole shop,' she threw over her shoulder. She laughed shortly, pleased with herself. She rinsed the sink noisily and then threw back a sliding door and searched through a row of tins.

For two years now, 'the usual time' for a Friday evening visit was soon after five as Colin could get away, collect the car, crawl through the traffic, pick me up in Botanic Avenue with the shopping, and get back across to the Stranmillis Road. It was seldom before five thirty. Often enough it was a quarter to six. But I knew from long experience the facts were not relevant. There was no point whatever in mentioning them.

She opened a tin of peas, flung down the opener and strode across the kitchen towards me. For a moment I thought she was about to strike me, so hostile was the look on her face.

'Excuse me,' she said, with exaggerated politeness.

I moved hastily aside as she wrenched open a cupboard behind me and pulled out a saucepan.

'Can I do anything to help?' I asked quietly.

She tipped the peas into the saucepan so fiercely the unpleasant-looking green liquid splattered the work surface. She tossed her head and smiled a tight little smile. 'Well, you might just think of putting a comb through your hair.'

Without a word, I turned and left the kitchen, collected my handbag and made for the stairs. As I passed the dining-room door, I looked in, smiled with a cheerfulness I certainly didn't feel and pulled an imaginary lavatory chain. My father grinned, looked somewhat relieved, and picked up his paper again.

I locked the bathroom door and glanced around. I felt like the hero in a B movie, looking for something to barricade it with. But there was nothing handy. Brightly lit and dazzlingly clean, all the room offered me was multiple images of myself.

I sat down on the pink velvet stool in front of the vanity

unit and stared at a face I hardly recognised. The dark eyes that had won me the part of Elizabeth Bennett in a school production were dull and lifeless, with deep shadows under them. My pale complexion looked much too pale and my long, dark hair had come to the end of the week before I had. I pulled the ribbon from my pony tail and watched the dark mass flop around my face.

'How about the witch of Endor?' I said aloud as I pulled faces in the mirror. 'You look just right for the part.'

But I couldn't laugh. My dear mother was no laughing matter. I sighed and tipped out my make-up on the immaculate grey surface in front of me. If I did a proper job I might just work off some of the anger I was feeling.

I slid open the nearest bathroom cabinet. My mother never throws anything away and I was sure I'd seen a bottle of cleansing cream the last time I had to look for an aspirin. There it was, at the back, a brand I hadn't used since I was a teenager. As the cold liquid touched my skin, the faint floral fragrance stirred layers of memory. I shivered.

Harvey's wedding. My mother in an expensive silk suit. Daddy looking handsome in tails. Everywhere the smell of carnations. Buttonholes for the ushers and sprays for female relatives. My mother had helped me into my bridesmaid's dress of pink organza and tulle. It was not what I would have chosen, but I had to admit it was pretty and the posy and garland of fresh flowers for my hair that Mavis had sent had quite delighted me. My best friend, Valerie, said the garland made me look like Titania.

I enjoyed the wedding. Managed to do the right thing at the right time. Drank my first glass of champagne and danced with all Harvey's colleagues after the meal. I even

managed to kiss Harvey goodbye with a fair imitation of
sisterly love, given how supercilious and condescending
he had become since his graduation from medical school.
Everything seemed to go so well that I was completely
unprepared for the storm that broke over me once we were
home from the reception.

I was standing in my slip in my bedroom, the pink
organza at my feet, when my mother stalked in and just let
fly. I still don't know what I said or did to provoke her
outburst. She said I was full of myself, didn't know how
to behave, was spoilt, big-headed, lazy and idle, and that
Mavis would never have asked me to be her bridesmaid if
it hadn't been for her. I'd made a real exhibition of myself
at the reception, hadn't I, smiling up at all the men and
chattering away to Mavis's family as if I actually knew
them.

Hurt and taken by surprise, I had demanded to know
what exactly was so wrong about the way I'd behaved.
What had she expected of me that I hadn't done? And if
I'd done something awful, why hadn't Daddy said
anything? That was when she shouted at me so loudly
Daddy heard her in the garage and came hurrying upstairs.
Then she turned on him.

It was all his fault. He had spoilt me since I was no
size. Running after me and giving me everything I asked
for. Always reading to me, and books not suitable for a
young girl. Now I was so full of myself there was no
standing me. I just did what I liked and walked over her.
And he was just as bad as I was. It was two to one against
her, all the time.

I applied a little lipstick to my chin and cheekbones

and pressed powder gently over fresh foundation. Sometimes the tricks of the drama workshop came in handy. A new face in six minutes flat. But new perspectives take longer, much longer.

From that day, in my seventeenth year, I was never easy at home again and seldom felt free to enjoy my father's company as I had before. We still did some of the things we'd done previously, theatre, concerts and poetry readings, but there was always a price to pay. Either my mother would insist on coming with us and then pour scorn on whatever we had enjoyed, or she would insist she knew when she wasn't wanted, stay at home and then sulk for days.

I escaped when I married. But for my father there was no escape. I put my make-up away and wiped up the flecks of powder with a piece of Supersoft toilet paper. Then I mopped up the drops of water in the handbasin. There must be nothing for her to complain about when I was gone. For a long time now, this kind of avoidance had helped me get by. But it didn't solve anything. As I walked slowly down the thickly-carpeted stairs, I knew I had problems that couldn't be avoided any longer.

'Come on now, George. At least come to the table when it's ready. That's your father's,' she said, handing me a hot plate.

She glared at me as I put it down quickly and picked it up again with my napkin.

'Thank you, dear,' he said quietly as I put it in front of him.

He did not look up at me. The effort of walking across the room and bending down to switch off the television had left him breathless. His skin had a slight yellow look.

But he seemed composed, at ease almost, as if nothing she did could trouble him any more.

'There isn't any pudding,' she announced as she sat down heavily, a drained look on her face. 'But there's plenty of fruit in the bowl.'

I passed her the potatoes. She waved them away. 'No potatoes for me, I'm dieting.' She spooned a large helping of peas on to her plate and studied the beef casserole minutely for traces of fat. 'You wouldn't know what to have sometimes,' she said in a pained tone.

An effort had to be made. I collected my wits, passed the peas to my father and said agreeably, 'Yes, I know what you mean, I usually run out of ideas by Friday.'

'Well, of course, Jennifer, you can't really complain now, can you?' She wore that facial gesture which always meant she was about to say something hurtful but expected it to be let pass, because she was actually smiling.

'I don't think you've much to complain about, one way and another. I wonder if sometimes you might not consider Colin just a little bit. D'you ever think it might be hard on him, workin' away all day and comin' home and no meal ready?'

I opened my mouth to speak, but she didn't pause.

'It's all very well havin' a job, and the extra money's very nice, I'm sure, but you can't just have everythin' your own way.' And she was off again on the old familiar circuit. She stood up abruptly and reached across the table for the jug of water before I could pass it to her. The gesture was a familiar one. It meant, 'No one so much as offers me a glass of water.'

'Mummy, you know I'm not teaching just because of

the money. I've had four years at University, at the
community's expense. I don't think sitting at home is any
way to repay that.'

'Oh, that's all very well. You can't tell me very much
about community, with all I do for the Church. But charity
begins at home, Jennifer, doesn't it? Do you not think it's
nearly time you were to show a little consideration to your
husband and his family?'

I grasped my glass of water and swallowed slowly. When
Karen Pearson from across the Drive had her second baby,
six months ago, my mother had spoken her mind on the
subject. But it had been all right then. Colin was there,
he'd laughed and told her she was far too young to be a
grandmother, and besides, we still hadn't got the house
straight. Now it looked as if she was going to have another
go at me with Colin safely out of the way.

'You have to accept, Jennifer, that Colin is the
breadwinner. He is the one with the responsibility. Surely
you give a wee bit of thought to his future. Just a wee bit.'

It was her squeezed toothpaste tone again. Like that
'please' in the kitchen. If she goes on like this, I'll pour
the peas over her blue rinse. She's still talking about
breadwinners in 1968. My stomach did a lurch as I tried to
control myself.

'Mummy, we came home from Birmingham because of
Colin's future. We took the house in Helen's Bay because
of Colin's future. I didn't want to give up the job in
Birmingham and I didn't want to live in Loughview
Heights. What do you mean, "giving thought to Colin's
future"? We give it thought all the time.'

She swallowed hard, like a blackbird consuming a piece

of crust that's too big for it. Her chin poked forward with the effort. 'Well, I don't see much sign of it. There's not much comfort for Colin with you correctin' exercises in the evenings or runnin' off to the theatre with those girls. I don't think Colin has much say in what you do. It doesn't look like it, does it, heh?'

From the corner of my eye I saw my father put down his knife and fork. He looked as if he were about to speak, but he paused, thought better of it and remained silent.

'Mummy, Colin and I discuss everything we do,' I replied patiently.

'Oh yes, I'm sure you do,' she retorted. 'And you make sure you get what you want. And I have to hear from another party that you can't go on holiday with your husband at Easter because you're busy gallivantin' with your friends.'

'Easter?' For a moment I was so surprised I couldn't even think where in the year we were.

'Yes, Easter,' she repeated, her voice rising a degree higher, her flushed cheeks wobbling with vehemence. 'It's a quare thing when I have ta find out from another party.'

'Another party' was Maisie. At least now I'd guessed what she was talking about.

'I'm going to a conference on English teaching,' I said coolly. 'It's got nothing to do with going on holiday. Colin didn't want to go to Majorca with Maisie and William John any more than I did.'

'Oh, is that so? Is that so indeed?'

And then she took off. Just like the day of Harvey's wedding. There were some new lines since then, but the refrain was basically the same. I wasn't behaving as she thought I ought to behave. I made my own decisions, which

73

clearly I had no right to do. She commented on my lack of
loyalty to my husband, my family and my country,
catalogued misdemeanours such as taking my A-level girls
to see plays put on by the Other Side, 'running around'
with Valerie Thompson and that arty crowd of hers, and
being ungrateful to the McKinstrys who had been 'more
than generous' to me.

'My fine friends', as she called them, were a recurring
theme. Everyone I knew and cared about came in for some
unpleasant comment. It was on that topic I finally took my
stand.

'You and your fine friends will get a comedown one of
these days,' she said, nodding vigorously. 'Let me tell you,
that Keith McKinstry is a real bad one, him and that
Catholic crowd he runs around with. I'll thank you not to
bring that dirty-looking beggar to my front door where any
of our decent neighbours might see him. Colin has more
sense than to have anything to do with him.'

She had to pause for breath, so I took my chance.

'Mummy,' I said firmly, 'I don't know what Maisie has
been saying about Keith, but whatever it was, it has nothing
to do with Colin and me. Keith and Siobhan are friends of
ours and will go on being friends of ours.'

'Nothing to do with you?' She twitched with fury as her
voice rose higher.

I poured myself another glass of water and tried to find
some logic in the flood of abuse and accusations she was
stringing together. But I couldn't. When she finally stopped,
I didn't know where to begin. But she completely misread
my silence. Encouraged by it, she began again in a tone
several degrees less hysterical than before.

'You know, Jennifer, we all have to accept that we only have one life to live and that life is for the service of others. I don't think if you had to give an account to your Maker, you could really say you've done the things you ought to have done, now could you?'

I listened hard. Not to the words, but to the tone. Did she really think that by lowering her voice and making the odd reference to God, her message would sound any different?

I waited till she stopped. My hands were stone cold and my stomach felt as if I'd swallowed a huge pork pie. Suddenly, a moment from my childhood sprang back into my mind and in the midst of the angry words and all my anxieties I felt a totally unexpected sense of unshakeable calm. I saw myself as a small girl, hand in hand with my father. I was trailing my feet through the puddles, utterly confident of the magical water-repellent qualities of my new Wellington boots. The memory was extraordinarily comforting. I took a deep breath. 'Yes, Mummy, I agree. We do have only one life to live.' My voice was so steady I couldn't believe it. 'Where we disagree is about who decides how you should live it. I think each person has to decide for themselves. I don't think you should let other people decide for you.'

She opened her mouth, closed it again, then sprang to her feet. 'Oh no, you'll not do that, Jennifer. You only want to hear what suits you. As long as you're all right, you couldn't care less about poor Colin, or me, or anybody. I might as well talk to the wall. All you're interested in is yourself. Self. Self. Self.'

She flung her napkin down on the table.

'That's all you ever think about. That, and making others like you. Well, I'm not stayin' here for you to make skit of me. You take me for a fool. Well, I'm not. You're not going to get everythin' yer own way. We'll just see who's the fool.'

With a final vicious stare at me, she turned and strode out. She banged the door so hard a collection of old plates on the dresser rattled ominously. In the silence that followed, a full-blown rose on a small table by the door shed its petals in a soft shower on to the carpet.

I turned towards my father. To my amazement, he was smiling.

'Good girl yourself. You didn't cry.'

'I think I might now,' I said weakly.

'Ach, not at all. We'll have a drop of brandy and I'll make us some coffee. I went down on the bus to Bell's for a wee bag of Blue Mountain this morning. How about that?'

I nodded enthusiastically and then hesitated. 'D'you think she'll come back?'

'No, not very likely. She's got a television upstairs now and there's something or other she watches at seven thirty. She might come down at eight. Shure there's plenty o' time.'

I looked across at him as he took the brandy from the cupboard. How could he be so cool, living with this woman, the fresh-faced girl he'd married thirty-five years ago, when he was my age and she a country girl from a cottage where they still used paraffin lamps and drew water from a well halfway up an orchard behind the single-storey dwelling.

'Would you eat a bit of cheese, Jenny?'

I shook my head. 'I've got terrible wind.'

'The brandy'll help that,' he said comfortingly. 'I don't
know what set that one off,' he went on ruefully. 'I'd have
said my piece if I'd thought it would've done any good.
I'm glad I didn't. It was better the way it was.'

We sat down together, glasses in hand and looked into
the fire. I thought of all the times we had sat by this fireside,
reading to each other. Plays and poetry and fairytales. Those
were the days, from my early years right up to Harvey's
wedding, when my mother seemed happy enough, with the
new house being done up to her liking, a round of coffee
mornings and sales of work at the local church, and Harvey
always wanting attention, help with his work, someone to
look at what he was doing, or making. It was always my
mother he called for. If Harvey wanted to go to the cinema,
she was quite happy to leave my father and me to make
our own supper. How we might amuse ourselves while they
were gone didn't seem to trouble her at all.

I knelt on the hearth rug, hands outstretched to the
leaping flames, and looked at him over my shoulder.

'Got offered a job today, Daddy.'

He raised an eyebrow and grinned. 'Headmistress?'

I laughed and shook my head. 'Head of English.
Connie's going to retire early. She recommended me. So
Miss Braidwood said.'

'You'll take it?'

'To take or not to take, that is the question. I've got to
decide by Monday.'

'How do you feel about it?'

'I feel yes, but it's not as easy as that.'

He looked slightly puzzled and I wondered if, like Mr
Cummings, he too might have forgotten all the business

about starting a family. Since his heart attack, I'd noticed he could forget things and then get very upset, once he realised what had happened.

'What's on the no side?' he asked quietly. 'Colin wouldn't stand in your way, would he?' he went on, more sharply.

I reassured him. Colin and I had agreed I'd pursue my career till I was well-established. No need to make a break till I was twenty-nine or thirty, he'd said.

'No, it's not Colin, Daddy. There are some parties who might think it's not considerate to wait any longer. Not just Mummy. I have a nasty feeling Maisie and William John have been getting at Colin.'

'But what do *you* feel about that?' he asked, very gently.

'I just don't know, Daddy. I really don't.'

'But you do know about the job?'

'Oh yes,' I said honestly. 'I'd love the job.'

He looked away for a moment and I wondered what he could be thinking. Suddenly my mother's words came back to me and I felt so uneasy.

'I'm not selfish, Daddy, am I?' The question was out before I'd even thought it. My voice had wavered dangerously.

'Selfish?' he repeated, as if the very idea puzzled him.

For a moment I expected him to say, 'Now don't be silly, Jenny.' But he didn't. He just sat looking into the fire. It was a look I'd seen recently that worried me, though I couldn't really say why. I waited for him to reply. In the firelight, his face looked very old and very tired.

He straightened up with a visible effort and turned back

to look at me. 'Jenny, dear, all human beings are selfish in one sense of the word. They have to be if they're going to be any good to themselves or anyone else. Your self is all you've got in the end. No matter how much you care about anyone else, it's you that you have to live with, for whatever time you've got.'

He paused. I could see he was short of breath, but he ignored it and went on.

'Your mother was right saying you had only one life to live. But you're right, too, about making your own decisions. It has to be you, Jenny, leading the life you choose, otherwise you end up living the life others choose for you.'

His breathing was rougher by now, and to my dismay I heard a sound I hoped I'd never hear again, the wheeze he was making in the intensive care unit at the Royal when I got there straight from the Birmingham plane. That was two years ago. They'd said then they didn't think he'd pull round, the heart attack was massive. I'd held his hand and prayed, the way children pray. 'Please God, let Daddy live and I'll give up the job and come home as Colin and everybody else wants, and I'll not complain about leaving a super school and kids I love.' He'd pulled through but he'd had to retire early. And I'd kept my part of the bargain. But at times like tonight, I wondered if I'd actually been very selfish indeed.

He took a deep breath. The ominous sound disappeared. He went on, 'Jenny, I've seen too damn much of living for others in my time. This island's full of it. Women living for the house, or the family, or the neighbours, or the Church; men living for the business, or the Lodge, or the

Cause. Any excuse so as not to have to live for themselves and make some sort of decent job of it. Shakespeare had it right, you know. "To thine own self be true, Thou canst not then be false to any man." Aye, or woman either. If that's selfish, Jenny, I wish to goodness there was a bit more of it around.'

He leaned back in his chair, his face flushed with the effort he had made. I wanted to say so much, but I could see how tired he was. So I just said, 'Thanks, Daddy, I'll remember that.' Then I offered to go and make the coffee, thinking he might well doze off in his chair.

He nodded gratefully and I was just putting my warm feet back into my shoes when the telephone rang loudly in the hall. I heard my mother's step on the stairs. Her voice was as clear from the hallway as if she was standing in the room beside us.

It was Harvey, we gathered, honouring Rathmore Drive with one of his infrequent family visits for Sunday lunch. My mother was positively purring after the first few exchanges. There were a number of nauseating references to her favourite grandchild, Peter, the usual inquiries about Mavis and the two girls, and then, to my horror, I heard her assuring Harvey that I would be there too, that she was just about to ask me.

The call ended. I heard the heavy tread of her footsteps, the rattle of wooden rings as she pulled the velvet curtains behind the front door. The sitting-room curtains would come next. If she were going to come in, she would come in then. And as likely as not she would behave as if nothing whatever had happened.

My father was leaning back in his chair, listening to the

pattern of the evening ritual. We exchanged glances and grinned ruefully at each other.

The door opened. She marched across to the fireplace, a smirk on her face. 'My goodness,' she exclaimed, 'you're sitting here all in the dark. Harvey rang a little while ago. They're coming for Sunday lunch. Isn't that nice? And Susie was asking for you, Jenny, so I said I was sure you'd be able to come, as Colin is away. Harvey will pick you up while I'm getting the lunch. I thought we'd have a leg of lamb for a change. What do you think, George?'

Chapter 5

I pushed the front door closed with my elbow, stepped over a pile of envelopes and dropped briefcase and basket on the seat in the telephone alcove. 'Thank God to be home,' I said aloud.

There was an icy chill in the hall and a pervasive, unpleasant smell hanging in the air. It felt as if I'd been gone for a month. I kept my coat on and went into the kitchen. It was exactly as I had left it at a quarter to seven this morning when Colin suddenly announced that we had to leave an hour earlier than usual, because he had to pick up his father on the Antrim Road for their nine o'clock flight.

Earlier, I was surprised and delighted when he wakened me with a mug of tea. Sitting up in bed, listening to him cooking his breakfast, I drank it gratefully and hoped it was a peace offering after the awful row we'd had the previous evening. Relaxed and easy as it was still so early, I went down in my dressing gown and to my surprise found my fruit juice and cornflakes sitting ready for me.

Now, I scraped the soggy residue of the cornflakes into the polythene box where I keep scraps for the birds and put it back in the fridge. I'd been halfway through them when he told me. That gave me precisely fifteen minutes to shower, make up, dress, organise the papers I'd abandoned in my study the previous evening and be ready to leave. The alternative was to leave on foot, twenty minutes after Colin, and spend an hour and a half travelling, three buses and a train.

I shivered miserably and tried to put it out of mind as I studied the control panel for the central heating boiler. It looked perfectly all right. On: morning, six till eight. Heat and water. Back on: Five. For getting home, early evening. Off, ten thirty. By which time we were usually in bed. I looked at my watch. It was only ten fifteen so why was it off?

'Oh, not one more bloody thing,' I said crossly as I tramped round the kitchen in frustration. The air was still full of the smell of Colin's bacon and egg. I prodded the switch on the extractor fan. To my amazement, it began to whir. It hadn't worked for weeks. I almost managed to laugh at my bad temper, but then I caught sight of Colin's eggy plate. The very thought of the relaxed way he'd announced the change of plan made me furious again.

'Come on, Jenny, concentrate. It was working this morning,' I said firmly.

Among the many delights of Loughview Heights, as advertised in the colour brochure from any McKinstry Brothers agent and free to all would-be customers, was a range of modern conveniences 'guaranteed to impress your visitors'. What the brochure didn't say was that they also broke down at the slightest provocation. There'd been such a crop of failures recently I was ready to exchange them for reliable Stone Age technology like paraffin lamps and water from a well.

I stared at the control panel again. Somewhere at the back of my weary mind a thought formed. I was missing something blindingly obvious. I peered at the minute figures on the dial. Then the penny dropped. Slightly to the right of the control box was a large switch. It said 'OFF'.

'Off?' I exclaimed incredulously. 'Who's bloody OFF? I'm not OFF, I'm here and I'm freezing.'

I pushed it down. The loud click echoed through the dark, empty house. A red light flowered. There was a woosh and a shower of tiny ticks, like rain splattering a window. I shivered, cleared and stacked the breakfast things, and went through to the lounge and found an even worse mess.

I stepped round the ironing board and drew the curtains across the black hole that echoed the chaos around me. I switched on the table lamps and turned off the top light. Even with softer lighting, the walls looked almost as grubby as they did under the glare of the overhead fitment. I pushed a pile of Colin's papers, magazines and instruction sheets off an armchair and sat down.

I'd had plans for those walls this weekend. Tuscan. A rich, earthy colour that might even bring out some quality in the hideous, mustardy velvet curtains. The tins of emulsion had been sitting in the garage since the summer. But it looked as if my mother had put paid to that little scheme. I sized up the walls again. Allowed for the mass of the stone fireplace and the picture window. Calculated how long it might take me to remove the adjustable shelving and all the books and objects by myself. Shook my head sadly. Bitter experience had taught me things always take longer than you think. The tin says 'one coat'. But when I did my study, the same dirty white had grinned through one coat. Some bits had ended up needing three coats.

If I didn't have to go to Rathmore Drive for Sunday lunch, perhaps I could have just managed it. But there it was. I did. One more weekend, to follow all the others. Something on. Not something we wanted to do, but one more 'must do' among all the many 'must dos' that had come to dominate our life.

I tried to remember when we last had a weekend when we could just be together, sit over breakfast, talk, drink cups of coffee, or pull on boots and walk down to the loughshore. We had had so little time together recently it wasn't surprising, really; Colin could be so thoughtless and I could get so anxious and agitated about things never getting done.

The room was beginning to warm up slightly, but the hot air pouring through the vents was blowing Colin's scattered papers all over the place. Wearily, I got up and gathered them together. Half were specifications for the new factory in Antrim, now his special project. I'd seen them so often, I knew them by heart. Then I found the instructions for making the homebrew. A pile of photocopies – *Which* reports on new cars. And down at the bottom of the pile still on the sofa I found an overflowing ashtray full of Neville's cigarette stubs and ash from Colin's cigar. At least that accounted for the peculiar, stale smell in the room. Accounting for the furious row we had when Neville finally left would not be so easy.

Neville had appeared from next door before we'd finished supper. He was laden with packets and boxes which he deposited all round the kitchen wherever there was a space. The weekly shop still hadn't been put away, nor the supper dishes stacked, when he breezed in, but Colin shooed me away. Not to worry, he said, he'd sort things out while they were getting the brew going. No problem.

I retreated to my study and tried to read essays. Not exactly what I had planned, when Colin was going to be away all weekend. But I couldn't concentrate. From downstairs, great bursts of laughter rose at regular intervals, together with an unpleasant smell which made me think of sodden haystacks steaming in the hot sun after heavy rain.

Time passed. There were noises on the stairs. 'Mind how you go, Colin, old lad. You'll give yourself a hernia, you will.'

'Steady on, Neville. Watch where you're putting your airlock. You can harm a young lad like that.'

By ten o'clock I felt desperate. I set off to go and tell Neville there was packing to do and plans to make for the weekend.

Colin hailed me halfway down the stairs. 'Oh, Jenny, just in time. We've made some coffee. Are there any biscuits?'

The kitchen was exactly as I left it, only now there were sieves, bowls and large saucepans, full of the drying residue of boiled hops, stacked all over the floor, and the pedal bin was overflowing. I picked out the biscuits from the carrier where Colin had put them himself, declined coffee, and started to clear up.

It was nearly eleven by the time Neville went and Colin strode back into the kitchen, looking pleased with himself.

'Oh, Jenny, you shouldn't have washed up. I'd have helped.'

'That's what you said at eight o'clock,' I replied sharply.

'Well, it doesn't matter, does it? I'll do it now.'

'Yes, it does matter. It's nearly eleven and we haven't had a moment to ourselves all evening and you still have your packing to do.'

He came and put his arms round me and nuzzled my ear. 'Oh, come on, Jen. It's not that late,' he began persuasively. 'I won't be two ticks packing. You go on up and have a nice shower and I'll be in bed with you in no time.'

At that moment the thought of a shower and of getting to bed without any further delay was utterly appealing. I nodded wearily but decided to finish drying up the saucepans while he packed. I heard him fetch his weekend case from the cloakroom and run upstairs whistling cheerfully. I bent over to empty the pedal bin.

The night air was cold as I replaced the lid on the dustbin, but looking up I saw the moon appear suddenly from behind a great mass of cloud. Light spilled all around me. A spray of yellow chrysanthemums gleamed in the big flowerbed at the end of the garden. Beyond the dark mass of the shrubs and the climbers I'd planted to hide the solid shape of the fence, the lough lay calm, a silver swathe laid across its dark surface. On the far shore, where the Antrim plateau plunged down to the coast, strings and chains of lights winked along the coastline like pale flowers edging a garden path. The still, frosty air was heavy with quiet.

'Jen. Can you hear me? Where are you?'

Reluctantly, I went back into the house and found Colin

peering down over the banisters. His good spirits had vanished and he wore a patient look that did nothing to hide his irritation.

'What have you done with my white shirts, Jen? I can't find them.'

'Which white shirts?'

'Any white shirts. They aren't in the drawer,' he went on quickly. 'I've looked.'

'They're probably all in the wash,' I replied steadily. 'I've been handwashing your drip-dries since the machine packed up. There are two or three of those on the fitment in the bathroom.'

'But they're blue,' he protested impatiently.

'Since when has there been a rule about wearing white shirts at conferences?' I asked crossly.

I went back into the kitchen, opened a drawer and pulled a pedal-bin liner off the roll. I heard him pound downstairs and turned and saw him glowering in at me.

'Jenny, you know perfectly well I always wear the white ones for conferences,' he said with a dangerous edge to his voice. 'What the hell am I supposed to do? Wash my own?'

'Colin, if you had let me ring someone two weeks ago about the machine neither of us would have to wash your shirts. But you wanted to fiddle with the damn thing. I told you I'd rather we paid to have it done so we'd have some time to do other things. But you said no. You'd order the part. You'd fit it yourself. Well, if you had, the drawer would be full of shirts. So don't go blaming me.'

The wretched pedal-bin liner wouldn't open. I stood there struggling with it as I watched him change gear. The glowering face disappeared and his tone was sweetness itself as he started to explain that he wasn't blaming me. I just didn't understand how difficult his position was. Didn't I grasp what a big responsibility this new Antrim contract was? Couldn't I see that he was run off his feet, he was so busy? And just how important it was for his future. He couldn't really use office time to make domestic phone calls, now could he? Besides, he was out on site so much. Surely I didn't expect him to be responsible for everything, even his own shirts.

Something about that rapid change of expression, perhaps, or something about that sweet-reasonable tone made me angrier and angrier. At one point, I nearly threw the roll of pedal-bin bags at him just to get him to stop. But I managed not to. Instead, I insisted he had plenty of other shirts. That he could have checked last night he had exactly the shirts he wanted. At the very least, he could have checked before he and Neville made both the kitchen and the bathroom unusable.

'Why on earth did you have to invite Neville in on the evening before a conference anyway?' I ended angrily.

'Because I prefer not to spend all my time working, unlike some people,' he threw back at me.

'Unlike some people?' I repeated furiously. 'And what about these last three weekends? Who was working then?'

He went quite white, but I scarcely noticed as the pent-up resentment of the last weeks poured out of me.

'Entertaining your wretched uncle from Australia because Maisie thinks he might just leave you something. And the bloke from British Steel, who might just wangle you a contract,' I shouted. 'Or maybe that doesn't count as work because you could relax and wave your cigar around just like your father does while I lay on the meals. I suppose you think that's what women are for. And I suppose you think I enjoy providing cut-price entertainment for McKinstry Brothers instead of having some time for us, like any working couple.'

Recalling the violence of my outburst, I shivered, although the room was now pleasantly warm. I looked at my watch. Ten fifty-five. The row had gone on for an hour or more. I ended up weeping from pure exhaustion. Colin apologised, insisted he loved me. Just wanted me to be happy. It would all be much better soon, he said. He thought he could promise me that. It might even be he would have some good news when he came back on Sunday night. Of course I was right about the shirts. They did look a bit creased but he'd manage with the blue ones. I was far more important than any old shirts.

So we'd made it up, and at half past midnight I got out the ironing board and did the bits of the blue shirts that showed. Going halfway, my father would call it. He always argued you have to go halfway to meet people, because we all make mistakes sometimes. No one's perfect.

Eleven o'clock. Warm at last, I took off my coat and went and sat by the phone. Driving into Belfast this morning, Colin insisted he hadn't told me about the early start because he didn't want to upset me. He thought I mightn't sleep as well if I knew we had to get up early. Hadn't he done his best to help me, when he had so much on his mind? Didn't I see how important this weekend was to our future?

I could see why it was so important for him. That was easy enough. After all, he'd talked about nothing else for weeks. He thought it would be the moment when his father offered him the dirctorship. And that was where our future came in, because it would mean more money, as he so frequently told me, besides the perks of his own office and a company car. Things would be easier for us. Of that he was sure. Why, I could even have my own little car, he said. Wouldn't that be nice for me?

Outside school, he put his arms round me and kissed me. 'I'll phone you tonight between ten and eleven. I promise. Just as soon as I get away from the evening session.' He drove off and I went slowly up the steps into the cold and empty building to put myself together for the day's teaching, a full nine periods, most of them with examination classes.

The phone rang a long way off. Colin. At last. I set out to answer it, but I couldn't find my way. I hurried, but didn't seem to get any closer. Its peremptory ring got louder and louder. I struggled on. Tripped over things in the darkness. My basket. My briefcase. Then a pile of saucepans, which fell down and made a noise even louder than the phone. I woke up and found myself in bed, the room pitch black.

Colin's alarm clock was still ringing its head off. And it was on his side of the bed. Desperate to stop the appalling racket, I fought my way through the tangled bedclothes, grabbed it one-handed and squashed its 'Off' knob against the crumpled pillow. I lay back exhausted, my heart pounding, the strident, metallic sound still vibrating in my ears.

I stared at the cold object in my hand, a wedding present

from one of Colin's friends. 'Extra loud', it had said on the box. A curtain of exclamation marks had been added. I was supposed to find it funny. Five forty-five, I read on its luminous dial. Yesterday's early start. That wasn't funny either. I just stopped myself flinging the wretched thing at the bedroom wall.

I switched on my bedside lamp, put my hands to my face and moaned, 'Oh, couldn't he have turned that bloody thing off instead of the central heating?' Tears of anger and frustration sprang into my eyes. I'd so needed a good night's sleep but the few hours I'd had were restless and dream-haunted.

Colin's promised call hadn't come till after twelve. The phone box he'd chosen was horribly noisy and the moment he spoke it was clear he only wanted to say he'd try again tomorrow, when he had more coins. I'd asked him to reverse the charges and quickly told him about the job and having to decide by Monday. But he couldn't have heard properly. All he said was, 'Well, if Monday suits you for doing it, that's fine by me.' Then I heard a voice call out. A woman's voice. Very bright and sharp. 'Do hurry up, darling, the taxi's waiting.' And he said, 'Sorry, Jen, no more money. It's all going fine, just fine. We'll have a chat tomorrow,' and hung up.

I sat up in bed and caught sight of my reflection in the glass-fronted wardrobes that lined the wall opposite me. I hardly recognised myself.

'Stop it, Jenny,' I said firmly. 'That way madness lies. It's dark and you've had a bad night. Don't think. Act. Do something. Anything. Don't dare think till you're feeling more like yourself. Come on. Get going. You're wide awake

93

and you may as well make the best of it. Shower. Breakfast. One thing at a time.'

I turned my face up to the shower's warm rain and felt my anger drain away. I let the water play on my aching shoulders and imagined my tension washing away down the plughole like so many slivers of metal. I shut my eyes and saw a sandy beach lapped by blue sea. A coral reef shut out the crashing breakers of the ocean beyond. In the sun-warmed waters of the lagoon, I could dive down and follow the flickers of tiny fish, jewel-bright against the pale silver sand, the fine residue of the reef beyond, swept in by the pounding waves.

Reluctantly, I emerged from my reverie and reached for a towel from the heated rail. The towel was cold, damp and smelly.

'I don't believe it,' I said as I dripped across to the airing cupboard for a dry one. The statement was purely rhetorical. It was only too easy to believe the towel rail had finally packed up. It had been on the blink for months. I pulled open the cupboard door, put out my hand for a bath sheet and swore vigorously.

Pushed in among the piles of towels, the bed linen and the table linen was an enormous glass bottle full of seething, yellow-green liquid. The bath sheets were squashed up against the wall behind it. As I reached past the intruding object, the airlock made a loud, hiccupping noise and released a tiny puff of foul-smelling gas. Only a few seconds later, it did it again. Even I knew it was going too fast. At this rate, it was only a matter of time before it blew out the airlock and spewed its contents all over everything. Unless, of course, as Colin had done, I turned off the central heating to keep it happy.

I scrubbed myself dry, ran back into the bedroom and pulled on some clothes. Suddenly the penny dropped. All that racket on the stairs, on Thursday night, and the great jokes about straining your privates. Neville in his element and Colin egging him on. That's what they'd been up to. And not a thought of 'Do you mind?' And now I was left to work out what in hell's name I was going to do about it, given there was no way I could move the damn thing.

'Damage limitation, Jenny. Damage limitation. That's all's for it,' I muttered. I fished out the clean linen, carried it into the guest room and stacked it up on the twin beds. Amazing how much the cupboard held. Enough sheets to furnish a dormitory. Those McKinstrys who weren't in construction were in textiles, which was handy for wedding presents. I ran my eye over the armfuls I had carried in and had a sudden appalling vision of having to wash the whole lot. Without a washing machine.

Another wave of fury swept over me. That was Colin all over. No matter what he did, it was always going to be fine. From the most trivial to the most important. Just fine. His only problem was, he said, that I didn't seem to see things as he did. If only I'd relax and not upset myself everything would be just grand. I was always upsetting myself, he said. Well, perhaps he was right. He never got upset, and I couldn't stop getting upset about the fact that he never got upset. I banged the guest-room door, ran downstairs and put the kettle on. I reached for the jar of coffee beans and nearly dropped it.

'Stop it, Jenny. Stop it.'

I took a deep breath and concentrated hard on measuring

the coffee beans into the grinder without spilling them. Then I searched through the carriers still parked on the garage floor and found some sliced bread. As I made myself some breakfast, the agitation slowly began to subside. I sat sipping my coffee and thinking about the day ahead. There was an awful lot to do, but it didn't trouble me. I had time, a whole, precious day to myself. No one to see, no one coming for a meal and nowhere I had to go.

I took up a pad of paper and made a list. It was so long, I laughed out loud. Long lists only intimidate me when there is no time to reduce them. Today, I could choose what I was going to do and in what order I was going to do it. I sat for a little while longer sipping my coffee and leafing through the week's accumulated mail, relishing the chance to be leisurely.

I put down my cup and got to my feet. 'Let's get this place straight,' I said to the empty kitchen.

I cleared breakfast and washed up. Thursday's shopping was put away, the fridge cleaned, the floor swept. I stepped out into the garage to refill the washing-up liquid and spotted the overflowing laundry basket beside the washing machine. I scooped it up, ran upstairs for the other two and shook their contents onto the kitchen table. It would have been easier to use the floor, but one look at it made me wonder when it had last seen soap and water.

I stared at the multicoloured pyramids which now decorated every freshly wiped surface in sight. 'Surely there hasn't always been this much to do.'

I thought back to January 1967 when we had first moved in. Yes, it had been a bit chaotic to begin with. Packing cases everywhere and that awful straw the movers used for all our china and glass. But that was only for a week or two. And before that there was Birmingham.

I remembered our furnished flat, the yellowed magnolia-patterned wallpaper on the stairwell, the draught under the living-room door, so fierce in winter it made the carpet flap, the tiny kitchen, so small we could barely get in together to do the washing-up. The first Saturday night we came back from shopping, the people downstairs were cooking bloaters. The smell was unbearable. We took one look at each other, ran all the way downstairs, had supper in a Wimpey bar and went to an early film.

That was typical of us, then. Problems had solutions in those days. Like the February week when the ancient heating-system packed up. We spent the evenings in bed, talking and reading and making love, our supper dishes left unwashed till morning, when we donned layers of woollens over our camping pyjamas until it was time to dress for work.

Perhaps distance lends enchantment, I thought, as I surveyed my pyramids. Perhaps Birmingham was different, almost an extension of student days. For fifteen months we had been a young couple in a flat. Nothing expected of us beyond our work, no appearances to be kept up, no ideal home to run or parents to visit, no contacts to be made, or useful acquaintances to be cultivated. There was just us. With new jobs and the challenge of new experiences. Encouraging each other. Sharing things, dreaming dreams and making plans. We'd talked endlessly about the future and all we wanted to do and see before we started a family.

'How about Abu Dhabi, Jen?' Colin had asked one Sunday morning as we lay in bed reading the papers.

'I don't even know where it is,' I'd admitted, laughing. I'd hopped out of bed, fetched my old school atlas and we'd worked through all the contracting jobs we could find so I could see just what the possibilities were.

Only a week later, the call came. Colin's uncle had died suddenly, leaving a space on the board. Colin could finish his traineeship within the firm and move into his uncle's place when his father thought he was ready.

'But what about all our plans, Colin?'

Of course he'd agreed it was a pity. And yes, of course it was too soon. But he could hardly turn down such an opportunity, could he? Not many men made the boardroom before they were thirty, did they? And yes, he agreed it was a pity about my school. But he was sure they'd understand and let me go.

I went on resisting. After all, it had been Colin's father himself who had said how valuable it would be to go away and get experience with other companies. Now all that was forgotten. Colin was needed at home, so that was the end of that particular idea.

I wondered now what would have happened if Daddy had not had his heart attack just a few days later. When that news came, I had flown home alone and spent a very unhappy three days moving between my father's bedside and Rathmore Drive. My mother had been appalling. Oscillating between self-pity and anger with my father for upsetting everyone, she had made it clear that if my father didn't make a complete recovery she certainly wasn't going to look after him. She had her own health to think of as well, she insisted.

Back at school, I taught lessons and couldn't remember

afterwards what I'd said and discovered a warm sympathy in both my pupils and my colleagues that I had never expected. Back at the flat, I stopped protesting. During my time in Belfast, I had realised there was no point. Now, with my father off the immediate danger list, I had my own reason for wanting to go home.

I filled the sink and shook the soap powder so fiercely that I sneezed. As I prodded the first of the shirts into the foaming mass, something caught my eye. At the far end of the garden, the first finger of sunlight picked up the golden spray of chrysanthemums I'd last seen by moonlight. In the pale awakening of the early morning, the dew on the grass was so white it looked like frost. I watched the sky lighten. Soon, I could separate the grey-blue of the lough from the darker blue of the Antrim Hills.

I pushed open the window and caught the throb of engines. Moments later, the black and white mass of the Liverpool ferry glided across the smooth water, heading for its berth in the centre of the city. Behind it, the wake oscillated, sending out its vibrating ripples to break as tiny waves on the Down shore. Minutes after and miles away on the far Antrim shore, gulls would bob up and down briefly on the grey water, their unexpected motion understood only by those who could connect such a distant event as the passage of the Liverpool ferry with such a small local happening.

When I looked through the porthole and caught sight of the Down coast the December morning we returned to Ulster, the lough was far from calm. I had wanted to go up on deck. Soon, we would be able to see the places we knew so well, the beaches where we had walked, the bays where we had sailed with our friends. But Colin said it would be chilly and that he'd see to the car, so I'd gone up alone and found myself a small, partly-sheltered space on the upper deck below the lifeboats. From there, I'd looked out at the grey, broken water and listened to the mournful cries of the gulls following in our wake.

The Antrim shore was dark and brooding and the crags of Cave Hill rose ominously above the red and grey sprawl of the estates at its feet. By the lough's side, the gantries stood, silhouetted against the sky like great mechanical birds feeding in the tainted water. Factory and warehouse, chapel and church, two-storey house and four-storey mill. So familiar, my heart leapt. But only with sadness. An unnameable sadness.

Words of Louis MacNeice suddenly came back to me. I could hear my father's voice reading them, and the thought of that well-loved voice, so nearly lost such a little time ago, released a flood of memories.

Long after I'd been able to read for myself, I'd still ask my father to read to me. And he had, so willingly. Anything I put into his hands. Books from school, or from the library, or his own, well-thumbed volumes of plays and poetry. He read to me and then he'd coax me to read aloud for myself. Soon, we were able to take it in turns to read and our reading together had become a ritual and a reassurance.

At that moment the ship had begun to turn. I went forward to the rail. The water was brown in the harbour area, beaten into an unlovely whirlpool, spattered with debris and flecked with oily waste. The water slapped and protested as the ship whittled away the remaining inches between itself and the slimy masonry of the dock wall. I heard the chains run out, saw the gangway rise, and felt the deck shudder as the engines died. Ship and land embraced. I had come home. As I turned to go below, the tears welled up so fiercely I could not see my way ahead.

I rubbed crossly at the collar of a white shirt, squeezed it out and piled it on the draining board with the others. Six of them, the hand-finished ones Maisie gave him that first Christmas home.

'Just a "little" present, Colin dear.'

I could still hear her voice, thin and bright, as the stack of gift-wrapped boxes was brought out from under the tree.

'Oh, Mum, you shouldn't have. After all you've done already.'

Colin's tone made me wince. Not just his effusiveness, but the particular way he chose to acknowledge the 'real' present, the awful furniture already installed in the new house. He had kissed her and sat with his arms entwined in hers as my 'little' present was brought out.

'Nothing like a nice white shirt to help on the way to the boardroom,' she said, in the sort of whisper that only the stone deaf could fail to hear.

The look of self-satisfaction on Colin's face was so sickening, I had to turn away. That look and the way they sat with their arms entwined upset me more than I could explain to myself. It was an awful moment, but worse was to come.

'I do hope you like yours as much, Jenny,' went on Maisie, as Keith passed over the beribboned box bearing my name.

With all eyes upon me, I fumbled with the ribbons and tore ineffectually at the wrapping. When I finally got the lid off the elegant box inside, I discovered two superbly finished garments in cashmere. Light as a feather, and more expensive than any item I had ever possessed, I found myself holding what Valerie and I always called a 'lady wife' twin-set. And as if that were not bad enough, the colour was the particular pastel shade we'd long ago christened 'knicker pink'.

I pulled out the plug and watched the dirty water settle to a flat calm. I braced myself and pressed a switch. The disposal unit minced the harmless water as if it were crunching chicken bones. The whole sink fitment vibrated, the soap holder moved crabwise across the draining board and the whirling vortex of water disappeared.

Well, the boardroom wouldn't be long now. And then what? I started rinsing the shirts. Of course, everything would be fine. It seemed once Colin had convinced himself that something was fine, or going to be fine, then that was it. Finished. Classified. No need even to speak of it again.

Just the way this house had been 'fine'. It was the show house for the Loughview and Kilmorey estates, and it had been Maisie's idea we should have it, all nicely furnished as it was and only a little grubby from the probing fingers of potential buyers. 'The last word in elegance,' she said enthusiastically. 'Everything you could possibly want and nothing for you to do but unpack your bits and pieces.'

We hadn't even seen it when Colin said yes. I objected, of course. And he agreed with everything I said. True, it wasn't what we'd had in mind, was it? No, it wasn't very convenient for my school. Yes, we had hoped for a little more privacy, hadn't we? And then he made his own position clear. It was such a good opportunity. The nominal figure his father had suggested in lieu of a mortgage would leave us very comfortable. We could travel, as I wanted. And we could always redecorate, and even refurnish, to our own taste, after a discreet interval. We'd be fools not to take it.

I dumped the first batch of shirts in a bucket and started on my blouses. That was the trouble. Colin always saw my point of view, said how much he agreed with it, and then paid no real attention to it whatever. How often had we discussed and planned some course of action, only for me to find that just the opposite was happening? Once, I used to think it was my fault for not making myself clear. But now I wasn't so sure. I was beginning to wonder if Colin ever thought about anything at all, or simply reacted to any situation as it happened.

I found myself rehearsing some of his characteristic phrases. 'But it's Saturday,' he would say, or, 'After all, we can afford it,' or his favourite, 'It's too good an opportunity to miss.' They seemed harmless enough, I had to admit, but the problem was the effect they had on me. Colin had only to utter one of them and I would feel I was quibbling, or being difficult or unreasonable. How was it he could manage to give such empty phrases the stamp of sweet reasonableness? And why was I always having to protest at decisions that materialised out of nowhere, as if there was no need for me to be involved in them?

The whole miserable business had begun that very morning we arrived home. Straight from the boat, en route to the flat our friends had lent us while they were abroad, we stopped off to see Maisie. She insisted we stay with them till the Christmas holiday was over. He had said yes for both of us, without a moment's hesitation.

So we quarrelled that night in our bedroom, hissing at each other across the thickly carpeted room, with its pink fringed lamps and fat, pink eiderdowns. Colin said he didn't see what else he could do when Maisie suggested it. He'd thought it would save me having to cook in a strange flat till after the holiday.

I would never forget that Christmas holiday. It was a nightmare from beginning to end, a continuous exposure to noise, food, and relatives. A continuous demand for sociability, small talk and team performance. And Christmas Day itself had been the worst of all.

The house was overheated and airless. Every room, even the bathroom, boomed with festive music piped from the new stereo, William John's latest acquisition. Over the top of it, William John himself sounded forth, his voice heavy with goodwill but edged with unease. As if by continuous action he could disperse the burden of Maisie's disapproval, he urged the company on from one celebratory meal to another and from one obligatory piece of jollity to the next. He circulated endlessly, enveloping himself with talk as if it were his only defence. He asked questions and paid no attention to the answers. He grew flushed, exhausted and irritable. His efforts made him so querulous that, in the end, I was hard-pressed to find any sympathy for him, even though I knew how much he feared the sharp edge of Maisie's tongue.

Maisie had been even worse, if that was possible. Less good-natured than William John to begin with, she shuttled between kitchen and lounge, tight with tension and breathless with effort, so resentful of what she saw as

William John enjoying himself while she had the worry of
the food, despite the fact she'd refused all help with it. Her
eyes darted about constantly without ever focusing upon
anyone. Her endearments flowed endlessly all around the
company, their emptiness as palpable as that of the gin
glass which seldom left her hand.

'What on earth am I doing here?' I asked myself as I
stood in the lounge on Christmas morning, watching Colin
mixing drinks at the bar and serving them out to William
John's cronies and their blue-rinsed wives. I looked up
and spotted Keith, grim-faced and uneasy, changing records
under William John's supervision. I went over to him and
tried to comfort him. He muttered something bitter about
'conspicuous consumption', and then Maisie bore down
on me.

Half the time I felt a failure for not being able to 'enjoy
myself' and the other half I felt a fraud for even trying to.
In the end, I hit on the idea of playing a film extra. That
way, I could put some life into a non-speaking part. Laugh
merrily over spilt champagne. Smile happily as mother-
in-law points you out as Colin's little wife. Accept
delightedly drink or liqueur, chocolate or crystallised fruit.
Or even a paper hat.

A few hours' exit were granted in the afternoon to go
over and see my parents and then back we went for the
evening performance. By bedtime, I was beside myself.
As we shut the bedroom door, I turned to Colin for comfort
and all he did was look down at me with amazement and
say, just as if he were humouring a fractious child, 'Oh
come on, Jenny, what's wrong? It's Christmas. It's the old
man's way, you know. He does lay it on a bit thick, but

he's all right. He's very fond of you, you must see that. They both are. That was quite a present you had from Mum, wasn't it? More than generous.'

I despatched another sinkful of grey water with a furious press of the switch.

'More than generous,' I repeated. Just what my mother said last night. That was it. Generosity was quite their forte, their well-practised technique, for getting what they wanted. When you had finished being 'more than generous' you could stand back, secure in your own good opinion of yourself, and expect repayment. How could anyone refuse you anything you wanted when you had had the foresight to be 'more than generous'?

I turned on the cold tap so fiercely that a stream of water bounced off the clothes in the sink, splashed me in the face and poured down the front of my sweater. I stood and shook myself, but it was no use. The ice-cold water was trickling down inside my jeans. 'Damn the bloody McKinstrys,' I hissed as I peeled off my wet top. 'Damn, damn their bloody generosity,' I fumed as I ran upstairs in my bra to find something dry to wear.

By the time I found a cotton top and an old wool sweater to go over it, my wet jeans had made a damp, cold spot on my tummy. I stripped them off and scuffled in the drawer where I keep my gardening clothes. As I pulled out my old green cords, I caught the lingering perfume of lemon geranium. I sniffed appreciatively, stuck my hand in the pocket and brought out a handful of withered leaves. They were the trimmings from the cuttings I'd set going for Valerie, after that splendid day at the end of the holidays up on the north coast.

Dear Valerie. The thought of my oldest and closest friend brought a sudden anxious stab of distress. Valerie and I hadn't seen each other all term and it was entirely my fault. Several times when I had come back from theatre visits or parents' evenings, Colin had said she'd phoned. She'd chatted to him, passed on bits of news and sent me messages, but I hadn't phoned her back. I couldn't think why on earth I hadn't. Every time I watered her cuttings, I vowed I'd do it right away. I thought of her so often, but I still didn't do it.

Why on earth not? I asked myself crossly. You're a fool. An absolute fool. She's the one person who'd really be able to help you.

I continued to scold myself as I pulled on the green cords. I zipped them up and found they sagged limply round my middle. 'Gracious, you have lost weight this term,' I muttered as I looked for a belt.

But all the belts I tried needed an extra hole and I didn't feel like searching the garage for a hammer and a sharp instrument, so I found a pyjama cord of Colin's, threaded it quickly through the loops and tied it in a bow. 'Like a sack tied in the middle,' my mother would say. Well, she wouldn't see it, would she? So there. No one would see it. I pulled my sweater firmly over my handiwork and ran downstairs to phone Val.

Why are you still puzzling over it, Jenny, I asked myself as I settled by the phone. Why do the reasons matter so much when you know she'll understand?'

As I started to dial her number, the hall clock began to strike. I dropped the receiver as if it had given me an electric shock, stood up and laughed at myself. Valerie is one of those people who can sparkle half the night but has an awful job waking up in the morning. It was still only eight o'clock. Well, at least today there'd be nothing to stop me ringing her. I'd have a good old blitz till about eleven, make a mug of coffee, and get her after she'd had some breakfast.

Feeling positively light-hearted, I collected my buckets and headed for the clothesline. The sun had come out from behind one of the bright, white clouds that streamed out of the west. I could feel warmth on my arms as I pinned up the first shirt. The dripping fabric inflated in the breeze like a wet sail, showering me with droplets as fine as spray from a toppling wave.

Suddenly, I was on the north coast, the beaches deserted, clean and empty, the summer people gone. I was walking by the sea, the real sea, the Atlantic, its breakers driven by the force of the wind out of the great empty spaces of mid-ocean, unmarked sand at my feet. The cry of the gulls filled the air. Pieces of driftwood caught in the black tangled masses of wrack, seashells small as children's fingernails, pebbles bright with moisture, fragments of glass, transformed by the cleansing sea from rubbish to tiny jewels, lay spread out before me.

'Hello, Jenny, you're up early this morning.'

I swore under my breath, disentangled myself from the sixth hand-finished white shirt and said, 'Hello, Karen.' One look at her face told me there wasn't the slightest possibility of her going away.

While the fence at the end of the garden adjoining the council estate is six feet high and backed by a fast-growing screen of willow, the fences on both sides of the Loughview gardens are only three feet high. Tastefully planted with low-growing shrubs, 'all part of the extra care which make these properties so desirable', it makes it possible to carry on a conversation with other young executive neighbours up to six houses away. If you so wished.

I didn't. The first time I'd seen the house, I'd suggested we put up a six-foot fence all the way round and plant honeysuckle and climbing roses, knowing that would add another couple of feet in time. Colin agreed immediately that it would look very nice. But that was before we discovered Karen and Neville lived next door.

'How are you, Jenny? We haven't seen you for ages.'

I went on pegging my way down the line, though I knew there would be no escape. Karen followed me along on her side of the fence, displeasure written all over her face.

'I'm fine thanks, Karen, just fine. How are you?' I added dutifully.

Not that I needed to ask. Karen was Karen. She was flourishing, as always. Newly-set hair, tailored slacks, floral pattern smock, well-made-up face. As my mother would say, and regularly did say, 'Karen Pearson always looks just immaculate.' Intimidating at the best of times, at eight o'clock on a Saturday morning it was positively indecent.

Karen has always been 'immaculate'. Ever since my first day at primary school, when she was detailed to look after me, she has been a model of propriety. Always tidy. Always in the right place, at the right time. And ever since that day, by virtue of her two months seniority, she has been ready to show me the right way to do things, exactly as she showed me my peg in the cloakroom and supervised my changing into my house shoes on our very first meeting.

I came to the end of the clothesline. There was nothing for it. I marched back towards the house and paused at the bald spot in the flowerbed where Colin and Neville stood to chat or hop over to peer under the bonnets of their respective cars.

'Look, Jenny, I can't stop now,' she began breathlessly as she caught up with me.

I breathed a sigh of relief but I should have known better.

'I think I hear Simon,' she went on. 'You must come in for coffee, ten thirty, and we'll have a proper chat. They'll both be asleep again by then.'

I opened my mouth to protest; but she was too quick for me.

'I have a parcel for you. Came yesterday. And a note from Valerie. I can give them to you then,' she ended firmly as she looked back over her shoulder and closed her kitchen door.

I worked off my fury on the garage and by ten thirty I was feeling quite pleased with myself. I had a huge pile of newspapers and flattened cardboard for the charity collection, two boxes of magazines for the local hospital, and three boxes of assorted objects which I would insist Colin went through and disposed of. As I swept out the cobwebs and last year's autumn leaves, I was amazed at just how large the double garage had become.

It was turning into the loveliest of autumn days, mild and blowy, with sudden bursts of warm sun. As I scrubbed my hands at the kitchen sink, blinking in the strong sunlight, I told myself that it was far better to do Karen properly and get it over than to try and dodge in and out of the garden all afternoon, never knowing when that sharp little voice would scatter my thoughts to the four winds. Once I'd done my duty visit, I could whiz through the rest of the house. Then I'd be free to go into the garden. I was dying to go down and look at the chrysanthemums. There might be enough in bloom for a big arrangement in the hall.

'My goodness, you have been busy, Jenny.'

The small, close-set eyes took in every detail of my appearance in one quick sweep as she directed me through to the lounge.

'You'd better sit down and have a rest while I perk the coffee. I've got it all ready.'

Somewhat taken aback, for Saturday morning coffees were usually served at the breakfast bar in the kitchen, I settled myself on one of the raft-like armchairs identical to the ones we'd inherited with the show house. I looked around me. The place was as pristine as a furniture showroom, even down to the crystal vase containing six long-stemmed red carnations with the regulation two sprays of greenery. And not the remotest trace of two children under three.

I dropped off my mules and drew my bare feet up under me. The seats of these ocean-going armchairs are so deep that my feet don't reach the ground unless I perch on the edge. And I wasn't in the mood for that. As I leaned comfortably back, I spotted the smoked glass coffee table. It had been placed squarely between the two armchairs and was laid with a bright red woven cloth and pottery coffee cups. On the pottery plates, matching red paper napkins were aligned precisely with each other.

Watch out, Jennifer, I said to myself, as I took in the

detail. Trouble in store. I stared at the two red triangles until their sharp outline blurred. I caught the smell of coffee and fresh scones and braced myself. Karen wanted something. I picked a stray cobweb off my trousers, concealed it in my pocket and sat looking out through the picture window which framed the Saturday morning comings and goings of other inhabitants of Loughview Heights.

Chapter 6

Karen pressed the switch on the coffee percolator and glanced through the serving hatch into the lounge. It was all looking very nice, even down to the flowers she'd bought after she'd met Mrs Erwin and Mrs McKinstry and had such a long talk with them in Brand's. Jenny Erwin really did look a mess. No wonder they were so concerned about her. No make-up, her hair lank and unwashed and as for what she was wearing, you'd think she'd picked it up at a church jumble sale.

One might have some sympathy if she couldn't afford to dress properly, but she and Colin were very comfortably off, two salaries, a firm's car and from what Neville gathered, hardly any mortgage either. She'd got everything, so why on earth was she still working?

She wiped a few drops of water from the polished work surface and spread the cloth neatly on the drying rack above the radiator. The percolator began to gurgle. It really shouldn't make as much noise as that, surely. Perhaps it was time to use the descaling powder again.

Well, she'd promised them she would do what she could. Having known Jenny so long, it wasn't surprising they'd felt she was the right person to say something. But it wasn't easy. Jenny could be awkward. And that was being

113

generous. With Valerie Thompson egging her on, she was downright stubborn. Talk, talk, talk, the pair of them, whenever you saw them together, making up their minds what they thought. Most of it pie in the sky. In the end, they'd just have to do what everyone else did and settle down.

The percolator gulped and spat out small specks of coffee onto the work surface. She retrieved the cloth and decided it really wouldn't do. A wedding present from one of the Baird cousins, it had been an expensive one but wasn't really modern. That was the problem with Neville's family. Even the ones who had done well, like his father, and moved out to detached houses in nice parts of the city, still didn't have much style. She really must look in Robinson Cleaver's for something more up-to-date next Friday when she had her day off from the children.

Still focused on the room beyond, her eye caught a movement. She saw her guest bend forward, pick something from the leg of those disgusting trousers and put it in her pocket. What were those strings hanging down below her sweater? The ends looked almost like the tassels on a pyjama cord. Probably it was some peculiar craft work thing Valerie had produced with her backward children in that school of hers. You could never tell what either of that pair would turn up in next. They'd wear anything just to be different.

Well, they weren't different, for all their great talk. Valerie always said she wanted to be an artist. And Jenny fancied herself as a writer. She'd had a couple of stories published in some little magazine nobody had ever heard of, but there was no mention of writing these days. And

Valerie wasn't going to have much time for being an artist now.

'There you are, Jenny, a nice fresh cup of coffee,' Karen began as she came in with the percolator and perched herself on the edge of the raft opposite. 'Now, do tell me all your news.'

For a moment I was quite taken aback. Then I thought of Maisie and recognised the familiar strategy. She would sit us down in her kitchen, say, 'Now, dear, we're on our own, tell me how you are,' and settle herself just as Karen was doing now. Maisie could ask questions about the job that looked as if she was really interested. But the interest never lasted long. She'd take just enough time to collect the information she needed, some detail like a job we hadn't managed to do or something I'd not got finished, and then she'd strike.

'You know, Jenny dear, men never understan' what it's like tryin' to run a house,' she'd begin, sincerity oozing from every pore. 'Colin's the best in the world, I know he is,' she'd go on, 'but no man has ony idea, ony idea, what a job it is.' Her eyes would gaze heavenward as if seeking the agreement of the Almighty Himself. 'An' you work so hard, Jenny, tryin' to do yer best for them girls. All that markin' and preparin' work. Even at the weekends.' I always knew she was about to get to the point when she lowered her voice confidentially, even if the whole house was empty.

'Jenny, ivery woman needs time wi' her husband an' time to herself.'

She would make a little bowing gesture with her head

that appeared to mean 'we married women know about such intimate things, so we don't have to say any more'. Then she'd pat my hand reassuringly and offer her advice. Maisie could see exactly how to solve my problems of time and conflicting activities. However often it was offered, the advice always came down to the same thing and it was always blatantly obvious that it was what Maisie herself wanted. I should give up work, start a family 'whenever it suited me', and devote myself to being a company wife and a mother.

'And what plays have you seen this term, Jenny?' Karen persisted when I'd despatched her request for my news with a few dismissive comments.

She moved the basket of fresh scones a little towards me. Reluctantly, I worked out that from my present comfortable position I couldn't reach either the individual butter pot or the cut-glass dish with the homemade strawberry jam. If I wanted a scone, I'd have to perch on the edge of my raft like Karen.

'Super scones, Karen,' I said, after I'd completed my manoeuvre.

'Do have another. I know you like fresh scones. You don't get time to bake very often, do you?' she asked sweetly.

I shook my head as I spread strawberry jam generously on the still warm scone. Eat, drink and be merry, Jenny, for she'll shortly get to the point.

But Karen was taking her time. First, I had an account of this super dress she had found in Brand's the previous morning. Then came details of the marvellous scheme she and Carol had worked out so they could each be free to go shopping and have their hair done once a week. After that, we moved to her new car, and how much easier it now was just to pop in the babies and their things and whisk them over to Rathmore Drive to her mother, or Malone Park, to her mother-in-law, when she wanted a day to herself. It was so nice being able to do things and go places again. She sat back and sighed agreeably as if resting after sustained effort. Now that she looked back on it, the year's teaching she'd done when she was first married really had been very demanding. Even Neville agreed how difficult it had all been and I knew how easy-going Neville was, didn't I?

'Is Neville working today?' I asked when she paused for breath.

She frowned slightly. Clearly, I had said the wrong thing. But she recomposed her smile and tossed her head. 'No, not likely. Rugger comes first on Saturdays. He's off to a lunch for some visiting team. They're playing at Ravenhill this afternoon. Goodness knows when he'll appear back.'

'Don't you mind him being away all day?' I asked, curious she should seem so relaxed about his absence.

'Goodness no. He works hard all week. He's entitled to a break at weekends. Of course, Mummy comes over on Saturday afternoons and stays the night, so I never mind if he's late or wants to "go out with the boys", as the saying is,' she ended archly.

I thought of the way Neville hopped over the fence at the slightest encouragement and wondered just how much he figured in Karen's scheme of things. She certainly looked as if she had got what she wanted. She sat, mistress of the smoked glass coffee table, entirely pleased with herself, a smile on her face that made me think of a well-fed pussycat.

Unlike me, Karen had always known exactly what she wanted. At school, she'd been quite open about it. Get her O-levels. Go to Domestic Science College. Marry. Have a lovely home and her own car. And four lovely children. And, presumably, live happily ever after. So far, she was right on target. Two down and two to go. Just the happy-ever-after bit to come.

'I saw your mother yesterday, Jenny,' she began, putting down her empty coffee cup. 'She was with Mrs McKinstry in Brand's and I was on my own, so I went and joined them.'

'Oh,' I said, noncommittally.

'Your mother said you were going up for a meal.'

I stared silently at the dregs of my coffee and found myself quite unwilling to say anything else. But there was no need to say anything. Karen had picked her moment and begun. There was not the slightest possibility of stopping her.

'Really, Jenny, she did seem so concerned about you. And Mrs McKinstry too. They both said you've been losing weight, and I must say I did notice it myself when you were hanging up Colin's shirts. Don't you think, Jenny, it's all getting a bit much, teaching and trying to run a home?' she asked sympathetically.

'Lots of my colleagues seem to manage perfectly well,' I replied as steadily as I could. 'Even the ones with children.'

'Well, of course, it depends what you mean by "manage", doesn't it?' she said, smiling indulgently. 'I don't think you'd much enjoy the mess some of them are happy to live in. You've always liked things to be nice, haven't you, Jenny? And you so love your garden and your photography and so on. You can't have very much time for those any more.'

'So what are you suggesting I do, Karen?' I asked quietly. I wasn't in much doubt what her answer would be and I'd no idea how I'd deal with it, but I was suddenly weary of the play being played. As I looked across at her prim little face, I had a picture of someone just so damn sure of herself, so confident that the little world she'd made for herself was the only one anyone could possibly want. I had the most passionate desire to do something quite outrageous.

'Well, honestly, Jenny, at your age you really should have begun.'

To my own surprise, I laughed. It was the tone that did it. Two months older than me and Karen was already a matron, full of gravity and wisdom. I wondered if her manner was a side effect of parturition.

'You make me sound like Methuselah. For heaven's sake, I'm only twenty-six.'

'But that's just the point. You *are* twenty-six. It's more than time you were thinking of your first. You know perfectly well that the ideal age is eighteen and after that, fertility begins to drop and complications are more likely. I'm sure that's what your mother and Mrs McKinstry are worried about. They're only thinking of your own good.'

'Oh, I know that's what they're worried about all right,' I replied agreeably. 'Whether they're thinking of my own good rather than their own good is another matter.'

Karen's sympathetic look disappeared like snow off a

ditch, but before I had time to enjoy my success, she'd collected herself again. She continued, her voice now much less persuasive, her tone demanding. 'But, Jenny, all the medical evidence is there. I mean, I do know quite a lot about it. Mr Jones is so good at explaining things. He says it's so much better to have your family young.'

'If you're going to have one.' My response had popped out without any permission from me.

'Jenny!'

I felt the colour drain from my face. From the look on hers, it was quite clear I had said the unsayable. And perhaps I had. That Colin and I would have children had always been part of our plan. It was there when we talked about 'when we came back from Abu Dhabi' or 'when we bought our house in the country'. Suddenly, it seemed I had put a large question mark against the whole idea.

'Perhaps I shall prove infertile,' I said quickly while I digested the implications of what I'd said. 'Don't forget, Karen, that one couple in six are unable to conceive.' If Karen was going to quote medical evidence then she might as well have a bit of something on the other side. But I might as well not have spoken. I'd forgotten that any fact or figure not a part of her own collection was always dismissed as hearsay.

She tossed my comment aside and went on remorselessly, 'But you haven't even tried, have you?'

'No, I haven't. And I don't intend to. Not until I've made up my mind about committing eighteen years of my life to what you call "enjoying yourself". You haven't told me what I do if I don't enjoy myself,' I said sharply. 'What if I'm not cut out for motherhood?'

She smiled patiently, as if this were no more than she expected. 'Honestly, Jenny,' she went on, secure in the knowledge that she had all the answers, 'it's no wonder we're all so concerned about you. You really are upsetting yourself quite unnecessarily. You're tired out. You're losing weight. You have far too much to do. Now, tell me honestly, have you ever met anyone who didn't enjoy having a family?' She sat back comfortably for the first time, confident she had made an unanswerable point.

'Yes, I have,' I replied promptly. 'I meet them all the time. Only they just don't admit it. They take it out on their husbands or the children themselves, and go on encouraging other women to do what they've done. Why not? If they've got it wrong, why shouldn't everybody else do the same? But it's grim for the poor kids. Perhaps the problems don't show up so much when you're teaching domestic science, but they certainly do when you're teaching English.'

Karen shook her head and smiled. 'All my girls were looking forward to being mothers and having a home of their own. Even the juniors,' she added as she began to gather up the coffee cups.

I hadn't set out to be provocative but I knew there was an edge in my voice. I was really puzzled and distinctly uneasy as to why she hadn't reacted.

'You know, Jenny, I have always tried to help you but it's not easy,' she said patiently. 'Why don't you talk to some of your other friends? Perhaps they could help you more than I can, though I've known you longer than any of them.'

She stood up and I hauled myself out of the raft, put my

feet back in my mules and thanked her for coffee. On the face of it, I had made my point. But as I followed her through to the kitchen, there was something about the set of her shoulders and her self-confident tone that reminded me of schooldays when Karen was well-known for passing on confidences and hurtful gossip. Envious of my friendship with Valerie, more than once she'd managed to create upsets between us.

'Here you are, Jenny. More poetry books. I don't know how you find time to read them,' she said sweetly.

I took them quickly and was about to open the door when she smiled again.

'Oh, you mustn't forget Valerie's note, must you? She came last night and said she hadn't seen you for ages. She was looking terribly well. Absolutely blooming.'

She was still using the sweet tone that was making me feel so uncomfortable.

'Oh good,' I said firmly.

She passed over the note reluctantly.

'Thank you,' I added as I stepped outside.

'Perhaps you'd better just glance at it, Jenny. It might be about tonight. You'll be wanting a lift, won't you?'

'Lift? Where to?'

'Valerie's party, of course. Don't tell me you didn't know about it?' she said in amazement.

I didn't look at her. I could imagine the satisfaction on her face only too well. I didn't answer her either, I just unfolded the note, which I was sure she'd read. It was written in Valerie's usual expansive manner with a purple felt-tipped pen and heavy underlinings. 'Dear Jenny,' it said, 'I'm *so* sorry to have missed you tonight – I came *especially* to see you. Karen says Colin is away and has the car, but you will still come tomorrow, won't you? Bob will collect you if Karen and Neville can't bring you. I *must* see you – I have *so much* to tell you. Love and hugs. Val.'

I read it twice, perfectly aware of Karen's small, hard eyes watching me. Valerie never sent me party invitations. There was no need. She always rang to make sure I'd be free before she chose the date in the first place.

'I think Colin must have forgotten to tell me when she rang about it,' I said quietly. 'But there's no harm done. Are you and Neville picking up anyone, or have you a spare seat?'

'Oh, we can fit you in going. But we may leave early. I don't like Mummy being kept up too late. Perhaps Valerie will drop you back if you stay on to talk. I'm sure she's got lots to tell you.'

She was smirking now and I was even more determined not to let her see how uneasy I was feeling.

'Of course,' I said brightly. 'When have Valerie and I not had lots to tell each other?'

I got myself out of her kitchen, but she went on standing at her door.

'I think you really should have a nice, long talk to Valerie,' she went on as I swung my leg over the fence. 'I'm sure it will do you good. You and Valerie always seem to agree about everything.'

I closed my own door firmly behind me, hurried to the phone and dialled Valerie's number. It was engaged. I tried again and counted the rhythmic bleeps in an attempt to calm myself. I remembered that Bob sometimes made calls to clients on a Saturday morning and they could go on a long time. After a while, I got tired of dialling, so I rang Colin's hotel and left a message asking him to make his promised call before eight o'clock. I tried Val again. Still engaged. I found the number of a local plumber and spoke to his wife, a friendly woman who couldn't give me much hope for a visit today, but was most sympathetic. Then I tried again.

Dear Bob. He must be designing a mansion. I pulled out the drawer in the telephone table and began to sort the contents between attempts.

Like an archaeological excavation, I thought to myself, as I lifted out the directories and went down through layers of bus and train timetables, flights to London, local pamphlets offering gardening and rubbish disposal services, and bits of paper with mysterious telephone numbers in Colin's handwriting. At the very bottom, I found a brand new calendar for 1967. Someone must have given it to Colin when we moved into Loughview. I dialled again and began to flick over the months of our first whole year back home. After three more attempts, I got to July.

'The best of summer weather on a crowded Irish beach,' it said under the picture. I laughed aloud, delighted by what I saw in front of me. On a great curving beach under a brilliant blue sky, with flocks of those little white clouds that make the sky look even brighter and more glorious, two tiny figures were walking along in the shallow water. The two little figures could have been Valerie and myself, for the picture was of our beloved Tra-na-rossan, our very favourite beach in Donegal.

The first time we had had a holiday together, just the

two of us, we had spent more than half of our precious week on that beach.

'Where shall we go, Jenny? Alan says we can have his car while he finishes his lab work. Shall we go round Ireland? Or cross to Scotland and head for John o'Groats? What d'you think?'

I could hear her now, her voice so full of excitement. It was typical of Valerie to think we could go round Ireland in a week in Alan's ancient car when we'd only just got our licences and were still terrified of driving in the centre of Belfast. But we'd worked it out together, set off with the car full of cameras and art materials and picnic things so we could feed ourselves and keep our money for finding interesting places to give us bed and breakfast.

It was July 1961, one of those weeks when the sun shines every day, a rare thing indeed on that wild north-western coast. We stayed in cottages and farms and were made so welcome. We rode in the turf carts and went out in the fishing boats. Kindly women filled our Thermoses with milk or hot water and whole families advised us when the car was reluctant to start.

On our fourth day, an old lady told us how to find Tra-na-rossan. We left her straggling village and drove out over a sandy lowland towards a rocky outcrop which she said had once been an island. The road ran on to the east of it, along Mulroy Bay, and then dived down precipitously between two low thatched cottages and became a rough track. Val was convinced we'd gone wrong and I was equally convinced we'd do something awful to Alan's car. But after a bone-shaking descent, we found ourselves on another sandy lowland. To our left, by a stone wall, a thread of path ran across a steep slope dotted with sheep and wind-blown bushes. It answered to the old lady's description.

We set off together, a light breeze and a murmur of sound hinting at what we would find. But when we came over the brow of the rocky promontory and looked down on the deserted bay, shimmering in the morning light, it was even more magical than we had imagined.

'Jenny, I shall remember this moment for the rest of my life.'

All I could do was nod as I took in the scene before me. The sun beat down on the shining white sand, the waves splashed softly at the edge of the calm, swelling sea, and high above me the skylarks soared, tiny specks in the bright sky, duplicating, dancing and deceiving, when I tried to look up into the dazzling light. Their song tumbled down around me, a cascade of perfect, rounded notes that seemed only to intensify the soft murmuring silence all about us.

'Jenny, I have to fetch my things. I can't wait. Do you mind?'

'I can't either. Come on, it won't take a minute.'

We hurried back to the car, rummaged round for what we wanted, picked up sandwiches and Thermos and returned as quickly as we could, almost afraid the vision might vanish if we delayed.

Val poured out sketch after sketch and I wrote page after page of my Donegal Journal. I took some pictures to go with what I'd written and then went back to scribbling furiously again.

'What are you going to do with all that, Jenny?'

'All my scribbles?'

'Mmm.'

126

'A story, perhaps. A novel, maybe. But that's really just a dream.'

'Why should it be?'

'Oh, I don't know. You have to be very clever to write novels.'

'But you are clever, Jenny. Alan says you're the only woman he knows worth talking to. Apart from me, that is.'

'Did he really? Goodness, and I'm always thinking what an idiot I must sound whenever he talks chemistry. I have to hang on by my eyebrows.'

'I'm lucky, he knows I'm a duffer so he doesn't bother.'

'No, you're not, Val. You mustn't say things like that. Look at those marvellous sketches you're turning out, as if it were easy.'

'But it is easy, and I am a duffer. Honestly, Jenny, I don't mind any more. Not now they've taken me at Art College.'

She was smiling so easily, sitting in a small hollow she'd made in the shingle, her board across her knees. With the sunlight catching her hair, it looked even more golden than usual. Her bare arms were already honey-coloured and freckled. I couldn't recall ever having seen her look so happy.

'You know something, Jenny,' she said musingly, without looking up from her work, 'there's only one thing more I want to make me happy *after* I meet Prince Charming.'

She paused for effect, took up a clean sheet of paper and swept a piece of charcoal in a long curve across it.

'And what's that?'

'You to marry Alan,' she said soberly. 'Then you'd be my sister and we could all live happily ever after.' She turned towards me and smiled and with a few deft strokes put me into her picture.

'I take it you have consulted him,' I retorted, laughing, as I put my writing things back in my duffle bag.

'I don't need to. I just know. I have a feeling.'

'Must be the heat. Poor Alan. I don't know how a sober soul like him managed to get a sister like you. Come on, let's go and paddle. There's a nice hole under this bush to tuck our things in.'

We flew along the beach, kicking spray from the tiny waves till we'd almost soaked each other. Then we lay on the soft sand, steaming slightly.

'Shall we remember this when we're old, Jenny?'

'Of course we shall. This is what one of my favourite writers calls a "moment of being". I don't think they very often turn up for two people at once. We're very lucky, Val. Whatever's in store for us, we've had so much that is good.'

I dialled again. This time the phone rang. I found myself smiling, already hearing the sound of Val's voice. I would ask her if she remembered that day on Tra-na-rossan and how we never got any further on our grand tour of Donegal because we loved it so. But the phone went on ringing. And ringing. I could almost see it vibrating in her empty hallway. She had gone out. I had missed her again.

There was nothing for it. I would just have to cope by myself with that horrible uneasy feeling somewhere down in the pit of my stomach Karen had created. Surely nothing Val would ever have to tell me could come between us.

Surely not. I just couldn't imagine how it could. But then, had I ever imagined anything could come to spoil the ease and happiness Colin and I had once had?

Chapter 7

There was far more to do upstairs than I imagined. As I changed the sheets on the double bed, I remembered both the single beds needed doing as well, thanks to Colin's Australian uncle and his 'useful contact' from British Steel. And that meant moving all the linen I'd parked there when I found the hiccupping bottle in the airing cupboard. I hate making beds. By the time I'd finished, the landing looked like a hotel corridor early in the morning, a scatter of wastepaper baskets, a pile of towels and a forgotten morning-tea tray parked amid the drifts of crumpled sheets.

I summoned up all my patience, folded the laundry into a neat pile, went down and stacked it in the garage, and came back and started in on the bathroom. My patience shredded when I discovered the grey dust on the shower curtain wasn't discoloured talcum powder after all, but a mould. It proved even harder to shift than the ring I found round the bath. While I was down on my knees, scrubbing away at that, I had a close up view of the carpet. Its once pleasant dusky pink was so full of well-tramped talcum powder, it shone smooth. It needed a stiff brushing to raise the pile before it was worth vacuuming.

Still sneezing from my efforts on the bathroom carpet and thoroughly irritated with the time it had taken to make it look half decent again, I opened the door on the last of the upstairs rooms. Colin's office.

While my study had been intended for 'the nursery', complete with teddy bear wallpaper and white, wipeable furniture, when the show house was furnished, this room of Colin's had actually been set up as an office. It contained the only pieces of furniture I might have chosen myself: a large Swedish-designed desk in teak with matching adjustable shelving and a pair of pale grey filing cabinets which toned nicely with the darker grey carpet. Leaning wearily against the door frame, I looked in at the chaotic mess of papers and objects which covered all the surfaces and spilled over into piles on the floor.

I strode across to the wide window ledge and looked at the plants I had chosen to bring a little colour to the room. Even in the watering tray where they stood, there was a scatter of Biros and small tools and the dismantled pieces of an electric plug. The yucca and the cacti which Maisie had given Colin were fine, if somewhat dusty, but the blooms on the bright scarlet geraniums had dropped. The tiny shrivelled remnants lay scattered among the debris below the wilted foliage.

'What is the point? Whatever is the point?' I fumed as I carried the geraniums into the bathroom and filled the basin with tepid water. I soaked them well, left them to drain, and went back across the landing. I stood by the door and tried to steady myself.

'All right, so my room is tidy, Colin's is a mess,' I reasoned. 'Isn't that a personal difference one should accept?'

I put together every single sensible thing I'd read about

accepting that different people had different needs. Clearly, our needs were different, so why was it such a problem for me? It certainly didn't seem a problem to Colin.

I went back to the window and looked out over the garden. The lawn needed cutting, I'd done no weeding or tidying for four weekends now, and so far today I still hadn't found five minutes to go down and look at my chrysanthemums. 'If I start to sort out this lot, I'll never get outside,' I muttered, glaring at the stacks of magazines, catalogues, newspapers and household documents piled up on the surface of the desk.

I knew what the writers in the women's magazines would say. Do what you want to do and let him sort out his own mess. Why should the state of his room have any effect on you? It was his room and his mess, wasn't it? End of story. But it didn't help me any. Either I couldn't forgive him for killing off my favourite geraniums, or the state of the room was spelling out something that I really couldn't yet bring myself to face.

I remembered the weekend, weeks back, when he'd said he was going up to have a good sort-out. I'd encouraged him, asked him if he'd like a little colour to set against the shades of grey and the dark tones of the teak. 'Yes, yes, that would be lovely,' he'd replied enthusiastically. I'd stopped what I was doing, lifted the geraniums carefully from the garden, scrubbed the nicest of my terracotta pots, settled them in and brought them up to him. I'd found him reading a motoring magazine which he dropped hastily when I appeared.

'Just checking on something,' he said quickly, taking the flourishing plants from me and placing them carefully on the window ledge. 'Super, Jenny, I'll have this place straight in no time.'

As like as not, they were now dead. Even if I'd caught them in time, I'd have to cut them back and they wouldn't flower again till next year.

Viciously, I pulled the vacuum cleaner into the room, switched on and shoved it round the small area of carpet still visible. I dragged out the swivel chair one-handed to get at the kneehole area and spotted three copies of a past edition of the *Ulster Tatler* on its dark grey seat. I switched off, picked them up, and dropped down on the chair myself.

'Three bloody months,' I proclaimed to the silent vacuum cleaner. 'That's how long these magazines have been sitting on this chair.' I flipped one open just to make sure it was what I thought it was. I found what I was looking for. A two-page spread. On one side William John McKinstry, cigar in hand, with a collection of the great and the good at a top hotel. On the other, banner headlines which read: 'Proud of his working-class origins'. The article below charted his progress 'From Backyard to Boardroom', quoted him freely on the virtues of hard work and foresight, and carefully avoided any mention of his absolute ban against employing anyone in his organisation who was not a Protestant.

Colin had bought three copies so he could send them to the Canadian relatives. And here they were. Abandoned and forgotten. Like the geraniums. I shook my head, put them back on the chair exactly as I had found them, and walked out of the room. I closed the door firmly behind me, carried the vacuum to the bottom of the stairs and picked up my poetry books from the table beside the phone.

'Lunch, Jennifer, lunch,' I said to myself as I made for the kitchen. 'You've had quite enough of messes for one morning.'

I made some coffee and a cheese sandwich, and sat down at the breakfast bar with a pair of scissors and the parcel I'd collected from Karen. A whole little pile of books from the Poetry Book Society. The R.S. Thomas I'd been expecting, some volumes from their backlist I'd bought with Daddy's birthday money, and a fresh copy of *Death of a Naturalist* because the copy I'd been using in school was dropping to pieces.

I love new books, especially new poetry books. I sat and gloated over them, picking them up one at a time and reading a little here and there. I promised myself a long read tomorrow, when I got back from Rathmore Drive. But my good intentions weakened. I was halfway through Derek Mahon's 'Spring Letter in Winter' when it dawned on me that the doorbell was ringing.

Confused, I put the book down and blinked at the kitchen clock as if it might tell me something about the unknown caller. I glanced back again at the lines I had just read, as if the book itself would disappear in the time it took me to answer the door.

Two years on and none the wiser
I go down to the door in the morning twilight.

It was three o'clock in the afternoon, but the words echoed in my head as if I had just received an urgent message. I hurried down the hall. Perhaps I too was two years on and none the wiser.

The brown figure on the doorstep had his back to me and was looking down the Drive towards a battered blue van parked by the kerb. I couldn't think what on earth he might want. As he turned towards me, a drip from the end of his nose fell among the oil stains on his dungarees. His pale eyes flickered towards mine momentarily and then darted away, as if he feared a refusal.

'Hello,' I said brightly as I focused on his too-large dungarees and the bag of tools he carried in one hand.

'Washer,' he said abruptly.

'Oh, Mr Taggart. I *am* pleased to see you,' I said, honestly. 'Your wife said you'd hardly manage it today. Do come in.'

He eyed the hall carpet uneasily as he began to wipe his feet meticulously on the outside doormat. One of his boots was a heavy surgical one. They were both perfectly clean.

'Oh please, don't worry. It's only clean dirt, as my father would say.'

A flicker of a smile appeared in his watery blue eyes and he limped down the hall behind me.

'And you needn't worry about this floor either. I'm not doing it till I've caught up on the rest of the washing. That's if you can fix the wretched thing.'

He hesitated at the kitchen door, his eyes moving over my half-eaten sandwich and empty mug of coffee.

'I'm disturbin' yer lunch, missus.'

'Not at all. I should have had it hours ago but some of my jobs took longer than I'd expected. Would you like a cup of coffee? I was just going to make some more. It won't take a minute.'

'Ah niver says no till a lady,' he said shortly as he

dropped his toolbag on the floor and sat down on the chair opposite mine.

In the few moments it took me to make two mugs of instant, he sat with his shoulders hunched, looking gloomily at the dirty floor tiles. I was quite surprised when he straightened up and managed a smile as I put his in front of him.

'I hafta go roun' the back whin a come next door.' He jerked his head in the direction of Karen's and I had to suppress a smile. I could not see Ernie being allowed to limp down the wall-to-wall Wilton in Karen's hall.

I mentioned the washing machine and the manner of its passing. He raised his eyes heavenward. 'Them's buggers, missus, ivery wan the same.'

I nodded encouragingly. 'Funny you say that. I've never liked it either. Not that I'm any good with household stuff,' I added. 'A nice two-stroke tractor engine now, I could have a go at that if I had the specification. But not that thing.'

'Begod, ye could do better nor me,' he said, staring at me in amazement. 'Is that yer job?'

I shook my head and laughed. 'No, I'm a teacher, but I used to work in my father's showroom when I was a student. Erwin's of North Street?'

'George Erwin? Farm machinery an' suchlike?'

'That's right. You know it then?'

''Deed an' I do. Tho' indirect like. Bro'er wrought there on a paintin' job, lass job he did afore he wos took ill. Said George Erwin was a powerful dacent man.' He drank noisily and wiped his drip with one brown arm.

'Was your brother's name Willy?'

137

'Aye, it twas. Did ye iver meet 'im?'

'No, but I saw his work. He made a lovely job of that old showroom. I liked his colour scheme.'

He nodded and tightened his lips. 'Han's for anythin', our Willy. Usta make lampshades for my missus, like somethin' ye'd see in a book. Aye, an' toys fer the childer, a wee fire engine with the ladder. Just the rale thing, only minacheer-like. Forty-three he was, an' a wife an' three we'ans. Cancer of the throat. All them clivir docters standin' roun' his bed and not a damn thing wan o' thim could do. Makes ye wonner, wouden it?'

I nodded silently as he finished his coffee at a single gulp and drew his sleeve across his lips.

'What about his family?' I asked, tentatively.

'Aye, now yer askin'. The missus an' I have thim wi' us. Six childer in wan house.' He raised his eyes heavenward as he stood up and laughed a hard little laugh as he followed me out to the garage. 'It's all graft, missus, 'cept Lodge nite an' Bann nite. Tha's the way, in't it?'

The job on the machine was clearly not a simple one. While I was mowing the back lawn, I heard vigorous banging, and when I brought the mower back into the garage, it looked as if the entire inside of the machine was spread out over the floor. I said a few friendly words and took myself off to the bottom of the garden.

There were three sprays of chrysanthemum in bloom. Not enough yet for a big arrangement, but stripped down to individual florets and mixed with foliage, I could fill a bowl for the lounge and have a few left over for my own room. I touched the heavy gold heads and smelt their spicy, autumn smell.

Two years ago, my own form in Birmingham had given me a pot of chrysanthemums as a leaving present. The pot had travelled with me from Birmingham to Belfast, carefully wedged between bags and boxes in the back seat of the Mini. It had sat in Maisie's hideous pink guest bedroom and in our friend's chilly attic flat. In late January, with all its blooms gone, I carried it up to the teddy bear room and vowed I would never part with it. I'd read up propagation in one of Daddy's books and waited anxiously for the first new shoots to appear.

Standing in the soft earth of the flowerbed, with the brilliant gold blooms in my hands, I knew very well that you can't hold on to the past. The second form who'd inscribed their names on a huge card for me would be leaving school next year. They'd scatter far and wide. But for just a little while they'd been 'my' second form and I wanted something to remind me of that past happy time. My cuttings had flourished. I had made something from what they had given me that would go on blooming for me every year at this time.

Behind the chrysanthemums, in the angle where the six-foot fence joins the three-foot fence, there was a place where you could look out over Belfast Lough, the houses of the estate invisible behind you. I pushed my way gently between the forsythia and the escallonia and climbed on the upturned bucket that gave me the extra bit of height I needed.

As I gazed out, a fleet of small boats appeared, sails taut triangles of sharp colour against the ruffled water. Then they were gone, as suddenly as migrating swallows. I sniffed the crisp air and caught the scent of woodsmoke from the council estate. The willows screening the shabby brick houses had begun to sway. As the breeze stiffened, the whole mass expanded, dipping and stretching, becoming the wind itself.

'I wish it was always like this,' I muttered to myself. The drills, the saws, the car-cleaning devices and the radios had all disappeared indoors as the temperature began to drop. Not a single child shouted or dog yapped across the whole expanse of well-trimmed gardens. I closed my eyes for a moment and caught the tang of salt on the wind. I saw myself standing on a rocky headland on the north coast of Donegal, the grey-blue mass of the ocean sweeping around me, the breakers swollen with the full fetch of the Atlantic behind them.

Inishowen and Lough Swilly, Fanad Head and Mulroy Bay, Rosguil and Sheephaven. The names came to me like the lines of a poem. As I spoke them softly to myself, the falling cadences brought back the crash of waves, I saw the seabirds circling below towering cliffs and the light suddenly spill across a misty hillside as a shower passed along the coast, leaving pools of brilliant light to flow over the sodden greens and vibrant yellows and the dark gashes of peaty streams, tumbling their way down steep slopes to the deep inlets that pierced that rocky coast.

Abruptly, the image was shattered. A neighbour's television blared out, then subsided to a nagging grumble. I opened my eyes and saw the beginning of the day's Sports News escaping through the open vents of the nearest picture window. Behind me, other flickering screens jumped into life. So close. So inescapably close. I felt my heart sink as I acknowledged the fact, for the umpteenth time, that there was no quiet to be had in Loughview, neither the quiet which comes from the absence of noise, nor the quiet which flows from the absence of intrusion.

No, it had to be faced. You came to Loughview to put your life on show. And like one of the new stage sets, there were neither wings nor backstage. You were visible all the time, and your performance was assessed even when you had no lines to say. All very well for the Karens of this world who chose this play and knew their lines, but different for me. I didn't choose the play, nor did I like it, and I refused to learn my lines. But what was even worse, I was beginning to feel I should never have let myself be cast for the play in the first place.

I got down from my perch, wiped my muddy feet on the edge of the lawn and walked back up the path. It occurred to me that Ernie Taggart probably didn't much care for his part either.

'How's it going, Mr Taggart?'

'Rightly,' he said, his face contorted with effort. He was lying full length on the cold concrete floor, struggling with something at the back of the machine. After a moment he sat up, wiped the sweat from his brow and looked at me. 'I think that'll do it,' he said, nodding to himself. 'There was a short surkit forby thon bit that 'id perished.'

'Just for good measure,' I said sympathetically. 'I didn't know you were an electrician as well.'

'Dear aye. Turn ma han' to most things, 'cept decoratin'. Jack of all trades they say, master a none,' he added dismissively.

'I wouldn't say that at all,' I replied firmly as he got to his feet awkwardly. 'Would you have a moment to look at a towel rail while you're here? Or is it too near teatime?'

'Aye surely,' he replied easily. 'Sure, I oney live doun the bottom o' the hill.' He stood back from the machine, eyed it as if he expected it to have a will of its own and then thumped it gently with his fist. 'Behave yerself now, when Ernie tells ye.'

He picked up his tools and followed me back into the kitchen. 'Missus, would ye mine if I got ma wee transistor from the van?'

'Not a bit. But don't bother fetching yours.' I picked up the radio from the breakfast bar and carried it upstairs to the bathroom. 'Are you hoping for a win?' I asked as I set it down and gathered up the clean towels from the rail.

'Ah, divil the win, missus. Iss the news I'm waitin' fer. Them buggers is marchin' in Derry the day. I wan till hear whass happ'nd.'

At the mention of Derry, a wave of panic swept over me. I had been so preoccupied with my own concerns, the march had gone completely out of my mind.

'You mean the civil rights march?' I said.

'Civil rights? Naa,' he said, his tone sour with distrust. 'A lota codology that. Pay no heed till that at all, missus, they'd tell ye anythin', them'ens – a crowd of Catholicks out fer what they can git. Stirrin' up trouble. That's all they're good fer. Sure, aren't they gettin' everythin' as good as we are and into the big jobs as well and lukin' more. Niver know whin they're well off that lot.'

I stared at the empty towel rail as he dropped to his knees. There was nothing unfamiliar in what he'd just said. I had heard the same thing put in different ways and in different accents all my life. Put most brutally by work people and cleaning ladies, small farmers and shop assistants. But I'd heard them too from those who could choose words more carefully to give an impression of tolerance and liberality. The feelings were the same. Maisie and my mother would line up with William John and agree wholeheartedly with what Ernie said.

My father was a different matter. Brought up as he had been in one of the glens of Antrim where most of the people were Catholic, he had always refused to categorise people. He had never joined a Lodge and never asked anyone applying for a job on his small staff whether they were Catholic or Protestant. He had been roundly abused by my mother for 'not being one bit loyal'. In the months after Harvey's marriage, she had argued furiously that he had made me as bad as he was, reading books and plays written by the Other Side. Once, when my father cut a poem out of the newspaper, there was a blazing row because it had been written by one of my English lecturers at Queen's, Seamus Heaney. She just looked at the name and exploded. Seamus was a Catholic name, and that was enough.

I shivered in the chill bathroom and busied myself with the towels. I had no words to offer the man who knelt at my feet. The taste of his bitterness was too much for me. I had too many memories of my mother attacking anything and anyone who threatened to change what she saw as the unalterable law of the universe.

'Can you fix it, do you think?' I asked, just to have something to say.

'Dear aye,' he responded easily, as he reached for a screwdriver. 'Don't ye worry yersel', missus. Ernie'll fix it, just like our ones 'ill fix them other buggers we wos

143

speakin' off. There's a lock o' the boys knows the sauce for them'ens. I'm tellin' ye, them'ens 'ill get all they're askin' fer.' He looked up at me over his shoulder, a glint in his pale eyes, an ugly twist on his mouth.

'You think there'll be trouble then?' I said feebly.

'Trouble, how are ye?' he replied shortly. 'There'll be blue bloody murder, if I know the lads. Them'ens needn't think the polis and Specials 'ill stand up for them. They'll get what they desarve, I'm tellin' ye. About time they wos taken down a peg or two.'

I stood staring down at him as he struggled with the cover of the rail. I knew perfectly well he was probably more aware of what was going to happen than anyone I knew. Except Keith, of course. Keith had no illusions about what was going to happen. He'd tried to reassure me, yes, but he'd not pretended all would be fine, just fine, like his brother would have done. No, he'd said the march was going forward and the cameras would be there. He left me to make up my own mind.

That was one reason I liked Keith so much. Even when we disagreed, he respected my point of view. He was interested in what was the case, not what people wanted to believe. One evening about a year ago, he'd come to supper and stayed on to talk to me when Colin said he had work to do. I'd taken out the ironing board and asked him about his canvassing for the Labour Party in East Belfast.

To begin with, he said little. Then he admitted how depressed he'd been by the blank hostility they'd met among the solidly working-class men and women they'd talked to.

'But Keith, are you surprised? If they're all loyal

Orangemen who always vote Unionist, what do you expect? You're asking them to turn their world on its head.'

He looked at me closely, as if he were trying to decide whether or not I was worth the effort. Clearly, he decided I was, because he launched into a detailed account of sectarianism and socialism, vested interests and political power, all set in the matrix of the social, economic and cultural history of the Province. And as he talked, for the first time I began to grasp that however important concern and compassion might be, without access to real political power all you can do is tinker with the big things, like equality of opportunity and social justice.

My political education had begun that evening. When next we met, I told him I'd try hard not just to be upset by what distressed me in future but to step back a moment and look at the underlying causes just as he had laid them out for me.

'Ah, missus, these'ns are buggers too,' Ernie said suddenly, tapping the metal bar with a spanner. 'Ah'll hafta turn the power off agane. Is that alrite?'

He stood up and limped back along the landing. I was halfway down the stairs, still thinking about Keith, when the phone rang.

'Helen's Bay, three—'

'Jenny, what's wrong! I've just got your message.' Colin's voice was loud and agitated and from the racket in the background it sounded as if he was using the same awful phone box.

'Nothing's wrong,' I said steadily. 'I left a message asking you to ring because I'm going out. I particularly said it wasn't urgent.'

'Well, this note says "Urgent, please ring your wife",' he replied irritably, though his relief was evident.

'Before eight o'clock,' I added shortly. 'You promised you'd ring, so we could talk, and as you hadn't, I thought you might try this evening,' I explained. 'It's Val's party. Had you forgotten?' I was amazed at how steady I was able to be, given how I was actually feeling.

'Look, Jen, I can't chat now. The old man's taking me out to dinner and you can guess what that means. He'll be down any minute.'

'Well, he can wait a couple of minutes, can't he?' I said sharply. 'I've been waiting to speak to you all day. You know there's something we need to talk about. Couldn't you have managed a few minutes this afternoon? The session ended at four thirty, I seem to remember.'

'Jen, you know how he hates being kept waiting,' he broke in, as if he hadn't heard a word I'd said. 'Look, I can see him coming now. I'll phone you later, when I get back, say between eleven and twelve.'

'No, Colin. That's what you said last night. Don't bother to ring. I'll make up my own mind and I'll see you sometime tomorrow,' I said abruptly, as I dropped the phone back in the cradle.

I sat staring at it, amazed and horrified by what I had done. I felt tears in my eyes. He'll ring back, I told myself. He knows he's upset me. He's sure to ring back and apologise. I sat and watched the phone, willing it to ring.

From upstairs, I heard the radio. The six o'clock news. I could tell by the pattern and tone. I sat on miserably, rigid with tension, waiting.

As the broadcast ended, I heard footsteps on the stairs.

'Screw loose,' Ernie said abruptly. 'I put them towels back, wos that alrite?'

'That was very thoughtful,' I replied weakly. 'I was afraid it might be another big job like the washer.'

'Naa,' he said, shaking his head. 'Wish all the jobs was that aisy.'

'Well, I'm very grateful indeed. Now how much do I owe you?'

I stepped into the cloakroom for my handbag, looked hopefully at the telephone and observed that Ernie was moving awkwardly from one foot to the other, his eyes firmly fixed on the carpet.

'Two ten all right?'

I was quite shocked. Three hours skilled work, work that was also physically demanding, and he felt he couldn't ask more than two pounds ten shillings. I wondered what Keith would say when I told him.

I opened my wallet and was relieved to find a five pound note at the back. I folded it and handed it to him.

'Saturday's double time,' I said as lightly as I could manage. 'Besides, that washer was bonus rated.'

He looked puzzled as he drew out a battered notecase from his back pocket. 'Ah niver says no till a lady,' he mumbled as he put the note away. 'Give us a shout, now, if ye have ony more trouble with yer man,' he added, jerking his head in the direction of the garage. 'The wife's usually there and ye have ma number.'

'Yes, I'll do that,' I nodded. 'I could do with someone to thump things for me.'

'Well, Ernie's yer man.'

I looked at the small figure, his face streaked with oil

from his dungarees and dust from the garage floor, and thought of the battered notecase with only a few ten shilling notes in it. Yes, Ernie was my man.

'Does your wife make apple tarts, Ernie?'

''Deed aye, she does. She's a great cook, tho' she says I'm no credit to her at all.'

I waved to him to follow me out into the garage. 'There you are, a little present for the children,' I said as I removed the paper cover from a box of Bramleys.

'Thems lovely. I coulden take yer good apples, missus.'

'They'll go bad if you don't,' I said cheerfully. 'I don't get time to bake these days and I don't see much sign of it in the future. I had them as a present from one of my father's customers. I can't let them spoil, now can I?'

We carried the heavy box out to his van and put it in the back with all his gear.

'The childer 'ill be rale glad to see me the night,' he said through his open window. 'Mind now, giv' us a shout if anythin' goes wrong an' I'll come and give it a wee thump for ye.'

'I'll do just that.'

Dusk had fallen and the street lights were flickering into life as the blue van drove off down the hill to the shabby brick house with its six children. I went back into my own dark, empty house, put on the lamps and collected up three armfuls of very cold clothes from the line.

Stars were beginning to appear in the clear sky as I came in, dropped the last chilly load on the kitchen table and set up the ironing board.

Suddenly, I felt overwhelmed with a sense of loss. Some nameless cloud of misery had descended upon me. I turned my back on the ironing board and went into the lounge, but it was so clean and empty, so devoid of any mark I could make upon it that I could not sit there, though my back ached and I was longing for a rest.

'Do something, Jennifer. Anything. Don't just stand there being miserable,' I said firmly, as I recognised the familiar symptoms. I turned my back on the room and took my secateurs from the kitchen drawer. In the blowy darkness, I went out and cut my chrysanthemums and some sprays of foliage from the shrubs. 'There's always something you can do, no matter how hopeless you feel,' I whispered to myself as I fetched a pottery bowl from the bottom of the kitchen cupboard and began to arrange my flowers.

Chapter 8

Although my hands were shaking, the flowers looked really good when I tucked the last perky gold bloom into place. I carried them into the lounge, set the bowl down on the coffee table and stood back to admire my work. Tears of disappointment pricked in my eyes. They looked about as pleasing as a dirty sock on a freshly-vacuumed bedroom floor.

I flopped down in the nearest armchair and stared at them. It was the fault of the glass and steel coffee table. What it needed was that cut-glass vase of Karen's with its six carnations that could just as well be plastic carnations for all the difference it made. My lovely pottery bowl looked completely out of place in this room.

It wasn't the only thing that felt wrong either. I drew my feet up under me and shrivelled into the unyielding imitation leather upholstery of the raft on which I'd descended. I looked round the clean and tidy room seeking some comfort, some satisfaction, after all the hours of cleaning and tidying. But there was none. Apart from the relief of having disposed of the mess, nothing in the room spoke to me. It had always looked like a miniature airport lounge and nothing I'd ever done had made it any better.

Suddenly, I felt quite desolate. Utterly alone in the empty house, surrounded by dark empty spaces. I'd been alone in the house before and enjoyed my solitude, the opportunity to do exactly what I felt like, in whatever order pleased me. I'd enjoyed being able to eat when it was convenient, or when I felt hungry, sleep late or get up early, exhaust myself in the garden and read all evening. But now, I felt my solitariness a burden, my space an emptiness, my freedom, dust and ashes.

Tears trickled unbidden down my face. I jumped to my feet and dashed over to the gaping black hole that reflected back at me the room and my own crumpled figure, a solitary, discarded object dropped in a chair by someone passing through.

As the curtains swished into place, the phone rang and my heart raced. It must be Colin, ringing from wherever his father had taken him to dinner. I dashed headlong into the hall and grabbed the phone, my hands shaking.

It was Karen. We hadn't arranged a time. In view of the fact that Neville had just phoned to say he'd been delayed we'd better make it eight thirty. Her voice was thick with sarcasm and she sounded just as if she was giving evidence against him in court.

Poor bloody Neville, I thought. However much Neville irritates me by turning up at the wrong time and distracting Colin from whatever he's supposed to be doing, I do like him very much. Truly good-natured and easy-going, I've never heard him say anything nasty about anyone, unless it was really justified. He works hard, is devoted to his children and provides Karen with all the goodies to which she feels so thoroughly entitled. What the hell's in it for him? I asked myself as I tramped back into the kitchen.

I flicked the light switch and surveyed the mountain of clean laundry I'd dumped on the kitchen table. 'Why not, Jennifer, why not? Whatever you feel, it's still got to be done. Might as well get on with it.'

I caught sight of myself in my dressing-table mirror as I put away the last of the shirts. I looked dreadful. Hardly surprising, given how dreadful I was feeling. But that was not the point. If I turned up at Valerie and Bob's looking like this, they'd be really worried. An effort would have to be made. Bath. Hair. Extra layer of foundation with blusher. The full treatment.

As I peeled off my clothes and dropped them in a tangled puddle on the floor, I thought what a relief it was to walk around in my skin in a warm room. When had I last wandered around naked, stretching my aching limbs and dropping things into the laundry basket? I sat down at my dressing table and spread moisturiser on my face. I could almost feel the tight skin relax, as if finally the day's work was over and I didn't have to keep myself going. For a few moments, I even felt a sense of warmth and wellbeing. Then the phone rang.

I grabbed for my dressing gown. Cursing roundly, I dashed downstairs, pulling it on as I went.

It was Karen again. Neville was still not back though it was now eight o'clock. I waited till her fury ran out and then said, 'No matter, Karen, I was about to have a bath.'

'Oh well, you can take your time, can't you, even with having left it this late,' she said nastily, as she rang off.

I lay in the bath, trying to relax my shoulders. My trailing ivies and ferns were definitely looking better for having been sprayed and tidied, but I felt no joy in them. The bath water was already getting cold. I climbed out, dried myself, did my hair and with little enthusiasm went in search of something to wear.

'Oh no,' I moaned, as I pulled out my black velvet skirt. It stank of cigar and cigarette smoke. The first whiff of it brought the whole business flooding back. Firm's dinners. Three of them since the beginning of term, the most recent only last Saturday night. Each firm trying to make a bigger splash than the others. Vast quantities of food, gallons of alcohol and unlimited decibels of noise.

I took the skirt into the bathroom, hung it on the shower fitment and opened the window. I must have been out of my mind to put it back in the wardrobe smelling like that. But then, I'm always out of my mind after a firm's do. No, not the alcohol. I only drink sparkling water at these affairs. What makes me feel so awful is the noise. The noise and the smoke and the boom. The boom, boom, boom of men doing men's talk. Whatever the topic of conversation the underlying message is the same: 'I'm a good chap, why not do business with me?' And the more urgent the need to put over the message, the louder the boom.

Last Saturday night's effort was even worse than usual. Rumour had it the firm in question was in difficulties due to over-expansion and badly needed new contracts. Perhaps that was why Colin and I were on the top table, with the directors. Consequently, Colin talked plumbing supplies for most of the evening and I was left to entertain a sad, grey-haired man who only showed signs of life when I picked up my cue and asked him to explain about a new cistern valve he'd mentioned. It allows your loo to fill without making a noise.

I stared at the contents of my wardrobe. Every single thing seemed to call up images I'd rather forget. At last, I put out my hand for 'old faithful', a turquoise skirt made for me years ago. I found a black velvet top with a wide scoop neck to go with it and added the little pendant with the turquoise stones Daddy gave me for my twenty-first birthday. I took my time dressing and making up and after the agitation I'd been feeling most of the evening, I began to feel steadier at last. I had a look at myself in the long mirrors and knew I'd chosen the right thing to wear.

Dear Valerie. She's always been so good to me, making things for me when I couldn't find anything I liked, or when I'd spent all my grant money on books. Long ago, she showed me how to change a dress by adding a different collar, buying new buttons or trying a different belt. She'd given me little presents to encourage me, things that she knew would match what I already had, scarves or ribbons or pieces of lace. I love clothes, but I hate shopping for them. I'm always totally intimidated by racks of skirts, or dresses, and those long mirrors that throw back multiple images of someone you don't recognise as you. Valerie has always helped me out, coaxed me to try things I would never have thought of, and told me honestly when something didn't suit me.

I came downstairs, got out my cloak and checked the contents of my handbag. Then I collected my poetry books and settled myself in the lounge where I'd hear Neville arriving back long before he knocked on the front door. I took out my bookmark and saw again the words on the page:

> Two years on and none the wiser
> I go down to the door in the morning twilight.

They seemed so familiar, as if I'd always known them, though it was only over lunch I read them for the first time.

Suddenly, I remembered 'the morning twilight' when I wore this turquoise skirt for the first time. My third year at Queen's. The May Ball. The first time Colin had asked me out, though we'd known each other for some time and he'd often run me home after rehearsals.

We'd all gone to the ball in a party, with friends from the Dramatic Society. Lovely, lively people I had come to know so well as we struggled to get our production good enough to go on tour through the Province. It had been such a happy evening. I'd danced until my feet ached and my hair fell down.

'Let's sneak off, Jenny. Just you and me. I've had to share you all evening,' Colin said, as we headed for the car park. Around us, our friends were squashing into cars together to drive up to Shaw's Bridge and watch the dawn come up over the city.

'All right, let's go.'

Once away from the university, there was nothing about. We zoomed through the empty streets as fingers of light began to touch the edge of the hills.

'Where are we going?' I cried over the noise of the engine and the rush of the wind.

'It's a secret. I'm carrying you off to my lair,' he hissed

in his best melodramatic style, as we drove westwards out of the city, and then north through the open countryside to the east of Lisburn. We sped along winding country roads, twisted through small hamlets and whizzed past large farms where even the cows in the fields appeared to be asleep. As we climbed higher and higher, I looked back and saw the city spread out below us. The street lamps had gone out as the light grew, but here and there a pane of glass or a slate roof flashed back a reflection from the rising sun. We got there just in time.

As we pulled off the narrow road at the highest point, we saw the sun break clear of the low cloud on the Castlereagh Hills and cast long shadows across the patchwork fields beyond the great sweep of the Lagan valley that lay far below, full of toy houses and miniature buildings.

'There you are, Jenny. You have the world at your feet. I give it all to you.'

He had taken me in his arms and I had not resisted. He was someone I liked, someone who made me laugh. We were friends who had had a lovely evening. And a lovely morning, too. We walked hand in hand along a rough track leading to the edge of the escarpment. The slight dawn breeze just stirred the long, lush grass and I could smell the scent of hawthorn heavy on the air, though the nearest bushes I could see were in a steep, narrow glen way below where we stood.

Neither of us wanted to drive back to the city but I was worried as to how my mother would react, even though I had told her I would be very late indeed. When we arrived at Rathmore Drive, the milkman held the front gate open as I waved Colin goodbye. I said hello to him and laughed. How often I'd heard the phrase 'coming home with the milk' and here I was, coming home with the milk for the first time in my life.

I took off my shoes, crept upstairs and slipped into bed, my mind full of the cool morning air, the sunrise and the song of birds. The thought that I'd spent the long, light evening and the short, May night with the man I should one day marry never entered my head.

'No further on,' I whispered to myself as I cocked an ear for a car turning into the road. But it wasn't Neville. It went on past. Besides, Neville always changed gear, did a point stop and crept into his driveway. I was always quite sure when it was Neville.

Later that morning after the ball, I woke with light streaming into my bedroom. My mother had drawn the curtains and now stood by the window. To my surprise, she was smiling.

'Did you have a nice time last night? I think I heard you come in,' she said encouragingly.

'Yes, it was super. We went and looked at the sunrise,' I offered, reassured by her tone.

'I'm sure that was lovely,' she said agreeably. 'Did Colin enjoy it too?' she asked, coyly.

'Oh, yes, I think so.'

'Well, I think he must have done. There's a little surprise for you downstairs. Why don't you have a shower and I'll make you some coffee and toast.'

I blinked when she left the room. After the way she'd been behaving every time I went anywhere, I just couldn't make any sense of this. Why, she was almost pleasant. I had to go back before Harvey's wedding for the last time she'd offered to make me breakfast on a Saturday morning or shown the slightest enthusiasm for anything I might do or anywhere I chose to go.

Consumed with curiosity, I rushed through my shower, pulled on my clothes and ran downstairs. I could smell real coffee. There on the kitchen table, beside the place she'd laid for me, was a transparent florist's box.

She raised an eyebrow at me as I caught it up, pulled off the ribbon, unpicked the Sellotape and brought out the spray of five perfectly matched pink roses. I stared at them in amazement, until she pointed out that there was a card. Well, of course there was, wasn't there, and she was sure to have read it already. I picked it up. It said: 'For Jenny. Thank you for a lovely evening. Love, Colin.'

'It's from Colin,' I said abstractedly.

'Well now, isn't that nice,' she said warmly. 'He must think a lot of you,' she went on, as she poured my coffee. 'Roses from that florist will have cost him a pretty penny. Aren't you the lucky girl to have met someone so thoughtful?'

When Neville rang the front doorbell, I was still sitting, my book open at the same page, staring at my bowl of chrysanthemums, trying to figure out why that particular Saturday morning should come back to me now, and why my mother's enthusiastic response to the pink roses and their sender was repeating itself over and over in my mind.

Chapter 9

'Hello, Jenny, sorry I'm so late. Are you cross?'

Even if I had been, I'd have lied like a trooper. Neville looked tired and miserable. I felt a sudden rush of warm affection for him rather like the way I feel about my little niece, Susie, when she comes a cropper rushing round the garden and has to be picked up and comforted.

'Not a bit, Neville. I've had a busy day and I was glad of a sit-down,' I said, as we took a short cut across the front lawn.

The night temperature had dropped sharply. It was so cold we could see our breath streaming into the clear air as we crossed the lawn. The bodywork of the car was already beginning to sparkle with tiny specks of ice. But that was nothing compared with the icy chill inside the car.

'I hope you've had some supper,' I added, as he opened the car door for me and tucked in a straying end of my skirt.

'Oh, there'll be something later,' he said hurriedly as Karen turned round to glare at me from the front seat.

As we drove off, I made some attempts at conversation. Neville did his best to respond and I lobbed a few harmless remarks in Karen's direction, but despite our efforts she managed to maintain almost a complete silence the whole way to the far side of Bangor.

When we stopped opposite Valerie and Bob's, she was out of the car and up the drive before Neville even had time to switch off. Valerie appeared immediately, her hands outstretched in greeting. As I hitched up my skirt and stepped cautiously out on the slippery pavement, I looked up and saw the porch light catching her blonde hair and fair skin. She was looking marvellous in a dress of mauve and violet, with floating panels, delicate and exotic, that flared out behind her as she turned towards Karen who was already at the front door.

'Karen, hello. How nice to see you,' she said warmly, as she drew her into the hall. She waved cheerfully at Neville who was still sitting slumped over the steering wheel looking gloomily at the lines of cars on both sides of the road.

'Would Neville like Bob to help him reverse round the back of the house?' asked Valerie quickly. 'We've saved you a space, but it's a bit tricky,' she said, as she blew a kiss to Neville.

'Oh, don't bother Bob. He'll manage,' said Karen shortly as I came up the drive to join them. 'He can park at the bottom of the hill. After all the bother he's caused this evening, I don't see why we should worry. Anyway, the walk will help sober him up.'

My eyes met Val's over Karen's dark head as she bent down to change her shoes. She raised one eyebrow a minute amount and I smiled in spite of myself. Val has always managed to cope with Karen far better than I ever have.

'You will be interested to hear, Valerie,' Karen began

as Val waved us towards the stairs, 'that the English team were quite unable to go drinking without Neville.'

I could hardly believe my ears. Karen was repeating word for word every single line she'd used in the course of her multiple phone calls. I wondered if she would go on playing the version she'd made, like a tape, all through the evening.

'Well, you're here now and that's all that matters,' said Valerie easily as we went into the bedroom.

But Karen had not finished. As she twitched at her tight-fitting wool dress and adjusted its collar at Val's dressing table, she watched us both in the mirror to make sure we were paying attention.

'May I ask what time it is, Valerie?' she began coldly. 'Just as a matter of interest.'

'It's somewhere after nine, but the night is still young,' Val replied, her tone as light as before.

How Val managed to keep a smile on her face and look easy and relaxed in the face of Karen's tight-lipped expression and acidic tone was more than I could imagine. I stood watching her with admiration. I knew perfectly well that one more remark of Karen's about Neville and I'd be looking for the nearest blunt instrument. But then, Val has always had a gift of lightness. When she's feeling right in herself she has an almost magical quality about her. My father always said that if Valerie Thompson put her mind to it, she could charm ducks off water.

'Isn't Neville Secretary of the Social Committee this year, Karen?' Val went on easily, as Karen peered at her pursed lips in the mirror.

Karen tossed her head and faltered as Val turned towards

her, a look of attentive interest in her unwavering grey eyes.

'Oh, I expect he is. He's secretary of so many things, I can't be expected to remember them all. I don't see it's any excuse.'

'But Neville is *here*, Karen, isn't he?' she continued quietly. 'Quite a few husbands have other commitments this evening, haven't they? Colin, for one. Let's be grateful for small mercies, shall we?'

Karen opened her mouth and closed it again, while Val turned towards me and put her arms round me.

'Jenny, dear, it's ages since I've seen you. I'm so sorry I haven't managed to catch you,' she said as she hugged me tight.

For a moment, the warmth of her body and the familiar floral scent brought such a sense of wellbeing, of so many good times shared, that the last thing I wanted to do was let go of her. But one glimpse of Karen's knowing look in the mirror and all my anxieties came streaming back.

'Don't you think it's time we were going down?' she said abruptly and moved towards the bedroom door.

'Why don't you go ahead, Karen?' said Val. 'I'll have to do something about Jenny's hair. She's gone and put it up and we can't have that tonight, can we?'

As she spoke, Val ignored my half-hearted protests, manoeuvred me on to the stool in front of her dressing table, and reached for her hairbrush. I was really very grateful, for I knew my hair didn't look right. I'd tried it down, lost patience with it, pinned it up and got it too tight. Besides, the thought of just a few moments alone with Val was very appealing.

Karen was standing by the door. 'Aren't you going to

tell us the good news then, Valerie? Or are you trying to keep it quiet a bit longer?'

I saw the colour drain from Val's face as she spun round to face her. 'What good news?' she asked quietly.

'Why, the good news you're planning to tell Jenny. Surely you're going to tell me as well. I'll be so pleased to hear when it's going to be, after so long.'

'When what's going to be?' Val's voice had dropped to a whisper and her face had a crumpled look that I knew only too well. I held my breath, dreading what was to come next. I had a moment's relief as Karen turned away, but then she delivered her parting shot, and it was just as upsetting as I had imagined it would be.

'I'll leave you two to talk it over,' she said sweetly. 'I'm sure, Val, you and I will have lots of time to get together now you won't have the job to cope with any more.'

As the door closed behind her, Val covered her face with her hands and collapsed on the edge of the bed. Her shoulders shook and she sobbed as if her heart would break. I put my arms round her and held her tight.

'Val, Val dear. What's wrong? Whatever is it? Tell me.'

It seemed like an age before she could get any words out.

'I didn't tell her, Jenny. I didn't tell her,' she kept repeating. 'You don't think I told her, do you?' she sobbed, looking up at me, her face streaked with tears.

It was by no means the first time I had seen Val as distraught as this, but it was the very first time that came into my mind as she continued to sob. It was winter, a chill grey day with flurries of snow. We had run home from school together, stopping only to see if we could catch a snowflake on our outstretched tongues. It was my turn to accompany her home, so we walked up her side of the Drive together. A little while later, after I had hung up my coat and put my slippers on, I heard a furious ringing at the door. I got there before my mother who had been baking and had to wash her hands.

Valerie stood on the doorstep, breathless, without a coat, the snow flying round her. Tears were streaming down her face and she was sobbing so I could hardly hear what she was saying as she flung herself at me. 'Jenny, Jenny, my mummy's dead and the little baby too. What shall I do? What shall I do?' We'd known each other for three years. We were only eight years old.

The loss of her mother, a gentle, rather faded woman whose sweet smile I've never forgotten, was only the beginning of Val's heartbreak. Within a year, her father, English by birth, a sturdy, no-nonsense character from the Black Country, who had come to Ulster to be headmaster of a boys' preparatory school well-known for its strict discipline, had married his school secretary, a hard-faced woman as different from Val's tender-hearted mother as it was possible to imagine. From that point onwards, Val's father, always overbearing and intolerant of any weakness, regarded his two children as an intrusion into his new life. 'Aunt Eleanor', as their stepmother chose to be called, had little time for Val and none at all for Alan, the long-legged, awkward thirteen-year-old who had come chasing after his sister that awful afternoon.

Alan was despatched immediately to an English public school. Val went on living at Rathmore Drive until she was eleven. Then she too was sent to board at the Belfast school where I was a day girl. While both the Thompson children suffered from their mother's loss and their father's neglect, it was Val who was almost driven to the edge.

Since that winter day when we were children, there had always been times when Val would suddenly become so distraught, she'd scarcely know what she was doing. It could be set off by something quite small, a harsh word or a disappointment. A slight upset, of no significance to another child, would affect her so badly, she could do nothing but weep inconsolably.

Her aunt and uncle in Ballycastle had insisted that she be sent to doctors and psychologists, and they themselves provided a welcome retreat for holidays, but it was only when Val discovered her talent for sketching and painting at grammar school that things began to improve. Without her aunt and uncle, one or two teachers who knew the whole situation, and her much-loved brother, Alan, Val might never have made it through her teenage years.

However she tried, she just couldn't get over the sense of total abandonment that had come with the loss of her mother, her father and her home. She longed for friends and made them easily. But when they let her down, the hurt it generated fell along the old fault line and so the price she paid for their failure was far greater than they could ever imagine.

I stroked her hair and talked to her, reminding her of promises we had made to each other as little girls, solemn vows and cross-my-hearts. I could have been talking nonsense, but it wouldn't have mattered. When Val went to pieces, the only thing to do was remind her she wasn't on her own. I had done this many times before. Gradually the sobbing subsided and she made an effort to collect herself.

'I'll be all right, Jenny,' she managed. 'As long as you don't think I told her,' she repeated, her voice wavering dangerously.

'But of course I don't, silly. You know Karen's fitted with a built-in pregnancy detector. She's a great loss to the medical profession.'

She managed a ghost of a smile and I asked the question I knew I had to ask, as gently as I could.

'Was it an accident, Val?'

'No, that's just the point,' she began, shaking her head vehemently. 'That's why I wanted to tell you before anyone, even Bob. It was because of you I finally got there. Time and time again, Jenny, I've gone through it all. My fears about dying in childbirth, like Mummy, and the worry of being an awful parent like my father, and not being able to cope, like just now. And letting Bob down, when he's been so wonderful. I went through it all again that lovely day we had up at Murlough,' she went on, wiping her eyes on a minute scrap of lace handkerchief. 'That's what did it, Jenny. It was that day.'

'What d'you mean, Val?' I asked, confused, not even able to remember which day up at Murlough, one of our favourite places.

She grasped my hands and swallowed hard. 'Just before the end of the holidays. That lovely sunny day. I didn't mean to start talking about it, but it just came out, and you were so patient. You just kept saying that I mustn't do anything till I felt right about it, whatever anyone said.

And you reminded me how Bob always says it was me he married and not someone to be the mother of his children. You said however much Bob might like to have children it wouldn't be right for him unless it was what we *both* wanted. Well, suddenly, a few days later, I just made up my mind it was going to be all right. I didn't even tell Bob at first. I just flushed my pills down the loo when I was packing for that bargain break we had in Spain. When we came back, I didn't bleed, but I thought it was just the heat. It was only when I missed again, Bob persuaded me to go to the doctor. I just couldn't believe it had happened so quickly.'

The tears had gone, the sparkle had come back to her eyes and I knew Val was going to be all right. Yes, there were things she was still afraid off, worries and anxieties about coping, but they'd been through it all together and made their plans. As I listened, I felt relief sweep over me.

'We're going to have a nanny to begin with, but when I can cope, I'll stop teaching and work at home. Bob says I must have my own studio, so we're looking for an old farmhouse we can rebuild or extend.' She broke off, her eyes shining. 'Oh Jenny, say you forgive me for neglecting you. Say I'm not an ungrateful wretch, after all the agonising you've listened to. You're not cross with me, are you?' she ended breathlessly.

'Of course I'm not cross,' I said, giving her a little hug. 'You just had me worried in case it was an accident. But if it was your decision and you're happy, that's all I need to hear.'

The colour had come back to her face and she was

smiling so happily it was hard to imagine the havoc Karen's exit line had produced.

'I'll only be cross if you lecture me now about my wifely duties, like Karen did this morning,' I went on.

'She didn't!'

'She did.'

'I promise you, Jenny, never, never, never. Brownie's honour!'

I started to laugh and found I couldn't stop.

'What's so funny, Jenny?' she asked, laughing too.

'I don't know. I really don't know,' I giggled. 'It might just be your mascara.'

Valerie looked in the mirror and threw up her hands in one of those flowing gestures that would seem contrived in anyone else.

'Eyes first and then your hair, Jenny. I've really messed you up, crying all over you like that. Sorry.'

We went on talking about her plans as she renewed her make-up. She and Bob had accepted that old fears don't just melt away, so they'd worked out how they'd meet them when they showed up.

'You know, Jenny, you were right about my work,' she said suddenly. 'You've always said it was painting kept me sane. And now, every time I get panicky about being at home with a baby, I just think about my studio and I'm all right. Isn't that an absolutely awful thing to say?'

'No, it's just very honest, thank goodness. The most unhappy kids I've met are the ones whose parents pretend things. You can't fool children. All you do is confuse them. They always see through an act in the end and that really does awful things to them.'

'Jenny, you promise you won't ever let me do anything like that. You'll tell me, won't you?' she insisted. 'I'm so afraid I'll be an awful mother.'

I shook my head and smiled at her. 'That's probably your best defence, Val. The really awful ones are the ones who think they're God's gift to motherhood. Look at Karen.'

We exchanged glances in the mirror.

'Karen's got a shock coming, Jenny. Wait till she hears I'm not giving up work.'

'And not caring for your own child!' I added gleefully.

'And not giving any more parties!'

'Val, do you mean it?' I cried in amazement.

'Jenny dear, it's not me any more. I wanted everyone to love me, but the people who love me don't need parties. That lot downstairs don't give tuppence about me. Good old Val. Great fun when she's on form, and definitely to be avoided when she's not,' she said sharply. 'Don't look so surprised, Jenny,' she said, laughing, as she finished brushing out my hair. 'It's all your own work, you know. You've been trying to tell me that for years. The penny's dropped at last.'

She put down the hairbrush, rummaged in a drawer full of small scarves and neatly hemmed fragments of fabric, chose one and held it against my hair.

'How about this? Just softly caught back, about here.' I nodded weakly and leaned my elbows on the dressing table. The scarf was a perfect match for my skirt and much nicer than the crumpled black velvet ribbon which lay in front of me, but suddenly I felt overwhelmed by weariness. The thought of going downstairs to face the noise and smoke and the need to talk to people was more than I could bear.

'Jenny?' Val's voice was full of concern.

'I'm fine, just a bit tired,' I said, making the effort to sit up straight again. 'I could do with a drink,' I added feebly.

'I did notice how pale you were before I started weeping all over you. Something's wrong. No secrets, Jenny.'

I bit my lip and sat twisting my engagement ring. 'No secrets' was a bit of our private language, like 'Brownie's honour'. I didn't want to hide anything from Val, but I just didn't know what to say.

'Something *is* wrong, Jenny.'

'No more than usual.' The look on Val's face told me I'd spoken far more sharply than I intended. 'Perhaps it is all getting a bit much,' I went on. 'Maybe I should be starting a family too. There's not much point putting it off if I'm going to. At least I'd have you for company.'

'Jenny! What on earth are you talking about? Has Colin's mother been getting at you again?'

'No,' I said weakly. 'But I've been offered the head of department and I have to decide by Monday. And Colin's so wrapped up in the directorship business he hasn't found time for a phone call to discuss it.'

Val paused, her expression full of concern. 'Yes,' she said thoughtfully, 'he talked about it all the time when I tried to ring you. And Alan said it was just the same the night he tried.'

'Alan? Phoned?'

Dear friend that Alan is, a phone call from Scotland was not something I would ever expect. To begin with, he hates the phone. Besides, we've always kept in touch by letter. And our famous postcards. We have an ongoing competition to see who can say most in the space available.

'Didn't Colin tell you that Alan phoned?' asked Val cautiously.

'No, he never mentioned it,' I said shortly. 'He didn't even tell me about your party. I found out from Karen this morning. You can imagine how pleased she was about that,' I said crossly.

'Oh, Jenny, I'm sorry. It's Colin, isn't it?' she asked gently, her voice soft, her eyes shadowed. 'Do you think it'll be better when he gets it? Is he just anxious?'

I shook my head sadly. 'No, Val, it won't be better when he gets it. I'd like to think it would, but it won't. It started going wrong as soon as we drove off the Liverpool ferry. Since then, not one single thing I've said has had the slightest effect on him. I've tried to make excuses for him. I've tried to blame myself, the job, his family, my mother, the time of the month, the season of the year. It's no good, Val. Colin's not going to be any different. And I haven't the slightest idea what I'm going to do about it.' I stood up and hugged her briefly. 'Val, the show must go on. Your show,' I reminded her. 'Do you realise what time it is?'

'Oh Jenny, what can I do to help? Let's have an evening next week. I'll pick you up from school and we'll have a meal together. I know I'm not as good as you at sorting problems, but at least let me try.'

We settled on an evening. It was only as we turned to go downstairs that I remembered Alan.

'Why *did* Alan phone, Val?'

'To ask you and Colin to come out for a celebration meal with us last weekend. Colin said there was a firm's dinner.'

'Oh, Val,' I said sadly, 'Alan was home and I missed him. Damn that bloody dinner. When did he go back?'

'He didn't, Jenny. That's the point. He's just got a job with the Textile Research Institute and he wanted to tell you himself. That's why he rang. But when he couldn't get you, he thought perhaps he should wait till tonight. He's probably skulking in the kitchen, wondering what on earth I've done with you. He'll have my life for making him wait so long. You know how much he loves parties,' she said wryly.

'You mean he's here?' I said stupidly.

'Yes, Jenny, he's here,' she nodded, taking my hands. 'And perhaps that's a very good thing. Maybe he can help you more than I can. You've always said Alan never lets his feelings get in the way of the facts. Not like me. I feel like murdering Colin because he's hurt you.'

I turned round to smile at her as she closed the bedroom door behind us.

'Val, every girl needs a friend who would murder for her. Don't think it doesn't help. It does.'

Chapter 10

A cloud of cigarette smoke rose to envelop me as I followed Valerie downstairs. Through the teak-framed glass panels that separated hall from lounge, I could see the close-packed figures gesticulating to each other, heads nodding, fingers pointing, their faces red with heat and alcohol, their voices raised in a crescendo of noise that assaulted me like shock waves from an explosion. I clutched the banister as I felt all the colour drain from my own face.

Val turned to me at the foot of the stairs, took one look and raised an eyebrow. 'Jenny, why don't you sit out here for a moment. I'll hunt up Alan and send him through to you.'

I nodded gratefully and watched her weave her way through the tight press of bodies that filled the long lounge from one end to the other. One glance at that room had been enough. The thought of being shut up with those people, their smoke, and their noise, was more than I could bear, but it was no problem to Val. Some instinct told her it was time to show herself and in she went. I watched her progress through the crowded room, amazed at the way solid groups parted before her lightest touch, responding to her smiles and waves as she passed.

And yet I had caught a look in her eye as she left me

which did make me wonder just how easy she really felt. Val is a superb actress. When she makes up her mind to do something, she can carry it off with complete conviction but that says nothing at all about what the effort may cost her.

Val's last party, I said to myself, as I sat down on the telephone seat. Mine too, perhaps.

I ran my eye over the familiar faces. Mostly our crowd, Colin would say. People from schooldays, or Queen's, or the Rugby Club, for Bob had been a keen player too, until recently. I looked around the student pairings, now turned into 'respectable young couples', with someone back at the new house to look after the babies. The room was full of up-and-coming young businessmen like Colin. Useful contacts, he called them now. Not people we knew and liked, and certainly not old friends. Not any more. Just contacts. Useful or not, as the case might be.

'An' I sez to him, "C'mon, Charlie, wha's this car got, solid gold bumpers?" And he sez to me, "All right, Nev, eight hundred it is. But yer a hard man."'

There was a burst of laughter as Neville slapped hands on the bargain. I looked around to see where Karen was. At the other side of the room, she was holding forth to a tight cluster of women, her podgy fingers busy with bright, precise little movements. As the laughter died, she paused, threw one disdainful glance across at him and went back to her story. Neville's face crumpled. Before anyone noticed, he buried his nose in his tankard.

My eyes were prickling with the drifting smoke. I closed them, leaned back, and felt the chill of the wall on my bare shoulders. I had known Neville for a long time, though I couldn't remember exactly when his family moved into Rathmore Drive. He'd been sent to a preparatory school somewhere outside Bangor, so we only saw each other at Sunday School and later on at church socials. It was when we were both press-ganged for the church choir that I really got to know him. Every Wednesday evening we'd walk to and from choir practice on the Lisburn Road. I learnt a great deal about sport on those walks, rugby in particular. But choir practice was grim. We only managed to stick it for a year and then used studying for A-levels as an excuse to make our escape.

The October we went to Queen's, Neville's family moved to Malone Park. 'A step up in the world', was my mother's tight-lipped comment. Neville, like Colin, was destined for the family business, glazing and double-glazing. Reluctantly, he read economics. We'd bumped into each other one day, gone to the Union for coffee and talked for ages. He admitted how much the course bored him but, as he said, there was the rugby. He had once told me that his greatest ambition was to be capped for Ireland and it was clear he was going to make it. Only a week or two later, Neville ended up at the bottom of a collapsed scrum and his broken shoulder put an end to his chances.

Now he was the father of two boys and the husband of a woman who didn't appear to care what secretaryship of the Rugby Club might mean for him. When I thought of the way she'd behaved today and her particular brand of carping criticism, I could only think of Maisie McKinstry. Karen was a Maisie in the making and if Neville threw himself into his work the way William John had done, he might indeed end up just as rich but he would certainly be just as unhappy.

'Jenny!'

Startled, I opened my eyes.

'Alan,' I cried. 'I thought you'd abandoned ship.'

'What, and miss seeing you twice in one year?' he retorted. 'No, I was on a mission,' he went on quickly. 'There's enough alcohol to float a liner out there, but we appear to have drunk all the milk.'

I laughed and moved along the bench to make room for him.

'I don't quite believe this,' I began. 'Your last communiqué from Kilmarnock said Patterson's had just made you an unrefusable offer.'

I watched him as he lowered himself on to the narrow seat, a familiar quizzical look on his face. As uneasy as ever in the first moments of meeting, his eyes were not quite able to meet mine, though his smile was warm and I knew he was pleased to see me.

'Indeed they did,' he agreed. 'A huge increase in salary, a seat on the board, a company car and a piece of carpet under my desk.'

'And you actually refused?' I was totally taken aback by the edge in my voice. It sounded as if I were criticising him for turning it down, which was the last thing I'd intended. The very words 'seat on the board' had set off the response without any help from me.

'I did,' he said quietly. He looked awkwardly up and down the hall and I was sure the sharpness of my reaction had hurt him. It quite overwhelmed me to think I could ever do such a thing to Alan of all people.

I tried to pull myself together, fought back the ridiculous tears that sprang to my eyes and swallowed hard.

'Oh Alan,' I said, touching his sleeve. 'How terribly unfashionable of you.'

This time I managed to get the words out as I meant them, light and teasing. As he turned back towards me, I smiled encouragingly.

'There aren't many in there who would have done what you did,' I said gently as I nodded towards the crowded room.

'But there's one out here who might.' He said it quietly, matter-of-factly, as he looked at me directly for the first time. For a moment or two, I wasn't even sure I'd heard what he'd said properly over the awful racket going on only a few yards away. But as I looked back at him, I seemed to hear the words again. Ordinary words. Unexceptional words. Suddenly, they took on a meaning I had not thought of before.

He was saying that I might well have done just what he had done. He was quite right, of course. He knew perfectly well how I felt about the endless focus on money that had become such a feature among the people Colin called 'our crowd'. Quite suddenly, I was so aware of the two of us, out here in the hall, sitting side-by-side, looking in at the party. I'd never understood Alan when he'd sometimes talked about being an outsider, the loneliness of feeling you didn't belong. Now, I understood. I hadn't been able to put any name to it, but this was what I'd been feeling for months. I was an outsider too. I didn't belong in there with our crowd. There was no part I could play in their lives, nor they in mine. There were no lines for any of us to say to each other any more.

Alan and I weren't just sitting outside, here and now, we were permanently outside. Both of us. Alan had known it for years, but until this moment it had never entered my mind that I too might be just as much of an outsider as he was.

I nodded slowly in reply and dived into the pocket of my skirt for my handkerchief. I was so shocked by where my own thoughts had taken me that just for the moment I couldn't think of anything whatever to say.

'Didn't Val give you a drink before she parked you here?' he exclaimed, abruptly jumping to his feet. 'I'll get us one before we get launched. What would you like?' he added, as I blew my nose and tried to behave as if nothing had happened.

'What is there?' I asked brightly. I glanced up at him and caught a look on his face that made me wonder if he'd spotted that something was wrong. If he had, he covered it beautifully while I collected myself.

'Just about everything. All the hard stuff, variety of homebrews. Hugh, Mark One, Alwyn, Mark Three, Neville, Mark Six, none of which, as a former chemist, I can recommend,' he said lightly. 'But there *is* a bottle of that dry sherry we had at Christmas. Bob produced it from the garden shed. Said he'd been keeping it till you came!'

'Just what I need, Alan. Just what I need.'

Relief swept over me as I watched him stride off down the hall and disappear into the kitchen. Dear Alan, he hadn't changed a bit. Not in the things that mattered most to me. For three years now we'd met only at Christmas, at the Annual General Meeting, as Val called her Boxing Night dinner. That last meeting seemed an eternity away and yet at this minute I felt as if I'd seen Alan only yesterday. It was nothing to do with how often you saw someone. It was all about what happened when you did.

I knew I could say anything I wanted to Alan. And he'd listen. Whether he agreed or disagreed, it didn't matter. It was the sheer blessed relief of talking to someone who actually listened to what you said. And someone, too, who always gave me honest answers to my questions, even when those answers had to admit doubt or ignorance.

If there was one thing that had been making me utterly miserable over the last few months, it was Colin's sureness about everything. From the fastest car in its class to the best place to eat out, from the time it would take to mend a washing machine to the golden future of the Province, he was so sure of himself and so completely free of doubt. All the time, he behaved as if he could map out his own future, and mine, as easily as he could plot a flow chart for a contract.

'Here you are, Bob's compliments. Sends his apologies. He's on supper duty.' Alan dropped into his seat beside me. 'To the good old days,' he went on, touching his glass against mine.

'Oh Alan, you said that just the way you did when I was still at school. You used to frighten the life out of me,' I laughed, as I sipped my sherry appreciatively.

It had taken me a long time to get used to Alan's ironic manner, but having mastered it, I found its dryness as pleasing as the sherry Bob had so thoughtfully set aside for me.

'Still at school,' he repeated thoughtfully. 'A long time

ago, Jenny. How long have we known each other?'

'Depends what you mean by "know",' I said lightly. 'I can tell you the first time we spent a day together. I'll never forget it.'

'Sounds ominous.'

'Yes, it was. You were in your first year at Oxford and I was only in the fourth form. Val asked me to come up with you to visit Aunt Audrey and Uncle John and she insisted I sit in the front seat. I couldn't think of a single intelligent thing to say the whole way up to Ballycastle.'

'Yes, I remember,' he said, stretching out his legs more comfortably. 'I'd had strict instructions to be nice to you and I thought I was going to cop it when Val got me home for making such a mess of it.'

'And didn't you?'

'No, for some reason she let me off. She said you needed time to get used to me.'

'Certainly I did. About three years!'

'Oh, come, Jenny, was I as awful as that?'

'Yes,' I said laughing. 'Everything you said seemed to be touched with acid. It was like trying to be friendly to a porcupine. But it wasn't entirely your fault. It just took me rather a long time to work out that you weren't quite as worldly-wise and cynical as you liked to make out.'

'Given your tender years, that was some achievement,' he said, looking down into his glass and shifting uneasily.

'Come on now. You're not that ancient.'

'Wouldn't you say I've mellowed in my maturity?' he asked, taking refuge in the teasing tone he'd used so often to get himself out of awkward situations.

'I hadn't exactly noticed,' I retorted.

'Oh, that really disappoints me,' he said, pulling a face. 'Only the other day, Val said I was almost fit for human consumption.'

He'd picked up my light tone and for a few, blissful minutes I'd put aside all my anxieties. I remembered just how easily we had always been able to talk about anything. If anyone could help me sort myself out, it would be Alan. I drained my sherry glass.

'Don't be disappointed, Alan,' I said quietly. 'Some people do appreciate your astringency. I could do with a spot of it at the moment. It's been in pretty short supply round here just recently.'

'That we shall have to address,' he said, jumping to his feet. 'When I've fetched us a refill.'

A couple of long strides and he disappeared through the kitchen door. I smiled to myself. Those long strides had once been a problem to me. When we went out taking pictures together at Queen's, on any reasonable surface those same strides had left me trailing far behind. We used to laugh about it, especially when I got my own back, for when it was wet rock, or seaweed, or mud, I came into my own. Alan always said he was quite intimidated by my sure-footedness.

A long time now since I'd scrambled over rock or mud in pursuit of a picture. I had forgotten just how much time we'd spent together, my first two years at Queen's, while Alan had been studying for his PhD. Some of the best times were up on the north coast when he and Val visited their aunt and uncle in their rambling old house that looked out across Rathlin Sound to Rathlin Island itself. Aunt Audrey and Uncle John were lovely people. They made me so welcome and sent the three of us off, walking and exploring, armed with vast picnics, sketchbooks and cameras.

When Alan and I joined the Photographic Society, we went off looking for pictures together for the monthly competitions. Often, we would go to the remote parts of Antrim, to places I knew through visiting with my father. One humid summer day, we found ourselves outside the churchyard at the foot of my father's glen. It was Alan who insisted we look for the gravestone my father used to see from his schoolroom window. And it was Alan who found it. He looked at it for a long time, took some pictures, and then asked me if I would take him to see the site of the old cottage where my father had been born.

At the time, I thought it a strange thing for him to ask, though I knew he liked my father and always listened carefully to his stories on the rare occasions when they met. We drove up the valley, parked on the road, walked down the rough track that led to what once was McTaggart's farm and worked our way cautiously along the hillside, for the path was so rarely used now, it had almost disappeared.

When we finally reached the fragment of gable still standing amid the tumbled walls and the invading bracken and heather, we became so absorbed in the view that we didn't notice the darkening sky behind us. As the first drops of rain splashed down, we dived under the lee of the gable and let the squall whip over us. We emerged, dishevelled but dry, continued our explorations and then got thoroughly soaked by a second downpour as we climbed back up the track to the road.

There had been so many happy times. I sat twisting my engagement ring round and round on my finger and asked myself whatever had happened at the end of that year to change everything. Alan had got his doctorate and the offer of a very good job in Cheshire. Val and Bob got engaged on her birthday in August and we had a marvellous celebration with them, and then, before Alan left in September, we had a whole series of splendid expeditions together.

In October I joined the Dramatic Society and that was where I met Colin six months later when he was drafted in to help with a difficult set and stayed on to help with the production. I'd seen Alan when he came home to visit Val and he came over specially the weekend of the Photographic Society's outing. But after that September, I realised, we had not gone out together again. Until this moment, I had never asked myself why that should have been so.

'Sorry about that, Jenny. Val needed some candle ends paring.'

'For her romantic gloom?' I asked matter-of-factly, as I pushed away the thoughts that had been crowding in upon me.

'"The last performance on any stage," was what she said this afternoon when we did the balloons.' He handed me my sherry and sat down.

'So you've come home, Alan. For good?'

'For good or ill. Which remains to be seen. I'm certainly committed to this new project for a year or two. It'll take at least that long to get it off the ground.'

'And after?'

He opened his free hand and looked at me very directly. 'Who knows? Can we predict who we're going to be in two or three years' time, never mind the circumstances we'll find ourselves in?' he said quietly.

I nodded. 'You've always said things like that, Alan, and I've been reluctant to admit that we can change so fast. Perhaps I've known too many people who never seem to change. Too many who know just who they'll be in three years' time. Or thirty. And where. And how wonderfully it'll all work out.' I stared at the faces beyond the glass panels and twisted my sherry glass in my hand.

'Jenny?' he said softly.

I glanced towards him. He was looking at me intently, on his face a look of gentleness I could not bear. It was a look I had seen before and had somehow forgotten. Alan had looked at me just this way more than once in that late summer before he went off to Cheshire.

'I was thinking of a nice set of prints,' I said hastily. 'For the annual exhibition. "Life on the way to the top" by Jennifer Erwin, Honorary Member. What d'you think?' I waved a hand at the screen dividing us from the lounge and was relieved when he turned away. Each panel framed the sort of image we'd once have entered as a 'candid'. He picked up my cue instantly.

'Mmm, I see what you mean. How would you light it?'

'Oh, available. On really fast film,' I said firmly. 'Those faces need big grainy prints. It would pull out the haze of smoke to stand for the haze they're creating. I'd soften the focus too, blur the shapes a bit. Just like they do.'

He nodded and waited.

'Alan, they don't talk to each other. They don't look at each other. They don't connect.' I heard the bitterness in my voice, but I went on. 'Is it me? Or is it them? What's happened to all those people I used to know and like?'

I saw him hesitate, but once he began, he was simple and direct.

'I think you've changed, Jenny. Changed very fast. But so have they. And you've not taken the same path.'

I glanced up at him anxiously, afraid of what was coming next. Yet I was even more afraid that he would let me down and evade my question.

'Most of the men in that room are living out a fantasy of some kind,' he began. 'Successful businessman. Jolly good chap. Real live wire. They don't think about it. They just go through the appropriate actions. Very labour-saving device. Simplifies life enormously. Eliminates effort and confusion and guarantees a sense of superiority over anyone who decides not to do likewise.'

'And the women, Alan. What about the women? What do they do while their husbands are acting out their fantasies?'

'That depends. Most of the ones I can see from here have fantasies of their own.'

'Such as?'

'Capable wife. Caring mother. Dutiful daughter.'

'And what happens if the wife hasn't got a fantasy of her own? If, for example, she were one of those unfortunates who want to do differently, to find out who they really are.' I knew he was looking at me, but I kept my eyes firmly on the pale liquid in my glass.

'She has a number of options,' he began. 'Do you remember me telling you about Iona Patterson? No, you probably don't. It must have been the Christmas before last.'

'Oh yes I do,' I replied quickly. 'She was your boss's

wife, the one who painted that splendid watercolour you bought Val for her birthday.'

'Right. Well, I asked Iona your question once. We were at a firm's dinner and she'd said some of the things you've been saying. She was very honest. Drink, bridge or sex, she said, were the options. Most of the women she knew had taken up one, or two, or all three. But in her case, it didn't work. She's allergic to alcohol, bored by cards, and still in love with Jamie. Hence the painting.'

'Hardly a substitute for a real relationship.'

'Depends what you mean by a "real" relationship, Jenny.'

I could see the point he was making, but I doubted if it offered me a solution. 'So presumably, as long as both parties play the rules of the game, all is sweetness and light,' I said without enthusiasm.

'Correct. Problems only arise if one party refuses to go on playing. Like my mother did.'

I looked up quickly. Alan had never mentioned his mother before, except in relation to Valerie.

'Alan, was it because of your parents that you've been so hostile to marriage? You've always been so cynical about falling in love. I remember you saying most men gave more thought to choosing a car than choosing a wife.'

'That remark couldn't have made me very popular.'

'No, it didn't. Nor did the comments you made, my last year, about all the pairing off that went on. Most of our crowd got engaged or married that year. You didn't think those marriages would last, did you?'

I saw his eyes flicker over the group nearest the lounge door. A burly figure broke away and dashed up the stairs behind us. The bathroom door banged shut but did not disguise the sounds of someone being violently sick. Only moments later, heavy footsteps re-echoed on the stairs and Alwyn McPherson elbowed his way back into the crowd as if nothing whatever had happened.

'It seemed to me the people involved hardly knew each other. As real people, that is. It looked just like a Paul Jones – you married the girl opposite when the music stopped.'

'Has it ever struck you, Alan, that the Paul Jones doesn't stop with the marriage?'

'Go on,' he said quietly.

But now I had seen it, I felt too tired to bother. It was all so obvious. Quite pointless to talk about it or analyse it. Over and done with. Only the harm left to face up to.

'Go on, Jenny,' he insisted. 'What happens then?'

'Well, as you say, you marry when the music stops,' I said, taking a deep breath. 'But, if you're a woman, the Paul Jones goes on. And on. The next time it stops, you're opposite velvet lounge curtains and a holiday in Spain. The next time, the new car and the washing machine. And the time after that, the second car and the first baby. But if you miss your cue and you're not in the right place at the right time, you start to think about the whole preposterous business. That's if you can hear yourself think with everyone telling you at the top of their voice where you've gone wrong and how you get back into the dance before it's too late.'

I paused. The strain of talking over the din from the lounge was making my voice crack, or so I told myself. I sipped my sherry, cleared my throat and tried again.

'You know, men deciding on marriage and women deciding on children comes to much the same thing in the end. Most of the women I know give more thought to choosing a new dress than having another baby. That's why Val has had such a wretched time. She refused to play the game.'

I stopped abruptly, aware of the build-up behind my words. Waves of anger were flooding over me. Alan could cope with whatever I threw at him, but whether I could was a different matter.

'Jenny dear! Sorry to butt in.'

I got one look at Bob's face as he bent to kiss me. He looked hot and agitated.

'Is anything wrong, Bob?'

'No, but I need reinforcements. Val's had to go down to the summerhouse. The smell of the pastry was making her sick. Would you come and direct operations if Alan and I fetch and carry for you? Val says we need to go ahead right away or the savories will spoil.'

'Yes, of course,' I said jumping to my feet. 'But is Val all right?'

'Yes, truly. She was just fed up she couldn't keep going. She says she'll be back the moment the smell's gone,' he replied, as we trooped along the hall to the kitchen.

Val's supper was certainly going to be memorable. She had made all the food herself, including the fresh cream gateaux I found when I opened the fridge. The oven was full of sausage rolls and vol-au-vents, and there were dishes of colourful bits and pieces on sticks and tiny sandwiches cut in interesting shapes. The only problem was where to put anything. The work surfaces were covered with bottles and clean glasses and the draining boards were covered with dirty ones. There wasn't time to wash up, for the savories were indeed ready. I could see why the smell had got to Val. The state my stomach was in, it was getting to me as well.

But things got better as Bob and Alan carried stuff through to the lounge. The smell in the kitchen got less and the noise from next door diminished magically.

'Jenny, could you manage for a few minutes if Alan and I go and open another keg of beer?'

I shut the oven door with my foot and looked at Bob over my shoulder. 'Fine. This is the last trayful. I'll take them through myself. What about the coffee?'

Alan plugged in the percolator and switched it on. 'We'll be back before that's through,' he said reassuringly as he followed Bob out to the garage.

I perched the hot tray on the edge of the sink so I could loosen the golden triangles with an egg slice. I looked for something to put them on but there wasn't a plate in sight, so I picked up the tray again and carried it in as it was.

Neville was leaning against the doorpost, munching devotedly, his broad back blocking the entrance.

'Neville,' I said quietly. He didn't hear me. He was looking across the room at Karen, where she sat, still surrounded by the same group of women. On her lap she held a well-filled plate of sandwiches and savories. Alwyn McPherson was leaning towards her, a dish of cocktail sausages in his hand.

'Oh no, Alwyn, I shouldn't,' she protested coyly. 'I really can't have any more little sausages. They're frightfully fattening.'

'Oh, c'mon Karen, treat yourself. You can work it off later. A skinny woman's no use. Give Neville something to hold on to.'

Karen's lips tightened as she stretched out her hand and took another sausage.

'C'mon, Karen. Bloody hell, what's the use of one? C'mon.' Alwyn's voice was thick and slurred. As he leaned further forward, the sausages skidded towards her outstretched hand.

'It's all right, Karen,' Alison Craig put in. 'It's only carbohydrate that matters. As long as it's protein, you can absolutely stuff yourself.'

Karen shrugged. 'That's fine then.' Her podgy fingers tightened round a handful of sticks, transferred them to her plate, and began to pop them whole into her prim little mouth.

'C'mon Alison, here y'ar, girl, have some bloody sausages. Build you up into a big, strong wench. Great for the figure. Don't tell me Jim doesn't fancy a nice round pair. Thassright, isn't it, Jim?'

Alison giggled and helped herself. She was already eyeing a lemon meringue which was disappearing fast as the plate passed from hand to hand across the room. 'You can't be careful all the time,' she moaned, as she filled her plate. 'You just can't. Why, I eat practically nothing and I still put on weight. So what's the point?'

I tightened my grip on the hot tray and wondered how I was going to get it safely across the room to the empty plates on the sideboard.

'Neville,' I began, 'could you walk in front of me? This tray's very hot.'

Neville jumped and turned round so quickly he nearly knocked it out of my hands.

'Jenny! Here, let me take—'

'Neville, it's—'

'Ooooww . . .'

All conversation stopped as Neville licked his burnt fingers.

'You being raped then, Neville?'

'Whassat? Who's being raped?' Alwyn turned round and made his way unsteadily towards us. 'I say, I say, and where have you been all evening, Jenny McKinstry? C'mon then. I saw you out there with Thompson.'

I moved briskly into the space left by Neville and slipped past Alwyn to the sideboard, ignoring him as best I could.

'Could I have those empty plates, please, Jim?'

'Anything for you, Jenny,' he said agreeably as he passed them along.

I started to unload the savories. Conversation had stopped and showed no signs of starting again. I could feel their eyes upon me and it was all I could do to keep my hands from shaking as I slid the last golden triangle on to a plate. I took up my empty tray, turned, and found Alwyn blocking my path.

'Whassis then, Jenny? Not talkin' to me tonight? Zat it?' He slid his arm round my waist and pulled me towards him. I could smell the whisky on his breath and his body reeked of sweat. He felt hot and damp against my bare shoulders.

An overpowering sense of claustrophobia swept over me. Silent figures surrounded me, munching, a vol-au-vent at a mouthful. A sandwich at a bite. Watching me. Waiting to be entertained. Even by a man who'd had far too much to drink making an absolute fool of himself.

'Where's McKinstry tonight, then?'

For God's sake humour him, Jenny. Keep it light, I said to myself as I felt his grip tighten on me.

'Off to the big city, Alwyn.'

'Ah-ha. So thass it. While the cat's away . . .' He slid his hand up from my waist till his thumb pressed into my breast. I gripped my tray and tried to press his hand away without making it too obvious to the watchers.

But he wouldn't move his hand or let me go.

'We all know 'bout London, Jenny. McKinstry's not sittin' in tonight, izzy? A fine upstandin' lad like Colin, he'll be living it up,' he went on, breathing in my face. 'UP,' he repeated, hiccupping. 'So what about you 'n' me havin' the lass dance? I'll see you gets 'ome all right.'

'Alwyn, you're standing between me and another pot of coffee. And some people's cups are empty,' I said, making a supreme effort to sound easy.

But Alwyn was past talking to. The needle had stuck in the groove and on he went. 'Oh, a pot of coffee, is it? Well, thass a new name for it. Jim, d'ye hear? She calls it apotocoffee.'

Jim sniggered. Beyond the solid obstacle of Alwyn's large frame, I caught a glimpse of Neville. He was looking very uncomfortable.

'C'mon Jenny, wass Thompson got that I haven't got? What d'ye want to sit out there for talkin' to him all evenin'? He's not one of our crowd. Oh, we saw you, didden we, Jim? We not fancy enough for you these days? C'mon, Jenny, less go an' 'ave a danse.'

'Sorry, Alwyn, I'm busy. Let me past, please.' I couldn't keep the thin edge out of my tone. I was getting desperate. 'Please, Alwyn,' I repeated, more sharply. I pressed the tray onto his hand as hard as I could. He belched and released me.

'She doessn' fancy me,' he announced to the whole room, waving his tankard in the air. 'Well, thass all right. Thass juss all right. You go off with nice boy Thompson. He'll spin you a fine yarn. Don' know who your frenss are, Jenny,' he called after me as I left the lounge as swiftly as I decently could.

I stumbled down the corridor, threw open the kitchen door and banged it shut behind me. I leaned against it, shivering violently, wincing in the brilliant fluorescent light. For a moment I thought I was going to be violently sick.

'Jenny, what on earth's the matter?' Alan put down the percolator, dragged out a stool from under the work surface and sat me down. I leaned back against the wall, my eyes closed, tears streaming down my cheeks. 'What's wrong, Jenny? Tell me what I can do. Shall I fetch Val?'

I shook my head. 'Alan, for God's sake get me away from here. Now, this minute. If you don't, I won't be responsible for what I do.'

'What coat were you wearing?'

'The black cloak.'

'I'll get it and tell Bob we're going. I won't be a moment.' He ran the water till it was cold and filled a glass. 'Here, that might help.'

I drank it gratefully. I looked at the glass, turning it in my hand. A pity it was one of Val's best. I couldn't bear to smash anything that was precious to her. Besides, if I smashed it, I wasn't sure I'd be able to stop there, and at this moment the kitchen was just full of glass.

Chapter 11

We slipped out by the back door and headed down the hill, past the long line of cars, to where Alan had had to leave his after his expedition for the milk. After the steamy heat of the kitchen, the cold, frosty air whipped my breath away. My teeth began to chatter, so loudly I was sure they'd be heard far and wide. I was quite terrified someone would appear and try to stop us getting away. But apart from an unidentified figure having a pee in a flowerbed by the front door, there was no one to see or hear us as we ran the last few yards to the car.

'Here, wrap this round you,' Alan said as he opened the passenger door. He grabbed a rug from the back seat, thrust it into my lap and hurried round to his own side. 'Where to?'

'Anywhere.'

I pulled the rug up round my neck, shut my eyes and tried to pretend I was warm, but I just couldn't stop shivering. At first, all I was aware of was the flicker of neon street lamps and then the festoons of coloured lights that meant we were now down on the road along the lough shore. Alan was driving fast. We turned right and began to climb. The gradient steepened and I could feel the darkness grow all around us. Only an occasional car broke the deep stillness of the countryside with the whoosh of its passing. In a little while, I felt warm air blowing on my feet. I stopped clutching the rug so fiercely and opened my eyes a little.

Alan was concentrating on the road, his face in sharp profile. When he had come walking down the hall with our refilled glasses, I'd thought how different he looked. I felt the difference even more now, but exactly what it was I couldn't put my finger on. Older certainly. But older than when? Alan had looked older than his years ever since I'd known him. Even as an eleven-year-old he had seemed solemn and responsible. I remembered him at one of Val's birthday parties picking up the torn wrappings from her presents, putting the presents themselves safely out of harm's way, and catching his mother's eye when it was time to bring the children to the tea table. He had always taken care of Val, and after their mother died, he still tried so hard to help her even when most of the time they were hundreds of miles apart.

Perhaps Alan had grown up quickly because of Val's need. After their father's remarriage he was all she'd got left of the loving home her mother had made for them. It had certainly made Alan different. I looked cautiously at the strong lines of his face, his eyes intent on the road ahead, and thought of the men at the party, the ones I'd been watching all evening. They seemed to me just like the crowd of rowdy small boys at that birthday tea, all of twenty years ago.

I shut my eyes again, grateful for the quiet and the sense of smooth, rapid movement. Usually, I don't like driving fast. I get frightened when Colin puts his foot down on the few bits of open road between the city centre and Loughview Heights. But Alan wasn't pretending he was driving a sports car 'with a bit of poke', he was simply taking me away as quickly as he could from the blare of voices and the choking smoke, the throb of the hi-fi, and a drunken man fumbling at my breast.

Alwyn had said I didn't know who my friends were. In one sense, he was right. I had forgotten just what good friends I had. One of the strangest things about these last two months was the way I had let myself be separated from the people who knew me best and cared for me most. I hadn't contacted Val, nor invited her and Bob to come for a meal. When I'd thought about it this morning, I'd still accepted that it was simply pressure of work. Now I saw a more convincing reason. If Val and Bob had come to supper and Colin had behaved in his usual manner, Val would have seen what I was trying not to see. The Colin and Jenny Show wouldn't have fooled her for a minute, even if I'd gone on letting it fool me.

'Are you taking me to the sea?' I asked quietly.

He looked surprised as he glanced across at me. He had been deep in thought, but now a smile flickered briefly. He seemed relieved I'd said something.

'Would that be a good idea?'

'Yes, I think so. If anything is.'

The moon was high in the sky. Ahead of us the road lay like a white swathe cut through the dark shadows of trees and hedgerows. Suddenly, I recognised the worn and weathered stump of a tree, snapped off in the gales of 1953 and grown more silvery with each passing year. As when you meet an old friend in an unfamiliar setting and a stream

of happy memories flows back to you, I had a sudden sense
of wellbeing.

'I don't know when I was last on this road, Alan. Could
we stop on Windmill Hill?'

Windmill Hill had what my father always called 'an
outlook'. Over the years, on an ancient ordnance map
coming apart at the creases, he had marked all the places
he knew that had outlooks. In the school holidays, when
he was 'doing his calls', visiting all his farmer clients
scattered around the countryside, I had gone with him.
There was hardly a road, lane, or farm track, in Down or
Armagh, we had not travelled together at some time,
sandwiches wrapped in greaseproof paper and tea in a flask.
And lunch always had to be eaten somewhere 'with an
outlook'.

Alan slowed right down and then edged cautiously off
the road at the highest point of the low hill where the
remains of the old mill still stood. Beyond the low hedge
that straggled along the edge of the wide grassy verge, the
whole of the southern Ards lay spread out in the moonlight,
the deep silence of the sea a palpable presence where the
shadowy carpet of tiny fields dissolved into darkness.

'What happened back at the house, Jenny?'

'I'm not sure. Alwyn McPherson made a grab at me.
Nothing new about that. But this time I couldn't cope.
Nausea. Panic. Suddenly I just felt my whole life falling
apart.' I heard myself speak as coolly as if I were describing
the symptoms of some everyday ailment, the kind of thing
some doctors prescribe for without raising their eyes from
their prescription pad. I took a deep breath, clutched the
rug more firmly around me, and tried again.

'Three years ago, I married someone I believed I loved. I set out to make a home and a life and a future. The home I have is the hand-me-down he accepted to keep his parents happy, and the life I have is the same. It's all about people we have to see and dinners we have to attend. Friends we haven't time for and things we never do. And the future? The future is what I saw in that room tonight. Alwyn gropes me to remind me what the rules permit in "our crowd". Colin has it off in London, a one-night stand, like any proper lad, without prejudice to the show back home. I am free to amuse myself likewise, should I so wish, but mark you, only with one of "our" crowd. There are even rules about that,' I spat out bitterly.

'And the women, Alan,' I went on, catching my breath. 'Those hideous women, stuffing themselves silly while they talk about their diets. Having babies to justify their good opinion of themselves. So self-satisfied they've got it all worked out just the way they want it. I don't know which is worse, their indifference to the men or the men's indifference to them. And the men are just as bad, swigging their beer and telling smutty jokes. Treating each other as objects. Treating everyone as objects, like Alwyn treated me. But that's Colin's world, Alan, that's where he feels comfortable, at ease, at home . . . and I can't stand it. I can't live like that . . . I can't . . .'

As I tried to get the words out, the pain in my throat broke in a great sob and tears poured down my face.

For a moment, he stared out at the moonlit landscape as if he were searching among the remote farms, the tiny, bright starflowers scattered in the darkness, for a particular one that he knew. Then he said, very quietly and very coolly,

'You don't have to live that life, Jenny. There are options, you know.'

'What options, Alan?' I hissed angrily. 'What options? You're not going to suggest Colin and I could do a Val and Bob, are you? Move out into the country? Break away from our crowd?'

'It is one option,' he replied steadily.

'Oh no, Alan. It isn't. Not for Colin and me. Colin's mummy wouldn't like it. It wouldn't help her dear son in his career. Too far away from the right people. And what about the grandchildren? She'd want them near her, so she could pop in often. And Colin would agree. After all, why not, with Jenny at home being a fulltime wife and mother. No, Alan, doing a Val and Bob wouldn't please Mummy at all. And as Colin has done everything Mummy has wanted since we drove off the Liverpool ferry, I don't think it's likely he'll change now.'

My voice packed up as I saw the enormity of what I'd spelled out. The sobs broke over me again and I had to gasp for breath. I couldn't do anything whatever to stop them and they were even noisier than my chattering teeth.

Alan's hand brushed mine and I saw he was offering me something. Blurred, but very white. An extraordinary object, gleaming in the moonlight. I stared at it for ages before I saw what it was. A clean and folded handkerchief. Quite unexpectedly, the sobs stopped, though tears went on pouring down my cheeks. I took it and blew my nose.

'I thought all men used their handkerchiefs to clean their cars with,' I said weakly, as I looked across at him.

'No, not all of them,' he said, turning away distractedly.

'Alan,' I began cautiously, afraid the sobs might jump

up and suffocate me, 'I can't see any options at all.'

He took in his breath so sharply, I wondered what he'd been thinking about while I'd been sobbing.

'Well, if you can't, I can at least lay out the possibilities for you. And I mean possibilities,' he said firmly. 'Only you can say which of them might become options,' he went on matter-of-factly, as if he were anxious to keep the record straight. 'Firstly, you can tell Colin how you feel, spell out the problems as you see them, and work out how you can change things. Second, you can make a life of your own while remaining married to Colin.'

'And third, Alan?' I said quickly.

He seemed almost reluctant to reply, stared out again at the wide landscape, but then went on as steadily as before. 'You can make a life on your own, Jenny. It's not easy, but you don't lack courage. You have your job. Friends. Things that are important to you.'

Each word dropped into place like the last piece of a jigsaw puzzle. Blue pieces to finish the sky and dappled bits to fill in the shade of a tree. Not the most important pieces in the puzzle, or even the most difficult ones, simply the last. I felt a stillness come over me; a strange composure took the place of all the agitation.

'Alan, do you ever imagine you're standing outside yourself, watching something happening to you and feeling that it must be happening to someone else?'

He nodded wryly. 'I know it well, but only in the bad moments. Never the good. What about you?'

I looked down and saw I'd been twisting my engagement ring, round and round, till it was quite loose.

'There don't seem to have been many good moments to

test it on,' I said honestly. 'Not for a long, long time, anyway.'

The tears began again and I mopped them up patiently. At least they flowed quietly now and didn't shake my shoulders and tear at my throat. I looked at the handkerchief in my hand. The fresh white linen was reduced to a limp, sodden rag, streaked with eye make-up. I giggled.

Alan looked alarmed. It occurred to me he might think I was hysterical, so I reassured him.

'It's all right, Alan. I'm laughing at a bad joke.' I dried off my tears again and held up his handkerchief by the corners. 'Behold, a massacred handkerchief.'

He looked so puzzled I began to wonder if he was right. Perhaps I was hysterical.

'Mascara. Val and I always call it "massacre". Hence a massacred handkerchief,' I explained. 'I told you it was a bad joke. Like my life at the moment,' I ended.

My snuffles had cleared and my mind seemed to be working again, but a deep silence had settled upon me. It made me uneasy, for I was afraid I couldn't speak again without weeping.

I looked out over the quiet countryside, my eyes moving from one spark of light to another. Each spark, a home. Each home, a person, or a family, sitting by the embers of a fire, reading, or talking, or drinking a cup of tea. Here were people whose lives were going on day by day, week by week, lives shaped by work and relationships, by the small fields, the bumpy lanes, the narrow roads, the links to hamlet, village, town or city. I felt myself as remote from the ordinary everyday events of my own life as I was from the lives of these unknown people out in the darkness.

Except for the dear friend beside me, I was totally alone in a dark world where there was no spark of light to welcome me.

I shivered again and twisted the damp handkerchief in my hands. Alan was staring into the distance, his eyes following the headlamps of two cars driving slowly in convoy along the deserted coast road.

Time passed. The second hand of the luminous clock on the dashboard clicked rhythmically. Say something, Jenny. Don't go silent. How can anyone help you if you don't offer something, I admonished myself.

'How did I get it wrong, Alan?' I asked, looking across at him. 'What did I do? Or not do? I thought it was real enough, three years ago. Not just vague notions of living together happily ever after. We did talk. We had plans and projects. We were happy in Birmingham. At least, I thought I was. Where did I go wrong?'

'What makes you assume it was you who did the going wrong?'

'I always do blame myself, I suppose, if things go wrong. Don't you?'

'Yes, actually I do,' he answered ruefully. 'But blaming oneself is not a good idea. I'm trying to give it up. There's no logical reason to assume that it's you who's got it wrong just because things don't work out the way you hoped they would. There are always elements in any situation that only the future can reveal.'

'But surely there's always something you can do. You can't just let events dictate to you. You have to struggle for what you want. Don't you?'

'Oh yes, you do have to struggle,' he agreed readily.

'But you have to be sure you're struggling against the right thing. Ultimately, the only thing you can really have any command over is yourself. You may be able to do precious little about events, but you can still act upon yourself. When you do that, all manner of things become possible.'

'So you're saying, if I change me, I can change the way I see the situation I'm in?'

'Up to a point, yes, you can. But you must also accept what you can't change in others. And even then, there are still situations that will resist all your attempts to see them in a different light. That's why you must never blame yourself for a failure that isn't yours.' He paused, and then continued very softly, as if he'd got to the heart of what he wanted to say. 'The only real failure, Jenny, is to disengage from your life. "Slipping the clutch" is what one of my tutors used to call it. Going into neutral and letting events do your living for you. Like your Paul Jones. That's what you saw at the party tonight, wasn't it? People letting the Paul Jones live life for them. And you know it's not your style.'

I looked out again at the scatter of lights. Some individuals were just like those bright points in the darkness. Only the ones who struggled to engage with life produced light. But it was an effort. Far easier to remain lost in the unlit background.

'So, if I get me right,' I said cautiously, 'then I won't go struggling in the wrong place, is that it?'

'I'd put it even more strongly. If you don't get you right, you can't get anything right for anyone, whatever your relationship with them.'

I laughed softly.

'You know Alan, that really cheers me. It's just what my father said to me last night when I told him I'd been offered the head of department and I was afraid I'd be selfish to take it. I got the gist of what he was saying then, but it all seems so much clearer now.'

He looked across at me and smiled, looking easier for the first time since we'd stopped the car. He nodded vigorously. 'It's what I call the K1 to K2 effect. Where K1 equals what you know, and K2 is what K1 will come to mean after time has passed and the future has added its egg. Awareness always grows by what it feeds on. And what your father said on Friday night has had quite a lot to feed on since.'

I laughed in spite of myself, delighted by his enthusiastic response and amused that he should have invented an equation to work out his insight. 'That's all a long way from treating loomstate and developing Easicare linen,' I said doubtfully.

He shook his head. 'Not as far as you might think, Jenny. Even ordinary everyday problems can look quite different when you live inside the skin you've chosen for yourself and not one people have forced upon you.'

If anyone had a right to say something like that, it was Alan. From the moment he'd lost his mother, he'd had to fight every inch of the way for his right to be himself. And even when he had succeeded academically and landed a well-paid job with excellent prospects, he'd still had his battles.

After two years with the big chemical company in Cheshire he'd felt compelled to leave because the project he had been asked to work on was exploitive, designed to boost sales instead of getting inexpensive medicines into the hands of people who needed them. He'd moved to Scotland, to a small textile plant desperately trying to survive in a hostile economic climate. He'd reviewed all their traditional methods of bleaching and dyeing, created a new treatment for the finishing of cotton, and helped them get back on their feet. Already at work on similar processes for the treatment of linen, he had turned down the seat on the board so that he could go on working on something he felt was worthwhile.

I smiled and fell silent, so grateful I didn't need to say anything in reply. I shivered again, but more with relief than cold. What he said next came as a complete surprise to me.

'Look, Jenny, would you like to see my new home? It's only about five minutes up the road.'

'What? Out here?' I was so amazed, my voice came out as a squeak. If I'd ever had to describe Alan's ideal home I'd almost certainly have plumped for a modern flat with the latest in Scandinavian furniture and a kitchen designed by a time-and-motion expert.

'Mmm, I've bought a fisherman's cottage down at Drinsallagh,' he admitted shyly. 'If there was a light on, you might just be able to see it over there,' he went on, waving a hand vaguely towards the south-east.

'But how marvellous! Of course I want to see it. Village of, or townland of?'

'Townland,' he answered as he manoeuvred the car carefully back on to the road. 'You'll recognise the lane down when we get to it. It's just before the turn to your favourite harbour, Ballydrumard, where you did those studies of the old breakwater. Remember?'

I had forgotten completely. Apart from the odd family group and some studies of Susie when she'd stayed with me in the summer, I hadn't touched a camera since before we came back. All my pictures of pieces of wood, ploughed fields, stonewalls and wildflowers were in a portfolio under the studio couch in my study. When we moved in, I'd had a couple of my favourites framed to hang on the wall by my desk, but since then I hadn't even got round to looking at the others.

A few minutes later and we were bumping down a rutted lane between overgrown stonewalls and windshaped hawthorns. We turned round a whitewashed gable and stopped on a wide, flagged area opposite the front door.

'Alan, I don't believe it,' I said, as I got out of the car and stood looking up at the gnarled branches of a climbing rose which half smothered the whole front of the low dwelling. 'I'm green with envy,' I went on. 'This is just what I used to dream about when I was a child. I was going to be a famous writer and live in a cottage by the sea, with roses round the windows and hollyhocks by the front door. I'd never seen a real hollyhock, but all my storybooks had them, so they were obligatory. My fantasies were always quite specific,' I added thoughtfully, as I watched him unhook a large key from behind a piece of drainpipe. It was at least six inches long and quite extraordinary in shape.

'I hope your fantasy allowed for rising damp, a leak in the roof and a complete lack of services,' he said, breaking into a broad grin.

'Good heavens, no. You can't go spoiling a good fantasy

with boring facts like that,' I retorted.

He opened the door. 'Sorry about the smell. It's been shut up for nearly three years, so it's not surprising. Val says it's the wallpaper and I need to strip it off and emulsion the walls so they can breathe,' he went on as I stood taking in every detail of the room, which was still furnished as it must have been at the end of the last century.

'You've even got a salt box!' I exclaimed.

'And there's salt in it too. Along with the spiders.'

The cottage had been offered to the Ulster Folk Museum by the executors of the old lady who had been born there in 1880, he explained. After a long delay, they'd had to turn it down. Bob heard about it from a fellow architect, thought it might make a studio for Val, and took Alan to see it when he came for his job interview.

'Why on earth didn't the Folk Museum have it?' I asked, as I examined the three-legged pots on the hearth.

'Too difficult to move and re-erect on their site, apparently. It's built of a crumbly mix with a lot of shingle.'

We went through the house together, and Alan outlined his plans for each room. While I listened, I opened cupboards and looked in drawers. Some of them were still full of delph and ancient kitchenware, while upstairs there were clothes and bed and table linens. I had never seen Alan so animated before.

'I didn't know you were a do-it-yourself expert.'

'I'm not. I'm a handless idiot. I've never put up a shelf in my life. Or rather, I did once and it was a disaster, as my father hastened to point out and never let me forget. That's partly why I took it. To find out if I really am handless, I mean.'

'But what will you do if you find that you are,' I asked
without thinking.

'Accept it,' he said cheerfully. 'Like the elderly virgin
who went to bed with the postman, I don't want to die
wondering. Besides, I've got Bob to advise me on what I
can tackle and what needs a professional. I thought I'd
make you my horticultural expert. That's if you'd be
willing,' he added hastily.

I nodded my agreement vigorously. 'You know that rose
will need a lot of pruning, don't you?'

'I thought you might say that when I saw you looking at
it.' He smiled broadly as he ducked his head and we went
into the larger of the two small bedrooms under the steep
pitched roof.

Immediately, I caught the gleam of water. I went to the
window, pushed it open, and heard the plash of tiny waves
on the sandy shore.

'Oh Alan, you can even hear the sea from your bedroom,'
I said wistfully. 'Can we go and walk along the beach?
I've been thinking about the sea all day.'

He looked at my long skirt and high-heeled gold sandals
and raised an eyebrow.

'I can turn it over at the waist quite easily, if you've
got any shoes or boots. Anything will do,' I said
quickly.

'I can do better than that,' he replied, with a look of
triumph. 'Val came down last weekend to see if it really
was safe to let me spend the odd night here, before any
work is done, and she left her painting clothes as an earnest
of intent.'

A little while later, he pulled the front door shut behind

us and we set off along a sandy path towards the sound of the waves.

'Can I help?' he asked as I stopped and bent over on the path.

'No, it's fine now,' I said, catching him up. 'Val's legs are longer than mine. There's lots of extra trouser to jump out of the boots.'

We scrunched across the storm beach and ploughed on through the very soft sand, totally absorbed in the quiet murmurings of the sea and the movements of our own thoughts.

A few moments later, I realised Alan was way ahead of me, striding out on the firm damp sand left by the retreating tide. I stopped where I was. In a moment or two, he paused, looked round and came hurrying back to me.

'Sorry, Jenny. Another bad habit. Comes of being on one's own rather a lot.'

'Don't you get lonely, Alan?'

'Yes, I do. Sometimes.'

'And what do you do then?'

'Different things at different times. You can't predict what will work because you don't know when it's going to happen. And you can't guess in advance what might be around to help you.'

'What things, for instance?'

'Well, there's music, of course. Sometimes you can get right inside a work and come out feeling better. And there's poetry too. When you read what others have written, when they've felt like you do, it often helps. And sometimes there's the completely unexpected. Like when I was up in the Highlands last year. I was on my own in a friend's cottage. Lovely place. Quiet, beautiful. I had some wonderful walks, took pictures, saw ravens and sea eagles. But one night, suddenly, I felt really down. I just couldn't cope. I tried to read. Listened to the radio. No good. Then I thought, Hamish must have a drop of whisky somewhere. I'll have that and get him some more. I searched for ages for that whisky. Never found it. I ended up making a cup of tea. It was only when I was drinking the tea I realised I was feeling better,' he ended, laughing.

I bent down and picked up a tiny shell, rinsed it in a pool of water and held it out on the palm of my hand.

He looked at it closely and said he hadn't seen one like it for a very long time. And then he waited patiently while I collected some more.

How long is it, Jenny, I said to myself, since anyone waited for you to collect shells? Since we'd left Windmill Hill, I hadn't given a single thought to the life waiting out there for me in the darkness away to the north. I looked at our footprints, two long tracks side by side on the wet sand. Soon, we should have to turn and follow them back. The thought of what I had fled from at Val's and what lay beyond at Loughview came in upon me and sadness overwhelmed me.

'Whatever was that sombre thought, Jenny?'

I couldn't bring myself to say anything and we walked on in silence. Quite unexpectedly, the line of the beach changed. Beyond the dazzle of the moonlight on the wet sand, we saw the bones of an old boat poking up through the sand.

'Look, Alan, look!' I cried, dashing towards it over piles of seaweed and soft sand.

I got there well ahead of him and stood gazing up at the silvered surface of a curved bow timber. I put out my hand and stroked it. The same wood as the old breakwater at Ballydrumard, I was sure, the bolt holes enlarged by the continuous ebb and flow of the tides and stained with the reddish oxides of long-corroded metal, the lower parts colonised by tiny marine animals, their shells clamped firmly to the smooth surfaces that lay between the deep holes drilled by unknown creatures now long gone. I took it all in, but it was not just delight in my discovery that held me silent as Alan caught up with me.

Behind me, I heard him slither on the wet seaweed and scrunch across the soft shingle, but I did not turn towards him. I went on standing, my hands grasping the textured wood of the long-foundered wreck as I felt myself sink fathoms deep under the weight of the memories that poured over me.

'How splendid, Jenny. Just like your breakwater at Ballydrumard,' he said enthusiastically, as he came up to me.

I made a noise in agreement, but I couldn't bear to turn and look at him. I went on clutching the silvery timbers as if my hands were frozen to them, and stared out across the calm, moonlit waters, seeing images I had not the smallest wish to see and not the slightest power to shut out.

I was back at Rathmore Drive. Downstairs, the phone was ringing. It had been ringing for some time, but I had been so absorbed in my work it had taken some minutes for it to impinge. I put my pen down and listened. With my bedroom door closed, I couldn't hear the words but I could usually pick up the tone. I hoped it might be Colin. If it was, then my mother's voice would take on that well-rounded note which only appeared when it was Harvey, or the new curate, or one or two other especially favoured individuals.

'Jennifer. Jennifer!'

Her tone was harsh and peremptory. It was certainly not Colin. I jumped to my feet and hurried along the landing.

'Jennifer!' she called again, without looking up.

I arrived at the foot of the stairs as she put her hand to the kitchen door.

'It's for you,' she threw over her shoulder.

I hurried to pick up the receiver. 'Hello,' I said breathlessly.

'Hello, Jenny, it's Alan,' he said quietly. 'Have I called at a bad moment?'

'Oh no, no, not at all,' I replied, flustered. 'I'm struggling with a long essay. It's lovely to hear you. How are things?' I asked, my voice recovering somewhat as I heard the kitchen door bang shut.

We talked for ten minutes or so during which my mother walked along the hall and into the sitting room once and crossed over into the dining room twice. Each time, she ignored me pointedly.

'I think I'd better be getting back to the great work,' I said reluctantly, as the atmosphere became ever more icy with each transit.

'Yes, of course. I just rang to see what day suited you best for our Easter expedition, the one we spoke about at the Annual General Meeting. Had you forgotten?'

'Of course I hadn't. I've been looking forward to it.

I've done no serious picture-making since last summer.'

We made our plans for the following Tuesday.

'Do you realise that Tuesday is April the first, All Fools' Day,' said Alan, laughing.

'Oh, that's wonderful. It will probably snow on us. You could get Val to send a St Bernard for us if we don't arrive back.'

I was still smiling as I tore off my scribbles from the telephone pad and turned back in the direction of my essay.

'Very nice, Jennifer. I'm sure you're pleased with yourself. Smiling all over your face. Making dates with your gentleman friends and you an engaged girl.' My mother was standing across the foot of the stairs, her face red with fury, her chin poked out vehemently as she began her tirade.

I had heard most of it before, her usual catalogue of my misdemeanours which ranged from reading disgusting books to wasting my time running to visit that Valerie Thompson and her boyfriend. She waxed eloquent on my lack of consideration for my family, my refusal to go to church, and my coming in at all hours from these carryings on at Dramatic Society. But these were merely preliminaries to the real object of her fury.

'Alan Thompson,' she spat out. 'That blighter. Like father, like son. The father was married again before his wife was cold in her grave, and his son's just as bad. Asking you out and you engaged to be married. And you standing there laughing away. Alan this and Alan that and "What do you think, Alan?" Well, I'll tell you what *I* think. We'll see what Colin has to say about this.' Colin was far too good for me. I didn't know how lucky I was. And if it hadn't been for her wearing herself out to try to get me to look decent, there'd be no Colin.

She went on and on, till I screamed at her to shut up. And that made her ten times worse. I pushed past her and ran upstairs to my room, but there was no lock on the door so she just followed me. She was still shouting at me when Daddy arrived home and came upstairs to see what was going on.

I lay and wept all through a long Saturday afternoon. I thought about just packing a case and walking out, going to Val and Bob and asking if I could move in with them for a little, but then I thought of Daddy and couldn't bring myself to do it. Downstairs, I could still hear her in full flight. Later, when I heard the front door bang, I went to the window and saw her drive off.

I went downstairs to find my father. He was in the dining room, lying back in his chair, his eyes closed, his face pale. I wasn't sure if he was asleep or just exhausted. He hadn't heard me, so I slipped away again. It was no use. If I were to leave, it would only make things ten times worse for him. I just couldn't do it. I couldn't go to Val and I would have to say no to Alan. I went back to my room feeling as if the last spark of brightness in my life had gone out.

I gripped the timbers of the old wreck even harder. I blinked at the moonlit shore, so aware of Alan behind me as the memory of that awful year between graduation and wedding reran itself in clips and jerks like an amateur video.

I was working for my Diploma in Education and continuing to live at home. Colin was in London on a special surveying course and only came back once a month. My Dramatic Society friends had scattered after graduation.

Val was newly married and working very hard at her first job. Worst of all, my mother, who had been sunshine itself up to our engagement, reverted to her most unlovely self the moment Colin departed.

Nothing I did was ever right. Unless I sat in my own room, working or reading, or writing long epistles to Colin, she found something to criticise. If I went out with my father, there were week-long sulks. If I visited Val and Bob, there'd be a row about my going and another when I returned. And if I dared to go out on my own, she would cross-question me as if I were a child. I began to exist for Colin's brief visits; counting the weeks, the days, the hours till his appearance would bring me some relief from this endless bombardment.

As the flood of recollection poured over me, suddenly I saw what had happened. I had completely lost my nerve. Exhausted by the relentless pressure to do only what she wanted me to do, and the burden of a course which was tedious and boring, I just didn't read the signs that things between Colin and me were not at all that they should have been. Neither Colin's letters, nor his phonecalls, nor his very existence had had the slightest effect in modifying the darkness of the depressions which came upon me continually throughout that year. It was all so obvious, now I could see it, and the enormity of what I had done overwhelmed me.

Just at that moment, Alan spoke my name. 'Jenny?'

The gentleness in his voice was the very last straw. Tears streamed down my cheeks and my shoulders shook, great gasping sobs welled up from my throat as uncontrollably as before.

'Jenny, what is it? Whatever's wrong, my dear? Tell me.'

I felt his arms round me. I leaned against him, not sure I could stay on my feet if he let go. I could smell the wool of his duffle coat as my tears soaked into it. He stroked my hair distractedly and tried to comfort me, but I was beyond comfort, bleakly aware at last of what I'd done. How could I have let matters take their course when it was so blindingly clear things weren't right between Colin and me? We made love for the first time on that Easter visit to London, and it had been a disaster. But then, as ever, Colin had simply said everything would be fine when we were married. I was tense, or tired, or premenstrual. It would all be so different when we could be together in our own nice double bed. It would be fine, just fine. And I let myself believe him because I could not face the alternative.

'Alan, do you remember the expedition we planned for Ballydrumard in April nineteen sixty-five,' I asked quickly in a brief pause between sobs.

'Yes, of course I do,' he said, looking surprised. 'You went down with a bad cold.'

I wiped my eyes on my sleeve. 'No, Alan, I didn't. I went down all right. All the way to the bottom. But it wasn't a cold.' I took the handkerchief he offered me and blew my nose. 'That's the second one,' I said.

'I'm not counting,' he replied softly, as he gently took his arms from around me.

I straightened up, did my best to steady myself, and began to tell him all that had gone on through my Diploma year. When I got to his March phonecall, I used my mother's voice. You don't have to be a good mimic to do my mother, you just need a harsh, driving tone and a hectoring manner, and you throw in as many well-worn clichés as you can lay your hands on. I saw him wince, but I pressed on, unable to stop now I had begun.

'That's what's so awful, Alan. It's bad enough having married someone I shouldn't have married, but it's even worse having done it because I was too worn down to stop my mother setting me up for it. From the minute Colin appeared, she was charm itself. Life was just so much easier. I'm sure I thought it was all because I had Colin. But that wasn't it at all. It was her.

'She really was as nice as pie because she wanted Colin as a son-in-law. She was so delighted when we got engaged, but then, as soon as he went off to London, she was back to her old self. She kept all my other friends away because she wanted to be quite sure I'd have no chance for second thoughts. Especially where you were concerned, Alan,' I croaked, my voice threatening to pack up. 'For once in her life she got it absolutely right. She saw something I couldn't see myself. She was afraid I'd turn to you and drop Colin, and that would be the end of all her hard work,' I whispered, my voice breaking at last.

'It's my fault, my fault entirely. I know now I could see it wasn't going to work. But I wouldn't face up to it. What we had in Birmingham was a honeymoon, that's all. Just an extension of student life with more freedom and no parents breathing down our necks. It was an escape, and as an escape it worked. But once we were back in the real world, with real responsibilities and a life to put together, that was the end.'

Shaking sobs overwhelmed me again and I collapsed

against him. He put his arms round me and held me tight.

'Jenny, I must take you back. You're frozen,' he said urgently.

'No, I don't want to go back. Please, Alan, no,' I protested desperately.

'All right, all right. Not back to the party, silly, just to the cottage. I'll make a fire and some tea. Now, come on, or you'll turn into an icicle.'

I felt just like an icicle. Brittle and fragile. And dripping. One more blow from my own bitter memories and I'd shatter into fragments and be washed away by my own tears.

He clutched my hand firmly and turned me round towards the shore. He coaxed me to lead us back over the seaweed and sand; once we were over that, he'd carry me the rest of the way if he had to. As we set off, I caught sight of the oil lamp we'd left lit in the bedroom window. Blurred by my tears at first, it grew clearer as we moved silently towards it. Such a little light, and yet how bright it was, all that distance away. Like a beacon in the darkness, a promise of safety and comfort.

I stumbled on the storm beach and felt his grip tighten.

'All right?'

'Yes, I'm fine.' I couldn't quite believe it. My voice was perfectly normal again and I was beginning to feel warm.

In no time at all we were tramping up the sandy path through the low, humpy dunes. I looked up at the cottage and saw there were a few late roses still in bloom, a little way below the upstairs window.

Just as we reached the front door, an owl called. A

haunting, lonely cry. Like the cry of a creature for whom there is no comfort, no companion of like kind. We stood perfectly still, hoping it might appear. But the next call was further away. A sad, desolate sound that made me long for the touch of Alan's sheltering arms and his clumsy tenderness when my tears had overwhelmed me down by the wreck.

The moon was sinking behind cloud. For a moment, a radiance in the midnight sky. Then it was gone. The darkness enfolded us where we stood, hand in hand, in the tiny patch of lamplight spilling down through the roses.

'I'll make us a fire while you go and change, Jenny. Unless you'd be warmer in what you're wearing,' he added thoughtfully. 'I can wrap you in the car rug,' he offered as he opened the door.

I shook my head. We went into the tiny hallway and I put my arms round him. Reached up and kissed him.

'You're cold too,' I said quietly. 'We could warm each other.'

I held out my hand and led him up the narrow stair to the tiny bedroom where my party clothes were laid on the bed, waiting for me. He took me in his arms.

'Jenny, my love. Are you quite, quite sure?'

I kicked off my boots, caught up my clothes from the bed and dropped them on a chair.

'Yes, I'm sure,' I said, smiling at him. 'At this moment, I'm absolutely sure. You don't want me to predict the future, do you?'

After we made love, I must have fallen asleep. I woke to find him stroking my wrist. He was standing looking down at me in his dressing gown, two mugs of tea perched on the bedside cabinet.

'Oh Alan, how awful. Have I been asleep long?'

'Yes. For hours and hours. I'm deeply offended,' he said, a broad grin on his face. 'I thought it was only drunken males in earthy novels about "oop north" who fell asleep after having their way with their women. Here, sit up and have some tea, before it gets cold.'

He picked up Val's sweater and tucked it round me as I straightened myself in the bed.

'What about you? You'll freeze to death out there. Come back in.'

He shook his head. 'If I did that, you mightn't get any tea at all.'

'I'll risk it. Come on.'

We sat up together in the narrow bed, pressed close against each other, and drank our tea. The air in the room was so cold we could see our breath rising to the low ceiling. The tiny windowpanes dripped with condensation.

'Not the greatest cup of tea, I fear,' he said, sipping the pale brew thoughtfully. 'I think the teabags were damp.'

I started to giggle, put my mug down hastily, and began to laugh uncontrollably.

'What's so funny?' he asked, trying to keep his tea from spilling.

'Alan, do you always say such passionately romantic things to the ladies you honour in your very cold bed?'

'No. Not to the best of my knowledge,' he replied grinning. 'Perhaps I just fall asleep and don't remember,' he added. 'Tomorrow, I may not even remember your name.'

He took my empty mug, parked it on the cabinet and

wrapped me in his arms again. We snuggled down and lay
entwined, warm and easy, my head in the hollow of his
neck. The lamp made a small hissing noise and threw long
shadows on the steep pitched roof. Quiet and darkness
enfolded the cottage. Even the murmur of the sea had faded,
the tide now far out on the flats. In a moment, one of us
would have to speak. Please, please, not yet, I said to
myself. I couldn't remember ever having felt such warmth
and such comfort. Some time in the future, when warmth
and comfort seemed an entirely impossible thing to hope
for, I would remember this moment.

'Which one, Jenny?' Alan asked as we turned into
Loughview Heights somewhere around three in the morning.

'That one. With the white gates,' I replied wryly. The
very sight of the house brought down a pall of misery upon
me.

'Next to the formidable Mrs Karen Baird,' he said
lightly. 'Does she keep permanent watch?'

I laughed in spite of myself. Alan had known Karen as
long as I had. 'If you see the curtain move, I suggest you
wave,' I said tartly.

'And what about you?'

'I hadn't thought about me. Do you think I have the
look of a fallen woman?'

My tone was light and ironic. He laughed and shook
his head as he stopped by the gates. But the ridiculous
phrase repeated itself inside my head. Fallen woman? I
supposed the origin must be Biblical as in 'fall from grace'.
I smiled to myself. You could only fall from grace, surely,
if you were in it in the first place. There was nothing in the

relationship between Colin and me that had the slightest touch of grace about it. That was one thing I was sure about.

'As far as Karen Baird's concerned, I think you fell a long time ago,' he said quietly.

'You could be right,' I said, as I rummaged in my bag for my keys. 'In fact, I'm sure you are. She'll think the worst anyway, so we needn't worry, need we?' I gathered up my party clothes and turned towards him. 'If I go and open up, would you bring my takeaway presents?'

'Of course I will.'

I put on some lights, dropped my things on the telephone table, went through to the kitchen, took bacon and eggs from the fridge, switched on the kettle and plugged in the toaster.

'You haven't changed your mind, have you?' I asked, as I turned round and found him standing in the doorway holding sprays of bracken and hawthorn with one hand and the few late roses carefully cupped in the other.

'No, I must confess I'm absolutely ravenous.'

'They do say making love burns up as many calories as a brisk walk.'

He laughed and put the full-blown roses gently down on the draining board. 'I think I'll just go and inspect your very superior plumbing.'

I took the sheaf of bronze and gold foliage from him. 'Do. Have a look round the house while you're about it. I won't be very long, but I'll call before I put the eggs in.'

He was back before I called.

'What do you think of the establishment?' I asked, without turning round.

When there was no reply, I glanced over my shoulder. He was looking very uneasy.

'Don't worry, Alan. I told you how I felt about it. You don't have to pretend you like it. Unless of course you do,' I added hastily, as I slid the second egg onto a plate and switched off the battery of lights over the cooker.

'I think it did take me back a bit,' he said, as I poured coffee and picked hot toast gingerly out of the toaster.

'You mean it wasn't quite what you expected?'

'No, that was the trouble. It was just what I had expected, given your description, only worse.' He paused and then added, very deliberately, 'It isn't really you, is it?'

'No, Alan, not me at all,' I said easily, as we devoted ourselves to our bacon and egg. 'Did you go into my study?'

'No, just the bedrooms and the bathroom. And a quick blink at the lounge. I liked your chrysanthemums.'

'I'll show you my study before you go. You can see the lough from there. It's not a patch on Drinsallagh, but it's something.'

I refilled our cups, dropped more bread in the toaster, and wondered when food had last tasted so good. It was some minutes before I realised how silent he had grown. I glanced across the table and saw a look which made me most uneasy.

'Alan?'

His eyes responded, but the sombre lines of his face did not soften.

'Alan, you look so . . . sad. You're not upset? I mean, you're not sorry . . .' I broke off unhappily.

He shook his head firmly and put his hand over mine. 'No, Jenny, I'm not sorry.'

'Then please tell me what you were thinking.'

'I was thinking about this house. And you living in it. With Colin,' he added, awkwardly.

'And that makes you sad?'

'Yes, it does. Does that bother you?'

'No. It's a great comfort to me. Until tonight, I didn't think that anybody cared very much what happened to me. Except perhaps Val and Bob, and my father. I don't know how things managed to get like that, but that's how it felt. Now I know something has to change once and for all.' I went on, more slowly, 'I felt awful when we stopped outside the house, but I hardly noticed it when we came in together. I don't think it can get at me the way it's been doing. But other things . . .' I broke off, my voice shaking dangerously. 'I'm not sure which things can get to me and which I can cope with. I suppose I'll just have to wait and see.'

'Does that frighten you?'

'I'm afraid it does . . . I . . .'

'Go on, Jenny, say it. Tell me. Please.'

'I'm afraid I'll see too much, that it will all come at me at once and I'll panic, or go to pieces, or give in . . . or something awful.'

He moved our coffee cups out of the way so he could take both my hands. They had gone stone cold.

'Listen, Jenny. I can't promise it won't happen like that, but you can use Thompson's Law. It's helped me out of many a spot.'

'Thompson's Law,' I repeated, weakly. I was so agitated, I wondered if Thompson's Law was one of those things you learn at school and forget as soon as you leave.

'Uncle John. In Ballycastle. Do you remember he was an income tax inspector before he retired?'

I nodded and waited for him to go on.

'Dear man that he is, Uncle John never tires of telling me that while tax evasion is a criminal offence, tax avoidance is simply good management. You have to avoid where you can, Jenny. Don't try to do it all at once. Save your energy for what really matters.'

'And remember what you said about not acting being a course of action.'

'Yes, never forget that. And sometimes you have to wait your moment. Waiting isn't letting circumstances dictate to you, it's making things easier by giving you more options. Once you're clear what you want to do, you choose your moment and then strike, swift and hard.'

'I know what I want all right,' I said sharply. 'I want to be me. I want to be free to make my own decisions. And to put an end to this whole shabby show.'

'Knowing what you want is more than half the battle,' he said encouragingly. 'You'll manage. I'm sure you will.' He looked so tired and the small movement he made reminded me that he ought to go. But the thought of his leaving was quite unbearable.

'Alan,' I said quickly, 'I know it's time you went, but please, come up and see my study. Please. It won't take a minute. Just let me put my roses in water so we can take them with us.'

I led the way upstairs, the small jug of roses in my hand. 'I won't put the light on. You can see the lough better if I don't. Here, sit down at my desk. That's the best view.'

The moon had reappeared, so low on the horizon that it poured light all around us. To the west, the waters of the lough were ink black. Strings and scatters of light marked the shore. To the east, the calm water was silver grey. Where the moon's path lay across it, tiny ripples flickered with dazzling brightness.

'I think I see some old friends.' I watched Alan as his gaze swept from the wide windowledge, where I keep my collection of stones and pieces of wood, rest a moment on the worn surface of my antique desk, and pass on to my sketches and photographs and Val's watercolours hanging on the walls.

'But of course you do. All my precious things are here. There's hardly anything new, except these lemon geranium cuttings for Val,' I said, laughing.

He turned to look at me. Suddenly, I was aware of the room as it must appear to him. A secret place, a place where I could hold together the shreds of my real self. The realisation filled me with anxiety. At least I had this. How on earth would I manage if I had to leave even this and make a life on my own?

'Alan,' I began, determined not to cry, 'Do you know why I can't bear to let you go?'

'I think so.'

'Then tell me, please.'

'I think you are a brave girl, Jenny, but you've been on your own for far too long. "Many fears are born of fatigue and loneliness," says the Desiderata. And it's true. You've been wearied by your life and you've felt your isolation. Perhaps you think if you can't see me, touch me, feel my arms round you, you'll be all on your own again. But you won't. I'll be there. I'll help you do whatever you decide you want to do.'

'I don't know what's going to happen,' I said, shaking my head. 'But I do need to know you'll be there. Does that bother you?'

'No. Not in the slightest. But it'll be best, I think, if you contact me. Valerie will always know where I am. And I'll come whenever you call.' He stood up, took me in his arms and kissed me gently. 'Don't come down with me. Stay here till I'm gone and then go to bed. I'll be thinking about you.'

'And I'll be thinking of you too, Alan. Whatever happens, I'll never forget Drinsallagh. And those two clean hankies.'

''Bye, Jenny.'

He kissed me once more, not so gently this time, and went quickly from the room, leaving me alone with the lough and the moonlight. I stood looking out over the still water, listening for the car. I heard it start and move off. I went on listening, long after the silence had erased entirely its fading ribbon of sound.

'Never again from this window by moonlight.'

The words came into my mind unbidden and I did not push them away. Fatigue, or insight, or was it premonition? There was no need to puzzle over what the words meant. Time would make their meaning clear enough. And I felt sure Time was not going to be long about it.

Chapter 12

The strange, rhythmic sound was the call of a bird with but two notes, a great tit, or a cuckoo. Standing in sunlight on the fringe of a pinewood drifted with bluebells, I thought what a pity one discordant note should break the tranquillity of the early spring morning. Near my feet, clumps of primroses bloomed on a small mossy bank, a tiny garden, perfect in itself, without weeding or tidying. A gift garden, I said to myself, given without asking and without effort.

'Come here, come here, come here.'

The call of the bird grew insistent. I hunched my shoulders and refused to look around. If I paid attention to the bird, the flowers would disappear. Magical gardens always disappeared if you took your eye off them, even for a second.

'Come here, come here, come here.'

I woke in the darkness and reached for the alarm clock. It was silent, but the telephone down in the hall was shrilling its head off. Daddy was ill. It had to be Daddy for anyone to ring in the middle of the night. I leapt out of bed, flung open the bedroom door and was blinded by sunlight as I raced along the landing and down the stairs. Brilliant golden beams poured through the south-facing windows and the frosted glass of the front door. As I skidded to a halt, I caught sight of the hall clock. Ten forty-five.

'Helen's . . .'

The familiar voice sailed in, without a moment's pause, in the familiar way. Surely I wasn't still in bed on a lovely morning like this. Harvey had arrived early and he was coming over right away to fetch me, so I'd better hurry up and get my face on. Harvey was looking so well and so was Mavis. So wear something nice and don't keep Harvey waiting. She rang off before I had time to think of saying coldly I was in the bath or had been working at the bottom of the garden.

I sat on the padded bench, my heart banging loudly, perspiration breaking out on my bare skin and waves of nausea flowing over me. Your own fault entirely, Jenny. You shouldn't move that fast. No wonder you feel like passing out. Stick your head between your knees.

I tried it, but it made me feel worse. A blinding headache had struck me as I lifted the phone. It felt as if the throbbing would blow my forehead off. I took some deep breaths and staggered into the kitchen for a glass of water.

As I sat, sipping it slowly, I stared at the red checked tablecloth and the eggy plates and thought of my early-morning breakfast with Alan. Slowly the nausea eased and my breathing calmed. 'That bloody woman,' I said aloud. 'Put your face on and wear something nice,' I mimicked. I didn't know which was worse: the everyday unvarnished hectoring tone or the sugar-coated version we got when Harvey was around.

'Why do you put up with it, Jennifer? Why ever don't you tell her exactly where to go?' I asked myself crossly.

'Why don't you just ring back and say you've too much work to do. School work or thinking work. Either way, there's a hell of a lot to do before Colin gets back.'

I stood up cautiously, took two paracetamol and drank some more water. After what I'd said about my mother last night, I shouldn't be surprised if all the old questions were turning up this morning. But however differently I saw her part in bringing about the disaster I now faced, the brute facts hadn't changed. If I told my mother exactly what I thought of her, it wasn't me that would suffer, but my father. And goodness knows, he had enough to cope with.

I washed up the dirty dishes and rearranged the table for a solitary breakfast. I had no wish to share the details of my evening with Harvey and at the speed he drives, he was bound to turn up long before I would be ready to leave.

'Why don't you call it off, Jenny? Do your dying swan act and say you've got a migraine.'

The prospect was very appealing and I knew I could carry it off. Five minutes' droop with half-closed eyes and hand on head, and another five listening to the professional advice Harvey would not be able to refrain from giving, and the rest of the day would be my own. Enough time to plan next week's work properly and still have a couple of hours in the garden to think things through before Colin appeared.

The idea was so enticing, I knew there had to be a catch in it. No, it wasn't worth it. My mother would turn it to her advantage somehow, Daddy would be genuinely worried, and Susie would be disappointed. Susie is my youngest niece. She is two weeks older than my marriage.

I first met her twenty hours after her birth and I've been her willing slave ever since. The thought of that small, vulnerable face crumpling into tears got me back upstairs and under the shower in record time.

Dear Susie. If ever a child were to tempt me to motherhood it would be Susie. But when I find myself going weak at the knees, I remember her sister, Janet, and her brother, Peter. That sobers me up immediately.

I opened the wardrobe door. 'Wear something nice.' I heard my mother's voice over my shoulder and I almost put out my hand for my jeans. 'No, Jenny, no. Thompson's Law.'

I smiled to myself. If I was going to hear voices, I was glad Alan's would be one of them. 'Save your energy,' he would say. 'Only tackle the issues you are ready to tackle or ones you can't avoid. Remember, avoidance isn't evasion.'

I flicked along my skirts and dresses and fingered the sleeve of a grey jersey-wool suit and laughed aloud. How about that, with the jumper from the knicker-pink cashmere twin-set? My mother had bullied me into buying the suit and when Karen saw it, the day of my interview for Queen's Crescent, she'd said how elegant it was and how exactly right for me. Since then I'd only ever worn it for speech days and parents' evenings.

I found what I was looking for, a soft wool dress with mohair in it, lightly checked in dark brown over cinnamon. 'The stroky dress', Susie calls it. I knew a dress I'd chosen myself would never meet my mother's criteria for 'something nice', but at least it wouldn't raise issues.

'I'm doing well, so far, Alan,' I said softly as I finished

my make-up. 'Hair up, or down?'

'Up.'

'Jennifer, for goodness sake,' I said, shocked by the speed of the response. 'You'll soon have as many voices as Joan of Arc. And you know what happened to her!'

As I began pinning up my hair, I saw why the answer had come so promptly. Lying in Alan's arms before we made love, he had stroked my cheeks, kissed my hair and gathered it in handfuls around his face. With my hair down, he said, I looked so vulnerable. Any man would rush to my defence, even an old cynic like himself.

But today was no day for being vulnerable and no one would rush to my defence, I said to myself as I hurried downstairs, switched on the kettle and dropped a slice of bread in the toaster. Moments later, I heard the roar of Harvey's Jaguar. Rather than rush to the door, as I once would have done, I went on quietly looking out of the kitchen window to where the pink and gold leaves were blowing into the garden from the chestnut trees on the main road. They fell on the newly-cut lawn, rested there briefly till they were stirred and whirled off once more by the next breezy gust. Huge clouds towered up out of the west, brilliant white snowcaps shaded with grey, set against the clear blue that holds the promise of winter ice.

The toaster popped just as a long shrill note vibrated down the hall. I pushed my toast into the rack and gathered my straying thoughts reluctantly. 'Right then, Jennifer,' I said briskly. 'Let's see what dear brother Harvey has come for.'

'Hello, Sis, long time no see.'

I smiled dutifully at the immaculately groomed figure

on the doorstep. Harvey has the knack of making his carefully chosen leisure clothes look just as formal as the expensive suits he dons for his consulting room.

'Hello, Harvey, I was just about to make coffee,' I said agreeably. As he stepped into the hall, he glanced at himself in the long mirror by the front door.

'Oh, just the thing, I'd love a coffee.' He followed me into the kitchen and settled himself at the table with practised ease.

'Biscuit?'

'Nothing for me, Sis, thanks. Just coffee. Black, please. Got to watch the old waistline,' he said with a jolly laugh.

Yes, indeed. No middle-age spread for Harvey. If we can't hold on to the 'boyish good looks' style, we'll have to go for the distinguished senior physician demeanour. Unfortunately, his hair wasn't going discreetly grey at the temples. It was just going. And mostly from the top.

I watched him sip his coffee appreciatively. For God's sake, I thought, it's only instant. You're behaving like one of those idiots in a TV commercial whose life is transformed by a steaming container of hot liquid. I concentrated on buttering my toast and spreading it liberally with honey.

'Late night, Jenny?' he asked, settling back in his chair as if we were about to have a long, pleasant chat.

I munched enthusiastically. I really was hungry this morning and I had no intention of facing Rathmore Drive on an empty stomach.

'Yes, it was rather,' I agreed, licking my fingers. 'Val had a party.'

'Been having a lot of late nights, have you?' He was

smiling at me encouragingly. If he were playing a consultant gynaecologist who fancied his technique with women, I'd be telling him he was grossly overplaying it. But I wasn't directing him, so I made myself another piece of toast and waited a moment before I replied.

'No, actually. It's ages since I've been to a party. I haven't got time these days.'

He nodded sympathetically. 'I expect the job is pretty damned hard work.' His voice oozed with understanding.

'No, I can't say it is,' I replied coolly. 'It was to begin with. Like any new job. But now I have the experience, it's fine. Time-consuming, of course. Like any profession.'

'Yes, of course, it must be. I do agree. In fact, Jenny, I thought we ought to have a quiet word. I've become a little concerned about you and your job, you know.' He paused as if he were considering judiciously just which aspects of me and my job concerned him most. 'It's never easy for a woman doing two jobs,' he went on. 'When I heard you hadn't been looking too good, I did wonder if I might be able to help. Perhaps it is time you were thinking more about *yourself* and *your* future,' he ended, underlining each pronoun heavily.

I concentrated on my toast. I had a horrible feeling that if I caught sight of his face switched into its professional sympathetic style, I might pour the rest of the honey over him to see if its actual sticky sweetness might have any effect on the phoney treacle in his voice.

'Harvey, Mummy's asked you to come and talk to me about starting a family, hasn't she?' I asked sweetly.

He looked startled and immediately uneasy. Harvey is a coward. If things don't go exactly the way he's planned them, he backs off rather than face up to what has happened. But this time there was a real problem. He knew as well as I did that he'd have my mother to deal with if he didn't tackle me.

'Well, yes, Jenny, you could say that in one way.' His easy manner had quite gone. 'She is very concerned about you, but naturally so am I. After all, you have been married over three years now and I wouldn't want you to think I hadn't offered you all the help I could. I know Mummy can be a bit sharp at times, but you do have to make allowances for menopausal women. She always has your best interests at heart, I'm sure.'

I watched him with growing disbelief. He was talking his way back into a very comfortable view of the way he was handling this little hitch in the programme. As I heard the professional unctuousness slowly creep back into the voice, I didn't know whether to laugh or explode with fury. But his final words decided for me.

'Best interests? Best interests?' I burst out. 'When have either of you ever let my best interests get in the way of your plans for me?'

'What do you mean, Jennifer?' he protested, the sympathetic look disappearing once more like snow from a ditch. 'You're surely not trying to suggest that I take the trouble to come and discuss your problems for my benefit?'

'You can hardly claim you've come to discuss them for mine when you haven't even asked me what I think my problems are,' I replied sharply.

'Oh, I think it's fairly obvious—'

'Yes, Harvey, of course you do. That's just the point. It's obvious to you and Mummy that my resistance to settling down and having a couple of children is what the problem is. I won't play the game properly, will I? It's a problem to her, and as she's no doubt been going on about it *ad nauseam*, it's become a problem to you. But it is not, Harvey, a problem to me.' Given how furious I was actually feeling, I ended far more calmly than I could have imagined. But to my amazement a look of relief swept over his face, wiping away all trace of the irritation he had allowed to break through. He smiled forgivingly at me and spread his hands in an expansive gesture that reminded me of multilingual Popes giving the Easter Sunday blessing to the assembled crowds.

'Well then, Jenny, if that's what's been the trouble, then it's no wonder you've been off colour,' he said warmly. 'Early pregnancy can be a most trying time for a mother who is still at work. I suppose you and Colin wanted to keep this to yourselves until this new job was all settled.' He sat there with a satisfied beam on his face, sure that all would be well and no ugly scenes would have to be coped with.

I stood up and took my time washing traces of honey from my fingertips. I couldn't believe it. How on earth could he reach that conclusion from what I'd actually said? Could I really have been so ambiguous? Or was the man so obsessed with motherhood he saw signs of it everywhere?

'Harvey,' I said, taking a deep breath, 'I am not pregnant and I am not likely to be pregnant in the foreseeable future. You can report that to Mummy, as planned, or I'll tell her myself. Take your pick.'

He swallowed hard, put down his coffee cup and

rearranged his face muscles. 'Now look, Jenny,' he began quietly. 'You really shouldn't be so touchy when someone is trying to help you. I've known lots of mothers who felt just like you do,' he went on quickly. 'Now, a few years later, with a couple of lovely children, they feel really fulfilled. All it needed was a little professional help. I'm sure, Jenny, that would make it much easier.'

'Easier for whom, Harvey?' I asked politely.

'Why, for you, Jenny. Obviously.'

I laughed as I dried my hands and stood leaning against the sink looking across at him. He really thought he had all the answers, didn't he. Well, it was time someone put a dint in his well-polished *amour-propre* and I felt just in the mood for doing it: 'Come off it, Harvey. When have you ever showed the slightest interest in me? The only thing you've ever been interested in is you, followed by the practice and then by a quiet life. And life hasn't been quiet, has it? Mummy's been a pain in the neck. Maisie McKinstry keeps dropping hints that I'm not doing my wifely duty, so she starts on you. And what do you do? Not having laid eyes on me for months, you do the brotherly advice bit and expect me to get you off the hook by doing what Mummy wants. Well, I'm sorry I can't oblige. I only have one life to live and I don't intend to live it for the benefit of the McKinistrys, or Mummy, or you.'

Harvey opened his mouth to protest, but having got launched, I found that I hadn't nearly finished.

'And the next time you're busy advocating motherhood to some hapless woman who comes to you with premenstrual tension, or advanced marital breakdown, or just a pain in her lower back, you might think of the women in your colleagues' surgeries queuing up for their Valium. And after you've looked at the figures for depression among women, you could take a look at the figures for child abuse and then teenage suicide statistics. It might just give you a less cosy picture of family life than the one you're so happy to peddle.'

'Cosy?' he threw back, when I had to pause for breath. 'If anybody round here's managed to make a cosy life, it's you, Jennifer,' he retorted. 'We don't all expect to have the benefits of marriage and a house like this without doing something to fulfil our obligations. We don't all manage to do exactly what we want without any regard for the wishes of our partner. I must say if your concern for Colin figured as largely in your conversation as your anxiety for various problem pupils then your comments on how other people fulfil their obligations might not seem so inappropriate.'

'As inappropriate, perhaps, as your suggesting that a wife is supposed to pay for her board and lodging by bearing children. Or that my role is to have children so that you and others like you can go on enjoying your own comfortable view of how you want the world to be.'

He stood up. 'I think, Jennifer,' he said in measured tones, 'that this conversation has gone far enough. I came here to offer you help and advice and you've used the opportunity to make an entirely ridiculous personal attack on me. I see no point in trying to discuss the problem in a rational manner. I can only put down your outburst to the inadequacy you have so often revealed in the past.' He drew himself up to his full height, adjusted his tie, which had not suffered at all in the dialogue, and moved towards the kitchen door.

I smiled at him. 'Inadequacy, Harvey? I would have thought that a man so obviously threatened by his sister's reluctance to become a mother, impelled to challenge her on the orders of his own mother, and apparently unable to relate to any woman except as a potential mother was in no position to talk about inadequacy.'

He dropped his eyes and walked out, banging the front door behind him. I heard the engine and waited for it to zoom off. But it didn't. It just went on revving.

'You've done it this time, Jenny,' I said to myself, as I picked up my coat and handbag from the cloakroom. 'You've really cooked your goose.'

Chapter 13

The journey to Rathmore Drive was mercifully brief and so precipitous, conversation was quite impossible. I was so grateful to arrive in one piece that I set aside all my worries and headed for the sitting room with a smile on my face, leaving Harvey to stride down the hall to the kitchen to give his report.

'Hello, Daddy. How's things?' I said and bent over to kiss his cheek.

His skin was rough against my lips and had a yellowish hue beneath his weather-worn complexion. I thought back to Friday night. I could have missed a change in his colour in the dim gloom of the dining room or later in the firelight.

'So far so good. Mavis has been summoned to the inner sanctum,' he said, raising an eyebrow. 'Janet looks set to join the second oldest profession. George Best has scored two direct hits on the azaleas.'

The light, bantering tone reassured me. It was always a sign that he felt well in himself and was in good spirits.

'And Susie,' he went on, pausing for breath and looking up at me with a twinkle in his eye, 'Susie, with her usual seriousness of purpose, has extracted a solemn promise from her grandad that he will tell her the moment her Aunty Jenny arrives. Cross his heart and hope to die.'

He folded his newspaper and turned towards the French windows with a broad grin. I followed his gaze and saw a small figure in a red dress and white lacy tights walking backwards along the path looking up at the huge blooms of his prize chrysanthemums which arched high above her blonde head.

'In that case, I'd better go straight out, hadn't I?'

'You had indeed,' he agreed warmly. 'I'm given to understand the children will lunch in the kitchen before we have our meal.'

We exchanged glances that said all we needed to say. I opened the doors and stepped into the garden. Before I had time to close them behind me, the small red figure spotted me. She raced back up the path and tripped on the edge of the terrace just as I managed to get there.

'Hello, Susie,' I said as she fell into my arms. 'Were you waiting for me?' As I picked her up and felt her small arms close round me in an energetic hug, Janet marched down the path to stand squarely in front of us.

'Hello, Janet,' I said pleasantly. 'No favouritism' was my rule, both in school and with my nephew and nieces.

Janet, at eight, had no such rule and had other things on her mind. She stared at us coldly. 'Mummy says you're not to run like that, Susie, and you're not to climb up on people either. Look what you've done to Aunty Jenny's hair. Mummy'll be so cross when I tell her.'

Susie's large brown eyes filled with tears.

'It's all right, Susie. It's all right,' I whispered to her as I returned her hug and made no move to put her down.

'Susie didn't climb up, Janet. I picked her up. Didn't you notice that?' I said easily. 'And my hair's always falling down. Long hair often does, especially when it's freshly washed. I'm sure you'll notice that when you grow up.'

'I shall have short hair when I grow up,' was her immediate reply. 'Like Mummy's. She says it's much more practical.' She turned her back on us and walked primly down the garden to where she had arranged two dolls and a teddy bear on a garden seat and set up a blackboard and easel in front of them.

Peter was kicking his football disconsolately round the rose beds and pretended he hadn't seen us. Like his father at the same age, he sulked when he had no admiring audience, and he had worked out long ago that I wasn't in the admiring audience business.

'Will you tell me the flowers again, Aunty Jenny?' Susie's eyelashes were still wet with tears but she was smiling now, her eyes bright with excitement. They looked at me steadily, so confident I wouldn't refuse her.

I carried her round the garden, intensely aware of the warmth and softness of her small body. No, I did not have Val's problem. I was not revolted by the thought of a small creature growing in my body, then clinging to me, needing my love for its growth and wellbeing. Since the first moment of holding Susie, still red and wizened like a very old lady, I had been entranced by her personality, her sheer passion for life, even when life involved only feeding and sleeping.

I remembered standing by Mavis's bed in the private nursing home, with Colin watching me, as I took her gingerly from Mavis's hands. One day, I thought. One day, I shall hold Colin's and my child. As I looked down at those shining eyes, I wondered if I would ever have any child to love other than Susie. What was certain was that it would never now be Colin's.

'Chrifanthemum,' repeated Susie, solemnly.

'Very nearly. Try again. Chrysanthemum.'

'Chrifanthemum.'

I smiled and moved a little further on. In the summer, while the Antrim house was being extended to provide more bedrooms and a new suite of consulting rooms, Susie had come to stay with me. Her vocabulary had expanded by leaps and bounds. Each day she demanded new words, rehearsed them and tried them out on me till she got them right. Susie never let a word defeat her.

'Begonia,' she said firmly.

'That's right. I thought you'd have forgotten begonias.'

She shook her head. 'That's a nother chrysanthemum.'

'Say again, Susie.'

'Nother chrysanthemum.'

'Good girl, well done. You've got it. Say it again for Grandad.'

'Chrysanthemum. Chrysanthemum. Chrysanthemum.'

She beamed with delight when I hugged her, but I had to turn my head away as we walked on. Tears had jumped into my eyes at the sight of that small, vulnerable face. So easily hurt. A pretty child. Along with the Jaguar, the new extension and the flourishing practice, I wondered if Susie was really only a delightful object to her father, just one more marker of his success. What was going to happen when she grew old enough to use her sharp little mind for herself and was no longer Daddy's little baby was a very nice question. I wasn't sure at all how Mavis would react to a Susie with a mind of her own, and there certainly wouldn't be much support for her from either of her grandmothers. Mavis's father had died some years ago. That left only Daddy and me.

'I like your stroky dress, Aunty Jenny. When I grow up, can I have a stroky dress just like yours?'

'Of course you can. But you might like a different colour because your hair is blonde and mine is dark.'

'I'll have blue, or red, or yellow, or green,' she began, counting on her fingers the colours she knew. 'Or perhaps crushed raspberry,' she added triumphantly.

'Come along, children, lunchtime.'

The saccharine tone reached us from the kitchen door where my mother stood with Mavis. Resplendent in a new wool dress with very high heels, she wore a minute frilly apron, the product of some long-forgotten bring-and-buy sale, as a gesture towards the cares of office. I walked Susie to the door and delivered her up for handwashing. I expected no greeting from her, nor was there one, and Mavis would not speak if my mother remained silent.

I turned back into the garden and walked the whole way round it, looking at my father's autumn planting and the new piece of crazy paving he'd laid in the summer. The air was mild for so late in the month and where the sun spilled onto the path through the trees and shrubs on the south side of the garden I could feel it warm on my shoulders.

I stood looking around me, the garden still bright with summer bloom, the flowers whose names Susie had finally mastered through her sheer persistence. With some things persistence really did pay off. I remembered the first cuttings I had made after I'd watched Daddy making trays full of them in the greenhouse. It looked so easy. Indeed, he assured me, it was easy. You just pulled off a new shoot with a little heel of old wood, trimmed it, and stuck it in some compost, or some soil. I'd tried it, produced a boxful that looked just like his and they'd all died. I'd firmed them in so energetically, I'd knocked all the air and moisture out of the soil. The next lot did better, but it was a while before I developed that knack of picking the right piece of new growth, at the right time, and sticking it in the right mixture of what would best encourage it to put roots down.

But sometimes persistence was not such a good idea. Like the way I had persisted in trying to make something of my marriage. I had certainly tried, I had gone on trying, as if, with practice, I could get the knack of it. But making relationships work was not at all the same thing as getting cuttings to grow. There were times when one just had to walk away. Admit defeat. Start over again.

I looked up at the bright sky, the sun glancing off the slate roofs across the Drive, the small clouds beginning to form on the crest of the hills to the north. I wondered what Alan was doing at this moment. Clearing up the mess after the party, or having lunch with Val and Bob. Or perhaps he'd gone down to the cottage.

I imagined him there, taking the key from behind the drainpipe, unloading stuff from his car. And as I thought of him, I knew I would have to be very strong, and very steady, because at this moment all I really wanted was to be with him, in his cottage, in his arms and in his bed. After all this time it just seemed so simple and so obvious.

I walked round the whole garden once again, gently putting Alan out of my thoughts. As I came back up the path, a wisp of grey cloud from the west blotted out the sun. The warmth was cut off for a few moments only, before the sun beamed out again, but I found myself shivering. A thought had shaped in my mind and repeated itself, over and over again. Never again in this garden. Never again in this garden.

Chapter 14

Apart from my father's comforting presence and the little stories he managed to slip in, whenever my mother paused for breath, the only enjoyable thing about Sunday lunch was the food itself. My mother is a good cook, when she chooses. Today, she had chosen. There was a formidable array of vegetables with the lamb, and on the sideboard she had lined up a trifle, a lemon meringue, and a thickly iced chocolate cake. Beside the dessert plates, a well-polished silver ladle lay ready for use with her largest Waterford bowl full of whipped cream. I thought back to Friday night's meal, the rock-hard, boiled potatoes and the tinned peas she'd not even managed to heat through properly.

Although she behaved as if I didn't exist, I knew from her tone that Harvey hadn't reported yet. If he had, then although she was being charm itself to Mavis and Harvey, the climate would have been distinctly chillier. I looked across the table at Harvey, absorbed in choosing the most delectable of the crisp, golden roast potatoes and wondered if he'd held back because Mavis was in the kitchen when he got there.

I don't pretend to understand my sister-in-law. I've never figured out whether she really is as bland as she appears to be, or whether there is some deep passion hidden far down below the calm, unruffled surface she presents to the world. Not for Harvey, of course. I can't imagine Harvey inspiring passion in anyone. But rather some esoteric interest, like early eighteenth-century antimacassars, or self-fertilising fuchsias. I've always had a fantasy that one day I would mention some subject or other to Mavis and find her suddenly transformed. But it's never happened. The nearest I've got on the rare occasions we've been together is a sense that she was on the verge of saying something to me, making some declaration about herself, or telling me some significant story about her past. I sometimes feel sad that she never has.

'No, Mavis, don't you trouble with that,' said my mother graciously, her tone well mellowed by Harvey's attentions and her share of a rather good bottle of Burgundy.

I watched her extract the dessert plates from Mavis's hands and pass them to Harvey.

'If anyone deserves a rest today it's you, Mavis,' she said, fulsomely. 'And I'm sure Jennifer has had a busy weekend too, covering up for not being there all week. You go and put your feet up and Harvey will give me a hand,' she ended firmly as she took up the untouched bowl of trifle and the remains of the lemon meringue.

Noting the change in tone as I was given my exit line, I rose obediently from the table. 'Covering up' was her usual way of referring to the hours of hard work put in during evenings and weekends by those who wilfully refused to do things properly and make housekeeping a fulltime job. It was on the same scale of unpleasantness as her referring to Bob Dawson as Val's boyfriend, or even 'fancy man', long after they were married.

I smiled to myself. No point whatever getting upset by the familiar barbs when a full-frontal assault was likely in the not very distant future.

'George, see you don't let that fire go out in the sitting room. It's not one bit warm today when the sun's not out,' she called over her shoulder as she left the room with Harvey in close attendance.

I followed Mavis across the hall and heard the kitchen door shut with a firm click. The sitting room was full of sunlight and beyond the French doors, halfway down the garden path, Susie was deep in conversation with some real or imaginary creature who lived under a late-flowering spiraea, bright with blossoms in both pink and white. I stood watching her for a few moments, turned round and found my father bending over the fire. Two bright spots of colour burned in his cheeks like badly applied rouge. As he placed small logs in the hot embers, he began to wheeze. Hastily, I turned away, pretended I hadn't noticed and stood waiting till I heard the squeak his chair always made as he leaned back into it when he had finished.

I looked out at the garden where the October sunshine was already casting long shadows across the lawn although it was still only three o'clock. This time yesterday I had been in my own garden, mowing the lawn, weeding, trimming edges. A mere twenty-four hours, but it seemed like a lifetime ago, so much had happened in the intervening time. And it seemed the pace was not going to slacken. Right now, Harvey would be making his report and I saw little likelihood of me leaving Rathmore Drive without a confrontation with my mother.

Confrontation was the only word I could find to describe what I felt sure lay ahead of me. 'Argument' and 'disagreement' both had connotations of discussion or interaction of some kind and that was something I could rule out. What was really troubling me was that I might not be able to find any way of dealing with her random brand of assertion, complaint and insult. Trying to use any kind of logic in reply to her was always doomed to failure.

I was thinking what the possibilities were for coping, for defending myself without making matters worse, when I heard my father wheeze again. And that was when I made up my mind. Whatever she said or did, however awful, untrue, or hurtful her comments, I would not let her see I was angry. I would not lose control. The one thing that would really upset my father was to see me in tears. I'd managed to survive her tirade on Friday night, well I would jolly well have to do it again.

As my father settled back gratefully in his wing chair, I turned away from the window and saw Mavis settle herself on the long settee opposite the fireplace. In one practised movement she smoothed the pleats of her skirt, touched her gold bracelet, straightened her sleeves and fingered her mother's cameo. She folded her hands easily in her lap, pressed her ankles neatly together and sat there looking as if every item she was wearing was either freshly laundered or straight from its wrapping paper. She entirely fitted my mother's No.1 category of approval: 'Just immaculate'.

Indeed, Mavis appeared to fit all my mother's categories, but it suddenly came to me, as I looked across at her, that she certainly didn't pay any attention whatever to the continuous flow of comment and advice my mother offered, particularly on the subject of Peter, her grandson, on whom she considered herself something of an authority.

I listened to what Mavis was saying to my father. There was nothing like a nice log fire now the weather was colder, and no, she wasn't at all cold, the room was quite warm, even if the fire had burnt down a little. She inquired about the quality of the logs this year, and whether the young man who delivered them had charged extra for stacking them along the side of the garage. When she moved on from logs to roses, I collected myself, came and sat down in the armchair opposite my father and prepared to do my bit.

'No, Grandad, no matter what I do, they still don't do well,' said Mavis earnestly in reply to my father's polite inquiries.

For the first year of her marriage, Mavis had managed to avoid calling my parents by any name at all. Then Janet was born and from that day on Mavis addressed my father as Grandad and my mother as Nana and me as Aunty Jenny. My father made no objection to his title and my mother embraced hers with delight. I still found being addressed as Aunty Jenny by a woman thirteen years older than myself rather curious, but I'd got used to it. It seemed all one with the way Mavis had chosen to play the game and if that was the way she wanted it, I was happy enough to do what was required of me.

'I'm sure it's that peaty soil of yours, Mavis. You'd have no trouble at all if you had a heavy clay like Loughview.'

'I didn't think you'd have time for gardening, Aunty Jenny. However do you manage to garden *and* do your housework?'

I smiled patiently for the question was a real one, it had none of the edge of criticism it would have carried had it been my mother, or even Karen Baird.

'Oh, I do what I can with weekends and holidays,' I said lightly. 'It's a question of priorities. You've got to be absolutely certain what's top of the agenda. I had a couple of hours yesterday for the garden, so it had to be cut the lawn and lift the geraniums. I didn't dare risk leaving either job for another weekend. Thank goodness too, I managed them before that frost. I hope that'll be the last cut of the season.'

'Should be, dear,' my father nodded. 'A few more frosts like last night will soon stop growth. Did you have a frost last night, Mavis? You're more exposed up in Antrim than we are here.'

Mavis seemed happy to do the bulk of the talking. She moved on from last night's frost to the size of the heating bills for the large house overlooking Lough Neagh, referred to the difficulty of getting a fulltime gardener and the extra cleaning lady that Harvey's new suite of rooms made necessary, and mentioned the problem of finding a garage reliable enough to be trusted to come and fetch her car and return it in time to collect the children from school in the afternoon. I kept an ear open for my cue, but in between my mind wandered.

Diagonally across the room from me, in the angle between the French windows and the long wall behind the settee where Mavis now sat, there's a china cabinet with a curved front. It's full of Waterford glass bowls, wine glasses and a collection of plated silver cups won by Harvey for cricket and athletics. But it was the two matching silver photograph frames on the top of the cabinet that caught my eye. Each designed to hold two full-plate prints, the one on the right has Mavis and Harvey on their wedding day, 'a lovely young couple', paired with the happy parents and Janet, Peter and a small bundle that is Susie, 'such a lovely family'.

I had to smile to myself as I heard the epithets repeat themselves. They were as obligatory as 'hero of Troy' or 'greatest of the warriors' in a classic story. The newer of the two frames held a similar wedding picture of Colin and me, another 'lovely young couple', but all there was to make a pair was a faded print of Granny and Granda Hughes outside the door of their cottage behind the forge.

Something about those two expensive silver frames said it all. That's the trouble, Jennifer, I said to myself. That's what all this is really about. You are refusing to earn your epithet and relegate your poor dear grandparents to the shoe box in the corner of the wardrobe. You won't play the game, and quite literally you won't fit the frame.

I remembered the conference going on in the kitchen and felt my stomach turn over. I burped discreetly, looked across at Mavis and wondered if anything this side of Domesday could upset her equilibrium. But then, I reminded myself, three years as a theatre sister no doubt taught you how to keep cool, whatever the stress.

Harvey had met Mavis at a hospital dance. He was twenty-six then and she was several years older. Three months after they met, they were engaged, and they married a year later. Mavis's father turned out to be a consultant gynaecologist, and it was no surprise to me when Harvey suddenly discovered his great ambition in life was to specialise in gynaecology.

Suddenly, and quite unexpectedly, I remembered the posy and headdress of fresh flowers Mavis had sent me on her wedding day. I could almost smell the delicate perfume as I thought of how I'd lifted them out of the florist's box and handed them to Val who had come to help me get dressed. I had planned to spray them with water when I got home from the reception and keep them moist, so Val could paint them for me. But that didn't happen. After my mother's performance, the only thing I watered was my pillow. I found the flowers next morning, limp and dying, beyond retrieval.

'Here we are then, Mavis, a nice cup of coffee,' said my mother brightly as she came in and put the tray down on the long table in front of the settee. 'How would you like it?'

'White please, Nana. No sugar,' replied Mavis, leaving what she'd been saying suspended in mid-air.

'Jennifer?'

One word was enough. Like the cell under the microscope to the practised eye, the tiny fragment said it all. The case was definitely terminal.

'Black, please.'

'It looks as if we're going to have another teacher in the family, Mavis,' said my mother charmingly as she looked towards the garden where the two dolls and the teddy bear were again under instruction.

'Goodness, yes. She practically takes that blackboard to bed with her,' said Mavis with a little laugh.

'Well, I do hope Janet will know when to stop, Mavis.

A career's all very well, as you yourself know, but I do hope she'll grow up to know better than to put her own interests before those of her husband and family.'

I took a sip of my coffee. It was only instant, and it was both tepid and weak.

'I think I will have some hot milk, please, Mummy,' I said, ignoring as best I could the unmistakable thrust of her comment.

'Oh, changed your mind, have you? Oh, well, they say it's a lady's privilege, don't they, Harvey? Perhaps it's a good sign,' she said with a small, hard laugh.

She turned to Mavis who was sipping her coffee carefully. 'Jennifer is a great one for making up her own mind, Mavis, without consideration for anyone else.'

My father put down his coffee cup and looked across at her sharply. 'Edna, Jennifer's a grown woman. Surely her decisions are a matter for herself?'

Mavis picked up her handbag, checked out sleeves, bracelet and cameo, and rose to her feet all in one easy movement, glanced at my mother, smiled vaguely and said, 'I think, Nana, I'll just go and have a little tidy up and see how the children are getting along.' She moved slowly across the room leaving a trace of Chanel on the air, and my mother promptly took her place on the settee at the other end from Harvey.

Stand by for boarders, Jenny, I said to myself. I saw Harvey shift uncomfortably at one end of the long sofa and my mother fiddle irritably with her coffee at the other.

'Cigarette, Harvey?'

Harvey jumped so visibly when my father's cigarette case appeared under his nose that I nearly laughed.

'Oh – er – no thanks, Father, I . . . I've given them up.'

'What, no bad habits at all now, Harvey?' Daddy sat down again and pulled out his lighter. I saw him glance from one to the other out of the corner of his eye. He busied himself lighting his cigarette and brushing flecks of ash from his trousers, but I knew he, too, was waiting. It comforted me to have him there. I sat looking down the garden, displaying a kind of calm I certainly did not feel.

Harvey cleared his throat.

A stream of clichés ran through my mind. This is it. The crunch. The big scene. I could almost hear the low drumbeat of the music from the climax of *Gunfight at the OK Corral* as I looked across the large Bokhara rug which lay between the fireside armchairs where my father and I sat, and the long settee where Harvey and my mother had taken up their positions.

'Jennifer, I'm aware that you seem to have some very clear plans regarding your future. Would you think it too unreasonable if your family were to inquire what they might be?' Harvey began, in the tone I imagined him using in his consulting room when he felt he was dealing with a really recalcitrant patient.

Susie was strolling along the path now, singing to herself. In the dead hush of the room, I could just catch an odd fragment of 'Twinkle, twinkle, little star'.

'No, Harvey, no, it's not unreasonable at all,' I said agreeably. 'My immediate plan is to accept the job of Head of Department I was offered on Friday, reorganise the English Department ready for the move to the new building, get the Drama Studio working there, and set up an English workshop. When I've done that, I'll take stock again.'

Harvey glanced at my mother, though he knew full well that wasn't the answer she had in mind at all.

'I hardly think, Jennifer, that the details of your job are quite relevant to the present discussion,' he said.

'Then we must disagree, Harvey,' I replied sweetly. 'Perhaps you still haven't grasped that I have no intention of giving it up. If you'd reported that part of our conversation this morning accurately, I don't think Mummy could have been left in any doubt.'

Harvey put his empty coffee cup back on the table with such force that the cup fell over and rattled noisily against the saucer. 'Now look, Jennifer, don't you go acting the schoolmarm with me,' he protested.

My mother silenced him with a look.

'And what does Colin think of all this, Jennifer, may I ask?' she began, with that veneer of politeness which I knew well enough to ignore.

'As I have told you many times, Mummy, Colin says it's up to me to decide.'

She was leaning back comfortably in the angle of the settee, pushing her gold wristwatch back into position and glancing idly round the room.

'And what age do you think you're going to be by the time you've done all this reorganising?' Harvey burst out.

'I haven't really thought about that, Harvey,' I began coolly. 'Age isn't very relevant to running an English Department, you see,' I went on steadily. 'Connie's done a splendid job and she's in her fifties, as far as I know,' I added wickedly, knowing that Harvey was having the greatest difficulty in keeping his temper.

'You deliberately misunderstand me,' he spluttered.

'You know perfectly well what I mean. What on earth age do you think that'll leave you when you do decide to start your family?'

I took a deep breath.

'Forgive me, Harvey, but have you forgotten that childbearing is not obligatory?' I began, very quietly. 'And thanks to the tremendous scientific advances in your chosen field, it is not inevitable either. You may not find it profitable to encourage choice among your clients, but choice does exist and I intend to exercise mine. No one is going to coerce me into starting a family when I don't choose to. Is that clear?'

The set of Harvey's shoulders and the way he was twitching the sleeves of his elegant lambswool sweater told me he'd got the message all right, but my mother left me no time to enjoy my small victory.

'Oh, I'm sure you've made that very clear, Jennifer,' she said, her voice rising an octave. 'Speaking to your brother like that. I suppose that's the way you speak to Colin too, telling him what you'll do and not do. I suppose you walk over him the way you walk over us.'

Daddy's logs had burned up in the grate and my left foot was being quietly roasted. I'd also developed a bad attack of wind. Neither discomfort was exactly helping me to seem cool and in command of the situation. I withdrew my grilled ankle very slowly, tucked it nonchalantly behind the other, and asked her what she meant by walking over her.

She tossed her head at me and I got a momentary back view of her recent perm, the grey-blue curls stuck tight to her scalp, lacquered enough to preserve them for all time.

'You know perfectly well what I mean, Jennifer, and you needn't use that sarcastic voice of yours with me.'

'Yes, Mummy, I do know what you mean, but I think we'd better get it straight just the same.' I paused deliberately and managed to continue in the same level and steady tone. 'What you actually mean by "walking over you" is that I'm not prepared to give up my job, have a baby and settle down to running a comfortable life for Colin, the way Mavis has chosen to do for Harvey. If that's walking over you, then you're quite right. I am "walking over you" and I shall go on "walking over you". I didn't marry Colin to turn myself into a wife and mother, or social secretary, or to lead the kind of life that you, or Harvey, or Maisie McKinstry, or Karen Baird, or any combination you think fit for me. What I do with my life, I am going to decide. Not you or anybody else.'

By the time I had finished, her face was twisted with fury, her cheeks a hectic red. The hostility she gave off was so tangible, I just had to look away. I turned towards the fire and watched a shower of sparks shoot up the chimney as a glowing log settled into the orange embers. From the corner of my eye, I could see my father watching me closely, a look of profound concentration on his face and an almost discernible twinkle in his eye.

'I, I, I, Jennifer,' she burst out, 'that's all we ever hear from you. Very nice, isn't it? I'm sure you're very proud of yourself speaking to me like that.' She glared at me, her eyes glittering. 'Well, let me tell you, my girl,' she went on, dropping her voice and nodding to herself. 'You're not just going to get everything your own way.'

I knew the tone and I didn't like it. Sometimes it was

bluff, but as often as not there was some reality behind the self-satisfied smirk. Probably there was something she knew that I didn't know, but how important it was I had no way of guessing. But she had managed to make me thoroughly uneasy, just like yesterday when Karen Baird had gone all sickly sweet as I was leaving after morning coffee.

'Perhaps when you're not so handy to your fine friends, you'll learn to think different,' she went on, continuing to nod to herself. 'You'll not walk over the McKinstrys the way you walk over me. No, nor make a fool of Colin either.'

She made a twitching gesture with her shoulders, leaned forward on the settee and poked her head out towards me. 'Entertaining your gentlemen friends till all hours of the morning. What have you got to say about that, heh?'

Her lips were compressed into a tight line as she threw a furious glance towards my father. It looked as if he was going to get blamed for this as well. Perhaps it was that look thrown across at my father, or perhaps it was that sneering 'gentlemen friends' but instead of being knocked off balance as once I might have been, I just felt an ice-cold fury generate somewhere in the region of Sunday lunch and spread out to envelop me. I actually felt the colour drain from my face and I knew my hands had gone stone cold.

I stared at her quite calmly. It was the 'gentlemen friends' that had done it. For a moment I was right back on the moonlit shore at Drinsallagh, my hands clutching the bare bones of the old wreck, the memory of that awful year before I was married pouring back into my mind like a flood tide. Those were the words I had mimicked when I stood there sobbing, telling him what had happened, and why I had lost the last chance I had to talk to someone I trusted about the way things were going between Colin and me.

It was that moment in the hall, in March 1965 that had sealed my fate. That was when I'd caved in, given up any last chance of avoiding the path she'd managed to set up for me. It was my fault all right for giving in. But who was it had made me so desperate to escape that marrying Colin had looked like some kind of heaven?

There was only one possible way my mother could know about Alan's visit to Loughview. The sheer bloody cheek of that damn Karen woman took my breath away.

'What did you say?' I asked very quietly, as I continued to look straight at her.

'I suppose now you'll tell me it took you three hours to drive back from the far side of Bangor to Helen's Bay,' she crowed, triumphantly. 'Like the story you told me on Friday, when you arrived here with Mister Keith.'

She spat his name out with another sneer, confident she had me cornered.

'Oh, so Karen Baird gave you a ring this morning, did she?' I asked, keeping my voice as lightly conversational as if I were inquiring about Mavis's use of Greensward on her lawn.

She looked distinctly taken aback, opened her mouth to speak, but I didn't give her the chance. For what seemed like the first time in my life, I was ready and waiting.

'And did she tell you that the plan you made last Friday in Brand's, when you discussed my future with her and Maisie, got nowhere?' I began. 'Well, she tried all right. Oh yes, she tried. I had the whole works on Saturday morning. Everything from how worried you and Maisie were about my health to the medical advantages of early pregnancy,' I went on briskly. 'You'd be proud of her, Harvey, she sounded just like you,' I added with a laugh, as I glanced along the settee to see how he was getting on.

I was managing so much better than I'd ever imagined I'd be able to. I couldn't quite believe it. But I did have a problem. All this self-control had given me the most awful cramp in my right leg. If I didn't do something to ease the pain I was sure the leg was going to twitch. Only one thing for it. I leapt to my feet as if I had intended to, parked myself in front of the fire and stood facing them.

'It didn't work, Mummy. Karen was a flop. And so was Harvey. And setting up family lunch so you can both have a go at me is just as big a flop. And I'll tell you why.'

Neither of them said a word. So I just spelt it out, very simply and directly. I told her that she'd been manoeuvring me ever since Harvey went off and got married, that she'd decided who I could bring home, who I could visit, which of my friends she would accept and which she wouldn't. I told her she'd used Karen Baird, and others like her, to keep an eye on me and that I wasn't having it. She herself had said on Friday night that we only had one life to live. From now on, she could be absolutely sure that it was me who would be living mine.

Although I managed to keep control of the anger, it did make me breathless. I just managed to get to the end of what I wanted to say before I had to stop. She was in at once, but to my surprise her voice was quite unexpectedly calm and her manner almost reasonable. Immediately, I was on my guard.

'Jennifer, there's no need whatever for you to get worked up over nothing. You've always done it and it really isn't good for you. If you go on like that you'll end up with your father's trouble. You're simply overworking, doing far too much, just like him. It's a pity you can't appreciate who really has your best interests at heart.'

'Best interests. Best interests,' I repeated, my voice an icy whisper. 'When have you ever let my thoughts or feelings get in the way of what you wanted? You've made up your mind what "best interests" suit you. You want me to pack up the life I've chosen for myself so I can step into the one that you and Maisie have cobbled up for me. It's a game called Happy Families. Colin doing well, a couple of lovely grandchildren for the pair of you to come and coo over, all arranged in a suitable, detached property, with plenty of money splashed around to give it a touch of class. I run the show and the pair of you sit back and feel pleased with yourselves. Well, it's not on. I'm not playing.'

My last words were drowned by the sudden shrill of the telephone, but neither of them were in any doubt about what I was saying. They looked at each other, my mother tight-lipped and flushed with anger, Harvey pale and uncomfortable. My father stubbed out his cigarette carefully in the ashtray on the small table by his chair. Usually he flicks the end neatly into the fire, but this way he could take a long look at them. Footsteps sounded on the stairs, unhurried in their descent.

'Hello, Belfast six four nine . . . Yes, yes, I see. Just hold the line, please.'

Mavis walked back into the room, glanced across at me and said evenly, 'It's for you, Aunty Jenny. It's Colin and he says he's got no more money, so you'd better hurry.'

I dashed into the hall, wondering why hotels bothered to install phones in bedrooms when people like Colin appeared to be incapable of using them. His voice was agitated by haste and irritation and the phonebox got the prize for the most appalling of the weekend. But even worse than the scream of jet engines and the boom of ethereal voices on the tannoy was Colin's news. Despite hearing one word in five and losing most of his final sentence, I got enough to go back into the sitting room pale and shaking.

My mother's face was enveloped in a large, monogrammed handkerchief. Beside her, Harvey muttered soothing comments about not distressing herself and having done all that any mother could do. My father looked up sharply as soon as he saw me.

'Daddy, could I borrow the car? I'll have to go up to McKinstry's,' I said, ignoring Harvey's stare.

'Surely you can. But would you not rather I ran you up? You're looking rather pale,' he said matter-of-factly.

I hesitated, so grateful for his offer yet uncertain as to whether I should accept it.

'You're surely not going off, Jennifer, without apologising to Mummy,' Harvey broke in.

'Apologise, Harvey? For what? For speaking a few of the home truths I should have had the courage to spell out years ago?'

My mother emerged from the handkerchief. Her face was very red but her eyes were bone dry. 'Oh, you can be very pleased with yourself, Jennifer, speaking to me like that and then running off. But I'll not forget today. Maybe by the end of it, you'll not forget it either.'

There it was again, that same tone of veiled threat. I put it firmly out of mind. Whatever she thought she had up her sleeve, I had more important things to think about.

'No, Mummy. I'm not likely to forget today,' I said coldly.

Her face bore a familiar look of complacency. It was the 'You just wait and see if I'm not right' look. Well, perhaps she would be proved right. So far, she had always managed to get the better of me. Either I was so lacking in courage that I always gave in, or she had some power I just hadn't recognised. Well, if that was the way it was to be and I had to accept defeat in the end, this time at least I would go down fighting.

'Nobody forgets the day when they come to understand at last how a certain kind of wickedness has been used against them,' I began slowly, my voice still managing to hold on to its cool, steady tone. 'Oh, it may not seem wicked to you, this scheming with winks and nods, bullying with words and gestures so that you can impose your will on anyone who is too young, too weak, or too inexperienced to stand up to you. But doing it to your own daughter is only the start of it. If enough people do to others what you have done to me, and if they're as determined to impose their will on them at whatever cost as you have been with me, then I'll tell you where it leads.'

My mother looked around the room as if she had lost something, stared out of the window and then consulted her watch. But I paused only to draw breath. However indifferent she pretended to be, she was going to hear me out.

'It leads to what happened in Derry yesterday. It was people like you, thinking and acting like you, who sent in the B Specials to break up the demonstration. Break it up by beating it up. A peaceful, legal demonstration. Of young people. Young men and women, unarmed. Committing no crime, except the crime I've committed of making up my own mind. Those young people wouldn't accept graciously what others had decided was in their "best interests" any more than I will. No, Mummy, there is no danger whatever that I'll ever forget today.'

With a final effort, I turned to my father who had been standing beside me. 'Daddy, Keith is in Altnagelvin with a head injury. Colin doesn't know how bad. Could we go right now?' I asked distractedly, suddenly so weary that I wondered how I was to get myself out of the house without another delay.

'I'll get our coats,' he said, as he crossed the room with a briskness I had not seen for a long time.

'If you go and anything happens to you, you've only yourself to blame,' my mother called after him as he disappeared into the hall.

I picked up my handbag from beside my chair, turned round and found him already holding out my coat for me. As I buttoned it up, she jumped to her feet and turned on him.

'You weren't listening to a word I said, George Erwin, running off to the Antrim Road. I said—'

'That if anything happened to me, I had only myself to blame,' he responded amiably. 'I am quite aware of what you said, Edna. My heart is a fairly dubious organ,' he went on, as he took his car keys from his pocket, 'but I'm happy to say both my hearing and my eyesight are still quite unaffected.'

'You know the specialist insisted you had to avoid stress and drive as little as possible. Harvey will bear me out. Didn't he say that, Harvey?'

'But of course he did, Edna,' said my father soothingly. 'There's no doubt about that at all. What seems to be involved is a matter of interpretation. And that being the case, I shall follow my daughter's splendid example and make my own decision. Should it be the last decision I make, I think I shall feel it most worthwhile.' He turned to me, a broad smile on his face. 'If we go out by the garden we can say goodbye to the children.'

My mother scowled and turned her eyes heavenward. I ignored her and went through the French window he held open for me.

Chapter 15

Down on the Stranmillis Road, students from Queen's University and the Stranmillis Training College were walking hand in hand in the sunshine, as they had done every Sunday afternoon since I was old enough to remember. There was a surprising amount of traffic around, along with the kind of Sunday drivers who force you to concentrate on them all the time. Despite that, Daddy seemed relaxed and in very good spirits.

'Shall I put my foot down?' he asked as the traffic cleared ahead of us.

'I'd rather you didn't,' I said wryly. 'I'll have quite enough of Maisie before Colin and William John get back.'

'You look tired,' he said quietly.

'I'm absolutely whacked but I didn't cry, did I?'

'No, Jenny, you didn't. Nor did you get drawn in and lose your temper. That's never the way with your mother. You were grand, just grand. And I'm delighted you've decided about the job. It's great news.' He turned towards me as we stopped at the traffic lights on the Grosvenor Road. 'Was Colin pleased?'

The question was put so easily and was so natural, I nearly said, 'Oh, yes, of course, he's delighted,' before I'd even thought about it. Then, as the full realisation struck me of exactly how things stood between Colin and me, all I could do was stare at the redbrick terraces of Divis Street and wonder what I could say. It even occurred to me that Daddy might have been checking out what Colin's actual reaction was.

'We didn't get much chance to discuss it, the way things worked out,' I said quickly. 'William John seems to have kept him on the hop from the moment they landed,' I added with a little laugh. Then I paused and chose my words carefully as much for my own sake as for my father's. 'Actually, I decided it was something I should make my own mind up about. I'm sure he'll be pleased when I tell him.'

But once I heard my own words, I knew how hollow they were. No, Colin would not be pleased. But the pretence had to go on for a little while longer. A time for Thompson's Law if ever there was one. This was neither the time nor the place to say anything to my father about how I now saw the disaster of my marriage.

'I gather the directorship is on the cards for this weekend,' he went on as we drove off again.

'Oh yes. Posh dinner on Saturday night and all that. He rang me before he left at six, but I was at Val and Bob's after, so I haven't heard the actual outcome,' I replied as cheerfully as I could manage. 'As you have gathered, I was entertaining a "gentleman friend",' I added lightly. 'He asked about you, by the way, and sent his best regards.'

He turned towards me and grinned. 'I was wondering who the lucky man might be. Bob Dawson?'

'No, but you're not far wrong,' I said, laughing.

I told him about Alan's unexpected appearance, the

reason he'd turned down the offer from Patterson's, the nature of the new job and his decision to buy the cottage. He listened intently when I told him exactly where it was, how we'd gone to see it and how so many of the things I'd seen there reminded me of childhood visits to Granny McTaggart and Aunt Mary and the various elderly relatives we had gone on visiting long after my mother had refused to go anywhere near them.

'You'll have to come and see it, Daddy. You'd love the outlook. Besides, there's a rose on the south side like nothing I've ever seen, stems as thick as my arm. Val's going to help him paint the place, but I'm going to be horticultural adviser.'

He nodded to himself and seemed suddenly very thoughtful. He said he'd get me an electric pruning saw from Bertie's new hire department and then asked me more about Alan's plans. He smiled when I went on to tell him about Val and Bob's as well, about their move and the baby, and how Val planned to cope with being a mother.

'You've got some good friends there, Jenny. It sounds like Alan's found his feet at last. Bob's a nice man and a very good architect. He'll do well whatever he puts his hand to.' He paused and then said something that really surprised me. 'I don't think I've ever met a more unpleasant man than Alan's late father, though one doesn't want to speak ill of the dead. How he could pack that lad off to England after his mother died and split up those two children when they were so bereft is more than I can understand. And then he marries that sour-looking woman from the school and just about ignores the pair of them. All credit to Alan for the way he stuck by Val, till she met

Bob. I don't know where that girl would have ended up, Jenny, if she hadn't had you for a friend and a brother like Alan. He sounds a lot happier than he used to be and I'm glad to hear it.'

He broke off as we came to a halt at the junction of Townsend Street and Peter's Hill. A policeman stood in the road, his back to us, his hand raised, while a crowd of people spilled off the pavements and onto the road in front of us. From somewhere a long way off, I caught the sound of a pipe band. My father smiled ruefully as he put on the handbrake and switched off.

'And I had a gentleman asking for you, too, the other day,' he went on as he settled himself more comfortably behind the wheel. 'Another of your admirers. Can you guess who?'

I named a couple of the old farmers we used to visit together, the ones who still left boxes of apples or bags of potatoes at the showroom for me. But each time he shook his head.

'I give up,' I said, smiling.

'Your Uncle Harry,' he said triumphantly.

For a moment I couldn't think what to say. Harry Morton is a lovely man and one of Daddy's oldest friends. But he is also his solicitor, and the last time we met was in the intensive care unit at the hospital, when Daddy sent for him to come and make an emergency arrangement about the business in the event of his death.

He turned towards me and caught the look on my face. 'Just routine, Jenny. Just routine,' he said reassuringly. 'There are still some bits and pieces to tie up from selling the business. Wills can be a great source of contention, you know. Think of all the good stories we've read. What would Agatha Christie have done without wills?'

He seemed so relaxed about it that I was able to push away the painful memory and ask about Uncle Harry. But I could see there was something he wanted to tell me.

'There's a bit of land, Jenny, I bought thirty years ago,' he began. 'To tell you the truth, I'd half forgotten it. I had the idea that when I retired I'd build a bungalow and a couple of greenhouses, one for fuchsias, one for chrysanths,' he added with a smile. 'But a few months back, a builder contacted me and made me an offer. Gave me a bit of a surprise, the amount he offered. I won't be able to move from Belfast now but one day you might like that bit of land. That's why I went to Harry. Your mentioning Drinsallagh reminded me I hadn't told you. It's not that far from there. Do you ever remember that road we used to take to Ballyhalbert?'

'The one that goes over Windmill Hill?'

'The very one,' he said, nodding and looking pleased. 'It's a long time now since we've been there,' he said wistfully.

'Don't laugh, Daddy, but I was there last night.'

'Were you now?'

'Yes,' I nodded vigorously. 'When we went down to see the cottage, I recognised that old tree stump we used to watch for and I asked Alan to stop. I was saying to him that it was such a long time since I'd been on that road.'

As I spoke, I felt a great sadness come over me. Without any warning whatsoever my mind filled with memories of all those drives we had done together and now did no longer.

'I do so miss the countryside, Daddy. Especially I miss those drives we used to do.'

He looked at me sharply, and I realised there were tears in my eyes. I blinked them away and stared out through the windscreen. Between the scatter of people in front of us, I could see a tall figure in a hard hat striding down the empty road, a silver-tipped staff in his hand. The pipe band struck up 'The Sash My Father Wore' and the plangent notes echoed back from the shabby buildings all around us, making conversation impossible till it moved away.

When the band had passed, my father took up our conversation again as we watched the long procession of Orangemen pour down from the Shankill Road, Lodge by Lodge, behind a succession of gaudy banners that gleamed in the afternoon sun. He explained that this piece of land was to be mine, in addition to my half of his estate and all his books. My mother was provided for, he said, for her lifetime, and as she and Harvey had cars, I was to have his, and he'd got Harry to write it into the will. 'You may not want anything as big as this Rover, dear, but Rovers hold their value well. You could trade it in for something smaller.'

The last of the Orangemen passed by and the policeman waved us forward. I was so grateful. There was no way I could think of saying thank you for gifts that would only come to me by the death of someone I loved so dearly.

'Are you very disappointed you can't build on your land, Daddy?' I managed at last as we moved slowly through Carlisle Circus and headed up the Antrim Road.

'Disappointed?' he repeated thoughtfully. 'No, Jenny dear, far from it.'

And then he began to tell me about when he was a wee lad going to the village school. The story seemed familiar, but I couldn't have heard it for years. He said it had suddenly come into his head on Friday afternoon when he was half asleep by the fire.

Once, he remembered, he met a lad he knew, riding on horseback. It was only a working farm horse, but the lad's family was well-off by my father's standards and he confessed he envied him. There my father stood, barefoot, a common enough thing in the 1910s, he said, with the backside out of his trousers, and he looked up at the lad and thought, One day I'll have a horse and a pair of good boots and a farm of land.

His eyes were twinkling with laughter as he turned to me. 'What fools we mortals are, Jenny. How we try to predict the future. I'd have been a lousy farmer. And I don't even like big horses. But I didn't do so bad, Jenny. If a gipsy had told me then my daughter would be a graduate of Queen's and Head of Department in a city grammar school, and I'd be driving her up the Antrim Road in a Rover, and I'd have a bit of land to leave her, I'd have laughed in her face. Life is full of surprises, Jenny, and some of them are great,' he ended.

He swung the car neatly off the main road and into the quiet avenue, beyond the end of which the McKinstry house stood, up a steep driveway.

'Would it help if I came in, d'you think?' he asked as he switched off the engine at the bottom of the drive.

I shook my head sadly. I'd have been so grateful for his company, but I knew only too well his presence might make matters worse. Maisie was quite capable of being unpleasant towards my father because of his tolerant way with things in general and Catholics in particular.

'Will you be going in to work this week, Daddy?' I asked, still reluctant to go, my hand on the door.

'Oh yes, all being well. Tuesday and Thursday. Bertie and I are still putting information onto this computer of his. I'd never have believed how much you can have in your head till he started asking me things,' he said cheerfully. 'Why d'you ask? Can you call in?'

'Yes. I know I haven't been down for ages, but I've just got my early afternoon again on a Tuesday, because Carol's come back from having her baby. Any chance of a cup of tea about three?'

'Indeed there is,' he said warmly. 'And Mrs Huey and Bertie will be glad to see you too. I'll ask Mrs Huey to get us a bun for our tea, shall I?'

I leaned over and kissed him and thanked him for driving me up. 'I'll let you know about Keith, Daddy, as soon as I can, and I'll see you on Tuesday. We can have a good chat then.'

'Good girl, that'll be great. Good luck with Maisie.'

He laughed, as I raised my eyes heavenward. I waved and watched him turn and drive off, still smiling.

When I turned away, I saw the front door of Myrtlefield House was already open. The thin, angular figure of my mother-in-law stood watching me, her eyes screwed up against the light, a gin glass in one hand, tension radiating from every part of her elegantly dressed and coiffed person. There was nothing for it but to take a deep breath, hurry up the short, steep driveway, and look as if I was pleased to see her.

Chapter 16

'Hello, Maisie,' I said as I reached the broad, shallow steps to the front door.

She poked out a cheek and I kissed it dutifully, but there was no smile or greeting in return. I followed her into the hall.

'Have you had any more news? I'm terribly sorry about Keith.'

'Sorry about Keith. Sorry about Keith,' she repeated in a voice full of bitterness. She took another swig of her gin as she tottered down the hall. 'More like it, Jennifer, if ye saved yer simpithy fer Willyum John and Colin. Wastin' it on that blighter. Sorry fer him? Huh. It's not him'll suffer if thisis all over the papers,' she began, her accent thick and harsh.

Out of the frying pan, Jenny, I said to myself as I followed her into the vast, empty lounge.

After the scene with my mother and the effort I'd made not to let my anger break through, I felt absolutely shattered. I had no sense of success to bear me up, for my departure from Rathmore Drive had been so hasty it wasn't clear at all whether I'd made any real impression or not. She hadn't said goodbye, but that was nothing new. In fact, as I listened with half an ear to Maisie who continued to pour out her fury at Keith, I remembered that it was only Mavis and Susie who had said goodbye to me.

Janet and Peter had disappeared indoors to play a game that needed the dining-room table. I'd waved to them as I stepped out onto the terrace, but they'd been so absorbed, they hadn't seen me. Susie had hugged me fiercely as I explained that I had to go because Uncle Keith had been hurt and his Mummy was worried about him. Mavis stood by, listening, a small, woolly garment in her hands.

'I hope you'll find things better when you get there, Aunty Jenny,' she said steadily. 'Susie and I were hoping you could come up for Peter's birthday next month, weren't we, Susie?'

'Yes, I'd love to come, Mavis. Thank you,' I said, looking at her over Susie's blonde curls. 'I'll see you again then, Susie,' I reassured her, as she looked up at me, reluctant to let me go. 'Only three weeks, Susie. Not long,' I said, as I disentangled the small, cold arms, gave her a kiss and hurried off to where Daddy was waiting, the engine running.

'An' poo-or Colin, poo-or Colin, workin' so hard to build up the bizniss. It's yer own husban' ye shud be thinkin' off an' not the same Mister Keith. An' don' ye ferget that.'

As she spat out 'Mister Keith' in the harsh accent that made it clear exactly which part of Belfast she had been born and brought up in, I suddenly realised where my mother had picked up the phrase.

My mother is never original. You only have to wait long enough and you'll find out where her new expressions come from, a sitcom she's been watching, some presenter on television, a visiting preacher, or an acquaintance she's been talking to. In this case, a day spent with Maisie, assisted by Karen Baird, having a go at 'Mister Keith', and then a go at me. I wondered what label they had given to me.

Fury swept over me as I thought of the pair of them, like the Witch of the West and the Witch of the East, crouched over their morning coffee, then over their very good lunch, and then, no doubt, over their afternoon tea. However different they might be from each other, in age, background and experience, and however much they actually disliked each other, there was no doubt that when it was a matter of misdeeds, and especially Keith's or mine, there was nothing but solidarity between them.

I took a deep breath, held on to my anger and followed her across the room to sit down in one of the huge black leather armchairs.

'I'm not one bit sorry for 'im, Jennifer, no more shud ye be. He only gat whit he desurves. He's a rale troublemaker. Tha's all he is. No respect for onywon or onythin'. Jus' walks over us. Trippin' off with that Cathlick bitch.'

So we were back to 'walking over', were we? I watched her drain her glass and bang it down on a side table scattered with discarded Sunday papers and the empty foils from a large box of expensive chocolates. Maisie is a size 10, shorter than I am, and despite her appetite for sweet things, skinny to the point of emaciation. Not yet fifty, she has a horror of looking old and compensates for the fact by choosing clothes which she thinks will make her look younger. She's never very successful, and even I have to admit that my mother's 'mutton dressed as lamb' is, if coarse, nevertheless accurate.

Today Maisie was wearing a cherry-coloured jersey wool dress with a broad, patent leather belt embossed with gold studs, and matching black stilettos. The dress, attractive enough in itself, clashed violently with her hair which, since it's gone grey, Maisie herself dyes to an unpleasant gingery colour, described on the box as Autumn Morning.

I've never liked Maisie very much but I have tried to see her good side. At times I've managed to find a lot of sympathy for the life she had before William John started making his money. But today, looking at Maisie, full of gin and self-righteousness, I could find little to mitigate my sense of loathing.

'I dunno what Willyum John is gonna say whin he gits here,' she went on. 'He's goin' ta go beserk. After all the work he's done . . . and that blighter . . .'

Words failed her and before she could begin again, I asked when she expected them to arrive.

'Oh, I dunno. Colin said they'd git the firss plane they cud. I know he'll do his best. If anythin's to be done, Colin'll do it. My poo-or Colin,' she lamented, as she jumped to her feet and marched across to the bar to refill her glass. 'An' yer not much comfort, Jennifer. All ye can ask about is Keith. Pur Keith, indeed.'

I stared out through the huge plate-glass window while she put together her drink. I heard her throw an empty tin of tonic fiercely into the waste bin. All the time, she kept up her flow of talk. She alternated between attacking Keith for his very existence, crooning over Colin and how wonderful he had been, and lamenting her own luckless fate that this should have happened to her after all her hard work. And just when things were working out so well.

I wondered if things really were working out so well for Maisie. On the face of it, she had everything money could buy, as my mother continually pointed out, but it often seemed to me that Maisie had little joy of all her possessions. She looked to me like a very lonely person. She saw little of William John, less of Colin, and now nothing at all of Keith. She had no hobbies except shopping, and no friends I had ever heard of except the wives of William John's cronies, who came to dinner and invited her to fund-raising events for their various charities and nothing more.

Over the years now, mostly when drunk, Maisie had confided to me the secrets of her family history, a history which Colin appeared to have no knowledge of at all. Her father, Hugh Dalzell, had been a seaman. Hard-living and hard-drinking, he had beaten up her mother regularly when he was on shore and kept them so short of money when he wasn't that often they had little to eat. When he fell off a harbour wall in a drunken stupor, onto the deck of a coal boat at low tide, his wife collected his tiny insurance and pawned everything she possessed to buy new clothes for herself and her daughters.

She then signed on at an agency for superior servants and found a position as a daily housekeeper with an elderly gentleman living alone in a large house, barely a mile away from the tiny house where she had eked out such a miserable existence. Within three months, her employer had suggested that she become resident. He made no objection when she said she could only move in if she could bring her two daughters with her.

From the minute the girls set foot in the Cliftonville house, Mary Dalzell set about making a new life for them. Maisie was no longer to be called Maisie, but Margaret. She was sent to a different school, attended a different church, and had elocution lessons. Edith, who had a good voice, had piano lessons and later the old gentleman paid for singing lessons as well. Both girls were instructed to devote their time and attention to the old gentleman.

They did so. When he died, he left their mother his house and both Edith and Margaret had generous legacies. Edith, the elder, used hers to go to London and pursue her singing career, but before she was there for very long she met a young barrister and got married. Margaret was summoned to visit the newlyweds and went to the large house in Bromley where Edith was now happily settled with new friends and a baby on the way. Margaret hated England, didn't like Edith's friends and felt awkward and uncomfortable all the time she was there. When she returned to Belfast, she went off to dances in the Orange Hall near her old home when her mother thought she was at church socials or the Floral Hall. And that was how she met William John whom she'd been at school with and who had been born in the next street to the one where she herself had lived.

What few people knew was that it was Maisie's money that had helped William John to get started and that it was William John, not Maisie, who had insisted they move out of the district where they had both started life and into the affluent suburb where they now lived.

Maisie never seemed easy with the life she had acquired. Sometimes, like that awful first Christmas when Colin and I stayed with them, she would act the lady and entertain generously, taking a huge amount of trouble and spending a great deal of money on the best of food and wine. Her voice would soften, her vowels round out and she would think before she spoke. When she put her mind to it, she could be quite charming. But it never seemed to bring her any pleasure. More often, she reacted to the effort she'd made and for days afterwards she'd tramp round the house in pink furry slippers, something which her mother had strictly forbidden her ever to do and something which she knew really irritated and upset William John.

'Least 'e got what he disurves,' she announced firmly as she sat down again, so abruptly that the gin slopped in her glass. 'Maybe whin he comes roun', he'll have had a bit of sense knockt intil him.'

A wave of nausea flooded over me. 'What do you mean, Maisie, "comes round",' I asked quietly, my whole body rigid with tension.

Coping with my sheer fury at her behaviour had already stretched me to the limit, but now I wondered desperately how I was going to go on keeping up any appearance of civility.

She turned towards me, her eyes sharp and malevolent. 'I mean, Jennifer, when he regains consciousness – since you are so very interested in his welfare,' she said, enunciating every word carefully, as if I couldn't understand what she'd said in her unmodified accent.

'Yes, Maisie, I am,' I said firmly.

Something snapped when I heard the heavy sarcasm of

her tone. I just couldn't go on sitting in silence, listening to her talk like this, whatever the consequences. 'Are you saying, Maisie, that Keith is still unconscious after yesterday's baton charge?' I asked in a whisper.

'How shud I know?' she shouted across at me. 'All the informashun I git is frum some Cathlick bitch who rings me up, thinkin' I might wanta know.'

'Do you mean Siobhan?'

'Shove-on? Shove-on? Don't you Shove-on me,' she cried, her voice rising to a hysterical scream. 'Don't you iver minshun that name in this house. A filthy little bitch frum some back street, runnin' after our Keith and gettin' him inta all this socialiss nonsense. I wonder ye haven' a bit more sense, Jennifer. You oughta know the kine she is.'

Suddenly, I was intensely aware of the hand clutching the gin. Its nails were long and immaculately painted in bright, pillar-box red. My head felt fuzzy as if I'd been downing the gin myself. And then, as if from a very long way away, I heard my own voice and wondered how I had managed to get it so cool and steady.

'And I wonder that you can speak like that, Maisie, about someone you've never met. Far from coming from the back streets, Siobhan lives near the Bairds in Malone Park and her father is a consultant neurologist. It was Keith who introduced her to the Young Socialists, not the other way round.'

'Oh, I see. I see,' she said nastily, jumping to her feet and heading for the bar again. She banged an ice tray noisily on the stainless steel sink hidden behind the studded, leather-padded exterior of the bar. 'I diden' know she was such a great pal of yours,' she said sarcastically.

'Of Colin's and mine, Maisie,' I replied, stressing the 'Colin'. 'Keith and Siobhan come to supper with us regularly.'

'I'd 'ave thought you an' Colin had plenty of fren's without the likes o' them. An' I'd 'ave thought you'd show a bit more simpathy for your own husban's famlee at a time like this,' she said sharply as she tipped up the last dregs from the gin bottle into her glass.

'But surely that includes Keith, doesn't it?'

Maisie's lips tightened to a thin line and her shoulders hunched as she dropped more ice into her drink.

'I think yer husban' shud come before any good-for-nothin' Cathlick, Jennifer, but ye've yer own ideas about that, an' yer father both, don't ye?' she said, as she marched past me and dropped down into her chair.

There was an extra edge to her voice that warned me I'd better not go any further down that road. I'd made it clear I wouldn't listen to her abusing either Keith or Siobhan any longer. As regards the subject of me and my husband, it was definitely back to Thompson's Law again.

I jumped up restlessly, went to the window and looked out over the nearby gardens to the bottom of the quiet avenue. I knew there was precious little hope they'd be here yet but I had to do something. 'I thought that was the car,' I said, turning back towards her. 'But I expect it's too soon. Why don't I make us a cup of tea? They could be ages yet.'

'Oh, make tea if ye like, Jennifer,' she said dismissively. 'I'm not sure I'll want ony. Ye know yer way roun' the kitchin by now.'

The relief of escaping to the kitchen was short-lived. I'd thought if I could just get away from her, I might feel easier, but as soon as I left the room I found myself calculating how much longer I would have to cope before Colin and William John arrived to create a diversion.

Given Colin had rung from Heathrow, I had to allow an hour's flight time, perhaps as much as half an hour for baggage and at least a half-hour's drive. As I didn't know what the flight times were on a Sunday, I tried to calculate from shortest possible to longest. As I pursued my calculations, agitated and weary, the simple business of laying a tray the way Maisie liked it to be laid and finding her second best china was almost too much for me.

Jenny, calm down. All you have to do is survive till they come, I told myself. This isn't the moment to deal with any other issue. Let her get stoned. Ignore her. You've done all you dare. Let it go.

It was while I was waiting for the tea to brew that I faced the fact I was seeing Maisie in a new light. At the same time, I could see that her view of me had also changed. She was no longer treating me as 'a nice wee girl'. I couldn't say exactly when the change had come. Perhaps when I had failed to wear the knicker-pink twinset, or perhaps the day she found the half-knitted matinee coat and was so upset when I told her it was for Karen's first baby. That was back in the early days at Loughview, when I was still trying to take the kindest view of Karen, along with a lot of other people.

I looked up at the white, steam-proof electric clock, its large, red second hand stopping momentarily between the individual seconds and then clicking rhythmically on.

Suddenly I thought of the luminous dial of the clock in Alan's car.

Oh Alan, I thought, how I wish you could spirit me out of this, like the way you did last night at the party. I smiled to myself, the very thought of him bringing me comfort. I remembered him standing in my study and saying that I thought if I couldn't see him he wouldn't be there. But he would. Yes, he was quite right. The very fact of his existence, someone who would understand the nightmare of being shut up in this house with this awful woman, made me feel better. I could imagine myself telling him how awful Maisie was, just like I'd told him about my mother. And he would listen. Avoidance, not evasion, that was the thing.

I thought of Alan's Uncle John and Aunt Audrey and how long it was since I'd seen them. I'd taken Colin to meet them when we were engaged and they'd come to our wedding, but somehow we'd never managed to visit them since we got back. I smiled wryly. No, Jenny, no more thoughts. Just avoidance. It can't go on for ever. Thus encouraged, I picked up the tray.

'Milk or lemon today, Maisie?' I asked pleasantly, as I put the tray down. To my surprise, the gin glass had disappeared, the papers had been tidied up, and the chocolate box was nowhere to be seen. Even more surprising, she had brought out some glossy building trade literature from the magazine rack and had left an illustration of the McKinstry development in Antrim lying open on the coffee table.

'There was cake in the tin,' she said as she ran her eye over the tray, noting that I had taken a fresh traycloth from the drawer and remembered the paper doily for under the biscuits.

'Oh, would you prefer cake?' I said, half rising.

'Oh no,' she said dismissively. 'A biscuit's enough for me. I thought maybe you'd be wantin' cake. You needn't have bothered wi' the lemon.'

I found my hand was shaking, so I concentrated on pouring the tea while we played the game I had become familiar with in recent months. The no-win game, I call it. Do it this way, and I'll tell you not to bother. Do it any other way, and I'll point out what you've missed. Well, playing the games Maisie wanted to play was all part of the job today. But letting myself play them didn't mean I didn't observe or didn't care.

'There they are. There they are,' Maisie shouted, jumping up so quickly that I nearly dropped her cup.

I turned and looked down the drive and caught a glimpse of Colin in shirtsleeves, swinging the car between the stone pillars. William John was in the passenger seat, a cigar between his fingers. Maisie disappeared at speed into the hall, leaving me holding the teapot. I put it down carefully and sent up an earnest prayer of thanksgiving.

'Hello, Jenny. Sorry about all this.' William John strode into the room, picked up the telephone directory and went over to the phone. 'Colin's putting the car away,' he said over his shoulder as he started to dial.

I took the hint and went out into the hall. Maisie was already at the front door.

'Colin. Colin,' she cried and flung herself at him as he came into the hall. She wrapped her arms round him and started to cry.

'There now, Mum. Don't worry. You mustn't be upset.

292

It'll be fine, just fine,' he said in his most soothing manner.

He dropped his briefcase, kissed her on the lips and bent his head to hear what she whispered in his ear. He smiled and nodded reassuringly. She looked very satisfied and added something more.

I stood at the lounge door, an unwilling and embarrassed spectator. The sight of the two of them with their heads together and their arms entwined, whispering confidences, quite nauseated me. I'd never before been just so aware of this sickening performance they put on when they were doing their Mummy's best boy routine. I couldn't step back into the lounge and I could hardly go and greet Colin, but I had to do something. I turned away and headed for the kitchen, but Colin caught the movement and called out a cheery, 'Hello. Where's my Jen then?'

His arm still round his mother's shoulders, he walked her towards me and held out his free arm. Reluctantly, I waited for it to close round my waist. I felt his lips brush mine.

'Now what have you two girls been up to?' he asked as he drew us both into the lounge.

'I've just made some tea,' I said, rather too brightly.

'Yes, Colin dear. Do come and have a cup. I'm sure Jenny won't mind making some more.'

I noted the transformation in Maisie's accent, and as Colin's arm released me instantly, I made for the kitchen.

No, not a bit, I said to myself. No, indeed. Jenny doesn't mind making more tea, or making more dinner, or making more anything, but what she'd really like to make is her escape. And she will. All in good time.

I put the kettle on again and looked back up at the clock.

A single hour had passed since Daddy dropped me off and already it seemed like an eternity. There would be worse to come, of that I felt quite sure. But if I could survive the last hour, I could probably survive the next one. And that was all I needed to do, an hour at a time, just for the moment.

Chapter 17

'Hello, hello, Bill. McKinstry here. How are you? Sorry to
butt in on a Sunday afternoon . . .'

I winced as William John launched yet again into his
now familiar routine. Each time he boomed into the
mouthpiece his voice seemed to expand inside my head so
that the pain of my headache oscillated unbearably. Could
there be anybody left to telephone? Since teatime, either
he or Colin had been talking to someone, establishing the
position, considering its implications, and attempting to
rearrange it more to their liking.

'A spot of bother, old man. I'd be grateful for a bit of
help. You know how these things are . . .'

Maisie stood up suddenly. 'I'll away and see how that
chicken's doing.'

I cursed the bloody chicken. I wasn't remotely surprised
when Colin agreed to stay for a meal. But having accepted
my fate, I discovered Maisie had decided to cook a chicken
she'd extracted, rock-hard, from the freezer. Bluish and
unappetising, the corpse now lay under a white napkin, a
small puddle of water marking its slow progress to the
point where it could decently be put in the oven.

I watched her go, tottering slightly on her very high
heels, as she always does whether she's drunk or sober.

Any last shred of sympathy I might have found for her had vanished entirely when Colin rang Altnagelvin Hospital. His brother, they said, was now conscious but still suffering from concussion. He'd had thirty stitches to the gash just above his right eye and they were now about to X-ray his ribs. Colin had repeated these details to her with about as much emotion as if he'd been passing on a train timetable. He hadn't actually said 'Fine, fine,' but his whole manner indicated the problem had been solved, there was nothing for any of them to worry about any more. And Maisie had just nodded, as much as to say, 'Well, that's that. As long as I have you, Colin dear, what does it matter?'

'Splendid, old man, splendid. I'm sure we'll be able to show our appreciation, if you can do that.' William John's voice filled the room. 'Gotta see these things in perspective. Boys will be boys. We've all done damn fool things in our time before we learnt a bit of sense, haven't we? Right then, we'll be in touch again about Beechcroft next week. Good. Right-oh. I'm sure it'll be good for both our companies. Gotta stick together these days, haven't we?'

He dropped the phone and clapped his hands so loudly that I jumped.

'That's done it, Colin lad,' he roared triumphantly. 'Good job we'd tipped off McWatters about the Beechcroft contract. He owes us a few favours.' He looked round at us both, radiating self-satisfaction. 'What we need is a drink,' he declared. He took out a fresh cigar and began the elaborate preliminaries before he actually lit it.

Colin looked up sharply from where he'd been scanning directories and making notes, slid the volumes off his knee, and immediately strode across to the bar and touched a switch. A battery of fluorescent lights stabbed the gathering dusk in the room. I swivelled round towards the window, trying to escape their glare, but I found the bluey-white light and the room itself reflected back at me, a mirror image set against the dark mass of the lawns and the shrubbery.

'The usual, Dad?'

'Just show it the tonic, son.'

'What about you, Jen?'

'Just tonic, please, with lots of ice and lemon.'

The light had almost gone. Only to the west could I distinguish a long streak of pale gold broken by the bands of grey-blue cloud that had begun to appear as the afternoon wore on. I stared out across the mature gardens and well-kept properties surrounding Myrtlefield House. Beyond the confining buildings and across the wide swathe of Belfast Lough lay the County Down shore. From the front bedrooms of Myrtlefield you can see Loughview and the low coastline as it continues eastwards to Bangor. But then the coast swings south and the long peninsula of Ards stretches protectively around Strangford, the inland lough with its scatter of tiny islands. Sheep graze in summer on the larger islands, but in winter only the wind disturbs the grass. How far, as the crow flies, I wondered, to one of those islands lying deserted amid the grey water? Fifteen miles. Maybe twenty. But at this moment it might as well be a million. Distance, like time, is such a variable thing. It is the situation of one's own life that determines whether you can travel those miles or be forever confined in someone else's reality.

The reality of this room had confined me for long

enough. But I knew now its power had gone. If it hadn't, then just being here would be totally unbearable. It wasn't. The sense of total isolation I felt, sitting here, an outsider, extraneous to the performance going on around me, did not distress me. It might irritate me, bore me, make me unutterably weary, but ultimately it did not touch me. Inside my head, I was free.

Knowing what you want is half the battle, I said silently to myself. Well, I knew I didn't want this. This house, these people, this man I knew I no longer loved, if ever I had actually loved him at all.

William John stirred restlessly in his chair, picked up the telephone again. 'Think I'll try McParland, Derry Chamber of Commerce. Just to be on the safe side. He's a JP. Bound to have contacts in the police.'

'Good idea, Dad. We did rather well by him on that local government contract. He must have made a bob or two on the earth-moving. Shall I get his number?' Without waiting for a reply, Colin crossed the room again, found the number, wrote it on a slip of paper and handed it to him. I watched his reflection in the window as he opened a fresh bottle of gin and filled the ice bucket from the built-in fridge behind the bar counter.

Relaxed, confident and infinitely pleased with himself, he was certainly playing the part of McKinstry's youngest director to perfection. Yet at any moment he was ready to jump to it like a hired lackey and do whatever his father wanted. Staring at the Cinemascope reflections, I remembered how once, a long time ago, I had thought this willingness to give to others what they wanted came from his inherent good nature. But after watching him this afternoon, the hugs and kisses for his mother, the face-giving gestures he made to his father, I could see now that it was policy. What he'd found worked he now operated automatically. There was nothing of caring or thoughtfulness for them, any more than there was for Keith; just a cool calculation as to what would best serve his own ends.

His father began to dial. Colin came across and handed me my drink. As I turned to take it, he mouthed, 'I love you,' and pursed his lips in an exaggerated kiss.

I turned away again as soon as I decently could.

'Ah, Tom, hello.'

The boom echoed in my head even louder than before.

'How are you? Sorry to butt in like this on a Sunday afternoon. We've had a little spot of bother this end which might affect the launch of the Derry office. I think it would help us both if we could have a quick word. Don't want to get off on the wrong foot, as the saying is . . .'

Colin lit a cigar, lay back in his armchair, his long legs stretched out in front of him, his glass within reach. I could see him congratulating himself on the way he'd handled things. William John must have gone up like a sky rocket when the news came through. Probably he'd have been happy to let Keith go to jail if he were charged and wouldn't even have stood bail for him if it was offered. But, from what had happened since, it looked as if Colin had calmed him and sobered him up by pointing out the advantages of avoiding any unfortunate publicity. He'd also managed to do it so that William John ended up thinking it was all his own idea.

William John laughed again and went on booming. I

thought of the Christmas we came back from Birmingham, and of all the times I had sat in this room, watching the McKinstrys play their parts. The very first time of all came back to me, the evening Colin had taken me to meet his family.

I closed my eyes as the memory swept over me. Nervous to begin with, I'd stepped into this lounge and been appalled by its ghastly furniture and the brashness of the bar which occupied one whole corner of the big room. William John boomed at me, asked what I'd like to drink, went 'Sorry' and 'Ho-ho' when I asked for sherry, and landed me with a stiff gin I hadn't liked at all. Maisie had been on her best behaviour, but I couldn't help noticing the way her vowels came and went, just like Eliza Dolittle on a bad day.

Only Keith, awkward and uneasy himself, had made me feel more comfortable when we were left to talk about his A-level texts. I had liked him immediately and really appreciated the sharp one-liners he made that no one else seemed to hear. We'd ended up talking about *Richard III* and political knavery and I'd offered him some of my own notes.

How easily we tell ourselves stories to explain our discomforts. After that evening I told myself I had been nervous, that gin on an empty stomach had upset me, that Maisie reminded me of a former teacher, someone I'd always disliked. No, I hadn't been dishonest. I simply hadn't let myself read my own best intuitions. It had taken over four years for those intuitions to emerge into the full light of consciousness. That light was now as brilliant as the flickering fluorescent tubes. There wasn't the slightest possibility of my going back on what was so clearly revealed to me.

The door opened and Maisie reappeared. 'It'll be a half-hour yet, and I'm sure you're starving.'

Colin was on his feet immediately. 'Never mind, Mum, it'll be worth waiting for. What can I get you to drink?'

'I'll just have a small gin and tonic, dear,' she said coyly.

I had a sudden uncontrollable urge to giggle. It was the 'small' that did it. Knowing how much she'd downed before she washed the glass, and how she'd finished off the chocolates to mask her breath, I just couldn't keep my face straight. In case anyone should notice, I reached hastily for my tonic and ice.

The shock of the warm, bitter liquid certainly removed the smile from my face. It was mostly gin. And what little tonic there was must have come straight out of the box by the radiator. A solitary ice cube floated on the warm surface. It made a small fizzling noise as it dissolved before my eyes. I put the glass down and looked across at Colin, comfortably stretched out again, cigar and glass in hand, chatting idly to his mother. Were he an unknown stranger seen thus across the proverbial crowded room, would I even wish to know him, let alone think of marrying him?

The chicken took even longer than Maisie had calculated and it was nearly eight o'clock by the time we sat down to the meal. Despite my commitment to patience and the fact that nothing much was required of me, I had become progressively more weary as the hours passed. I thought about the work for school I'd planned to do, and worried a bit about how I'd manage if I couldn't find time to do it, and I wondered about how I'd get through the time back at

Loughview, when presumably Colin would regale me with a blow-by-blow account of the good news.

Then I remembered Thompson's Law and scolded myself for thinking about the future and worrying about something that might not even happen. For a few brief moments, I allowed myself to think about Alan and to remember the feel of his arms around me. But I put that memory out of mind quickly. It was too important, too disturbing, too precious. Somehow, I just had to keep my mind on here and now, however awful it was.

I did my best to eat what Maisie put in front of me, but between my headache and the stringiness of the chicken I made a pretty poor job of it.

'Come on, Jenny, another glass of wine. Do you good. Put some colour in your cheeks, girl,' said William John as he leaned across the table.

'Perhaps, Daddy, Jennifer isn't feeling too well today,' Maisie said, as she promptly thrust out her own empty glass. 'She's been very quiet. Hardly said a word since you arrived, have you, Jennifer?' she went on, looking at me sharply.

I had noticed earlier how much her vowels had lengthened since Colin's arrival. Now I observed that 'feeling' too had a 'g' on the end of it, just like 'starving' had had earlier. Her mother would be proud of her, I thought uncharitably, as she glanced at me sideways, a far from friendly look in her eye. Always, when Maisie was going out, her mother would tell her to remember her name was Margaret, to use only the lace-trimmed hanky in company, and to make sure she minded her 'ings'. That way, she might do as well as her sister Edith had.

'Oh, not a bit of it, Mum,' Colin broke in. 'We haven't given you much chance to say anything since we arrived back, have we, darling?' He turned towards me with his most engaging smile and I felt his knee rub against mine under the table. 'Tell us now, how were things up at home? Tell us all about it. Especially Susie. How was she?'

'Oh, they're all flourishing,' I said lightly.

'And can Susie say the names of all the flowers yet?' Colin turned to his mother. 'You know, poor old Susie can't say long words yet and Jen's been trying to teach her. She gets all mixed up, doesn't she, Jen?'

'Actually, it's only the sounds she has any difficulty with, Colin, not the words themselves,' I replied, rather tartly. 'She's quite clear about what she wants to say.'

'That's what I meant, love. She keeps getting her words all wrong. Absolutely delightful and very funny too. Of course, Mum, Susie thinks Jen is the greatest thing since the sliced loaf . . .'

And with that, he was well launched into a Susie Saga. As I listened, I wondered if he hadn't missed a great career in writing for television. He had an unerring talent for failing to understand what had actually been said and an even greater talent for trivialising what he thought he'd understood. Only someone with a real gift for sitcom could turn Susie's intelligent and determined efforts to overcome her difficulties into jolly family entertainment.

'And do you remember, Jen, the day we took her to Bellevue and she wanted to see a gillaffe? A gillaffe,' he repeated, as he downed the last of his wine and leaned back so that his mother could clear away the dinner plates.

Well, Jen, there you have it, I said to myself, your bit of the action. He plays *wunderkind* to himself, lackey to William John, golden boy to Maisie and indulgent husband to you. 'Dearest' and 'darling' and 'Jen love' to keep me as sweet as he keeps them. And all with absolutely no expenditure of effort on his part. Perhaps this afternoon's little performance was worth having after all, just for the record.

I was still thinking about just how clearly I was seeing Colin's new, upgraded director-oriented style when I realised, to my intense surprise, that Maisie was dismissing us. It wasn't that she wouldn't like us to stay for coffee, she said effusively, but she realised how much we would have to talk about, and besides, she knew there were always things to do on a Sunday night and that I had to be up early in the morning for school.

A couple of looks passed between Colin and Maisie as she spoke that puzzled me, but I was so relieved to find we were going that I didn't really pay much attention. For the first time in living memory, we left the house without one of them remembering something to tell Colin, or something we were to take with us, or something to be arranged for the future.

I got into the car, leaned back in my seat and closed my eyes.

'Headache?'

'Mmmmm.'

'Taken anything?'

'Yes, twice.'

'Well, you just lie back and have a rest till we get home,' he said sympathetically. 'I think I've got some news that will get rid of that nasty old head. But good news can wait a little longer.'

I saw him smile to himself as he turned out onto the Antrim Road and settled down to drive at an unusually moderate pace. I kept my eyes shut and gave thanks. At this rate I'd have at least forty minutes of relative quiet before the action began again. Feeling as I did, I reckoned I'd better make the best of it.

Chapter 18

I woke with a jerk as we hit a familiar pothole at the junction between the main road and the private road down to Loughview. The green fields and the gentle sunshine of my dreams was replaced by the darkness of nightfall, and the feeling of freedom and wellbeing disappeared without trace as we drew up with the bonnet of the car almost touching the wrought-iron gates.

'Got your keys, Jen?' Colin asked, looking across at me and smiling. 'We may as well put her away now and have done with it. We'll be otherwise engaged later, won't we?'

I scuffled in my bag, got out of the car, and opened the gates. As I stood aside to let him drive through, the full impact of his words struck home. 'Otherwise engaged' was his usual way of indicating that sex was what he had in mind.

As I hurried up the drive and struggled with the up and over door, I felt a sudden violent nausea. Given how I was feeling, it wouldn't matter what he called it. I knew I didn't love him, and I most certainly didn't desire him. But I couldn't see how Thompson's Law was going to help me this time. If Colin insisted we made love, I was sure I would react violently. I could not bear him to touch me ever again.

Not after last night. Not after experiencing the difference between really making love and being involved in Colin's particular brand of sexual engagement. Perhaps 'otherwise engaged' was a good way of describing it, after all. But that reflection wasn't going to help me if the question of lovemaking should arise this evening.

My headache had subsided for the moment. It was not a migraine, but I knew from experience it was one of those heads that sits, like a dragon, waiting to pounce. Treat it with kindness and respect and it will lie down quietly, or even go to sleep. Upset it and it will go on the rampage. It had protested vigorously enough at the scrape of the unoiled hinges on the garage door. Let that be a warning.

I put on the hall light, hung up my coat, and dropped my handbag in its usual place on the chair in the cloakroom. I heard Colin close the garage from the inside and come into the kitchen, just as I got there myself.

'What's all that vegetation in the garage, Jen?' he said jovially. 'I nearly did myself an injury when I got out of the car.'

'Vegetation?'

'Yes. Wretched spiky stuff. You must have been pruning. Look!' He picked up a small frond of bronzed bracken from his trousers as he flopped down onto a chair.

The whole bloody double garage to park in after I've cleared it out and he has to land right up against my branches, I thought. Aloud, I said, 'Oh, did you tramp on it? I thought I'd left it well out of the way.'

There was an edge in my voice which wouldn't do. It would be just like us to have a row about him tramping on my bracken and hawthorn when there were much more pressing issues on the agenda. Thompson's Law, I said to myself, hastily, like a mantra for warding off evil.

'It was bracken and hawthorn I brought back for the stone jar in the hall,' I said, more steadily.

'Brought back from where?'

'Drinsallagh. Alan's bought a cottage down there.'

'Oh yes,' he said, without showing the slightest sign of interest. 'Why don't we make some coffee and take it into the lounge and then I can tell you all about the weekend.'

The tale of his dinner with William John went on and on, full of blow-by-blow accounts of what he'd said to William John and self-congratulations as to how well he'd put it. It seemed he'd done very well over the last twelve months. Now they were to set up a new branch in Derry, they needed to increase the number of directors, so he'd been given his place on the board. He told me about the salary, the company car and the extra weeks of holiday we would have, and the details of his own expense account and our entertainment allowance.

He had rehearsed so many of the details, so often, there was little I'd not already heard many, many times before. And yet I found myself listening hard, strangely attentive, even while wondering why I was listening so closely to something that surely could have so little relevance for me.

'So, there you are, Jen,' he wound up at last. 'That's the good news. Now let's hear all about your weekend. Did Val and Bob have their party down at Alan's new place?'

I laughed in spite of myself. 'Goodness, no. The cottage is far too small. It hasn't even got a bathroom yet.'

'So when did you see it?'

'We went down from the party. It has got electric light.'

He shifted uncomfortably in his chair. 'I say, Jen, you don't honestly mean you went sloping off with old Thompson, at dead of night, to some cottage in the back of beyond?'

'And why not?'

'Well, I mean to say . . . no reason at all, Jen, if you felt you wanted to,' he said, trying to appear easy about it. 'But you know how the crowd talk. I mean, if someone spotted you, I'd get a bit of a ribbing, now wouldn't I?'

A bit of a ribbing, I repeated silently to myself. 'And would that matter, Colin?'

'Well, no, of course not. But you know what the crowd are like. Someone might get the wrong idea.' He paused, flustered. Then he rattled on even more hastily, 'I mean, I never would for one moment, Jen. But you can't expect everyone to understand as I do. You know you can't be too careful with that lot. I don't give a hang for other people, any more than you do, but it does make life easier if you give them no opportunity.'

'Easier for whom, Colin?' I said, my voice quiet and perfectly calm. 'And no opportunity for what?'

'Well, everybody,' he said blandly, shrugging his shoulders. 'And people do talk. Especially if they get the wrong idea, you know. I mean it's obvious, isn't it?' he added as he got up to pour himself more coffee.

'It's obvious to me, Colin, that you think, in your new position, you cannot afford for your wife to be seen with an old friend who happens to be male, unless of course he's one of the crowd, which clearly Alan isn't. Is that it?'

I watched him bluster and try to get himself out of

the mess he'd made. I could predict his lines. A general-purpose collection of clichés that would indicate just how reasonable, liberal and understanding he was, and how, of course, I really hadn't quite appreciated his point, had I, or I would have had to agree with him immediately.

'So how could you imagine I'd think anything of you going off with old Thompson just because I said it might have been better if you hadn't gone to the cottage after the party?'

He had been struggling with one of those miniature cartons of cream that are so hard to open. Now, having succeeded, he tipped the whole lot into his cup and leaned back comfortably in his armchair, his legs stretched out full length, the coffee cup perched on his stomach. He looked completely easy and relaxed.

'And what about me and old Keith?' I asked quietly. 'Now that you're a full director, would you rather I wasn't seen in his company either? He could hardly manage to seduce me in his present condition, but perhaps his politics might.'

He said nothing, but the grin disappeared.

'What do you think?' I went on. 'Would you rather I stroked him off my list too, just to be on the safe side? Like the way you and your parents did, this afternoon?'

Whether it was what I actually said or the icy tone that had crept into it, he moved his coffee to the arm of his chair, sat up sharply and began to pay real attention to what I was saying. Such a rare event was fascinating to observe but even more so was the way he really exerted himself to put me straight and show me what had actually happened. 'Do you want Keith to serve a prison sentence?'

he asked. 'Do you want him sent down in his third year?' Surely I appreciated he'd done everything he could to help Keith.

'Keith or McKinstry's?' I retorted, shortly.

'Now, Jen,' he said, a note of irritation creeping into his voice at last. 'I know it's been a difficult day but we're not going to argue over Keith, are we? Keith and I do see things rather differently, but that's not unreasonable, is it? Everyone's entitled to their opinion, and if Keith and I don't quite see eye to eye, then surely we can still be friends.'

'So he and Siobhan will be welcome to supper one evening this week, if Keith is well enough?'

'Well, yes . . . yes, of course, if you want them,' he said hurriedly, 'though I'll have to be away most of the week.'

'Oh, why so?' I was genuinely surprised. I couldn't imagine what would take the newest director of McKinstry's away from the pleasure of setting up his new office, collecting his new car, and christening his new expense account.

'Oh, I shall have to spend some time with our people in Derry before the branch opens,' he said easily.

That was the third time, today, the Derry branch had been mentioned, and until today, I'd not heard a word about it. With a sudden, sickening sense of dread, I saw a possibility taking shape that would put an end once and for all to any further attempts at avoidance.

'Derry? Why Derry?' I asked, with an ease I certainly did not feel.

'That's where I'll be in charge from next month. I'll be running the show up there.' He smiled cheerfully, as if he had just added a further perk to the list he'd announced earlier.

'But you can't commute to Derry,' I protested mildly. 'Not till the M1's a lot further on anyway.'

'Oh no, there's a house with the job. A very nice house, I'm told,' he grinned, reassuringly. 'But if you don't like it, we won't have it,' he went on quickly. 'We'll find our own, whatever it costs. Don't worry, Jen, I know you've never liked this house, but there's going to be no problem this time. It'll be fine, this time, just fine,' he ended confidently.

So that was it. The last piece in the puzzle. I heard again my mother's voice telling me I'd not walk over the McKinstrys the way I walked over her, and how I might see things very differently if I wasn't so near to my fine friends. Then I saw Maisie's head bent to Colin's ear, whispering when he'd arrived, and the looks they'd exchanged as we left. So this was the grand plan, ship me off to Derry, sans job, sans friends, sans everything, the one option left to me to get pregnant and fill up my empty hours with the fulltime job of company wife and mother. To my great surprise, the anger that welled up at the sheer enormity of it was a stone-cold anger that left me startlingly sure of my self-control. And what I said next was said so coolly that Colin misread it completely.

'Haven't you forgotten something, Colin?'

'Have I?' he asked, a little puzzled.

'I'm afraid you have. You've forgotten that my new job will keep me in Belfast.'

'New job?' He looked at me in amazement.

'Yes, the one you were hurrying home to discuss with

me tonight because you were too busy on Friday and Saturday to spare me even a few minutes on the phone.'

'But you only said there was some job you had to do for the Head of Department on Monday. You didn't say anything about any new job.'

'Yes, I did, Colin. I did indeed. On Friday night, at something after midnight, and on Saturday, at two minutes to six. After that call and your total lack of interest, I decided to make up my own mind, and I have. I'm accepting the job of Head of English I was offered on Friday.'

He opened his mouth and closed it again several times over. He reminded me of Susie's goldfish at feeding time. I watched, fascinated.

'But . . . but you can't, Jen. I mean, how can you . . . What about us, about you and me?'

'Us, Colin? You and me? The "lovely couple" of my dear mother's fantasies? Well, I'll tell you about us,' I began, jumping up from my chair and pulling the lounge curtains together so fiercely that the wooden rings rattled like castanets.

'Once upon a time, Colin,' I began quietly as I faced him across the length of the room, 'we set out on a life together. We were going to make it for us, our way. Then Daddy called, and Colin came running. Since the moment we came off the Liverpool boat, Colin's done whatever Daddy and Mummy have wanted because that was the way to get what he really wanted. He'd get on the board. Not just to be one of the directors, oh no, that's only a stepping stone. What he really wants is to be chairman and managing director. And the way William John smokes and drinks and eats his head off, he shouldn't have to wait all that long before he gets that too,' I said, raising my voice as he tried to interrupt.

'Meantime, Mummy thinks it's time Colin's little wifey settles down and does the big thing. Should have done it sooner, Colin dear, shouldn't we, to keep her sweet. But never mind, Mummy'll fix it. All she has to do is feed William John the idea that you could do the Derry job and, bingo, two for the price of one: her golden boy is a director and his little wifey is carted off to where she'll be safely away from her friends and that dreadful liberal old father of hers, who brought her up to have a mind of her own and actually encouraged her to think Catholics are human beings too. Then the McKinstrys can really live happily ever after. Or rather, Maisie can. Keith out of the way, William John playing his harp, her dear son with "such a lovely family" and now able to make a complete fool of himself over his children the way he did over Susie tonight.' I paused and glared at him. He stared back at me, his expression a mixture of sheer incomprehension and growing hostility.

'There's one small problem with that cosy scenario, Colin, just one little problem,' I went on, dropping my voice to a whisper. 'I'm not going to Derry with you. In fact, I'm not going anywhere with you. It's finished, Colin. The show's over, over and done with. No more playing the lovely young couple, no more Edna and Maisie ganging up to decide my future for me, and no more of your endless self-regarding talk to endure. I've had enough of all of it.'

The last words came out as a croak, as my voice finally packed up on me.

'Jen, for goodness sake, what on earth are you talking about? You're tired . . .'

Suddenly the sight of him, visibly pulling himself back together and reaching out for his all-purpose verbal fire extinguisher made me so angry I could have hit him. Sitting there, his shirt buttons straining over his flabby midriff, I could see him lining up all the old well-worn, soggy phrases I knew so well I could have said them for him.

'Yes, I am,' I shouted, ignoring the ache in my throat. 'Yes, Colin, I'm tired of the whole shabby show. Tired. Tired. Tired. And most of all, I'm tired of seeing you manoeuvre and manipulate your way to wherever you want to go. And I'm sick of seeing you try to humour and sweeten me the way you humour and sweeten everyone else. Offering me goodies, houses and holidays, good dinners and my own little car, as if that was what it was all about. Can't you see, all I ever wanted was you to be yourself. Well, I've got what I wanted, with a vengeance. You're yourself all right, but it's a self I can't live with. I got it wrong, Colin. I got it wrong. And when you think about it, so did you. You should have asked Mummy what sort of a girl you needed for the part before you got mixed up with me. When she did get a good look at me, she only let you sign me on because she thought she could train me up to do the job properly, with a helping hand from my own dear mother. Like a bloody performing seal. Well, I won't be trained, coaxed, brow-beaten, bullied. Not any more. So I'm no good to you. And I'm putting an end to it. Now. This minute.'

My throat was so dry it forced me to stop. And the dragon in my head had woken up and was tramping around, breathing daggers into my forehead, making it pound so furiously, all I wanted to do was close my eyes.

'I need a drink of water,' I croaked, and strode out of the lounge.

I ran the water hard until it was really cold, filled a glass and stood leaning against the sink, drinking it slowly. In the unlit kitchen, a faint light from the sky reflected back from the white surfaces. Beyond the window, the lough lay dark, the moon obscured by cloud. There was such comfort in the dark, and such comfort in the silence after the brightly-lit lounge and the sound of my own voice.

I heard Colin run upstairs. The bathroom door banged shut above my head. I heard him pee. It seemed to go on for ever. Then the loo flushed. I heard him on the stairs again, then in the hall, and then at the open kitchen door. I winced as he touched the switch. Batteries of lights in the ceiling, over the cooker and under the eye-level cupboards flashed into life. He stood there watching me as I ignored him and went on drinking.

'Look, Jen, I do realise I should have told you about Derry first. I was going to tell you tomorrow evening, when we'd more time to discuss it. I'm sorry I've upset you. Really I am,' he said earnestly.

I smiled weakly. Colin was very good at apologising. I supposed he got lots of practice. I could even believe he meant it. But he was wasting his breath.

'Jen, I know you're not feeling well. Why don't I phone school tomorrow and tell them you've a bad head?' he went on smoothly, as if I was open to being persuaded. 'I'm not going into the office tomorrow, I'm meeting Robinson at the Crawfordsburn for lunch. You could come too. They do a very nice lunch. And we'd have lots of time to talk in the morning. I'm sure we can sort it all out. Come on, Jen.'

The glass was empty. I looked at it and thought of throwing it at him. Hard. Instead, I found myself speaking quite quietly, as if I were actually responding to the tired old routine.

'All right. I'll come.' I paused and he brightened visibly. 'But only if you'll ring William John now, tonight, and tell him we're not going to Derry.'

In another play, that could have been a genuine last appeal. But in this script, it was purely for effect. I had made my appeals long, long ago. Time after time, back in Birmingham and in the weeks after the call came that would take us back home to Ulster. And again and again once we'd returned. He had refused me then, and he had gone on refusing me ever since. And now the outcome I had feared so much, only last night, was already an accomplished fact.

The end of our life together had not come out there in the car with Alan on Windmill Hill, weeping as if my heart would break. Nor had it been here, tonight, in this brightly lit kitchen. The end had come and gone, quite unnoticed, before ever we got on the boat. All I was doing tonight was spelling out for us both what had been over and gone for a long time now.

'Not go to Derry?' he stuttered. He looked completely horrified and rather frightened. William John had never been a man to say no to, and never forgot or forgave anyone who did. 'But Jen, I can't do that. I mean . . .'

'I know perfectly well what you mean, Colin, it's only

too obvious, but I don't think you've yet grasped what I mean. I'll say it once more and then I'm going to bed. It's over, Colin, the charade we've been playing out these last two years. I'm leaving you. I'm going out of this house tomorrow and I'm not coming back.'

I rinsed the glass, left it to dry in the dishrack and slid past him into the hall.

'Jen, be reasonable,' he called after me.

I marched upstairs without looking back and went straight to the wardrobe in what had once been our bedroom. I heard him locking up. By the time he came upstairs, I'd draped tomorrow's clothes on a hanger, collected underwear and make-up from my dressing table and taken them into my study. As I carried in my dressing gown and nightie, we met face to face on the landing.

'Now look, Jen, there's no need to be like this,' he started, something like desperation creeping into his voice. 'We're both tired out. It'll all look different in the morning. Come on, come to bed.' He put out his arm, just like the way he'd offered me his free arm in the hallway of Myrtlefield House. I ducked under it and slipped into my room.

'Goodnight,' I said, furiously, as I shut the door.

I sat on the bed, rigid with tension, afraid he would knock or come in, as the door had no lock, or start talking through it. But as the minutes passed and no sound came, I began to relax. It was just possible he was 'being sensible'. I could imagine him telling himself that I was best left alone. It would all be different in the morning. All we needed was a good night's sleep and all would be fine, just fine.

After a little, I got up and put out the light which was hurting my head, took off my shoes and crept around making preparations for bed. As each minute passed, I felt easier. Eventually, I sat down at my desk and drew towards me the tiny vase of full-blown roses I had brought back from Drinsallagh. One of them had shed its petals and I collected up the scented leaves from the windowsill, held them in my hand, and breathed in their faint, distant perfume.

Only last evening, Alan had stood here with me, looking out at the moonlight on the lough. He had done his best to reassure me. He'd given me Thompson's Law. I had seen such a long and bitter disengagement ahead of me, I had feared for my own stamina, my ability to cope with what I expected to have lined up against me. But there would be no battle. It was already past. Over. So soon, so incredibly soon. Words had been spoken that could not be recalled. However Colin might argue or try to persuade, there was no way back from the point I had reached. I was out. Out into a space where I could breathe again. And as if to underline my thoughts, the moon came out from behind a cloud and filled the whole room with its radiance. Then it was gone again, but the brief moment lingered like the faint fragrance from the fallen petals I still held in my hand.

Chapter 19

When I was quite sure that Colin was asleep I drew the curtains, put on a lamp and began to put my things together for school in the morning. I had just closed my briefcase, set my alarm for six thirty and got into my nightie when I realised I was thirsty again. I'd been thirsty all evening, after the packet sauce Maisie had poured so liberally over that wretched chicken. The more I thought about it, the more thirsty I became. A glass of water from the bathroom had no appeal at all, but the idea of a pot of tea, all to myself, began to beckon as invitingly as a mirage in a desert.

Don't be silly, Jenny. It's after eleven, I said to myself as I pushed my feet into my slippers, tiptoed to the door and listened. There was no sound at all in the house. Even the central heating had stopped clicking. Encouraged, I crept soundlessly downstairs. As I reached the foot, the telephone rang. My hand went out for it so quickly I hardly realised what I'd done as I lifted it to my ear.

'Jenny?'

The voice was quiet yet familiar. For a moment, I didn't recognise it.

'I'm sorry if I wakened you. Mavis and I have been talking and she insisted I phone you . . . and I think she's quite right . . . and you won't be upset with me . . .'

Harvey. A Harvey who'd been talking to Mavis. Surely he wasn't going to apologise for his part at lunchtime or this morning. And yet his tone sounded distinctly chastened, as if he really did regret something he'd done.

'No, of course I won't, Harvey,' I said, still confused.

'I'm afraid, Jenny, Daddy's had another heart attack. He's in intensive care, but he's quite stable. Mavis felt you would want to know tonight, though there's nothing any of us can do till the morning. He's heavily sedated.'

I sat down on the telephone bench and looked at the dappled shadows on the hall carpet. It's the chestnut tree on the main road, fluttering across the light from the lamp standard, that makes the pattern, I thought. Then the words sunk in and I wondered whatever I was going to say next.

'Are you all right, Jenny?'

'Yes. Yes, I'm all right,' I said very quietly. 'Is Mummy there with him?'

'No, no,' he said quickly. 'She's much too upset. She's gone next door to Mrs Allen and taken a sleeping tablet. I've told her I'll ring the Royal at seven thirty for a full report. Would you like me to ring you too, Jenny?'

'Yes, Harvey, I would.'

He said something quite kindly about trying to get some sleep and I asked him to thank Mavis for persuading him to ring, that I'd rather know. I put the phone down and wondered quite how I'd come to be sitting here beside it when the call came.

It seemed a long time later when I opened the reminder pad at the card I'd sellotaped to its back cover the day after we'd moved in. 'Helen's Bay Taxis,' it read. 'Anytime. Anywhere. Distance no object.' It sounded like the lyric for a popular song.

'Taxi.' A woman's voice. Abrupt. With a strong Belfast accent.

'I need a taxi to the Royal Victoria, as soon as possible. Can you manage that?'

'Name and address?'

I had to spell out most of it for her and it seemed to take a long, long time. There were noises in the background. Surely she wouldn't say they couldn't do it after taking so long over the details.

'Ten minits be alrite?'

'Yes, oh yes. Thank you . . . oh, and could you ask the taxi man not to ring the bell. I'll be watching for him.'

'Aye, surely, I'll tell 'im. Goodnite now.'

'Goodnight.'

I stood up, took a deep breath and ran silently back upstairs. I dressed in the clothes I'd left out for the morning, put my make-up in my handbag and reached for my briefcase. As I shut the study door quietly behind me, I realised I ought to leave a note. I grabbed a sheet of A4 from my desk and wrote:

Dear Colin,

Daddy is ill and I've gone to the Royal. I won't be back, but you can contact me via Bob Dawson when you want to sort things out. Talk it over with Maisie. I bet she'll say 'Good riddance'. Good luck with Derry.

Jenny.

As I came down the stairs I heard the whoosh of tyres. I picked up my handbag, remembered I'd almost no money and cursed myself. Long ago, after being caught in Birmingham without the cash for a ticket home, I'd carefully hidden £25 in an evening bag in my dressing table. But I couldn't go up and get it now. I'd just have to manage.

I looked around me, as if there were something I might have forgotten, but no, clear in my mind that only one thing mattered at this moment, I went to the door. As I put my hand to the catch, I saw a shadowy figure on the other side and opened it hurriedly, in case he should press the bell.

But I need not have worried. The man who stood there had his hands in his pockets, his eyes firmly on the ground. For a moment I didn't recognise him. Only when he looked up at me and said, 'Father?' with an upward jerk of his pale blue eyes, did I realise it was Ernie Taggart.

'Afraid so,' I said.

He reached out his hand for my briefcase. 'I heard yer call when I was waitin' at me brother-in-law's. Soon as I heard ye, I thought, that's the father.'

He marched me down the drive so quickly I could hardly keep up, put the briefcase in the back seat and me in the front.

'Is he bad?'

For a moment I couldn't speak. There was something about his hasty, minimal utterances that carried more real sympathy than yards of Colin's sympathetic flannel.

'Not good, Ernie. They say he's stable. But I'm not so sure.'

No wonder I hadn't recognised him, I thought, as I looked across at him. His face was so clean it almost shone, his hair was sleeked back, and he was wearing a navy suit, with a bright Fair Isle pullover underneath. But the suit still hung on him, like his overalls, as if he had inherited it from someone much better covered than he was.

'Don't let the bad leg worry ye,' he said, shortly. 'I'm a gude driver an' I oney need that'un fer the brake. Will I put me fut down?'

Hours. Was it only hours ago Daddy had asked the same question. And I had said no, because I wanted his company for as long as possible crossing the small, private space between Rathmore Drive and Myrtlefield House.

'Yes, please, Ernie. The sooner I get there the better,' I said, as the tears sprang to my eyes and poured unheeded down my cheeks.

The dark clouds that cut off the moonlight as I stood drinking my glass of water in the kitchen at Loughview had built up in the hours that had passed. Now, as we moved swiftly into the city, rain came sheeting down. Gusts of wind caught the car on exposed corners, buffeting it and sending the raindrops streaming across the top of the windscreen out of the reach of the wipers.

There was little traffic about and not a soul in sight as we swished through the empty streets, the gutters streaming. We stopped at traffic lights, the only car at notoriously busy junctions. We drove on over the myriad reflections of shop windows, road signs and pedestrian crossings into yet more dark and deserted streets. Beyond the windscreen, the world was chill and unwelcoming, bereft of all comfort.

'Will ye stay all nite?'

My tears had dried on my cheeks and Ernie's eyes were

fixed firmly on the road ahead. I swallowed hard and moistened my dry lips.

'Yes, I'll stay. If he's no better in the morning, I'll ring school and ask for some time off.'

'Are they dacent about that in yer place?'

'I don't know, Ernie. The headmistress seems a very cold person. But she's very fair. You can't always tell, can you?'

''Deed no. There's many a one would surprise ye when things is bad, like yer father,' he said thoughtfully. 'They've rooms now fer close fam'ly. Ye'll maybe get a wee sleep whin ye've seed him and set yer mind at rest.'

I found myself smiling. I liked 'seed' as the past tense of 'see'. It made me think of my job, the work at Queen's Crescent, the books I carried in my briefcase. Work with words and with the understandings only words can carry. How very strange that such a thought should come to comfort me, speeding through this empty, hostile world.

'I'll certainly be better when I get a look at him,' I replied, grateful to find words again after the tearful silence that had come upon me.

'Nat far now. Am takin' ye to the Falls Road entrance. It's not as far ta walk wonst ye get in. Ye coud walk miles in thon place.'

For all Ernie's thoughtfulness, it still felt like miles when I did start walking down the familiar corridors, the tap of my heels echoing back from tiled walls, their vibrations speeding ahead of me to collide with the parked trolleys and the closed doors labelled in large letters. The further I walked and the nearer I got to my destination, the more endless they seemed. By the time I arrived, cold sweat was breaking on my brow. I pressed the bell and waited for someone to come and let me in.

It was the sister herself, a small square woman with the kind of chest that would accommodate a row of medals. I looked down at her and identified myself. She nodded abruptly, waved me into her office, sat me down and looked me over. I dropped my eyes, not able to cope yet with what I read in her expression.

'Your father's a very sick man, Jennifer. Do you realise that?'

I nodded, relieved, for I had begun to fear I was already too late. 'I've been here before. Two years ago. I know about the spaghetti and the monitors . . .'

'Good,' she said firmly, with a hint of a smile at the mention of the 'spaghetti'. 'Would you like to sit with him? He's heavily sedated, as you'd expect. He's unlikely to come round before morning.'

I stood up, made it clear that I understood, and waited for her to lead the way. She paused, took up her case notes, and put them down again.

'I'm afraid he is also on a ventilator,' she said gently. 'The breathing was erratic, even after sedation. There is also a kidney problem. We shall have to begin dialysis in the morning.'

'Thank you for telling me, Sister. But I really would like to see him.'

'This way.'

She turned on her heel and led me down the short, crowded entrance corridor, double-parked with equipment, linen trolleys, and oxygen cylinders, into the very large space that lay beyond. The lights had been dimmed for the night and the whole place glowed with a greenish hue. There were only four beds tonight in all that huge space, but as I ran my eye round, I caught sight of a young woman sitting in one of the glass-fronted alcoves. Our eyes met for a moment and softened in sympathy. In the bed where she kept watch a small blonde child lay asleep, its thumb in its mouth, its tiny body constrained by the mass of tubes and wires, the 'spaghetti', which could mean the difference between life and death.

'I think this side will be easier for you,' Sister said crisply.

I looked down at my father's pale face. A tube hung out of his mouth on the right side, distorting it. The squarish machine beyond looked just like one of the drinks trolleys parked in the corridor outside, except that it made a rhythmic noise, huffing like a blacksmith's bellows. Most of the usual tubes for hydration and medication were bandaged into his right arm or the right side of his neck. There were wires taped to his bare chest. They criss-crossed like a spider's web, feeding into the monitors that printed their ragged messages across flickering screens. Beyond them, his left hand lay inert but intact, outside his covering of textured cotton blanket.

I sat down on the moulded plastic chair which had suddenly appeared and took his hand in mine. It was warm and mine were stone cold, so I took them away again and rubbed them together. When they were less cold, I took up his hand again and told him that I had come.

Minutes passed, each one so full of thoughts and memories. I watched his face, taught myself not to see the sad distortion of his mouth. I watched the monitors, well able to translate their messages, a language I had learnt in this same classroom two years ago. Figures that recorded the minute rise and fall of blood pressure, oscillating lines that continually created and then recreated mountains with foothills and unbridgeable oceanic chasms. A pattern, rock steady, despite all its variations. So stable. As my father's presence had been throughout all of my life.

Time passed. My hands were warmer now than his. Hardly surprising, when the ward sat at seventy degrees and I was still wearing my three-quarter length winter coat. I slid it off, one-handed, so that I didn't have to break the precious contact that had strengthened between us as the minutes had slowly turned into hours.

I closed my eyes for a moment and saw him smile. 'Look,' he said, laughing, and there on the hillside stood a lad, barefoot, the backside out of his trousers, which were short but still too long for him. I waited for the neighbour to appear. Sure enough, there he was. A big boy on an enormous horse, its back as broad as a table. 'Wee Georgie Erwin,' he called, looking down, and I felt cross. 'How dare he?' I said to my father. But my father just laughed. 'Sticks and stones can break my bones, but names can never hurt me,' he chanted, singing out the old rhyme that all we children knew. 'Don't worry, Jenny. It's all right. It's all right.'

I jerked awake, his words still in my ears. It's the warmth, I thought to myself, and the purr of the ventilator. Now I'd got used to it, it was rather soothing. Reliable, too, doing its job. Breathing for Daddy so that he could sleep in peace. And tomorrow, surely, he would feel better.

Chapter 20

I heard footsteps, firm but very soft, and saw Sister had come to scan the monitors. She looked down at me, a small smile on her face.

'I hear you went to school with Maureen Coleman.'

'Yes, yes I did,' I responded, surprised by a name I hadn't heard for four or five years.

'Maureen was here when your Daddy came in. She's a ward sister now. Did you know that? She's having her break now and I think you ought to go and have a cup of tea with her,' she added firmly. 'You need a wee break yourself, but I'll stay here till you come back. I'll come for you if there's any change at all,' she said reassuringly as she saw my flicker of anxiety.

I hesitated, but I knew I could trust her, so I tiptoed down the ward, aware how noisy my heels would be on the tiled floor as I passed the sleeping child. Once in the corridor, I headed for the visitors' room.

'Jenny!'

I stopped, confused, as a dark-haired young woman stepped out of the office and took my arm, leading me into the empty staffroom.

'Jenny, I'm so sorry about your father. Here, sit down and drink a cup of tea.' She poured it out and handed it to me.

'I thought you were still in London, Maureen,' I said awkwardly as I tried to collect my thoughts. 'I couldn't even think for a moment who Maureen Coleman was when Sister came and said your name. I am sorry, I'm a bit through myself, as my mother would say.'

'Never you mind, sure you've good cause,' she said, pressing my arm. 'I have a message for you from your daddy,' she went on quietly.

I looked up, startled, as she took my hand.

'Jenny, dear, he was quite lucid when he came in. I don't actually think he had an awful lot of pain and he recognised me right away. Sister didn't want him to talk but he wasn't going to let that bother him. He said to tell you "It's all right". He made me repeat it twice, so I'd get it right. Not "I'm all right" but "It's all right". Is that any help to you, Jenny?'

I nodded hard, because the tears had jumped up on me again and were pouring down my face without my permission. I had no hanky in the pocket of my skirt and my bag was down in the ward beside my chair.

'There, love, it's hard. It's very hard,' she said as she put a ragged slice of kitchen roll into my hand. 'We're supposed to have tissues in here, but people borrow them and don't bring them back,' she explained. 'Come on now, drink your tea, like a good girl.'

I laughed in spite of myself and blew my nose. 'All part of your job, Maureen?' I said, as I mopped myself up.

'It is, Jenny, it is. But it's not often it's someone I've known as long as I've known you. D'you know, I remember going round Erwin's when we were at primary school. Your father let us all take turns sitting up on the high seats of the tractors and the reapers, and he gave a prize for the best drawing of one of them. Valerie Thompson won it. Do you remember?'

Maureen talked on easily as I drank my tea, but I felt myself go quiet and the effort of responding to her warm friendliness grew harder and harder. Suddenly, I just so wanted to be with my father.

'Maureen, I must go back,' I said, standing up. 'I'm so grateful to you for that message. I'll explain about it later, before you go off duty.'

'Go ahead, Jenny,' she nodded. 'I'll be down to see you in a while. I'll be starting up the dialysis before I go,' she added as I made for the door.

I slipped my shoes off and moved hastily over the polished floor. Sister saw me come and rose to meet me, my coat over her arm.

'He seems quite steady,' she said, looking down at the still figure. 'If you feel like a wee sleep, there's a room ready for you. Just come when you feel like it,' she said, as she walked away.

The back of his hand had the brown blotches that come with age, the fingers very slightly stained from his few daily cigarettes. The lines on his palm were strong and deep etched, though the palms themselves were soft and little marked. They seemed a little colder than before.

I shivered and looked again at the sleeping body, the face unfamiliar in its impassivity. I shut my eyes and saw him smile, his face mobile, the lines round his eyes crinkled with mirth. I opened them again and spoke sharply to myself. I must not close my eyes. I must keep watch. Watch and pray.

The words came into my mind unbidden. The Bible. We had read that too, over the years. Once, I had made a collection of his favourite verses and copied them out in italic script as a present for him. The page with 'Consider the lilies of the field' I had taken to Val, and I brought it back covered with cornflowers and flag iris, primroses and bluebells. He had smiled then, too.

Watch and pray. Watch and pray.

I found my mind wandering into strange places, backwards and forwards across my life. Trivial incidents suddenly came to me, long forgotten events. And always there were images of my father smiling. When I went to him in distress, he would always say 'It's all right.' 'It's all right,' the very words I had used when Susie's little face crumpled at her sister's harsh rebuke. They were his words. I had comforted Susie as he had comforted me. But who could bring comfort to him, with his body failing as it was failing now.

Watch and pray.

The large hand of the ward clock slid silently across another minute. A quarter to four. The small hours were growing larger, the individual minutes seemed fraught with a meaning I sensed but could not grasp. Last time, I had prayed. But what was I to pray this time? Please God, let Daddy live? Was that to be my prayer?

My eyes flickered around the ward. Saw the lights and the monitors at the other beds. Saw Maureen pause by a machine, check its function. Tomorrow, a like machine would stand here. Through larger tubes, my father's blood would pour into the machine, circulate, and be returned to his inert body. A body that could no longer serve the thoughts of his mind or the wishes of his heart.

The words spoke inside my head in the old-fashioned language I had known from Sunday School and church, before I was even aware of having shaped them. 'Please God, take this good man, thy servant George, into your safekeeping, that no harm may come to him, and he may be free of all ills. Amen.'

It seemed to grow quieter in the ward, though nothing I could observe had changed. Nurses moved silently in the glass-walled side ward where I could just make out the shape of the young woman still watching by the bedside of the sleeping child. A staff nurse had come to sit at a desk in the centre of the big open space near me. She was using a small spotlight to fill in forms and study charts. Light reflected upwards from her papers and cast a warm glow on her fresh and pleasant country girl's face. The ventilator huffed gently.

I stood at the door, looking into the dark. Behind me, the sunshine spilled down on a straggling village. From a broad, shallow stream beyond the dusty trackway where I stood I could hear the sound of children's voices. Gradually, my eyes grew accustomed to the darkness. A great coil of creamy smoke rose from a raised hearth. The soft sound was the bellows, huffing air so that the mound of smoking fuel began to glow at the centre. I watched the glow, fascinated, till suddenly the whole place rang with sound. A hammer danced on the anvil, strong, heavy blows interspersed with light caressing taps, rising to a crescendo and then falling away to silence. I saw the glowing heart of the fire pierced with metal.

'Aye, Georgie lad, I'll miss ye sore on Munday. Ye've

been a gran' worker and grate cump'ney.'

I drew my eyes from the fire and saw the young man who leaned so lightly on the bellows. His face was brown from wind and sun, his forehead streaked with soot. His eyes sparkled with pleasure at the older man's words.

'An' ye've been a grate fren' te me, Robert, an' te ma mather whin she was poorly. I'm sad ta gae,' he said warmly.

'Aye, but ye mun. This is nae place for a lad the likes o' ye. Ye'll make yer way. But yer a mite braver than ye wer whin yer come. That'll stan' t' ye.'

The smith drew the metal from the fire with heavy iron tongs and held it, vibrant with colour, on the anvil. At the first blow, the sparks arced and flew around me, but before I could draw back they had dissolved harmlessly in the warm air. The forge rang again with the rhythmic music of the hammer.

Once more the metal went into the fire. The gentle huff raised the orange glow to gold. The young man leaned effortlessly on the bellows and looked across at the smith, a tall, broad-shouldered man wearing a battered leather apron, its strings tied at the front.

'D'ye mine my first day, Robert?' he asked.

'Aye, I do lad,' the older man replied, laughing. 'I thocht I'd kilt you, yer wer tha' tired. Yer were so willin', I wasnae watchin' ye half well enow. But I caut mesel' on. I tawt ye a trick or two forby.'

'Ah, moren a few. I'll be iver in yer debt,' the young man replied. His cheerful grin disappeared and he became thoughtful. He had grey eyes and a shock of black hair. 'Do ye mine, Robert, sayin' to me, "Georgie, pace yersel'.

No use goin' at it like a bull at a gate. Give it the time it needs. Don't rush it."?'

'Aye, Ah do. An' I mine me father sayin' the same words to me, the first day I stood here. The auld pepil had ther own wisdom, Georgie. It's a foolish man fergets it whin times change. But ye'll nae ferget, I'm thinkin'. There's more to ye, Georgie Erwin, thin a pare o' hans.'

I blinked sharply. I was sure I had not taken my eyes away from the still figure whose hand I held in mine. But I had been in the forge. I had seen the young man who had set out from the glen to take the job in Ballymena that would launch him towards having his own business. The forge was long gone, my memories and the name of a modern bungalow built on the site its only trace.

I looked down at the dear familiar face, so pale, so peaceful, and then, to my surprise, I found myself addressing an audience of shadowy figures who seemed to have joined us. They were all people he knew, like Robert, my grandfather, of whom he was so fond, and Ellen, his mother. And aunts and cousins, and people he'd worked with, and farmers he'd shaken hands with and passed the time of day with. Many of them I knew, many more were just names I had heard and remembered for his sake.

'My father is a countryman,' I began, silently. 'One of his greatest joys in life is to walk in the sunshine on a fine spring morning,' I continued, as I saw a path rise before me. 'Up a green slope, with the birds singing in the hedgerows and the light glancing off the dewdrops hanging from the hawthorn hedge. Up and up to the brow of the hill, a hill with an outlook.'

I glanced up myself, prompted by my own words, and saw a small mountain on the monitor screen had become a jagged peak. In absolute silence, it fell to the ocean depths and rose again, yet higher. I looked across to the desk, and for what seemed an eternity of time could not remember the word I needed.

'Nurse,' I said urgently as I stood up and pulled my chair away from the bed.

She was the first to reach him. I saw her take the tube from his mouth and lean across him. But by then the place was full of people. I stood mesmerised as I saw a trolley race down the ward, propelled by four young people. How could they know to come, and move so fast, when I had taken so long to speak one word?

'Jennifer, I'm Helen, would you come with me, please? We mustn't get in the way.'

I protested feebly, knowing well enough what the rules were. 'Please, don't worry about me. I know my way. You may be needed here.'

She smiled and put an arm gently round my shoulders. 'The full team's here, they don't need me. I'll keep you company. Would you like a cup of tea?'

'No, thank you, but that's very kind. I think this may be the last one.'

She nodded gently. 'You might be right.'

We sat in the visitors' waiting room and talked about her summer holiday and her boyfriend. I inquired about the little blonde girl and heard that she was going to be all right. It seemed the most normal thing in the world to sit here and chat to a pleasant unknown girl with all my mind fifty yards away.

'You're very brave, Jennifer,' she said suddenly, after a little.

I shook my head. 'No, I'm an absolute coward, but I don't want him to suffer.'

'Would you like me to go and see what's happening?'

'Yes, please.'

Minutes passed. I wiped my damp hands with the crumpled piece of kitchen roll from my skirt pocket. Figures passed the open door. The young people who had sped down the ward with the trolley, like students in a charity pram race, returned more slowly to wherever they had come from. A tall doctor strode past going the other way, the tails of his white coat flying, a stethoscope round his neck.

I was staring out of the window when I heard a firm but soft footfall at the door. It was the sister, a small smile on her face.

'Has he gone?' I asked, turning towards her.

'Yes, Jennifer, he has.'

'I think I'm glad.'

She came towards me, and to my surprise gave me a little hug. 'Sometimes we're glad too. Would you like to go and see him?'

She came with me to the entrance to the unit and then slipped away into her office, leaving me free to walk alone towards the large circle of screens which had appeared around my father's bed. Like a settler's encampment, I thought, as I found the small gap and went through.

All the machines and tubes and wires had gone. I could walk up to him, take his hand. It was warmer than mine now. It was joined with the other across his chest and the right one had elastoplast on it.

You look as if you've been pruning, I said silently, as I observed the chair, a proper chair, not a plastic stackable, that had been left for me. I looked down at it and stayed standing.

'You managed it, Daddy, didn't you? You nipped off up the hill to the top before they caught you. I hope it has a good outlook,' I said quietly.

I patted his bare shoulder, kissed his cheek and went back through the barricades. He wasn't there any more, so why should I stay? I'd know where to find him whenever I wanted him, now he was free.

I waved and smiled to the young woman by the little girl's bed and walked on out of the ward, feeling life flowing back into me again, bringing me a joy and a light-heartedness I could not begin to understand.

Chapter 21

It was just before six o'clock when the dark-haired student nurse pulled the door shut behind her and left me alone in the small, hospital-clean bedroom. A white towelling bathrobe lay on the narrow bed. On the bedside cabinet, a Gideon Bible, a flask of water, and a small posy of flowers. To each according to their need, I said to myself, as I sat down on the edge of the bed and let my shoes drop gently to the floor.

I went round the room opening cupboards and drawers, curious to see what other provisions might be made for those who kept watch in the night, or were released from their vigil, as I had been. All I found were some wire coat hangers and an almost empty jar of Nescafe.

I drew back an edge of curtain to see where I was, for once I was inside the hospital I had lost all sense of direction. It was still dark but the rain had cleared. A fresh breeze rippled the large puddles and had already dried large stretches of the Grosvenor Road. A milk float went past with a strange whining noise and a rattle of crates. Then a newsagent's van.

I looked at the bed. It was too late to think of sleep but too early to go to the chaplain's empty room where I was to make my phone calls. Sister said it would help no one to ring at five thirty. There was nothing to be done that could not wait till seven.

I undressed quickly, hung up my clothes on one of the empty hangers, and ran the bath. Water gushed from the taps so fiercely I had to dash back into the tiny bathroom to turn them off. I lay in the warm water and thought of the bath at Loughview. The taps ran so slowly the bath was always tepid by the time it filled. Besides, there was never enough water to fill the bath like this, for the hot water tank was too small in the first place.

My father is dead and I'm lying here thinking about the water pressure in the Loughview bedroom, I said to myself, reprovingly. Surely one ought to be thinking higher thoughts at moments like this. To be meditating upon the nature of mortality, at the very least. But there it was. My mind was full of thoughts, but none of them seemed particularly elevated. Hardly what I would have predicted.

I closed my eyes and saw my father smile at me again. 'If a gipsy had told me,' he began, and I was back in the car, driving up the Antrim Road, with Maisie and her gin glass at the end of it. And William John booming down the phone and Colin playing dutiful son to perfection. 'I'd have been a lousy farmer,' he went on, and it was my turn to smile.

'Yes, Daddy, and I'd have been a lousy company wife, wouldn't I? But I've said no and there's no going back on it.'

'Good girl yourself,' he said, with that little nod he always gave when he was especially pleased. 'Life is full of surprises and some of them are great.'

I had just finished drying myself when there was a tap

at my door. Surprised, I pulled on the gown and opened it to reveal a large woman in a green overall holding a tray.

'Here yar, dear. Sister says yer to eat it all.'

Under the metal cover there were scrambled eggs and bacon. And real coffee and toast. I couldn't believe how hungry I was and how wonderful it tasted. I had no difficulty at all doing as Sister ordered. As I ate, I reflected that someone, somewhere, was trying to tell me something. Whatever awfulness lay ahead of me in the days to come, there would be good things too. Some of my difficulties would resolve themselves. Some wouldn't. But what was really important was what I did with whatever came to me. I was free to live my own life as never before.

The chaplain's office didn't look any tidier, and certainly no more holy, than most offices I've been in, except for a poster on the wall which said, 'The Lord will give you strength'. I hoped He would. I dialled Harvey's number.

'Hello, Mavis, I'm sorry to ring so early.'

'Your father, Jenny?'

'Yes.'

'Jenny, I'm so sorry. Were you with him?'

'Yes, I'm at the Royal now. In the chaplain's room.'

The voice was Mavis's all right, but there was a softness and a warmth which was quite new. She really wanted to know exactly what had happened. That wasn't surprising in itself, I suppose, and even less so remembering her training, but as we went on talking, her questions made it quite clear that what she wanted to know about most of all was me. How did I feel when it happened? What had I done between five thirty and seven? How was I feeling now?

I answered all her questions as honestly as I could, and as I did, I saw myself standing again in the hall at Loughview, amazed to hear Harvey say, 'Mavis and I had a talk and she insisted . . .' And at last, the penny dropped. What had mattered most to Mavis was her father. I had never met him, because he was already a sick man when she first met Harvey and he died only weeks after their engagement.

'Jenny, what can I do to help you?' she asked quietly. 'Would you like me to tell Harvey, or do you feel you must do it yourself? He's still dressing.'

'There is something, Mavis,' I began hesitantly. 'Harvey and I had a row yesterday. He's probably still very angry with me. And we've got to cope with the funeral . . .'

'Of course you have,' she said sympathetically, 'and with your mother as well,' she added sharply. 'Jenny, your dear brother hasn't even begun to come to terms with your mother, as yet, but he's going to have to. And now's a very good time to start. I told him that last night. I gather you stood up to her quite successfully yesterday.'

'Daddy thought I did rather well,' I replied. 'It helps me now that he did,' I went on, horribly aware that the unexpected warmth in her voice was drawing out the tears I had said a firm no to. 'Mavis, there's something else I think I'd better tell you,' I said, collecting myself with an effort.

I heard an encouraging noise.

'Things have been very difficult between Colin and me for some time now. But it all came to a head last night. I won't be going back to Loughview, Mavis, and I won't have Colin at Daddy's funeral. I just don't know how I'll cope with my mother when she has to be told,' I ended limply.

There was a silence at the other end of the line. For one awful moment I thought I'd done the wrong thing, that she was so shocked she would withdraw the support she'd so unexpectedly offered.

'Mavis?' I said tentatively.

'Sorry, Jenny. I'm just a bit taken aback that you've got this to cope with as well. It seems so unfair,' she said gently. 'To tell you the truth, I'm not really surprised. I thought things were bad back in the summer when I came to collect Susie. But it's an awful lot to cope with all at once. Oh, I *am* sorry, Jenny.'

I knew that she really meant it and I was touched. But the result was that yet more tears coursed down my cheeks. She must have heard my sniffs, or the fissle of my kitchen paper, for she went on speaking without waiting for any reply.

'I knew how anxious you were about your father yesterday when he bent over to put the logs on the fire, but there was nothing I could do then except keep talking,' she said sadly. 'Look, Jenny,' she went on, as if she'd suddenly made up her mind about something, 'can you ring back in about ten minutes? Let me talk to Harvey. You've got quite enough to cope with. There are some things he's going to have to get straight, right now. All right?'

'All right. Thanks, Mavis,' I said feebly.

I put the phone down and looked at it in amazement, as if the unexceptional instrument had been in some way responsible for this transformation. Then I took a deep breath and dialled Val's number. Poor Val, she was going to be so upset. Of all my friends, she was the one who knew Daddy best and was most fond of him.

The voice which replied immediately was unfamiliar and sounded so English, so formal and distant, I thought I'd misdialled and sat silent, confused, while it repeated the familiar Bangor number.

'Bob?' I said, weakly.

'Jenny, what's wrong? Are you all right?'

'Alan, I thought you were at the cottage, I didn't recognise your voice . . .'

'Jenny dear, what's wrong?' he said gently. 'Can you tell me or shall I get Val?'

Tears streamed down my face and I shook my head helplessly. I thought I could manage, but the slightest gentleness and back they came.

'Jenny, you're crying. Where are you? Can I come and fetch you?'

There was nothing cool about Alan's voice now. He sounded as distraught as I felt.

'It's all right, Alan. Really, it's all right,' I said quickly. 'Hold on a minute, till I find my hanky.'

I couldn't open my bag one-handed so I tried my skirt pocket and drew out again the familiar screwed-up piece of kitchen paper. So strange that it was not grief that made me weep but any show of kindness or tenderness.

'I'm all right now, Alan,' I managed at last. 'I do have very sad news, but that wasn't what made me cry.'

I told him about Daddy and he listened quietly. And then I told him I'd not been able to avoid as much as I'd hoped, though Thompson's Law had helped a lot. Things had been said that could not be avoided. I'd told Colin I was leaving him, and I was hoping to stay with Val and Bob till I found somewhere to live – if Val had room, that was.

'But of course she has, Jenny,' he said quickly. 'Where are you now? Are you really all right?'

He sounded so anxious about me I had to explain how grateful I actually felt that my father had died and how relieved I was that I never had to go back to Loughview again. I told him I was actually quite in command of myself as long as no one was sympathetic.

'I do believe you, Jenny, if you say so,' he replied. 'I think I just desperately want to see you.'

'And I want to see you too, Alan. I'd have come over this evening even if I couldn't stay,' I replied honestly.

'Just take care today, Jenny. Remember I'll be thinking about you,' he said gently, as he went off to fetch Val.

When she came on, Val was lovely, and then dear Bob made it quite clear that if I needed a mountain shifting, he would arrange it immediately. I thought of what Daddy had said about my three good friends, but this time I did manage not to cry. I said I'd be over sometime in the late afternoon, Val reminded me which plant pot the key was under, I said goodbye and dialled Harvey's number before I could begin to feel anxious again.

He answered immediately.

'Jenny, I'm sorry, so sorry. You've had such a difficult time and I hope you'll let me do . . . you'll let me make up for my . . . thoughtlessness yesterday. You were always closer to Daddy, so you'll know what he would have wanted. Whatever it is, you tell me, and I'll see that's what's done.'

I had never heard Harvey sound so unsure of himself in my life and to my amazement I discovered I was feeling a sympathy I'd never expected to feel. Quite suddenly, I realised that my mother's excessive love and uncritical approval of all he did had been just as damaging to him as all her manipulating and her perennial expressions of disapproval had been to me.

'Thanks, Harvey. It's going to be pretty grim the next few days. Daddy won't mind too much about the practicalities and I'm not too worried about them either. But I don't think I can cope if Mummy attacks me about Colin, at least until after the funeral.'

To my surprise, he promised quite firmly he would make sure she didn't. From that moment on, we were able to be easy with each other and make the decisions that had to be made before he rang my mother to break the news.

'It'll probably be late morning by the time I get up home, Jenny. Can you manage till then?' he ended.

'I'll manage somehow, Harvey,' I said gently. 'I think you've got the rough end this morning.'

'No, not a bit of it. I've ducked out of it for too long. 'Bye for now,' he said hastily, as he put the phone down.

I finished my calls, said my thank you to the sister, and began the long march back to the entrance. The corridors were already full of people, sunlight streamed in through the windows and skylights, and somewhere, beyond the clatter of breakfast trays, I heard a voice singing. Once again, I felt my spirits rise. I walked out into the fresh air, felt the sun on my face, and hailed a taxi as if I were greeting an old friend.

* * *

I blessed Ernie as I sat back in the large, black, city taxi.
He had refused to take any money last night when he
noticed how little I had in my purse. 'Ye might need that
in the mornin',' he'd said. He was in no hurry, he'd see
me again. And so he would. But now there was another
job to do. I collected my thoughts as best I could as we
negotiated the traffic round the City Hall and made for
Queen's Crescent.

It was only a few minutes after eight o'clock, but the
elderly school secretary was already at her desk. She
frowned when she saw me. Staff were a trial to her. They
only appeared when they wanted something. And that
invariably meant more work for her and her assistant. Even
Miss Fletcher, the vice-principal, thought twice about
asking her to duplicate her world maps.

I took a deep breath and said that I would like to see
Miss Braidwood as soon as she came in.

'She's in already, but she's busy,' she said sourly,
looking me up and down. 'What about lunchtime?'

'I'm afraid I can't be here at lunchtime, or at three thirty.
That's why I need to see her.'

'Oh.' She rose from her chair, glared at me, and walked
out of the office in the direction of the head's study. I took
a few deep breaths. I was so nervous, the lines I'd rehearsed
in the taxi had gone completely. I knew there were four
things I had to say, but at this moment I could remember
only two.

'Miss Braidwood will see you,' she said shortly. 'But
she's very busy.'

I picked up my briefcase and tapped along the bare
wooden corridor. When she called, 'Come in,' I opened

the door and saw her move a pile of papers from a chair on to her already crowded desk.

'Do sit down, Mrs McKinstry. You have a problem,' she said briskly.

'Yes,' I said. 'I have a number of things to tell you and some of them may cause problems.'

She shifted uneasily in her chair and glanced at the pile of papers she had just moved.

'My father died this morning in the Royal Victoria. I shall need some time off, but I don't know what the rules are.'

'Was this expected, Mrs McKinstry?'

'In some ways. He did have a severe heart attack two years ago, but he'd made a reasonable recovery. He was in good spirits yesterday when I saw him. The attack came at bedtime and he died at five twenty this morning.'

'So he did not suffer?' she said, her tone softening.

'No, he didn't. It helps me,' I said quite steadily, though I had to swallow afterwards.

She paused. It gave me time for another good deep breath.

'When I saw you on Friday, Miss Braidwood, you offered me the job of Head of the English Department. I made my decision at the weekend and I should like to accept.'

'Good. I'm pleased that you have. You made the decision before your father was taken ill, did you?'

'Yes, I did. I was able to tell him yesterday afternoon and that helps me too. He was very pleased about it.'

To my surprise, she smiled. 'You were clearly close to your father, Mrs McKinstry, and I think I understand why he was so pleased. You are really rather young, you know, for such a position, but we've been very impressed by the impact you've made. We've not had as much enthusiasm for your subject in many years and Miss McFarlane is the first to acknowledge it. I expect your father was very proud of you.'

I nodded, but I didn't dare say a word in case I dripped. 'The third thing is to do with Millicent Blackwood,' I said quickly, a wave of relief sweeping over me as I remembered. 'I know Miss Fletcher is coming to see you about her at lunchtime. I think you should know that her mother has left the family. Millie has four brothers and she's doing all the washing and ironing and most of the housework. I think the problem with her work is simply exhaustion. She's not getting enough sleep and certainly not enough time for proper study. She's an able girl but just can't manage.'

'And her father?'

'He seems kind enough, but thoughtless. I don't think it ever crosses his mind that this will wreck Millie's chances of getting to university. It's probably never occurred to him in any case, because she's a girl.'

'You think she is university material?' she said, surprised.

'Yes, I do. Before this happened, her work was really very good indeed.'

She made a note on a pad and looked up at me. 'And the fourth thing?'

I hesitated a moment and then decided the best thing was to put it as plainly as possible. 'I have left my husband, Miss Braidwood. From today, I shall be staying with friends until I find a home of my own.'

She nodded sharply and considered. 'Has the question of your job precipitated this?'

'Yes, I think it has. But it's only pulled out the underlying problems which could not have been resolved in any case.'

She smiled slightly and stood up. 'The rules about leave are discretionary,' she said abruptly. 'If you can return in a week I shall be very glad indeed. You know our limited resources only too well. But if you do need longer, please telephone me and we'll discuss it. Don't trouble to come in. Have you been up all night?'

'Yes. Yes, I have.'

'I appreciate your coming in. If you leave now you'll avoid having to speak to your colleagues. I can tell them about your father for you. Would that help?'

'Yes, it would indeed.'

She reached a hand across the table and shook mine firmly. 'I shall see the funeral details in the newspaper and I shall think about you at that time,' she said in a businesslike voice. Then she sat down again and took up her papers.

The staffroom was empty, as I expected, so I was able to unload most of my briefcase on to my shelf, leaving it a lot lighter to carry. I hurried along Queen's Crescent and into Botanic Avenue, just as the first cluster of brown figures appeared from the platform of an Ormeau Road bus.

I was about to turn into University Street when I suddenly saw the gates of the Botanic Gardens were wide open. Moments later, I was walking past the huge circular bed opposite the tropical greenhouse.

'Morning, miss.'

'Beautiful morning, isn't it?' I replied easily as the elderly gardener bent again to his task.

The summer bedding was gone and boxes of winter pansies sat on his trolley, one or two of them already in bloom. A deep, rich blue. And I thought of Debbie, my lovely, soft-spoken Jamaican friend who had taught with me in Birmingham. Once, in a Wimpy bar, following a theatre visit, we had talked about loss. After her mother died, she had left the hospital by bus, and looking down she'd seen a woman sweeping her front doorstep. 'How can she do that?' she'd asked herself. 'My mother has died, and she just goes on sweeping her doorstep.'

Debbie had loved her mother, as I loved my father, but only now, as I stood and watched the bent figure tap the pansies from their pots and firm them into the soft earth, did I really understand what she was trying to say. Life goes on regardless, season by season, whatever one's grief or joy.

I walked on slowly, found a seat in the sun and sat down. I drew up my collar against the sharp edge of the breeze. My eyes blinked and half closed against the brilliant light. My heart was breaking with unassuagable longing, a longing for a life of love and security which I knew none of us ever actually have.

Although I got very cold, I went on sitting there till after nine. I wanted to be sure my mother had returned from her neighbour's house before I set off up the Stranmillis Road. The ten-minute walk helped to warm me, but did nothing to ease my growing anxiety. My mother would be expecting me by now. Harvey would have broken the news and told her I had to visit school first. Then he would have to contact whatever undertaker she chose. But he still wouldn't be free to come to Rathmore Drive until he had dealt with the death certificate from the Royal and its registration.

I was about to put my key in the door when it opened and revealed my mother immaculately dressed and made up.

'Jenny, my poor Jenny, you must be exhausted,' she exclaimed, more warmly than I had heard her speak to me for years. 'And you look frozen. Come in quickly and get warm.'

A wave of Helena Rubenstein's Apple Blossom enveloped me as my mother drew me into the sitting room where a bright fire already burned. Two women rose from their armchairs and made leaving noises, but my mother would have none of it.

'Jenny, you know Mrs Allen. She's been so kind. I don't know what I'd have done without her when your poor Daddy was taken ill last night. And this is Mrs Brownlee. You don't know Mrs Brownlee, dear. She's from Balmoral Presbyterian. Jenny used to be in the choir, Mrs Brownlee, and she taught Sunday School too, you know, before she was married,' she went on, smiling her bright public smile, as Mrs Brownlee shook my hand and said, 'I'm sorry about your daddy, Jennifer.'

I sat by the fire as I was bidden while my mother went to make coffee. I smiled to myself as Mrs Allen and Mrs Brownlee made the kind of gentle and inconsequential conversation the rules prescribed for the situation. My mother's extraordinary behaviour suddenly fell into place.

Custom provided the role of widow nobly bearing up under her sudden loss. I knew it was a role my mother would play for all it was worth.

'Your mother's taking it very well, isn't she?' said Mrs Brownlee gently.

'Yes, indeed, she is,' I agreed, as I spread my frozen hands to the blazing log fire. 'Do you think it's likely the Reverend Bryson will be able to call to see her sometime today?'

'Oh yes, indeed, Jennifer,' she answered, patting my hand to reassure me. 'He'll be here quite soon now. He'll want to say some prayers with both of you,' she added, her voice lowering confidentially.

Somehow I managed to keep a straight face as I nodded, but inside me a bubble of gaiety bounced up and down so energetically I thought I should burst. But I didn't. I just said a few more of the polite and irrelevant things expected on these occasions while I offered up a prayer of my own. 'Dear Lord, thank you for these ladies and for the said Reverend Bryson, and for all those others who will come and go this morning and keep me safe from harm. Amen.'

If my mother had been an actress, the morning of my father's departure must surely have won her an Oscar. With a fluency that amazed me, she held centre stage all through its interminable length. As each caller appeared, she greeted them, set them where she wanted them, placed them for the other persons with a few neatly turned epithets, and issued them with the script she considered most suitable for the occasion. Karen's father from across the Drive provided the trial run.

'Ah, Mr Pearson,' I heard her say sadly in the hall. 'Do

come in. You and dear George were such good colleagues when you served together on the Churchyard Maintenance Committee,' she continued as she led him into the sitting room. 'He always used to say how knowledgeable you were about lawnmowers. You will have some coffee, won't you? Mrs Allen has just offered to make some more. How very kind.' She dismissed Mrs Allen with a nod.

'Now I think you know everyone here,' she ran her eye round the room. 'You won't have seen Jenny for some time, such a busy girl with her teaching and a home to run. And Mrs Brownlee, she came round as soon as I phoned the Reverend Bryson so I would have someone from the church with me right away.'

I sat and watched the performance, came in promptly on my cues, and began to make a collection of the sayings attributed to my father. As the morning wore on, I noticed how they became ever more fulsome, but only at one point did I have to take my life in my hands and intervene.

The Reverend Bryson had been given his opportunity to pray. The coffee cups were parked reverently and the dispatch of yesterday's chocolate cake suspended. I half opened my eyes and had a good look at him as he launched forth in fine style. Small and rather plump, he had a loud, bass voice which he had cultivated for the benefit of his profession. After his first two sermons, delivered in a tone much less agreeable than the one he presently employed, Daddy had resigned all his church offices and ceased to attend services. 'That man,' he declared, 'stands in the long tradition of bigots who will wreck this Province in the end if they ever get their way.'

Now, 'that man' was well into his stride. He implored

the Almighty to take care of the funeral arrangements, ensure the wellbeing and good order of our beloved Province, and assist the bringing of the Good News of the Lord Jesus to every nation and every tribe, however lowly. He announced that we must strive to fill the whole world with the Glory of God, as did our dear brother George who had been so committed to the work of the church, even if illness made it difficult for him to be present at worship in recent years.

After a few more flourishes, he amened, the coffee cups were refilled, and I heard him ask my mother about hymns for the funeral service.

'Oh indeed, Mr Bryson, my husband so loved music. He loved all hymns. And psalms too,' she added quickly, just to be on the safe side.

'I made a little list, Mummy. I thought it might be useful to the Reverend Bryson,' I said quietly, my eyes directed modestly towards the Axminster.

'Well now, Jennifer, that was indeed thoughtful,' said Bryson. I couldn't say he boomed like William John, for the note was lower, more bass and less treble. What he most reminded me of was Tubby the Tuba. But I tried to put aside such thoughts as he glanced down the list of Daddy's favourite hymns.

He nodded in a knowing way and I had to suppress a smile as my mother craned her neck and tried to read it sideways. Without her glasses, she couldn't see much, so she contented herself by saying, 'Well, really, all hymns are lovely, aren't they?'

'And, no doubt, burial afterwards in your family plot?'

'Of course,' said my mother, pressing her hands together

in a gesture of sincere agreement.

That was when my stomach did its quick somersault. Before it landed back in place, I had already spoken. 'Mummy, I think perhaps you've forgotten in all the distress that Daddy wanted to be cremated.'

'Cremated?' For one moment, she nearly lost her script, but she recovered herself and picked up the prompt just in time. 'Oh, Jenny dear, your Daddy didn't really mean it,' she began, confidingly. 'He was so concerned about land and the use of land,' she went on, turning to the Reverend Bryson. 'A conserv – ationist, I think, is the correct term. But he certainly would not want burial without the full blessing of his church,' she went on firmly. 'Look how hard he worked on the Churchyard Committee. Why, he raised the money for the new lawnmowers almost single-handed.'

Bryson laid a pastoral hand on her shoulder. 'My dear Mrs Erwin, a cremation is not inconsistent with the full rites of the church. All it involves is a slight delay between funeral service and interment of ashes. We normally do that privately about a week after the church service.'

Before I had time to breathe a sigh of relief, she had turned to me again. 'Are you sure, Jenny, that was what dear Daddy wanted?'

I reassured her and restrained myself. For one wicked moment I had thought of quoting my father's actual words as confirmation: 'Well, Jenny, when I go, I don't want to take up six feet of good earth. Just pop me up to the crem and get me turned into a wee plastic jar of rose fertiliser.'

I had just finished drafting the obituary notices for the *Belfast Telegraph* and *The Newsletter* at a small table in my old room when I heard the Jaguar stop. I opened the window, leaned out and waved silently, but Harvey didn't see me. I watched him get out of the car, go back for something he had forgotten, and walk up the garden path with his eyes firmly fixed on the crazy paving. I was shocked to see how pale and distressed he was.

I hurried to the stairs. Halfway down, I heard my mother begin her routine for the benefit of those neighbours who could now reasonably depart, their duty done.

'Where's Jenny?' he said abruptly as she released him from her embrace.

I came across to him, smiled at the small queue patiently waiting for their exit visas, and said, 'Mummy, could I possibly borrow Harvey for a moment? I need to check the notices with him before I take them into town.'

Harvey followed me upstairs and sat down hurriedly in the chair I'd just been using. I propped myself on the window ledge and waited, as he covered his face with his hands. It was hardly grief for my father, but whatever it was, it was real.

'Harvey, you look dreadful. Can I get you something? Water, whisky?'

He looked up, shook his head and smiled feebly. 'You don't look half bad, Jenny, to have been through what you've been through.'

'I'm a dab hand with make-up, Harvey,' I said easily. 'You look as if you've been through the wars yourself.'

He nodded. 'Mavis spelt it out last night. She knew Daddy hadn't got long. She said she'd been patient with me, she'd waited and waited, but I'd got to get free of Mummy before he went. She wasn't going to have Mummy messing up our family the way she'd messed up you and me, and she's seen signs of it already in Peter. She said if I didn't sort it, she'd leave me.'

For the first time in my life, I considered giving him a hug. But I thought better of it. He looked so upset I was afraid he might cry, and he hadn't got time for that. A couple more minutes and we had to be on parade.

'Look, Harvey,' I said gently, 'Mavis won't leave you, not unless you really make a mess of things, and you won't do that, not if you listen to what she's saying. But you can't do it all at once. Just one thing at a time. Avoid what can be avoided. That's what I've been doing and it works. We've just got to get through the next few days, then we can talk. If you want to,' I added tentatively.

'Yes,' he nodded, 'I think we need to talk.' He hesitated, tried to look at me, but couldn't manage it. 'I've not been much use to you, Jenny. I'm sorry.'

'We've not been much use to each other, Harvey,' I said quietly. 'Perhaps it's not entirely our fault. Let's not be too upset about it.'

I saw him collect himself and I took my chance. I showed him what I had written. He glanced at it briefly, asked what we needed to do next, and sat listening as I filled him in on where we were up to. A few minutes later, when we went downstairs together, he had rearranged his black tie and his persona and looked as if he could cope.

'I'm going to call on Bertie and the staff,' I informed my mother when the door had shut behind the last of the morning visitors. 'I'll take the notices to the newspapers and go on from there, if that's all right with you, Mummy, now that Harvey's here.'

'Yes, you do that if you feel you have to, Jennifer,' she said dismissively, her face making it quite clear how unnecessary she felt it was to show any consideration towards mere staff. 'Harvey and I will have some lunch together,' she went on, much more enthusiastically. 'I presume you'll be back over again this evening with Colin?'

'No, Mummy,' said Harvey. He was in so quickly, I didn't even have time to panic. 'I think Jennifer has managed very well to do all she's done, but she had no sleep at all last night. I really must insist she goes home and stays there until tomorrow morning,' he said in his crispest consultant's voice. 'Mavis will come down this evening, as soon as she's given the children their tea. She'll be able to do whatever you might have wanted Jenny to do.'

She was so busy agreeing with Harvey, she didn't even bother to object when I collected Daddy's car keys. I said my goodbye, reminded Harvey with a glance that he knew where to find me, and manoeuvred the Rover gingerly out into the Drive and down on to the Stranmillis Road. By the time I got to Erwin's, I felt quite comfortable with the car, which I've always liked, but distinctly uneasy about what I would find in the place where my father had worked for over twenty years.

I parked between Mrs Huey's elderly Morris Minor and Bertie's new red sports car and walked down the yard to the back entrance to the upstairs offices. I saw a movement at a window, looked up and waved to Loretto, the newest clerk, a cousin of Bertie's from the nearby Falls Road. Before I got to the door, Bertie came rushing out to meet me, hauling on the jacket he seldom wears as if it were an obligatory token of respect.

'Gawd, Jennifer, I'm sorry about yer father, rest his soul,' he said, crossing himself. 'There's bin no work done in this place the day. Mrs Huey's in a bad way,' he went on. 'Her an' Loretto hasn't had a dry eye among them all mornin'.'

He put his arms round me and hugged me. Short in stature and tending to plumpness, Bertie has shoulders on him like a rugby forward, and his hug left me breathless. He led me up the stairs to the office that had remained my father's even after he'd sold the business. During the handover, he and Bertie had got on so well my father suggested he return to work two days a week to help Bertie carry through the changes he'd planned. For his part, Bertie had insisted my father's office was not to be disturbed. While staff were retrained and computers installed, it kept its slightly old-fashioned and very informal arrangements.

'Haul on a minit, will ye, an' I'll away an' get Mrs Huey,' he said as he opened the door.

I took in the strange, familiar blend of the smell of old, well-polished furniture mixed in with the odour of shiny new machinery catalogues, dust, and chrysanthemums. A large, fresh bunch sat in a copper jug on top of a filing cabinet.

'I think I shud leave yis till yerselves a minit, but I'd like till take yis for a bite o' lunch. A've got a quiet wee table at the Royal Ave'nue wheniver yer reddy,' he said hastily, as he left me.

I walked across to my father's empty desk and sat down, and I was still sitting there, lost in thought, when Gladys came into the room. A warm, friendly woman, long widowed, I had known her all my life, and she had always been so very kind to me. One look at her gave me the answer to a question I'd had in my mind for many years, and it explained her great interest in my life. I walked across to her, put my arms round her and cried as if my heart would break, because I knew she had loved my father.

'Now, now, sweetheart, don' cry, don' cry. Sure Daddy would hate to see you cry,' she said, the tears streaming down her own face. I heard the door open and shut again behind us.

'I'm sorry,' I sniffed, 'I've left make-up on your lovely clean blouse.'

'And sure what matter that,' she said, wiping her own eyes. 'Now, com'on, Jenny. We'll hafta to do better than this. Poor Bertie doesn't know whether he's comin' or goin'. He wants to come to the funeral and he's afeard to menshun it, bein' Catholic like. Ye may say somethin' to the poor man.'

I nodded and put my hand to my pocket, pulled out the piece of kitchen paper once more and looked at it.

'D'you think Daddy would lend us some tissues?' I said, wiping my eyes again.

'Surely, he woud. Sure he has everythin' in that desk of his,' she went on, pulling out a drawer and handing me a box of Kleenex. 'No matter what ye'd ask him for, he'd have it in that desk – if ye waited long enough. What'll we do without him, Jenny?' she said quietly and burst into tears again.

'Gladys,' I said, hesitantly. I'd never used her Christian name before, for my father had always called her 'Mrs

Huey'. 'Gladys, if Daddy hadn't died last night, he'd be wired up to two machines this morning, a ventilator and a kidney machine. I prayed for him to go. You would have too, if you'd been there, wouldn't you?'

She nodded, but could not speak.

'Shall I tell you what his last words were?'

She looked up at me, surprised, and I told her about driving up the Antrim Road in the sunshine, and hearing the story of him standing barefoot, with the backside out of his trousers, looking up at his neighbour on the horse. She stopped crying and began to smile and said she knew the story well.

'I asked him if he'd be in work on Tuesday, and I said I'd come down from school. The last thing he said to me was, "Good girl, that's great. I'll get Mrs Huey to get us a bun for our tea".'

I had to re-do my make-up yet again before I could go and speak to the rest of the staff, but I managed it fairly well. Bertie had already told them the showroom would close so everyone could attend the funeral, if there were no objections from the family. Over lunch, I reassured Bertie and Gladys that if it were the last thing I were ever to do, I would see that all Daddy's friends from work would stand together in the pew behind the family, Catholic and Protestant alike, exactly as he would have wished.

Lunch was surprisingly enjoyable. Any group of businessmen casting an eye over the strangely assorted group we made in a quiet corner of the large dining room would not have guessed at the sadness which was our common bond. We talked about anything that came to mind, but returned again and again to remembrances of my father.

Gladys told us stories about the early days of the business I had never heard before. With little capital of his own, my father had rebuilt old farm machinery as well as importing what was new. Bertie had done differently. Coming from a home no less poor than my father's, he had worked in the building trade all through his teens and twenties, first in Glasgow and then in London. He'd worked every hour he could to build his capital, because his ambition was to have his own business. Erwin's was just what he wanted, for he shared my father's passion for farm machinery.

After lunch, I drove out of the city, free at last from telephone calls and arrangements that had to be made. I looked around at the autumn trees and the sparkle of the lough and wondered yet again how a day could still be so lovely and yet Daddy gone. I thought of the blue pansies in the Botanic Gardens, and the jug of chrysanthemums Gladys had put in his office that he would now never see. And then I remembered the tiny jug of late flowering roses in my study at Loughview where I would never work again.

I parked the car outside the gates and looked across at the neighbouring houses for any signs of life. Mercifully, there were none. I remembered that Monday was Karen's cleaning day. The babies were shipped off to her mother in the morning. By now, Karen would be on her way to collect them. She'd not be back for an hour or more.

I walked down the hall and into the kitchen. The breakfast table looked just as it had on Friday night, except that there was no half-eaten bowl of cornflakes, just Colin's eggy plate and the dregs of his coffee in the percolator. I turned my back on it and went upstairs.

What did you expect, Jenny? I asked myself when I saw

the unmade bed, the scatter of underwear on the floor, the abandoned pyjamas on the bedroom chair. I sat down at the dressing table and looked in the mirror.

'Harvey was right,' I said aloud. Although I was pale and had dark circles under my eyes, there was a lightness about the face I had not seen for some time. When I smiled experimentally, the solemn face in front of me responded with a twinkle that was quite unexpected.

'Sitting admiring yourself.' That's what my mother always said if ever she caught me peering in a mirror. But she was wrong. I laughed aloud. How wrong she was about so many things. How wrong all of us could be, even about the biggest things.

I cleared my dressing table except for the knicker-pink twin-set and the silver brush set which was Maisie's engagement present. Then I had a go at the bathroom. I removed all signs of a female presence, down to the last tampon. I ignored the matching luggage we'd taken on our honeymoon and pulled out my old suitcases from under the bed. What was left over I packed in a box from the garage which said 'Old Bushmills Whiskey'. I left my summer clothes in the wardrobe for another time and carried all my winter things to the car on hangers.

Then I turned to my study. Too many books to take today, so I picked out all the new poetry and just a few others I might need for school. I looked at my collection of stones and driftwood and could not bear to leave it, even for a few days. I packed it carefully and took it to the car. When I came back, the room seemed strangely bare already. I unhooked Val's sketches from the wall, and then my own. Less good than hers, they were still precious because they encapsulated the time and the place of their making – a sketch of the surviving gable wall of the cottage where my father began his life and one of the worn and weathered baulks of wood down at Ballydrumard, both of which I'd made on days I'd spent out with Alan.

The car was full when I'd finished. I had to put Val's lemon geraniums on the passenger seat and wedge the little jug of late roses in the door panel where Daddy kept his maps.

I went back into the house one last time to go to the loo. There in the bathroom were the three red geraniums, very dead. Like my relationship with Colin. No need to spend time lamenting what had been. It was over. Finished. Long ago and in another country.

I washed my hands, dried them on the warm, dry towel, and pulled open the airing cupboard. Covered in slimy ooze, the homebrew bottle now sat quiet. The smell was horrible. As I shut the door on it I had to laugh. Not with a bang but a whimper, I said to myself as I ran lightly down the stairs.

I pulled up out of Loughview and pointed the car east. Another day I would go and see Ernie and pay him what I owed him and tell him about the possibility of a job with Bertie. But not today. Today, I had done as much as I could.

I looked at my watch and saw there was time to drive down to Windmill Hill and look out over the green fields and work out which patchwork piece was mine. Or I could park somewhere and sit in the sun, or walk by the shore, or I could pick up the key from under the plant pot and go into a house that would welcome me.

I could lie down and sleep and Val would cook my

supper. I could worry about finding a home and Bob would tell me exactly how it was to be managed. I could ring Siobhan and make a plan to drive up to Derry and bring Keith home. I could falter and find my courage disappear and Alan would comfort me.

I sat for a moment thinking about Alan. Not thinking in a deliberate, logical way, more allowing myself to be aware of him, remembering all that had been between us over the years and what had happened in these last incredibly extended days. His tenderness was no longer a threat to the job in hand, it was a gift, so unexpected, and so precious, I could hardly believe it was mine.

Now that my life had been given back to me I was beginning to realise just how many wonderful things were mine for the taking.

Chapter 22

It came as a surprise when I saw the broken tree stump I'd glimpsed in the flare of Alan's headlights on Saturday evening. Somehow I'd managed to overshoot the turn to Val and Bob's. I was now heading south to Drinsallagh.

Well, and why not? I said to myself, as I opened the window and felt the rush of fresh, autumny air.

In no time at all, I came to the laneway. I reckoned I could probably get the car down to the cottage, but whether I could get it back up again was another matter. So I pulled off the road between the huge round pillars that had once supported a farm gate, scuffled in the back of the car for some flat shoes and set off down the lane.

It was wonderful to be out, the air still warm though the sun was dropping towards the horizon. I paused by the tumbled stone wall where Alan had helped me choose fronds of gold and bronze bracken on Saturday night. The ancient hawthorn where I'd added a few sprays of brilliant red berries was bent with age. It curved protectively over a tangle of grass sprinkled with harebells, their delicate blue flowers swaying on fragile stems.

Tears of joy sprang to my eyes. I felt as if I had emerged from some black and airless cave and been given back all the things I most loved: the space of the sky with the sea beyond, the glancing light on the turning leaves, and the flowers, the harebells that had been here all the time, but hidden by the darkness.

I tramped on, my eyes moving over the hedgebanks. Nodding seedheads on the grasses, bright red globes on the honeysuckle, shiny black beads on the elderberry. Golden hawkbeards. Brambles laden with ripe berries. Such richness, I hardly knew where to look. And then, as I turned a corner, the cottage came in sight. Tiny windowpanes caught the westering sun. The plaster was peeling, shabby in the bright light, but the place was sturdy. A cottage with its feet in the earth, its back to the wind, its door opening to the south.

I came round the gable and stood beneath the gnarled branches of the climbing rose and remembered how long ago, on the exposed side of a windy glen, my grandfather had planted a rose for my grandmother. 'To comfort her, for what she had lost,' my father always said. Ellen had been an educated girl from a comfortable home who married for love. She never regretted it, he said, though her life had been hard and she had suffered great loss.

I took the key from behind the drainpipe and turned it in the lock. I smelt the clean, sour-milk smell of emulsion paint as I came into the big kitchen. One wall had been stripped of its peeling paper and was freshly painted. Its rugged plaster surface, pitted and scarred, gleamed in the dim light. I sat down in a wooden armchair by the hearth and stared at the row of cooking pots lined up at the back of the broad sunlit space below the smoke-darkened canopy.

I tried to remember the name of the metal arm that swung out over the fire, so you could attach a pot or a griddle to

the chain that hung from it. The name teased on the edge
of consciousness. Then I thought of one of Daddy's books
with drawings of hearths and cooking equipment. He had
taken it from the shelf that July day when Alan and I got
soaked up at his old home and I'd come back feeling so
sad that nothing now remained but a piece of gable wall.

'And the climbing rose, Jenny?' he reminded me.

'No, Daddy dear. That's just it,' I said, almost in tears.
'Alan and I spent ages looking for any trace of it, but it's
gone.'

'I'm sure it has, dear,' he said easily. 'But those four
pink ones at the bottom of the garden are all cuttings from
it, and there are plenty of younger ones I've taken from
those,' he said reassuringly. 'That's as well as the ones in
Scotland and England and America, and a few more back
up in the glens. Your Aunt Mary has a splendid one on her
old home, though it's only a storehouse now.'

I thought of dear Aunt Mary, my favourite Hughes
relative, with her large, unruly family, 'my big cousins' I
had always called them, and Uncle Paddy, her good-natured
farmer husband. I hadn't been able to see them since before
I was married and now they'd be coming to the funeral,
with Jamsey and Paddy, the two youngest sons, the only
ones who had chosen to stay in Ulster when their brothers
and sisters had gone off to seek their fortunes, as so many
Ulster offspring do.

Harvey and I would make them very welcome, for my
mother would no doubt ignore them, as she always did.
She'd never forgiven her younger sister for marrying a poor
Catholic lad from the next valley when she was only
seventeen. But Mary and Paddy had been happy together.

Now, surrounded by their grandchildren, Jamsey and Paddy's sons and daughters, they were still happy, their new bungalow a focus for all the family, as their old cottage, and later their new farmhouse, had always been.

I sat looking up at the sky through the smoke hole above the hearth. Their first home had been a cottage just like this one. When I visited it as a little girl, I'd sat on a low three-legged stool by the hearth. The stool was called a 'creepie', and my aunt used 'piggins' and 'noggins' when she measured milk and made butter. I learnt all the unfamiliar words she used every day and treasured them, but even as a very little girl I knew never to use any of them in front of my mother.

'Yer mather, Jenny, wos always a great un fer progress,' said Aunt Mary one day when she was baking soda bread at the kitchen table. 'But what yer mather mint by progress wos muney. Gettin' muney, or havin' muney. That wos what wos importan' ta her. She'd no time atall for yer pur feyther whin he wos oney a prentice in tha smithy. Oh no, deer no. Amerikay wos tha whole go thin. Annie wos goin' ta send her a tickit. But Annie got married insted.'

I could see her kneading the bread, her touch so light, her fingers knobbly and bent from farm work.

'I alus mind yer mather comin' in fra work wi' somethin' some young man or ither had give her. Sweeties, or choclits, or some wee gift. "Oh," says we, for Annie and I were powerful nosey, "are ye gane out wi' him thin?" "We'll see," says she, as cool as ye like. And ye know, Jenny, she niver went out wi' anyun less she thought they'd a gude bit a muney ta spend. She wos very hard.'

Aunt Mary had dusted the flour from her hands, laughed

easily, and slid the cake of bread onto the waiting griddle.

'A right eejit she thought me for marryin' yer Uncle Paddy. She'd a skipt the weddin' if yer grandfayther hadn't put his fut down.'

And then she had showed me her wedding picture, a studio portrait with Grecian pillars and ferns in pots, Patrick McBride looking handsome but uncomfortable in a stiff collar and Mary peering over a huge circular bouquet of roses that looked exactly like a wreath.

Quite suddenly, I saw myself back in the kitchen at Rathmore Drive, in my hand a spray of five perfectly-matched roses. It was the Saturday morning after the May Ball and the roses were Colin's first gift. Now, sitting here, in Alan's cottage, remembering my Aunt Mary's words, I saw again that coy look on my mother's face. I couldn't remember her exact words, but it was about how much the roses had cost, 'a pretty penny from that florists', was what she'd said.

I got up quickly and climbed the steep wooden staircase to the larger of the two small bedrooms. Everything was exactly as it had been when I last saw it by the light of the paraffin lamp on Saturday night. The room might look the same, but everything else had changed. I saw now that it had all begun that morning when Colin had sent the roses. Now it had ended the only way it could.

I crossed to the window to open it and look out at the sea, but as I put my hand to the catch, I heard a noise below. I peered down through the branches of the rose and saw a tall figure struggling with an aluminium step ladder. So thick was the foliage that it was only as he began to climb I could be quite sure it was Alan.

'Young man,' I began severely, in my best Betsy Trotwood voice. 'Are you trying to gain access to these premises?'

He laughed and climbed higher. We regarded each other across several feet of rose canopy. He was looking at me quite directly and for the very first time I noticed that he had splendid grey eyes. They were full of surprise and delight.

'I wondered where you were when I saw the car,' he said, smiling. 'I thought you might have gone down to the beach.'

'How did you know it was me?'

'I didn't for a moment. I thought it might be the estate agent. Then I used my superior powers of deduction and decided he probably wouldn't have brought his Panda with him.'

I laughed and ran downstairs. He met me in the doorway, caught me in his arms, kissed me and held me.

'Jenny, I've been thinking of you all day,' he said, his voice full of relief and tenderness. 'You were so steady on the phone this morning, but I was afraid it might all catch up on you and you'd be distraught.'

I shook my head gently. 'That may come, Alan. I'm sure it will. I'm going to be so very sad at times, but right now I'm just so grateful Daddy's gone. He's free. And so am I,' I added, simply. I reached up and kissed him again.

'Jenny,' he began tentatively. 'Do you remember the day we went to the old church at Meevagh?'

'Yes,' I said, puzzled.

'I made such a bad mistake that day. I knew what I felt and I hadn't the courage to tell you. And you've been so unhappy . . .' He broke off, looked away from me, as if he couldn't bear to put into words what was troubling him.

'Alan,' I said, 'I think we *both* got it wrong.'

He hugged me, but the look on his face was still one of utter distress. I could not bear to see him so upset.

'How would it be, Alan, if we didn't blame ourselves for what's happened? There were things out against us. Things from your past and things from my past. But we're together now. Why don't we just start here, friends and lovers, and see what the future brings?'

I saw a look of such relief sweep across his face and then he smiled. 'Yes, Jenny. Yes, let's do just that.'

He drew me out of the doorway where we'd been entwined in each other's arms and over to where the stepladder stood abandoned.

'Alan, what are you doing?' I cried as he began to climb.

But it was perfectly obvious what he was doing. He took from his pocket a brand new pair of secateurs and began to cut the roses he hadn't been able to reach from the bedroom window on Saturday night.

We carried them back up to the road in a bucket of water and wedged them carefully in the front seat of his car, because there was no space at all left in mine.

'If you follow me up to the crossroads we can go back the quick way,' he said as he walked beside me to the Rover.

He bent down and kissed me again. I got in and switched on, waited till he came slowly past, then swung out after him. I could see he was watching me in his driving mirror. At the crossroads, we turned onto a road I had driven a hundred times with my father. He drove steadily, making sure I was never far behind. The light was fading fast and long shadows fell across the road, but the car was warm from sitting in the sun. It was full of the smell of lemon geranium and fallen rose petals.

Ahead of us the road swung right, straightened and ran along the Strangford shore, heading north, smooth and empty but for Alan's car and mine. He put his foot down and a few moments later so did I. The Rover moved smoothly forward, and as it did, I heard again the sound of my father's voice: 'Life is full of surprises, Jenny. And some of them are great.'